Age is Just a Number

Mor Love

ISBN: :9798335729703

DEDICATION

To my angel in the sky, Aunt Carmen.

You were the first person to give me an "adult" book. I read it in 2 days, and you laughed at how excited I was about it. I remember you telling me that maybe you will read one of my books one day and I always thought how far-fetched that idea was. It was always in the back of my mind though. When you left this earth, I kept thinking about all the things you didn't get a chance to do, and it dawned on me that you will never get to read my book. Now that it's here I hope you would have liked it, I love and miss you Auntie.

Thank you for everything!

ACKNOWLEDGMENTS

To my readers...

If you are reading this, thank you! Whether you end up liking it or not, thank you. This has been a bucket list item for a while now, so I am proud that I finally saw it through. These characters have grown with me for years, and I wanted to tell their story. Some parts are fictional, but some hit close to home. The moral is that at any age life hits HARD, no matter how good you think someone has it. I have to say that some parts could be triggering as this book touches on some hard-hitting topics, and although I consider it a coming-of-age novel there are some explicit scenes that may not be suitable for all ages.

Special shout out to my friends and family who have supported me, listened to me talk about this over the past few years, thank you for the excitement that was expressed, it honestly kept me going when I wanted to trash this whole idea more than a few times. My mother brought me my laptop so I could get started typing, and I am forever grateful for all her love and support. Thank you to Antionette. M, who was the first person to read this and helped me iron out a few things that I was stressing over. Thank you to Dr. Angela G., and Cathy M., who helped me put the final touches on this project.

I'm so blessed to have the support system that I do, I'm forever grateful.

CONTENTS

EVERYONE HAS A SECRET........

MOR LOVE

TIA

"What do you think your father wants to talk to us about?" I asked Derek, as he came and plopped down on the couch next to me.

"I'm not sure what OUR father would like to talk to us about." he replied, with putting an emphasis on, "our". I rolled my eyes.

"Like I said, YOUR father; he needs to hurry up. I have shit to do."

"Like what...all you do is shop and talk shit, Tia."

"Derek, shut the hell up! I really don't feel like hearing you or him talk, quite frankly, so I'm about to leave." As I tried to get up, I heard Derek's father.

"Damn baby girl, you can't give your father a few minutes of your time?" his voice boomed, as he entered the room. My eyes reached the ceiling again, as I reluctantly sat back down.

"What up pops?"

"Hello DW." I said, with a flat tone.

"Tia, how many times do I have to tell you to stop calling me that? Everyone calls me that, but I don't want you to. I am your father, whether you are fan of it or not!"

"Yeah, TIA stop being so disrespectful." Derek teased.

These two get on my damn nerves. They have the same name, same face, and the same annoying ass personality. I get a migraine when I have to be with both of them for an extended period of time. But I can tolerate my brother just a little more.

"Can you please say what you have to say, so I can leave?" I asked.

My father chuckled and shook his head.

"Well children, I wanted to see how you two felt about moving back to Baltimore?"

"What?" myself and my brother screeched.

"Calm down, just hear me out, okay. Y'all, know I have been flying back and forth between here and New York. I was offered a full-time job there and I thought…"

"You thought what?" I asked, cutting him off. "You will ship us back to Baltimore, while you live out your fake ass musical dreams in New York? You already aren't here half the time anyway, so what's the purpose in us moving back to that hell hole…" I ranted about get in his ass.

"TIA STOP…. just listen to me please!" he pleaded.

I folded my arms and sat back.

"As I was trying to say, I accepted the job in New York, and I know I've been gone, but that's why I was giving y'all the option. Move back to Baltimore, or I would love if y'all considered moving to NY with me or stay here with Aunt Pam."

"We will move in with, G?" Derek asked.

"No, I will get you two an apartment to share close by, I trust y'all to live on your own. Of course, when I come into town I will stay there, which I will try to come, every weekend."

"Yeah right." I mumbled.

"Tia please, I really want y'all in New York with me, but I thought it might be a bigger adjustment, so the next thing will be Baltimore where y'all actually know people. At least we can be on the same coast." my father stated, with sad eyes. I'm not falling for that bullshit though.

"Yeah, New York seems a bit much and I'm for damn sure not staying with Pam erky ass. Plus, I wanna get away from the shit here, so Baltimore is cool with me." Derek said.

I remained silent; I just couldn't even fathom the thought about going back to Baltimore.

"Alright baby girl, where is your head at?" DW questioned.

Still silent, but now I was giving him the death stare. He already blew up my life once by moving us all the way out here to California, and now 4 years later he wants to move us back.

"Tia, our dad is talking to you!" Derek said as he nudged me.

"What about school?" I asked flatly.

"Well, you have already been expelled from 2 schools for fighting, you're skating on thin ice with the one you are at now, and you don't seem to have any friends out here. I know it's your upcoming senior year, but I figured spending your last year with Keyarra would be nice." DW replied.

Hearing Keyarra's name made sadness wash over me and this nigga knew that me and her were not talking. So why in the fuck would he think that I would want to spend my senior year with her. At that moment I got up and proceeded to walk to my room.

"I'll be staying here." I stated on my way out the living room.

"Tia wait..." my father shouted.

"Just give her a few minutes pops, I'll go talk to her." I heard Derek tell him.

Fuck both of them for real, the thought of going to Baltimore and facing whatever issue Keyarra has with me, had me seeing red. Keyarra WAS my best friend literally since we were born, we are only 2 months apart in age and were raised more like sisters. Our mothers were best friends, but you couldn't tell them they weren't sisters so that's how they always carried it. They were so in sync that they both had 2 kids a piece, one boy and one girl. My auntie, Kiara, had Matthew 1st, then 4 months later, Derek was born. So, Derek and Matthew are also best friends, but again more like brothers. Fast forward 3-ish years, and my mother gave birth to me, which was the ultimate blessing to everyone if you ask me. Then 2 months later, Keyarra was born. My mother and aunt somehow managed to be pregnant twice together, carrying the same gender in the same years.

The 6 of us plus GG lived together, up until 4 years ago. Our mothers were involved in a tragic car accident that took their lives. Our perfect little family was ripped apart. DW, also known as Derek Williams Sr., finally decided to step up and be a "real" father after the accident. He was always around, but he could have done more, so he got custody of us.

Keyarra and Matthew's mother were the only family they knew of besides Matthew's father, Mark, who was always in and out of prison at the time. Keyarra's dad was basically non-existent. Since GG was the adoptive mother of our mothers, Tina and Kiara, she was granted custody of Matthew and Keyarra. She adopted our mothers when they were 14, so that they could stay together. GG was a well-off widowed Christian woman, who often visited group and foster homes of teen girls to minister and just assist in any way she could. She had become very attached to Kiara, but was having trouble connecting with my stubborn mother, Tina. When GG decided to finally adopt my aunt, she begged for her to bring Tina too. GG finally obliged, but the story is that my mother was a straight up asshole, and it took a long time for them to all finally blend. By the time we all came along, things were a lot better, even though GG was very upset that both of her girls had become young, unwedded mothers, with 2 kids before the age of 21. But our GG was the best grandmother you could ever have asked for. She spoiled the 4 of us rotten, we never even knew we weren't blood related until after the accident.

We all leaned on each other closely, for the 1st year after the accident. The 4 of us grieved together and shut the rest of the world out, until my sperm donor decided to be a selfish son of a bitch and move myself and Derek to California for his "career". We were devastated, but he said that he didn't want to leave us behind and that 4 pre-teens were just too much for GG to handle by herself. I already hated his ass but that right there took me over the edge. I did everything I could to stop the move. Hunger strike, running away, hiding his car keys, anything my little mind could think of to stay with my family, but nothing worked. He shipped us to Cali and got a house with his weak ass sister, Aunt

Pam. She just reaped the benefits of my father's budding career and really could have cared less about what we did; which is why I was a mean ass fighter, and my brother was a hoe who was out there getting in all types of trouble with these fast ass girls. Things were ok at 1ˢᵗ, me and Keyarra made sure to talk every single day, no matter the time difference, Matthew and Keyarra also visited often, even if it was just for a weekend. But almost 2 years ago something happened, Keyarra became distant, and she slowly cut all communication with me. I finally convinced my sperm donor to let me go see her, which was a mistake. It ended in a fight, me and my sister, my best friend in the entire world, had fought so badly that I had broken 2 of her fingers, and she had fractured my arm and gave me a black eye. I cried the entire flight back. She had reached out once to apologize, but I swear GG made her do it. I hung up on her and that was the last interaction we had, up until recently. So now, here I am debating if I want to return to my hometown and face the bullshit again.

"Knock knock." my brother said, as he rudely entered.
"You are supposed to wait for someone to actually tell you to come in." I replied, with my usual attitude.
He walked into my room and pulled my desk chair out to sit down.
"Well, I wasn't gonna hold my breath on that little sister."
"What do you want?"
"Tia, you already know you aren't staying here with Pam. How many times have I had to step in and break up y'all arguments? If I'm gone, then y'all might kill each other."
"Well, you clearly weren't thinking about that a few minutes ago."
"Tia, that was the obvious decision. You know I can't stay here with all that past bullshit; I still haven't heard the last of it. And you know I won't leave you, so just stop being difficult for once and get on board."

"Derek, how exactly am I being difficult? You KNOW I can't go back to Baltimore, so it's fucked up that you expect me to. You're selfish just like your got damn dad." I fumed.

"Listen I apologize for being hasty and not fully considering the position that would put you in, but you aren't going there alone. We gonna face all of it together, like we always do." Derek said, honestly.

Me and Derek may bicker and tease each other non-stop, but he is the only person that I trust wholeheartedly. He is the best big brother that a girl could ever ask for. He would lay his life down for me and I would do the same for him, so we are extremely close. When we first moved out here, I was in the 8th grade, but when I made it to the 9th, we were almost inseparable, we were in different grades, but we had lunch together every day and of course rode to and from school together. Derek always loved the girls, and they loved him right back, so when he lost his virginity at only 14, he got girl crazy. I felt abandoned because he always was with some new girl. I tried to make friends, but time and time again girls wanted to only be my friend just to get close to Derek. And the girls who didn't want to fuck my brother wanted to hate on me so they ended up getting fucked up because my patience was thin, and my hands were quick.

"Tia, are you listening to me?" Derek asked, interrupting my thoughts.

"I am really trying not to."

"Ok cut the bullshit, your little fucked up attitude is getting old man. I know it got a little rocky this past year but I'm here Ti. Talk to me, you don't have to hold everything in. Tell me how you are feeling, instead of acting like a child." Derek voiced.

I can hear him getting frustrated with me but sometimes I just can't help myself. I use my anger and sarcasm to scare people away, at least my therapist tells me. If they weren't family, I'm sure my brother and sperm donor would have jumped ship. Well, actually I don't give a shit about DW's big head ass, but Derek is all I have.

"I'm sorry Derek, I just don't know how to feel about this. The school year ends in 3 months, so by September we will be back in Baltimore and what? I have to fight all my classmates again so they can know not to mess with me, I don't feel like that all over again. At least here I can go about my school day in peace."

"Yeah...you've had 2 fights this year already and just got sent back the principal's office a few days ago, so I wouldn't say you are at peace by any means. Let's go to Baltimore this summer get you and Keyarra back right and you can enjoy your senior year like I enjoyed mine.... for the most part."
"Why do y'all keep bringing up her name." I questioned, "she doesn't want to see me just like I don't wanna see her."
"That's not what I'm hearing." Derek said with a smirk.
"What have you heard?"
"Key misses you and she has been trying to reach out."
Keyarra has called me from a private caller a few times, but I hung up every time. I was hurt and the only way I would talk to her was if she hopped on a plane and faced me, like I did her. I never mentioned that to Derek about her calling me though.

"I'm not sure what you're talking about." I said lowly.
"Yeah, ok sure.... Tia, I got you, we gonna get through the summer together and even if I gotta pose as your aid throughout the school year to make sure nobody messes with my baby sister then so be it, I'll sacrifice my classes to do so." Derek joked.
I rolled my eyes. "First, I'm not a baby and 2nd you are full of shit. Soon as we touch down you will be running the streets with your ugly ass girlfriend and forget all about me again. That's the only reason you were so quick to agree to go back to Baltimore."
"Well first, I never forgot about you so stop saying that and 2nd, you know damn well Katrina is not ugly, stop playing with me. But

I pinky promise you will come first, I won't let you down." Derek said, putting his pinky out.

We only pinky promised on really important things. We've done it since we were kids and never grew out of it. The last pinky promise he broke and I still haven't forgiven him for it.

"Derek if you break this one, I swear I will break your pinky finger...both of them." I threatened seriously as our pinky's intertwined. Derek smiled!

"I promise, I got you BABY sister."

He better or there will be hell to pay, and I put that on my mother's grave.

DEREK

I walked back out into the living room and sat across from my dad who was finishing up a conversation on the phone.

"Yes love, I'm still coming tonight. Just be ready when I do." He said with a slight smile.

I shook my head because my father was a dog. He had women out the ass. He was an audio engineer, who worked with some of the most popular musicians out now. So, with him being in the industry came women, and he loved living the life of a rich bachelor. He said he was never going to get married because my mother was the only woman who ever had his heart. He never got into anything serious with any of them, and if they got too clingy, they were cut off.

"What did your sister say? Is she really gonna stay here?" He questioned with concern.

"Naw, she's gonna come to Baltimore and tough it out."

"How the hell do you do that? She listens to your ass, but barely gives me the time of day." My father said as he fell back into his chair.

He hated that Tia barely spoke to him, and he really hates that she won't even acknowledge him as her father.

"Just give her some more time, she will come around...eventually."

I tried to sound convincing, but the truth was my sister was a tough cookie and talking to her about our father was like talking to a brick wall.

"Yeah sure, I just wish she will let me in and get pass the past bullshit."

Tia and my father have a very rocky relationship. When I was born my parents were together, my mother was 16, and my pops was 18. The story is that they were madly in love, my father worshipped the ground she walked on, but before she fell for him fully, she would constantly give him her ass to kiss, but eventually she came around. On her 19th birthday he asked her to marry him, she said yes but in return she gave him a positive pregnancy test. He was so excited about expanding their family until he found out about my mother stepping out on him about a year prior, after a fight they had. She said it only happened one time and it meant nothing, but my father didn't care, he was convinced that the baby she was carrying wasn't his and he called off their short engagement. He even had my ass tested and I look just like the nigga. He missed Tia's birth and refused to sign the birth certificate until she was tested as well. After proving that she was indeed his he still was being an asshole, coming to the house and only spending time with me or taking only me and Matthew out to ball games and shit. Tia did everything that she could to get my father to acknowledge her, but he was so focused on trying to hurt my mother that he didn't even realize that Tia was slowly becoming distant and making mental notes at her young age. By the time he started coming around the damage was done; Tia had written him off.

I watched my mother and father fight over the fact that she wouldn't force Tia to talk to him or spend time with him. The tables were turned, and my father was livid. I even stopped fucking with him for a while because I didn't like how he was doing my little sister or how he talked to my mom at times. But the truth is I love my pops, he really is my best friend. He taught me so much. He was smart and quick on his feet; he also taught me how to sway the ladies, which is probably why my ass got into some deep shit a little while back. When my mom died, I didn't want to leave Baltimore, but I wanted to be wherever my father was, so I didn't fight the move like Tia did. I just had to make her as comfortable as possible. I did good the first year or so, but I got caught up in all the perks and shit that came with my father's lifestyle.

"Son, did you hear me?" my father asked.

"No, what did you say?"

"Do you think I should give her some money to go shopping?"

I sucked my teeth. "No man, that's all you do is give her money. Just let her be, she will be fine." I fussed.

"Ard fine, I'm about to go meet my lady for the night." he said, getting up. "You good? You need some money?"

I chuckled. "Naw pop, I'm good."

"Ok just asking, I know business is still treating you well." he said as he dapped me up and left out the house.

I didn't just get my good looks from my parents but their intellect as well. I was the elected valedictorian at my school, but I let the person after me have that, I'm not into speeches and shit. Numbers were my niche; I was literally doing some of my old teacher's taxes. My father met so many people and spoke so highly of me, and that sent plenty of business my way. So, I started my own little tax service which kept my pockets heavy. I was in school to be an accountant, but I mainly did it online because walking around campus was stressing me out. I didn't mind transferring to another college in Baltimore because fuck Cali, I'm tired of the people here for real. My ringing phone brought me out of thoughts. I looked down and saw it was Katrina.

"Fuck!" I mumbled.

I hadn't called her back like I said I would earlier, and I knew I was about get an earful. I really liked her, and she helped me through some shit, but she could be extra and clingy as fuck sometimes. I some-what enjoyed having a long-distance relationship but moving back to Baltimore meant that she would be on my ass like white on rice, and I wasn't sure if I was ready for that just yet.

THREE MONTHS LATER
KEYARRA

I was sitting in the front seat as my brother drove to BWI, so we could pick up Tia and Derek. I literally could not keep still. My leg was shaking, and I was trying to talk myself down. I was so nervous to see Tia. I was prepared for her to punch me right in the face as soon as she saw me, and I was ok with that. I deserved it. I treated her like shit these past 2 years. I just couldn't face her because I knew she would see what I was hiding. She knew me better than anyone, so I had to push her away. I just never expected it to come to blows. When she showed up at the house, I was shocked and happy at the same time. I wanted to throw myself in her arms and cry, but I decided against that and tried to push her out of my room, and things just got out of hand from there. I could tell Tia didn't want to fight me; I just wanted her to leave but she wouldn't take no for an answer. Tia was a better fighter than me for sure, so the fact that I only walked away with a few broken fingers said a lot. She held back while I let all my frustration and anger out on her, and I felt terrible for months. I still feel like a shitty person. I called once to apologize because GG made me, but I just didn't want to explain myself at the time. But Tia hung up on me which was understandable.

The last few months I had reached out a handful of times but again I was met with silence, then the sound of her hanging up on me. When I was told about Tia and Derek moving back, I was mixed with emotions. I missed my best friend, but I knew it wouldn't be easy to get back in her good graces. I felt like now I was able to put on a good poker face and convince Tia that I was fine and just needed to "find myself".

"Why are you over there talking to yourself?" Matthew questioned, with his face all screwed up.
I looked over at him and rolled my eyes. I didn't have the best relationship with him either but that was mainly his fault. He could be a genuine asshole and after our mother died, he just took a turn for the worst. He started fighting and hanging out with the wrong people. GG had her hands full with the 2 of us, but she did the best she could honestly.

"Don't start with her." GG defended from the back seat.
Whenever Matthew drove, she wanted to sit in the back seat because she felt safer that way.
"I'm just saying G! She's shaking and talking to herself like a weirdo."
"Matthew you can go straight to hell." I quipped.
I felt a light smack on the side of my head from GG. She may have been a holy woman, but G would be quick to put her hands on us if we got out of line.
"Watch your mouth little girl!" GG scolded.
"Sorry." I mumbled.
"Are you nervous that Tia is gonna black your eye, like you blacked hers?"
"If G wasn't in this car Matthew, I would black your fucking eye." I spat coldly.
I was met with another smack to the head but a lot harder.
"KEYARRA, HAVE YOU LOST YOUR MIND?" GG shouted.

"Tell him to leave me alone G, I'm so sick of him." I yelled on the brink of tears. I was so stressed about being in Tia's presence and this dickhead wasn't making it any better.

"Matthew, I swear. Leave your sister alone before BOTH of y'all have black eyes."

"Sorry mam." Matthew apologized dryly.

"Don't apologize to me, say it to your damn sister. Stop acting like a bully!"

I felt Matthew's hand on my shaking knee, and I flinched slightly, I tried to smack it away, but he didn't move it.

"I'm sorry Key, ok? I surrender."

"Yeah whatever."

"See G, I try to be nice to her and she always acts like a brat." Matthew whined like a little bitch.

"You two won't be happy until I have a heart attack."

The rest of the ride was silent, we sat in the telephone lot for about 20 mins before Derek called Matt and told him that they were ready. My heart was beating so fast, and I felt like I was finna pass out. We got out of the car and waited to greet them. I was literally shaking. I felt a hand on my shoulder, and I looked up and it was Matthew.

"Calm down Key, I won't let her fuck you up too bad." he said, trying to make a joke, but I didn't find shit funny.

"Please get away from me." I snapped, stepping away from him.

I heard him suck his teeth. GG shouted with excitement as she saw the Williams siblings step out of the airport looking like they had just stepped off a runway. Tia was a dresser, she followed trends, then made them her own. I had been secretly stalking her socials and she posted constantly all her latest inspos and outfits that she wore to literally go nowhere. Her naturally curly hair was pulled up into a high ponytail, some oversized sunglasses adorned her face, which I'm sure were designer. She had some tight black ankle length jeans, with a cropped tie-dye shirt, she also had on some chunky wedges. She was carrying a Louis Vuitton duffle and walked like she knew she was the shit. Tia always had confidence even when we were kids. I always admired that. I was a little on the shyer side, but I popped out every so often. I looked over at Derek and I promise I drooled a little. He was beautiful, like picture perfect. I mean he was always a cutie, and I will admit he was my very 1st crush, but the pictures I had seen over the years didn't do him any justice. Derek looked to be about 6"1 and was built! He had on a blue Nike shirt, with Nike sweatpants shorts and a pair of the Retro French Blue Jordans. I was a sneakerhead, so I was jealous because I couldn't get a pair of those. He was dressed down compared to Tia, but he still looked like a model. I got a funny feeling in my stomach when we locked eyes for a second.

"Look at my babies." GG screeched, as she ran towards them. Derek caught her in his arms and swung her around.
"Aw G, I missed you." He beamed, when he finally put her down.
"When did you get so tall boy?" She questioned looking him over.
Fuck being tall when did he get so fine?
"Stop it G. I've been this tall forever now, you just saw me a few months ago for Tri's prom and you said the same thing." Derek laughed.
"I know but I can't get over it and look at my diva girl." GG said, turning her attention to Tia, who I'm sure was burning a hole in my face behind her dark shades.
"Hi GG, I missed you." Tia responded sweetly, as she greeted her.
"Brotherrrrr." Derek roared as he pulled Matthew into a bear hug. They were always close and stayed in contact over the years. Matthew visited constantly even after I had stopped, he loved it in Cali. DW had offered him multiple times to move in with them, but he refused because he didn't want to leave me behind. I called bullshit but whatever.
"What up brother?" Matthew asked with so much enthusiasm. That made me sick. He treated me like shit but was happy as hell to see Derek!

Derek approached me next, and I stuck out my hand like a dumbass so he could shake it. I hadn't seen him in about 2 years as well. When he came to visit, I would always make sure I wasn't around so he wouldn't try to press me about Tia. He squinted at me slightly and pulled me by my hand into his strong arms for a hug.

"Stop playing with me girl like we not family." Derek said.
I almost melted in his arms; he smelled good as hell too. I held on a little longer than I should of, when I finally let go, I was met with an intense pair of eyes. They were turning me on but made me nervous at the same time.
"It's been too long Keyarra, you look good." Derek complimented me as he gave me a look over.

I had on a white v neck t-shirt with a pair of black spandex shorts that showed the ass, that I had grown by just sitting in my room for days at a time and eating. I was a good size 10 and I was surprisingly happy with my weight gain. I thought I carried it well.
"Thank you, Derek." I replied lowly.
His staring was making me more nervous. It also didn't go unnoticed that he bit down on his bottom lip slightly. We stared at each other for a few seconds before I complimented him back.
"You look good too, um I-I like your Js."
"Thank you love." He flashed me a smile that would bring any woman to her knees.
I felt my panties getting wet and I was embarrassed, what the hell was wrong with me. This man is like my brother and here I was getting horny over him.
"Boy stop playing with me." I heard Tia say as she smacked Matthew in the chest and pushed him away from her.
"I'm serious Ti, you know you in ghetto Baltimore again. You don't have to dress like you're with the bougie white folks out in Cali." Matthew teased.

"What are you even talking about? This is me being dressed down." Tia said spinning around.

"Naw for real, that is her casual look." Derek chimed in.

"Well hello to you too Keyarra." Tia snipped zooming in on me. She removed her shades and cut her eyes at me. My voice got caught in my throat as I just stared at her.

"Oh, so you can blow my phone up but can't speak in person?" Tia spoke with an attitude, but I can hear a hint of playfulness in her voice.

Before I knew it, I ran over to her and hugged her so tightly, I couldn't fight the tears that fell from my eyes.

"I'm so sorry Tia, please please forgive me." I said between my sobs

It took her a second before she finally hugged me back. We stood there for a few minutes just embracing.

"Girl, I forgive you but we gotta talk…and I have to get my lick back." Tia broke our hug, put her glasses back on and turned on her heels, making her way towards the truck. I let out a huge sigh of relief and silently thanked the Lord.

"See baby, worried for nothing" GG said as she linked arms with me as we walked back to the car.

The worst was over…. I think.

MATTHEW

I have to say, I was happy as hell to have my brother back in town. Derek was my better half. He was a lot more levelheaded than I was and we just always got along. We were raised as if we were brothers and that's exactly how we carried it. When they moved, that shit pushed me over the edge. I was already still grieving the loss of our mothers but losing 2 more people that were close to me made me lose it. My grades slipped and I started lashing out, which caused me to fight. I was kicked out of my high school 2 weeks before graduation, which sucked but I didn't care. GG kicked me out for a few weeks at one point, but I just stayed with my dad. My dad, Mark, came around after my mother had died. At first, I was apprehensive because he never really was part of my life, but I really didn't have a choice. We grew closer, and even when G let me come back, I still spent a lot of time with Mark. He was cool and was more like a friend than a parent but that was cool. I felt like I needed a friend more than anything. Mark tried to get close to Keyarra too even though he wasn't her father, and she was open at first, then her ass just started tripping. She was irritable and mean as hell all the time. I love my little sister more than life itself, but I wanted to knock her out more than a few times. The only person that she would talk to was GG, but she was very short with her. All she did was go to school, come home from wherever and stay in her room. I tried so many times to get her to talk to me, but it was a lost cause. My patience was non-existent, and I didn't have time to deal with her temperamental ass, so I just let her be.

When she and Tia had that fight a few years back, I was disgusted with her. I wouldn't even look her way for at least 3 months. I didn't know what was going on with her. Tia came all that way just to talk to her and Keyarra just picked a fight for no reason; I had felt so bad for Tia. She looked heartbroken. I remember when me and G took her to the hospital so her arm could be looked at, she just sobbed, and asked why did Keyarra hate her and what did she do wrong? I came home and cussed Key out so badly. She seemed very unphased and just stared at me blankly. I begged G to get her professional help. She went for a few months, but now she barely goes. About 8 months ago, Keyarra came around and stopped acting like an omen child. She joined cheerleading and even got herself a little high yellow boyfriend. I was confused on why she did a 360 out of nowhere but G didn't care, she was just happy that Keyarra was acting like a normal teenager for once.

"What time is your father coming Derek? Our dinner reservation is at 7." GG stated as we drove back home.
"He should be here in an hour or so. He left NY around 2." Derek answered.
"Oh great, I can't believe I will have all my babies at one table. That hasn't happened in a few years." GG voiced.
"I wonder why that is?" I mumbled lowly.
I glanced at Keyarra in the rearview mirror, and she was giving me the look of death; I'm not sure why because it was true. She is single-handedly, the reason why we all haven't been in the same room for almost 2 years.
"It's all good man, we're all here now and that's all that matters." Derek said from beside me.

Out of the 4 of us, Derek was the most positive, he had the better attitude about everything. He could get very angry at times, then his eyes would do some mutant shit, and everyone knew to leave his ass alone. But he always tried to keep that at bay. Derek could beat the shit out of someone, then act like everything was ok the next minute. Now me on the other hand, once I got angry there was no stopping me. I was a wild card for sure, but I have been trying my best to work on my anger issues; another reason I was glad to have Derek back in town. He knew I was a hothead, but he always had a way of defusing situations better than I could before I went hulk on someone.

"Where are we eating?" Tia inquired.
"Don't worry princess, it will meet your standards." I answered as I gave her a quick wink in the rearview mirror, while everyone else was busy on their phones.
She gave me a slight smile and turned her attention away from me. I admit, I am happy to have Tia back too. I have a soft spot for her. She has a mean ass attitude which I don't tolerate but once she calms down, she is the easiest person to talk to. She is a great listener and really gives the best advice.

We lost our virginities to each other 2 summers ago; right before my wreck and kind of around the time Keyarra had started acting a little funny. So she hadn't come with me that summer but had promised that she would visit in a few weeks, which of course she never did. Tia and I have been sneaking around ever since; whenever I came to visit, we found a way to spend time together which wasn't hard because Derek was always out getting his dick wet. DW was never home, and Pam was a drunk who didn't know what was going on half the time. Tia swore up and down that Keyarra had found out about us and that is why she had stopped talking to her, but I promised that wasn't it. She stopped talking to me for a few months until I was able to convince her that Keyarra knew nothing about us. That also prompted Tia to come to Baltimore when she and Key got into that fight. That's why I was so upset because seeing Tia distraught like that and not being able to comfort her the way that I wanted to was hard.

Tia was a hard ass on the outside, but she liked to be babied and talked to gently; at one point she was the only person who brought that soft side out of me. I enjoyed kissing on her and making love together. Us being so inexperienced at the time was good because we were able to explore and see what we liked and disliked. I hated leaving Cali for that reason, I wanted to have sex more and once or twice a month wasn't cutting it. I added a few more bodies just because I became horny as fuck when I was home. I usually controlled those urges pretty well, before I started having sex because the thought of messing with any of my fast ass classmates would turn me all the way off, but I once I dipped in Tia, I was addicted. I didn't turn into a hoe like Derek, by any means. So I was very selective about who I gave dick to. Women ran their mouths too much and I just didn't want any drama. I'm not in a relationship and don't want to be in one, but I do have a little situation going on with someone; and with Tia being back I wasn't sure how to go about balancing the two. All I know is that my family is back together and that's all I've wanted for the past 4 years.

TIA

We finally pulled up to the house on Kings Ridge, and a wave of emotions came over me. I instantly thought of my mother, then I thought of the fight that me and Keyarra had. I felt myself getting hot. This bitch was really sitting next me like everything was ok just because she has said sorry. No mam it wasn't. Yeah, I forgave her or whatever, but she still had to answer to me about what the fuck her problem was with me.

"Alright family, we are home." Matthew announced.

His voice alone turned me on, I was so in love with Matt, and I hated it. I knew he had some little bitches because Derek told me when he lost his, "virginity". Which meant he made something up to tell Derek because he couldn't tell him who he really lost it to. I would overhear conversations about some girl he was fucking, and I would become infuriated, but I played it cool because I can't control what he did just like he couldn't control what I did. So, in return, I started sleeping with this guy I could tolerate at my school. I remember one time Derek was on facetime with Matthew and I purposely told him that I was going to hang out with Daniel, so that way Matt could hear. I heard him question who Daniel was and Derek just said, "some Spanish talking nigga she been studying with lately". Matthew blew up my phone the rest of the night; he was pissed when I finally answered him. He said that he understood that we weren't in a relationship, but it was too soon for me to be fucking someone else considering the fact I had just lost my virginity to him. I told him that he had some nerve to even tell me that because he was already fucking someone else. But of course, he turned the heat off him by saying that it wasn't anything serious, and that men didn't catch feelings so easily like women, when sex got involved. Matthew was telling me a bunch of bullshit that I didn't wanna hear. He must've forgot who my brother and sperm donor were; they were two hoes in a pod. And I have heard them sweet talk plenty of women out of their panties, so I wasn't ignorant to the games that men played. Matthew could play games if he wanted to, but I definitely would play them back. A piece of me was hoping now that I was back, we could make things official but I'm sure the excuse of Derek would come up again. But I call bullshit because he knows that my brother wasn't the issue. Matthew just wanted to hoe off, and that was fine because best believe I wasn't going to sit around this summer and wait for him.

I stepped out of the truck and removed my Chanel shades. I looked up and down the block and couldn't help but smile. This was my childhood. I remember running up down the block playing with the other neighborhood kids. I remember playing with sprinklers out in the front yard. I remember everything. I loved our home and our little family, but everything changed after the accident, and I had blamed God because of it. I was raised in the church, thanks to GG. I liked Sunday school and showing off my cute dresses every week. Keyarra and I were on the youth choir and praise team; we had so much fun, but of course all that ended when we moved. Aunt Pam claimed to be all holier than thou but would be drunk as a skunk. GG said we just had to pray for her, but I never did. I stopped praying a long time ago. I lost my mother, my aunt, my home, then my best friend; so, I was angry with God and had no plans on re-building a relationship with Him. I expressed this to GG plenty of times and she said that he makes no mistakes, and that I just needed to continue to pray and read

the Bible. That was my problem with the older generation now, half of them were hypocrites, then the other half just didn't fully listen to us; they told us to pray and things would get better, and I hated that. I loved GG though. She adopted my mother and aunt and made us all a family, but sometimes she just didn't listen, and that made me not want to talk about everything with her. That's why it hurt so much when Keyarra turned on me; we told each other
everything. When I told her I lost my virginity she barely cared; of course I didn't tell her to who, but she just was very uninterested anyway, shortly after that she stopped returning my calls and texts. I started feeling hot again at the thought of it.

"The neighborhood looks the same doesn't it, Ti?" Keyarra asked as she stood in front of me. I was finally getting a good look at her since I removed my shades, she had gained some weight but all in the right places. Keyarra always had the prettiest face with her cinnamon color skin. She had similar facial features to Christina Milian; she also had the sweetest personality to match. We were like yin and yang. She was always nice, and I was nice too just with a slight attitude problem. But I got it honest because my father could be an asshole, and my mother was never the one to play with.

"Yeah...it does look the same" I finally answered.
"The house looks totally different though, c'mon let me show you."
She grabbed my hand and made me follow her like she did when we were kids. I looked behind me at Derek, and he mouthed, "its ok". The last few weeks we have talked and talked about every scenario that I could come up with in my head about how things would go with me and Keyarra, I had a panic attack on the plane, I hadn't had one of those since the night Derek had got arrested. I didn't know what I was walking into and that made me nervous as hell. Derek talked me down and told me repeatedly, that everything was going to be ok, and he was going to be right by my

side. When we got into the house, I was floored. This was not my childhood home anymore. The carpeted floors were now replaced with this laminated wood, but a beautiful plush lavender area rug was laid in the middle of the floor. The wall was mirrored all the way up the staircase, the railings were black and shiny as well. We climbed the stairs until we got to me and Keyarra's old room. I walked in and laughed to myself because she still had some of the same Chris Brown posters that I hung up so many years ago. I was a diehard Chris Brown fan, and I was team breezy for life. I saw that her room was painted a dark grey with black trimming; it gave off a very cool vibe. I noticed the pictures on her wall and walked over to them, she had so many, and they all were shaped so they could fill out a heart. There were tons from our childhood; some from our birthday parties and class trips. Then I saw more recent ones, where she had on a cheerleading uniform and looked…. happy. There were a few with her and this high yellow boy, then I saw a lot with this cute girl who looked like she could be black, but I wasn't sure. They were all posing and cheesing like they were best friends.

"That's Sharin, we cheerlead together." Keyarra said from behind me.

The thought that Keyarra made new friends while she treated me like shit didn't sit right with me. I turned around and faced her, before I could even give it a thought, I smacked fire out of her ass. Tears fell from my eyes as I anticipated her next move, I was ready for a fight. She held her cheek and looked at me with almost an amused look. I know this bitch didn't take me as a joke.

"Ok, since that is out the way can we start to repair what I broke." she said.

I just stared into her eyes, and I knew that something was there, I could feel it and I could see it. I pulled her in for a hug and we stood there for a minute. I was finally feeling like I could get through this, and I was kind of happy to have my best friend back.

"Keyarra, I know that you are hiding something from me but I'm going to leave it alone for now." I said as I broke our embrace. She cleared her throat and turned away from me.

"So, when is y'all apartment going to be ready?" she asked, not even acknowledging my statement.

"A few days." I answered.

"Where is it again?"

"I think it's called, The Southerly."

"But that's in Towson! You wouldn't be going to Parkville then." She said, with sadness in her voice.

"I can when I pass this magnet test."

"Ok cool, when are you going to take it?"

"I'll have to schedule it; I wasn't sure how I was going to feel about your fickle ass, so I didn't want to waste my time." Keyarra chuckled. "That's understandable, are you changing for dinner?"

"Where are we going?"

"Kobe's, on the avenue."

I thought about it for a second. I didn't feel like changing, but I wasn't wearing plane clothes to dinner plus I wanted to look good for Matthew.

"Yeah I want to, but I don't feel like going through my luggage, is there something of yours I could wear?" I said walking over to her closet.

"Oh yes, I have just the dress. It will match your shoes too." Keyarra said excitedly, as she jumped up and started to rummage through her closet. She finally pulled out this light blue strapless midi dress, it was a little stretchy, so it would cling to me nicely.

"It's not designer or anything but it will compliment your skin tone." She said handing it to me.

"I'm not a label whore Keyarra. I've found some of the toughest shit in thrift stores."

I held the dress out to examine it. Me and Keyarra were always the same size for most of our lives, but she looked to be slightly thicker than me now. I admired the dress; she was right, it would look nice on me. I had pecan color skin, so I enjoyed wearing

29

brighter colors. A lot of people have said that I could be a dead ringer for, Reagan Gomez.

"Girl I know, I be seeing your little fits that you be putting together."

"And how did you see those?" I questioned, with my head slightly cocked to the side.

Keyarra looked guilty as hell. Her ass was watching me on IG and shit.

"Uh huh, you watching me online but I didn't get a like or nothing." I teased.

"I'm sorry Ti, I really did miss you." She said with her head down.

"You sure had a funny way of showing it, but listen we cool. I wouldn't have come back here if I thought you were gonna be on the same bullshit. Now come show me the rest of the house." I said, laying the dress on the back on her bed.

Keyarra smiled and led the way. GG had re-done the entire house. She showed me the renovations through FT but seeing it in person was just different. The finished attic is where our mothers had stayed but it was always nice being up there, so she didn't switch it up too much because she wanted to keep their memory alive. She just added a few more windows to brighten it up. The kitchen had granite countertops and state of the art appliances. The basement, which was GG's room, was all decked out; it looked like a mini apartment down there now. I remember it being a little cramped with all 7 of us being there at once. Our mothers wanted to move us out at one point, somewhere nearby still close to GG but we begged them not to, it was our home, and we had no complaints. They said they would re-visit it when we were all a little older. GG's mother left her this house and even though she had money to purchase a new one, she never wanted to give it up, so she just added her own touches to it.

We finally made it out back, and there was Derek and Matthew jumping on that got damn trampoline, with their overgrown asses. I remember being surprised with this trampoline one day after my asshole father took Matthew and Derek on a trip with him. My feelings were hurt because he barely talked to me, let alone took me anywhere. Me and Keyarra jumped all day every day and when the boys finally came home, they jumped with us. The 4 of us would have a ball on it; our mothers would have to pull us off it.

"Y'all are gonna break it." I yelled out.
"Come jump with us." Derek yelled back.
"I wish I would."
"C'mon Derek, you know the princess can't break a nail."
Matthew teased exiting the trampoline.
Matthew knew I hated that nickname, so of course he called me that whenever he got a chance; but what he didn't know was that my heart fluttered a little every time he did. He climbed the steps and grabbed Keyarra in a bear hug, making sure to get all his sweat all over her.
"Get the hell off of me…. ugh what the hell is wrong with you!" Keyarra shrieked, as she struggled to get out of his grasp.
Matthew just laughed, as he finally let her go.
"You are all sweaty now, might as well go jump for a little bit." Matthew said.
"Yes, c'mon Key, come jump with me!" Derek yelled, as he flipped in the air. I'm so glad that net was still up.
"You coming?" Keyarra asked as she started down the steps.
"I think, I'll pass"
"Come pick me out something to wear." Matthew said as he opened the door to go into the house.
"You are grown, you can pick out your own clothes" I replied crossing my arms in front of my chest.
"No Ti, please help him, he dresses like an old man." Keyarra added as Derek was helping her onto the trampoline.
"Come in the damn house!" Matthew gritted lowly.

When Matthew closed the door, he pulled me all the way upstairs. When we finally got into his room, his mouth covered mine. I hadn't felt his lips in about 4 months, and I was longing for them. I have made out with a few guys, but he was by far the best.

"I missed you Ti." He whispered against my lips and started to kiss me on my neck.

"I missed you too." I moaned lowly.

"I really wanna feel you right now." He said as he started to lift my shirt, but I pulled it back down.

"No, what if they come in, and where is G?"

"We can hear them." He said pointing to the window. I could hear the creaking of the trampoline and Keyarra's laughs.

"And G is getting dressed, you know she takes forever. But you are wasting time." He added.

"You gonna get your sweat all over me." I whined.

"Tia shut up!" He said as his mouth covered mine again. We began undressing each other as we made our way to his bed. He laid me down and stood over me for a few minutes. He licked his lips slightly and that alone could have made me cum. Matthew was so sexy to me, he reminded me of Romeo, with his beautiful umber skin and full lips. I loved to rub my hands through his soft waves, and I always ran my fingers down his toned body. Matthew was maybe a half of an inch taller than Derek, and he worked out often. We would work out together when he came to Cali. Derek would come sometimes but he wasn't big on the gym.

Matthew started to trail kisses down my body, then I stopped him.

"Matt no, I just got off of 7-hour flight."

"C'mon Ti, I'm sure it's fine." He assured.

"No!" I protested. I was not about to let him go down on me without freshening up first.

"Ughhhh!" He groaned.

He turned around, then I heard the fumbling of a wrapper and before I knew it, Matthew had filled me up. His size was something that I never thought I would get used to because along with the immense pleasure came pain, but it was so worth it.

"Shit!" He hissed as he closed his eyes.

Matthew rocked in and out of me slowly at first, then he started picking up the pace. I struggled to muffle myself.

"That feel good baby?" Matthew asked as he bit down on his bottom lip.

I nodded my head yes.

"I wanna hear you say it."

"Yes." I whimpered.

We suddenly heard the creaking from the trampoline stop.

"Ti, I need you to cum."

He leaned down and started sucking on one of my nipples, pumping in and out of me faster. I was on the brink of cumming.

"Please cum with me." I moaned as I pulled his face up and made him kiss me.

"Naw, get this one off and I'll cum with you in a few." He gently bit down on my bottom lip and stared into my eyes. I came in seconds.

"Good girl, Ti." He praised me with a devilish smile.

I felt lightheaded.

"C'mon princess, I want you to cum with me now…. please."

He kissed me and picked up the pace again, we were moaning into each other's mouths as quietly as possible.

"I'm about to nut Tia, let one more go." Matthew groaned in my ear, he started sucking on my lobe and that was my undoing. He knew exactly how to touch me, and it never failed. My hand flew to my mouth as I came hard.

"FUCK!" he growled as he shuddered a little.

He collapsed on top of me, and we laid there for a minute as we tried to catch our breaths.

"C'mon Ti, get up before we get caught up."

Matthew pulled out of me and pulled the condom off. I could barely move; my head was spinning, and I just wanted to go to sleep. He pulled me forward by both of my arms.

"Nooo, I just wanna lay here." I whined.

"Stop playing Tia, they gonna catch us."

"And why would that be such a bad thing?" I questioned.

"Ti, please don't start this."

33

Matthew walked over to the other side of the room to look out the window.

"Oh cool, they still on there...why they so close though?" He spoke out loud as he damn near stuck his head out the window.

I looked at the floor and saw the box of condoms. I picked it up and saw that it was a 16 pack and there only had to be about 9 or so left in there. I started getting hot.

"Ohhh so this is why...you wanna keep fucking all your other little bitches." I said throwing the box at his back, I knew Matt was fucking other girls, but the reality just set in, and I was pissed. He turned his attention back to me.

"Aye watch that shit Tia, don't come out here and start tripping." He growled walking towards me. I didn't say anything as I started to gather my clothes. I was so worried about how things would go with Keyarra, that I barely thought about what would happen if Matthew didn't want to be with me.

"C'mon Ti, don't act like that." Matthew pleaded as he wrapped his arms around me. He kissed me along my shoulder.

"Please let me go, so I can run to the bathroom and shower. I would hate for our siblings to catch me ass naked in the hallway." I snapped with an attitude.

"How could you possibly be upset after cumming as hard as you just did?" Matthew asked letting me go, he then turned me around to face him. He cupped my chin to make me look up into his eyes.

"After dinner I wanna spend some more time with you...ok?"

"How are we going to do that?"

"Don't worry, I'll take care of it."

He leaned down and kissed me again.

"Now go get ready. The washcloths and stuff are in the same place."

I didn't say anything as I left his room and walked across the hall into the bathroom, I started the shower and stepped in. My hair was already a curly mess so I would just blow-dry it when I came out. I stood under the water and thought about how I was going to make Matthew tell Derek and Keyarra about us. I don't care what he said. He was going to be mine.

DEREK

Me and Keyarra laid on the trampoline trying to catch our breaths, we jumped for a good 10 minutes, and were wiped out.
"This shit hit a little different when you older." I expressed.
"Right, I haven't been on this in years." Keyarra said in between ragged breaths.
"That's like the pool we had in Cali, I never got in there for some reason."
"Oh, see that's different, I would have been in there every day. Remember, y'all couldn't get me out the pool when I was coming out there." Keyarra reminded me.
"See my memory a little foggy about it because it's been a while since I seen your ass on the west coast." I teased.
She suddenly sat up straight.
"I guess, I owe you an apology as well. I didn't mean to ghost y'all the way I did, I um had some stuff going on." Keyarra explained with her head down. She looked uncomfortable and I couldn't help but wonder why.
"Like what, Key?"

There was silence. I sat up and moved next to her, probably a little closer than I should have, but something about her demeanor made me want to comfort her. I can't lie, when I laid eyes on Keyarra at the airport my dick got hard. She was beautiful! And she had the body that most women would pay for, I loved women that were thick; it gave me something to hold on to and to be honest, they took dick a lot better.

When we hugged though, I felt a mix of things. I felt like I didn't want to let her go, she was tense, and I wanted to hold her until she released whatever bullshit she had built up. No doubt I was attracted to her but not just in a sexual way, which was rare; I felt like I wanted to get to know her all over again, I don't even know if I felt that way about Katrina at any point. The relationship I was in now was my very first; after I lost my virginity, I hit the ground running. As Tia would say, I was like our hoe ass father, but I didn't care. I loved women but more importantly, I loved sex, and I had a lot of it. But currently, I am a one-woman guy. This shit is new to me, but I am trying my hardest. I promised my sister and GG that I would stay out of trouble but looking at Keyarra was making me feel like I might have a slip-up.

"Listen Key, I'm not tryna press you because I know you gonna get enough of that from Tia mean ass, but whatever you had going on, I hope you good now. I'm here if you ever need to talk." I voiced genuinely.

She turned to me and smiled slightly. I admired her pretty ass face and radiant brown eyes.

"Thank you, Derek I really appreciate that a lot."

We stared at each other for a little while longer. I knew when a woman wanted me, and Keyarra was no different, except she was off limits. I was in a relationship plus she was supposed to be like my little sister as well; even though we were each other's first kiss. I remember it was the night before me and Tia were leaving for Cali. I came downstairs to get water and Keyarra was sitting on the couch damn near in the dark crying while holding the teddy bear her mom had got her a few years ago for Valentines Day.

"What are you doing Keyarra? Why are you crying" I asked as I walked over to her.

"Everything is ruined, y'all are leaving tomorrow and nothing will be the same." She sobbed into her bear.

I wasn't sure what to say, I was kind of excited about the move, but Keyarra and Tia were devastated. Matthew wasn't thrilled about the idea, but he understood just like me. I sat down next to her and gently pulled her bear away her face.

"Keyarra, yes, we are going away but don't worry. My dad said he will pay for y'all to visit anytime y'all want and we will be back here to visit too." I said, trying my best to reassure her.

"It won't be the same." She wailed.

"I know but we have to make it work."

She just stared at me with teary eyes, so I did the only thing I could think of. I leaned in and kissed her lips gently. I saw my father do it to my mother so many times when she was upset, so I figured that was a way to make a girl happy again. We pressed our lips together for a few seconds until she broke our kiss. There was an awkward moment of silence, I was hoping I did it right because I had never kissed a girl on the lips before.

"Thank you, Derek." she finally said with a smile.

She leaned over to hug me then stood up, grabbed her bear and made her way back to her and Tia's room.

"Maybe we should go and get ready for dinner." I said breaking our staring contest. I looked at my watch and saw that it was almost 5. I made my way out of the trampoline then turned around and helped Keyarra get out.

"Matthew and Tia should be done with the bathroom; I can go downstairs and use G's, while you use the upstairs one." Keyarra suggested as we entered the house.

"Ok that's cool." I replied.

As we climbed the steps Matthew was just stepping out of the bathroom with a towel wrapped around his waist.

"Damn, you just getting done? What was you in there doing?" I asked.

"PRINCESS TIA" He yelled so that she could hear from the room, "took forever as usual." He continued.

"GO TO HELL MATTHEW!" she hollered from the other side of the door.

We all laughed. Matt loved to pick on Tia, and it never got old. Tia would fall for it every time.

"Well, imma go grab my clothes, and shower downstairs." Keyarra said as she slid past us and walked into her room.

"Y'all have fun? It sure sounded like it." Matthew said as I followed him into our old room. I saw the renovations he had done last year when I was here, but it still was wild to me that it looked nothing like the room we used to share. The walls were painted a dark green, but he kept the trimmings white. He had all new chocolate brown furniture and rearranged how everything was set up from the last time I had seen it.

"Yeah, it was cool…. Tia pick you out a fit?" I asked.

"Naw, her ass was tripping as usual." He said with a mug.

I laughed because as much as Tia loved to dress everyone, she hated to be asked. She was just complicated like that sometimes.

"Well, imma just shower then get dressed in the bathroom." I said, grabbing my duffle off the floor.

"You sure? I'll be dressed in like 10 mins."

"Naw you good bro, I don't mind."

I headed out the room and straight to the bathroom.

About a half hour later I heard GG's voice.

"Alright its almost 6, I want to be there on time children." GG announced.

I came out of the bathroom looking and smelling good. I put on a black Ralph Lauren short sleeve button up, I didn't want to risk messing up my shirt at dinner by putting on a lighter color; they be throwing shrimp at you and shit. I had on some khaki shorts with my black Armani Kombat sneakers. I had just finished spraying some Tom Ford Noir cologne. I hit the steps, and I saw Keyarra and Tia on the landing taking pictures in the mirror. I had to admit, mirroring the walls was tough. I met them at the bottom and stood between them, draping one arm across both shoulders and pulled them in.

"My turn." I cheesed.

We flicked it up a few times before Matt came down the steps.

39

"Aw Ti, good job. He doesn't look like a 40-year-old man." Keyarra complimented.

Matthew always kept it simple. He had on a grey polo, black cargo shorts, with some grey and black Jordan 1s.

"Thank you." Tia said.

"I thought you didn't pick out anything." I asked looking at her through the mirror.

Tia looked at me puzzled.

"I mean she pointed some shit out but she really ain't put nothing together like she would for you. She was holding out on me." Matthew said before she could respond.

"Yeah, he has the most basic shit in there." Tia added.

"Watch your mouth, Tia." GG said as she re-entered the living room.

That was something I would have to get used to again, filtering myself. My pop was cool, he never got on us about our language as long as we didn't cuss his ass out, and we tried to keep it respectful around Aunt Pam, but she cussed us out all day long, so in return we gave it back to her a few times. GG didn't play though; she may have cussed here and there if she was really fed up but otherwise, she was old school and would pop us right in the mouth no matter how old we were.

"Sorry." Tia replied.

"Where is your father, I don't want to be late." GG fussed as she looked at me for an answer. GG was hip to not asking Tia about our dad because she always had a smart comment.

"He texted me while I was in the shower and said to just meet him there." I replied.

"Oh great." she said with an eye roll.

"Chill G, the restaurant only like 10 minutes away." Matthew re-assured.

"Yeah, come take some pics with us." I said as I reached out for her hand.

It was a little tight for us all to be on the landing together, but we made it work. GG always reminded me of Angela Bassett, just a little shorter. She had this golden-brown skin, with long black hair that reached her mid-back, she had this grey-ish white strip that was on her left side, it was like her birthmark she had that strip since she was born, and she embraced it beautifully. You never would think she was almost 70, she barely had any wrinkles or fine lines. She always dressed classy, but with the help of Tia she stayed up to date with trends. Today she had on a mid-knee flowy blue dress, with gold sandals and matching gold jewelry. Keyarra and Tia used to play dress up in her clothes all the time.

"Ok ok, that's enough, can we go please." GG insisted.

She was always on time for everything. We all piled in Matt's truck and headed to The Avenue. We arrived about 15 minutes later; we all went in, and GG went to see about our reservations. Kobe's was one of our family's favorite restaurants. We went there for every special occasion, just about. It was crowded since it was a Saturday night. We had arrived half an hour early thanks to G rushing, but to our surprise, we had a private party room which I didn't even know they had. My father had a habit of throwing his money around because I'm sure you needed a bigger group for this room.

"This is dope." Matthew admired, as we all looked around the room.

The set up for the grill was different so we were all able to sit a little closer together. We all sat down; I pulled out GG's chair as she sat closer to the end. We left a chair open for my dad. Me and Matthew sat next to each other, and the girls sat across from us. Keyarra was directly across from me, we locked eyes for a second and she smiled. Again, I couldn't help but stare at her, she lightly did her make-up even though she didn't need it at all, but it enhanced her natural beauty. She put her auburn twists into a high bun, and she had on these big ass silver hoops. The long yellow dress she had made her cinnamon skin pop. She also had some glittery lotion or something on that made her shimmer a little every time she moved.

"Derek!" Keyarra said.

"Yeah?" I asked.

"The waitress is talking to you." she giggled.

I didn't even hear her; I was too busy lusting over Keyarra.

"Oh, my bad." I turned my attention to the waitress. "What did you say?"

"What can I get you to drink?" the waitress asked.

"Oh, can I get a coke please?"

She went around the table and took everyone else's order, then left.

"FAMILY." My dad's voice boomed as he entered the room a few moments later.

"He is so embarrassing." Tia said as she left out a deep breath.

"Don't start Tia." I warned.

"Look at my beautiful family." he said as he just cheesed and admired all of us. He drove from New York earlier that afternoon to meet us for dinner. He said he was staying for about a week to get us settled in the new place. My pops made his way to each one of us and hugged us. When he went to the girls, Keyarra stood up and embraced him. That's when I got a better look at the ass she had on her. I instantly got hard again; I imagined what it would be like as she threw it back on me.

He held on to Keyarra a few extra seconds since it had been a while since he seen her. He facetimed every now and then to check up on her; he also went to her first cheerleading game. Everyone except Tia was excited when she got out of whatever funk she had been in for that time.

"I'm so happy to see you, Keyarra." my pops said with a wide smile.

My dad loved Matthew and Keyarra as if they were his own. He would do anything for them just like he would for us. When he brought me my 1st car, he did the same for Matthew. When he first met my mother Tina, he met my aunt Kiara shortly after, and they instantly clicked and became best friends. She was the main one who advocated for him and would beg my mother to give him a chance. When they both passed my father was beyond devastated, not only did he lose the love of his life, but his best friend as well. He swore on their graves that not only would he be more present for me and Tia but he would take care of Keyarra and Matthew as well.

"I'm happy to see you as well, DW." Keyarra replied sweetly.

He let her go and moved on to Tia who hesitated to get up. I shot her a look and she got up and gave him a half ass hug. I just shook my head.

"About time you made it." GG fussed.

"My bad G, I hit traffic." pops said.

GG partly helped raise my father as well since he was around all the time. If you ask me, she saved his life because he was in the streets when he first met my mom. GG told him that if he wanted to date her baby then he would have to get his life together. He was so in love with my mother that he would do whatever so he could get close to her. He got a legit job then went to school for audio technology. He loved G like a mother. He would do anything for her and always tried to pay her bills, but she constantly denied his money because she had her own. All she wanted for him was to be a good father.

"Why did you reserve a party room?" I asked.

"Because I didn't want to scream over top of each other, it's been a while since we were all together."

The waitress came back with our drinks. She took his drink order and told us that she would take our order when she gets back. For the next hour in a half, we all conversed, laughed and reminisced; the cook did a bunch of extra shit when making our food. He did the usual throwing of the food, and the girls caught it in their mouths, Matthew and I did not participate.

"Let's say we catch a movie after this." My father suggested.

"Oh Derek, it's too late for that." GG said as she looked at her watch.

"Yeah Pop, and I have a date." I added.

"Derek you can see that hoe anytime." Tia said smartly.

Keyarra laughed.

"Shut up Tia, and don't laugh Keyarra. My girl not a hoe."

"She sure ain't a saint." Keyarra mumbled.

"What was that?" I questioned.

"Nothing." she said quickly

"Yeah, that's what I thought."

"Well Derek, I would like for y'all come to church with us tomorrow." GG said.

"Church?" Me and Tia questioned at the same time.

"Yes church, you heathens. That place where you paise and worship, remember that? I know y'all aren't under my roof but that's what I would like. At least 2 Sundays a month plus holidays." GG stated.

"It's really not that bad, plus I sing tomorrow." Keyarra said to the both of us.

"I'm ok with going to church tomorrow." Tia expressed.

"That's my girl." GG cheered.

"Yeah, I guess I'll come to." I added.

I really didn't want to, but to be honest, I just wanted to be in the same room as Keyarra again.

"Oh, and Tia, I was going to ask if you wanted to go to a party with me tonight." Keyarra asked as she turned in Tia's direction.

Tia was silent for a few seconds.

"Keyarra, Tia doesn't want to hang out with your weird friends." Matthew teased.

"Yet, you're sleeping with one of them." She retorted.

Tia peered at Matthew with one of her infamous looks.

"Keyarra shut the hell up!" Matthew yelled.

"No, you shut the hell up. No one was even talking to you so why you felt the need to insert yourself in my conversation has me confused...you erky as hell!"

"Because you in here being fake as fuck, inviting this girl to a party with your friends and y'all haven't even been cool again for 24 hours."

Next thing I know, water was flying across the table causing Matthew and I to fly out of our chairs. Keyarra threw her water right into Matt's face.

"ENOUGH!" GG screamed, as she stood up.

"I AM SO SICK OF THIS SHIT WITH YALL , ALL THIS BACK AND
FORTH HAS TO STOP. YALL TREAT EACH OTHER LIKE STRANGERS
INSTEAD OF SIBLINGS!"

"It's not me GG, it's always him!" Keyarra expressed as her voice
cracked.

"ITS BOTH OF Y'ALL!" GG continued to yell.

"Calm down G, sit down." my pops said as he tried to get her back
in her seat.

"I'm done with this brady brunch bull shit." Keyarra said as she
got her purse and proceeded to walk out of the room.

"Keyarra, I swear on my dead husband that I will knock you out."
GG spat as she tried to get back up but was stopped by my dad.
We all sat there silently for a minute trying to process what just
happened. I'm not sure why Matt and Key were so hostile
towards each other, but it wasn't cool at all.

"I'm going to go check on her." I volunteered, breaking the
silence. I got up and jogged out the door in search of Keyarra. This
side of the avenue wasn't too crowded. I looked both ways to try
and spot her. I finally saw her after a few minutes.

"Keyarra, wait up." I yelled a little so she could hear me. When I
caught up to her and she was crying.

"Aw come on Key, don't cry."

"I'm so sorry I ruined dinner."

"You didn't ruin it, shit just got a little out of hand." I tried to
reassure her.

"Derek, I got you wet. I'm sorry."

I guess she could see some of the wet spots on my shirt.

"It's all good, it's just water Key."

"Matthew really has the habit of bringing the worst out of me."

"I can see that.... what's up with y'all?"

"I don't know, after y'all left, our relationship just.... changed."
She sniffled.

"Well, y'all need to figure it out. I didn't come back to Baltimore
to be a referee." I joked, trying to lighten the mood.

She laughed a little. She held her phone up to look at herself in
her camera.

"Ugh I look a mess."

"Naw, you still look beautiful." I complimented, as I wiped a tear from her cheek.

She looked up at me and smiled.

"Thank you, Derek. You have always been one of the nicest guys."

"I try to be."

Again, we were having a staring contest, the urge I felt to kiss her was stronger than before. Just when I was about to give in, an alert popped up on her phone causing it to ding.

"My uber is about to arrive."

"You wasted no time doing that." I laughed.

"There was no way I was getting back in the truck with Matt."

"Where are you going?"

"To my boyfriend's house. He's having a party."

Matthew mentioned that she was hanging out with some football player, but I didn't know that was her nigga.

"Oh, I didn't know you had a boyfriend."

"Is that a problem?" She chuckled.

"Naw, naw, of course not." I replied, trying to play it off. But for some reason I was mad.

A red Honda pulled up next to us.

"Here is my uber. Could you do me a huge favor?"

"What's up?"

"If Tia decides to come to the party, could you drop her off before you go out tonight? I will send her the address. It's not far." She pleaded

"If I do, you better stay with her the whole time, Key. She doesn't know anybody." I warned.

Matthew may have been an asshole to his sister, but I didn't play about mine.

"I promise." She said smiling widely, then she held out her pinky finger.

I chuckled. "You better."

We intertwined our pinkys.

"You are the best!"

She jumped up and wrapped her arms around my neck. I wrapped mine around her waist and picked her up a little.

Damn she smells good!

I put her down then opened the car door for her. I stopped her before she got in.

"Now, you do me a favor, put my number in your phone and text me when you get there safe."

"Are you sure that's the only reason you want my number?" She asked, with a raised eyebrow but she still had a slight smile on her face.

I flashed a smile at her and stepped into her space.

"Keyarra, are you flirting with me?" I asked lowly.

I stared into her eyes and licked my bottom lip which was just a habit I had.

"Now why would I do that, I have a boyfriend remember." She replied, with the same flirty tone as before.

"You tell me."

We kept eye contact the entire time, she held her phone out, I took it and called my phone until I felt it vibrate.

"Make sure you text me, Keyarra."

"I will."

She got in the car and when I closed the door it pulled off. I was about to go back in the restaurant when I noticed everyone standing outside.

"Where is she?" my dad asked.

"She took an uber."

"Is she ok?" Tia asked with a look of concern.

"Yeah, she is cool. Are you going to that party...she asked me to drop you off?"

"Yeah, I'll go. She just texted me the address."

"Ard cool, where is Matthew?" I questioned, as I noticed he wasn't outside.

"He went to pull the car around." Tia answered.

"GG, is it still ok I borrow your car tonight?" I turned to ask her.

"Yes, anything to get y'all out my hair." She said with annoyance.

"G, what I do? Don't be mad at me." I said with amusement.

I could tell she was done for the night.

"Yeah whatever, just make sure you are back by 8am tomorrow morning. Church starts at 9 and I like to be there early."

"I got you, G."

"I'm not playing, Derek." GG said pointing her finger at me.

I threw my hands up in surrender.

"I said I got you G." I smiled.

Matthew pulled up, I hopped in the front and Tia in the back. GG didn't get in.

"You not riding with us?" I asked.

"No, I'm riding with your father. He is going to take me to the grocery store so I can cook tomorrow....and Matthew, your ass better be in that kitchen tomorrow too." GG said, as she looked past me at him.

He continued to stare straight.

"Yes ma'am." He replied, dryly.

"Take these keys, Derek, and remember what I said.... Tia, you know I don't allow spending the night out. Keyarra knows what time y'all should be home."

"Yes ma'am." Tia responded.

"G, why don't I wait with you, while my dad pulls the car around." I suggested.

"Because I can walk, damn it." GG said as she waved me off and started walking away.

Me and my pop chuckled.

"Y'all done pissed her off." He laughed.

"Ain't no y'all. I haven't done a damn thing."

"Me either." Tia added

"Can we go?" Matthew snapped.

"Aye Matt, get it together." my father warned, "Y'all kids have fun, but be safe tonight. Love y'all."

"Ard Pop." I dapped him up through the window. Matthew pulled off and we made it home in record time. The whole ride was silent. Matt was pissed. He has a short temper, so he could go from 0 to 100.

"Tia, imma go get my bag real quick, then I'll be ready…. you can go sit in the car if you want." I said, handing her the keys.

"Ok." She replied.

I ran upstairs to grab my carry on, I had packed it with 2 outfits. One for tonight and the other for tomorrow I felt like my second outfit wasn't really for church, but shit they say come as you are. I was going to take Katrina out to breakfast since we were staying in tonight, but I guess I would do that after church now. I grabbed my bag then went back outside. Matthew was talking to Tia outside the car, her arms folded in front of her, and it looked as if she wasn't listening to what he was saying.

"Matthew, I barely listen to the man who's ball sack I came from, what makes you think imma listen to your ass." I heard Tia say.

"Listen to him about what?" I asked.

"I was trying to convince her not to go to this party, until she meets them in a different setting."

"What's wrong with them?" I asked.

"They just can be rowdy sometimes."

"But you're fucking one, so they can't be too bad." Tia snapped.

"All that doesn't matter, I just want you to be safe."

"Maybe you shouldn't go Ti. Matt knows them better than us. We don't know what type of company Keyarra is keeping." I spoke.

I would lose my mind if something happened to my sister, and Matt seemed really concerned about her going.

"Derek please, you know I can handle myself, but I will call you if I get uncomfortable ok…. can we please go?" she insisted, as she opened the car door.

Matthew looked annoyed.

"Ard whatever." He said, as he walked off.

"Yo bro, is you good?" I questioned.

I was confused as fuck. I mean, I understand he was concerned but he was acting like a little kid.

"I'm straight." He shot back.

I turned to Tia, who looked amused. I didn't have time for this shit. Katrina already was blowing my phone up, it was almost 10 and I told her I would be there by 9:30.

"Where is this house at?" I asked as I got in the car.

"It's like 10 mins away, by Halstead." Tia answered.

"The hood of the county…. great." I said sarcastically, pulling off. As we hit the block, I slowed down a little, we saw a house with a bunch of people on the porch, so I assumed that was it. Tia started to get out the car.

"Aye, text Keyarra and tell her you're outside."

"Are you being serious right now?" Tia asked clearly irritated by my request.

"Dead ass, I will pull off and you will be at Katrina's house with me." She didn't say anything but did what I said. Two minutes later Key came out of the house. She started skipping to the car. The sight of her breasts jiggling made me swell.

"I'm so happy you came." She said excitedly, as she opened Tia's door.

"Yeah, I was almost being held hostage by our dumbass brothers."

"I thought I told your ass to text me when you got here?" I said to Keyarra.

"Damn, my bad I forgot."

"Fucking up already…. Tia, you remember what I said?" I told her on our way here to watch her surroundings, and to call me if she needed me to come get her.

"Yes father…damn."

I turned my attention back to Keyarra; her eyes were a little glossy.

"Have you been drinking?" I asked wrinkling my forehead.

"No, Derek."

"Don't make me fuck y'all up. Remember what you promised me Key."

"I got youuuuu, come on Ti." Keyarra said, as she linked arms with her, and they walked up to the house.

I waited for them to disappear inside before I pulled off. Katrina lived the opposite way, literally down the street from Parkville High about 5 minutes from GG. I pulled into the driveway, grabbed my bag and hopped out the car. When I had hit the top step, the door went flying open.

"I was about to go to sleep on your ass." Katrina said with a mug on her face.

Here we go!

"And you would have been woken up by me kicking this damn door down." I replied, as I pecked her lips and walked past her.

I walked into the living room, and it smelled like cinnamon and vanilla. I loved sweet smelling shit. The lights were dimmed, and soft Latin music was playing in the background. I put my bag down and turned around, Katrina was standing by the door with a somber look on her face. I then noticed she had on this lace robe, and I could see that she didn't have too much underneath. I licked my lips.

"Come here." I said in a low tone.

She just stared at me. Everything with her had to be difficult.

"Katrina...come...here." I said with a little more bass.

She walked over to me slowly. When she got within arm's reach, I wrapped my arm around her waist and pulled her towards me until we were chest to chest.

"Why don't you like to listen?" I asked, almost above a whisper.

I palmed her ass; she had on a thong so I started toying with the little material that was there.

"Because you be making me mad." She replied, in a small voice.

"I told your ass I was coming, so I don't know why you tripping."

"Derek, you said...." she started to talk but I ended that when my lips connected with hers. She immediately gave me her tongue. We stood there and made out for a few minutes. My dick was hard as fuck, and I was ready to show Katrina how much I missed her. I started to back her up to the couch but she broke our kiss and stopped us from walking.

"No baby, I wanna show you something first."

"Tri, can you show me after, I need to bust this nut."

"Derek, that's not fucking romantic." She argued, pushing me away from her.

I blew out a frustrated breath.

"Fine, what is it?" I questioned.

"It's upstairs. Wait 2 minutes and I'll tell you when to come up." She said excitedly, as she ran up the steps.

"Don't take all damn day!" I yelled.

I sat on the couch and laid my head back; I haven't had sex in a little over a month and it was driving me crazy. I kept replaying some of the words my therapist told me repeatedly in my head.

"Don't let the thoughts consume you. Focus on something else that brings you comfort when you get stuck in your head."

I started saying random multiplication tables out loud.

"123x12 is 1476

133x13 is 1729

143x14 is 2002"

My other comfort was numbers, and it worked most of the time. Figuring out math problems put my brain into a different mindset, so it would get me away from the sexual thoughts that would take over.

"Baby, I'm readyyy." Katrina sang.

I turned the lights and music off then climbed the steps, I saw the flickering of lights and heard music again. When I reached her room, she had candles lit all around. She stood in the middle of her room with just a see-through black bra and a thong on.

"Do you like it?" she asked me.

"Yeah, I like what I see." I replied as I eyed her lustfully.

"Nooo, the room."

I looked around the room and besides the candles, she had decorated it a little bit. There was a welcome home banner hung above her headboard. I noticed there were a few more pictures of us hung up throughout the room.

"Yes Tri, I like the room. But your grandmother's gonna kill us if you burn her house down."

She sauntered over to me and took my bag to sit it down on the floor. She wrapped her arms around my neck and gazed up at me.

"Well, if you would of let me get a hotel room, then we wouldn't have to worry about that now would we."

"Hotels are dirty, I keep telling you that. Why would you want to lay your head where 1000s of other people have." I said as I wrapped her in my arms.

"Derek, stop it. They clean the rooms every day."

"That's what they want you to think."

I hated hotels. I stayed in them whenever we traveled but I brought my own sheets when we got there and left them there too. I would Lysol the fuck out of that room, I didn't trust that were cleaned well.

"You're being silly." She said as she started to unbutton my shirt. Once it hit the floor, she led me over to the bed and pushed me back causing me to fall on to it. She had put some red satin sheets on the bed, so they felt cool against my back. She started to unbuckle my belt and my shorts. Once she pulled them down, she discarded them on the floor.

"Take that off for me." I said softly.

Katrina sensually started to dance in front of me as she unhooked her bra, her perky size C breasts were perfect. She turned around and bent over to give me full view of her ass and pussy. She played with the sides of her thong until she slid them down and stepped out of them. Now she was completely naked.

"Ven siéntate en mi cara." I said in perfect Spanish.
(come sit on my face)

Katrina was Dominican and black, so she taught me a lot of it over the years. Plus, I have been taking Spanish since the 8th grade and its basically my 2nd language now.

"Quieres probar esto?" she asked, as she climbed onto the bed.
(you wanna taste this)

"Sí." I answered.

Katrina was making her way up to my face when I put one of her breasts in mouth, I sucked on her nipple for a few seconds. A moan escaped her mouth, as she looked down at me. Katrina reminded me of Eva Mendes, she was pretty and exotic looking. Her looks and body made up for her immature ass ways sometimes. When I released it, she finally made her way up to my face. I couldn't wait to taste her. She slowly lowered down until she met my mouth.

"Oh, fuck baby." I heard her call out, as she started to slowly ride my face.

I started licking up and down, then I latched onto her clit and sucked hard.

"OH MY GOD, DEREK!" she shrieked.

I released my dick from my boxers and started stroking slowly. I was still attacking Katrina's clit as she started to jerk a little. She was about to cum already.

"Derek, Derek I'm about to cum baby!" she said.

She started riding me a little faster. I felt her juices running down the side of my face now.

"AAAAHHH FUCK." she moaned

She started to slow down some. I smacked her ass hard with my free hand.

"Ow." She yelped.

"Come see how sweet you taste." I said, as I pulled her down towards me.

"Derek nooo, you know I don't like that." she protested.

"Stop playing with me." I covered my mouth with hers as we swapped spit again. She knew I was a nasty nigga, and I liked all that shit. She finally pulled away and wiped her mouth. I laughed and wiped mine as well.

"See, don't you taste good? Now come take this dick." I said as I removed my boxers.

Katrina did as she was told and straddled me then slowly lowered herself down on to it.

"Oh baby, it's too much." she whined.

"Stop acting like it's your first time, Tri." I said as I inched inside of her.

Katrina started to grind slowly. I gave her a few seconds to adjust but I was ready for her to start bouncing on my dick. Katrina talked a good game all the time, but when the time came, she couldn't take dick the way she said she could. She wanted to do cute shit and not sweat but I wasn't on that type of time, especially not today. I grabbed her waist and started moving her a little faster.
"Mmm te sientes tan bien bebe." she moaned.
(you feel so good baby)
"Montar tu polla."
(ride your dick)
Katrina started to pick up the pace. She planted her hands on my chest as she started to bounce up and down. I closed my eyes and relished the feeling. This shit felt so good; I always felt like I couldn't get enough of it. After a few minutes Katrina was screaming my name as she came. I felt my nut building up, so I had to switch positions. Without warning, I flipped Katrina over, which took her by surprise because she yelped. I was now on top and started pumping in and out of her.
"D-derek I think imma cum again you hitting my spot." she screamed.
"Let that shit go Tri, cum for your man."
I looked between us, and I was covered in her juices. I pulled out real quick and started to devour her again.
"Derek, no...please." Katrina pleaded, as she tried to push my head away.
I grabbed each wrist and held them by her side. I wanted every drop of this good shit.
"OH MY GOD, OH MY GOD, NO PUEDO NO PUEDO!" She yelled.
(I can't, I can't)
When she went back and forth between Spanish and English, I knew she was about to cum hard. Her legs started shaking, and I continued to lick her up. Katrina started to yell all types of

obscenities, as she came in my mouth, yet again. I came up for air, wiped my mouth, then re-entered her.

"Derek, I can't take anymore." she whined as she tried to push me back. I noticed tears in her eyes.

"It's ok Tri, I'm almost done." I reassured, as I took her legs in the crooks of my arms.

I picked up my pace and stared up at the ceiling. I was about to bust any second.

"El semen para me papi." Katrina said breathlessly.

(cum for me daddy)

Hearing that made me nut hard as hell.

"Fuckkkkkkkk." I grunted, as I pulled out and bust all over the inside of her thigh. I collapsed on top of her and was out of breath, but I instantly felt comfort and relaxed. This was a feeling I chased; it was almost like a high.

"Shit." I mumbled.

Katrina wrapped herself around me.

"Hmm I love you baby." she purred, as she stroked the back of my head.

I remained silent, like I usually did every time she said that.

"Did you hear me, Derek?" she questioned.

"Yes, I did. Let me up so I clean us off."

She held her grip on to me tighter.

"No, why are you ignoring what I just said?"

"Please don't start this shit, now let me go." I said, as I forcefully got out of her tight grasp.

Before she could say anything else I walked out to the bathroom to grab a washcloth. I opened the closet and searched for one. As I picked one up, I noticed something silver from underneath the pile. When I moved the stack out the way, it was a men's watch. It was just Katrina and her grandmother that lived here, so I was confused. Her father stopped by occasionally, but as far as I knew, he never spent the night. But even if it was his, that didn't explain why it was hidden. Plus, this shit looked cheap, and her dad had an expensive taste. I thought about if I should say something, but I was going to leave it alone for now. When I walked back in, I noticed all the candles were blown out. Katrina was sitting up with her arms folded. She had this mean ass look on her face. I smirked at her and climbed on the bed. I attempted to open her legs to wipe her off, but she resisted.

"Katrina, stop playing and let me wipe you off. Then you can cuss me out, like I know you want to."

She opened her legs, and I washed the inside of her thighs with a wet rag. I made eye contact with her as I made my way up to her opening. I slowly rubbed over it and she flinched.

"Sensitive?" I asked, with a raised brow.

"Fuck you, Derek." she spat.

I chuckled. "I mean I'm ready for another round when you are."

"You are never fucking me again, since we clearly don't feel the same way about each other."

"Is that right?" I questioned, as I got off the bed.

I went in my bag and got out my basketball shorts. I threw them on, then looked for Katrina's present. She was still fussing at me, but I tuned her ass out. I walked over to her and placed the box in her lap. She opened it and when she laid eyes on the gold diamond tennis bracelet, her hand flew to her mouth. She looked up at me then back down to the bracelet, like 4 times.

"I see that shut your ass up." I laughed.

I have brought Katrina a few different gifts but never jewelry. I wanted to get her something special.

"Derek, oh my God. It's so beautiful." She cried.

She jumped up and wrapped her arms around my neck, kissing me passionately.

"I guess that means you like it."

"YES, baby I love it." She said excitedly, "Put it on me."

I took the bracelet out the box and clasped it on her wrist.

"OMG, it's so pretty." She beamed sitting on the bed staring at it in admiration.

"I'm glad you like it, Tri."

"Look at all the diamonds....is it custom?"

"No, why would it be custom?" I asked, with a little irritation.

"Well, you got Tia and GG custom jewelry."

"They are my family."
"What does that matter?" she queried, with her hand on her hip.

Katrina was an only child and she acted just like one; she was spoiled rotten. Her father was a businessman who had a whole other family in a different state. He got caught up with Katrina's mom and got her pregnant. He so called loved Katrina, but he could not let his wife know about his secret love child. So, he visited her when he could but for the most part, he just supported her financially. Now Katrina's mother was just a gold digger who had a habit of sleeping with married men, then trying to blackmail them. That's how she kept her pockets laced. She traveled often, with whatever man she was with at the time; so that's how Katrina ended up living with her grandmother. Granny B wasn't much better because she was a frequent gambler and was barely home to parent Katrina. All 3 of them would just throw money at her to keep her happy, so that allowed her to get whatever she wanted, when she wanted. Tia and I would be given whatever we wanted as well but we were humble and grateful. Even though Tia hated our dad, she never was a brat about material things.

"Katrina, please don't piss me off right now." I said, seriously.
"Derek, all I'm saying is I don't want to walk around with the same bracelet as some other girl at my school."
"You sound fucking ridiculous. That is a $1500 bracelet. I highly doubt anyone at dusty ass Parkville will have one, but even if they did, so the fuck what." I shouted.
"Derek, you know the shit I wear…. I don't want no bitch wearing what I have on."
"I really want you to listen to yourself. You say that goofy shit, but you and 100 other girls wear the same color Ugg's and Michael Kors bags. So, what the fuck are you talking about?" I argued.
"That's basic shit. All I'm asking is why am I not good enough to get custom jewelry?" She questioned, with a straight look on her face.

"The same reason, I won't tell your ass that I love you. Because you are ungrateful and petty as fuck."
I was pissed off. I started to gather my shit to leave because I felt like I was going to fuck her up in a minute.
"Wa-wa-wait, where are you going?" she stuttered, as she jumped off the bed.
"Home, you are tripping right now." I said, heading for the door.
"No no no, please don't leave. I'm sorry, ok?" she apologized.
She went to stand in front of her door to block my way.
"Move Katrina." I spat, in an angry tone.
"No baby, I'm really sorry you are right I'm tripping, I missed you so much...don't go." She reached up to pull me down a little and started raining kisses all over my face and neck.
"Naw, imma go and hit you up tomorrow." I said, trying to move her out the way.
"Nooo, Derek please. What do you want me to do? I'll do anything." she pleaded, with water in her eyes.

I just stared at her blankly, there was only one thing I wanted her to do when I was pissed off at her. She stared back at me and pushed me back a little, she got on her knees and slid my shorts down to my ankles. She started to stroke my dick until it came to life in her hand. She started to lick the tip, then put as much of me in her mouth as she could fit. I stared down at her intently. She was struggling as usual; I gathered her hair in my fist and started to push myself deeper into her mouth. Tears welled up in her eyes again as she gagged. I didn't let her give me head often because one, she wasn't good at it and two, I didn't feel like she needed to do that. She grabbed my waist and tried to push me back.
"Naw, you wanna talk that hot shit, swallow this dick, Tri."
I made her gag a little longer before I took my dick out her mouth. I pulled my shorts up, then went and laid down in the bed with my phone. She stood up and came to lay under me.
"You didn't cum." She said in a small voice.
"I never do." I spat coldly.
"I really am sorry Derek; I love my bracelet."

I sat quietly as I continued to scroll on Instagram.

"I made lunch reservations tomorrow at 11:30." She continued.

"I'm going to church tomorrow morning."

She sat up and looked at me with a confused expression.

"But we agreed to go out in the morning."

"Things change." I said, with a flat tone.

"Well, when the fuck were you gonna tell me?"

I glared over at her without turning my head, she was skating on thin ice with me.

"Katrina, I highly you suggest you shut up for the rest of the night. I will see you tomorrow after I'm done." I said, turning my back to her.

"Derekkkk." She whined.

I ignored her until I felt her hand down my shorts. She knew sex was my weakness.

"I know you're not that mad at me?" she asked, seductively.

The feel of her soft hand caressing my now hard dick caused me to blow out a frustrated breath, I placed my phone on the nightstand and turned towards her.

"All 4s." I demanded.

I was about to blow her back out with no mercy. I slid in her and started to go to work. We fucked for the next 45 mins, but for most of the time my mind kept going back to that watch. Something wasn't sitting right with me about it but everything that is done in the dark, will eventually come to light.

KEYARRA

It had been a few hours into the party, and I was passed tipsy. I wasn't drinking anymore because I had to sing at church in the morning, and I didn't want to embarrass myself by sounding like a frog. Every few minutes I was asking Tia if she was ok. By the 5th time, she cussed me out. I just didn't want her to feel like I was ignoring her or anything. The last time I checked on her she was talking to my friend Chris, which I was happy about. He is a cool guy, and I knew he wouldn't try any slick shit with her.

"Stop staring at them, she doesn't need a babysitter." my boyfriend, Tre said as he handed me another shot.

"No, I'm done for the night. And I know but I just wanna make sure." I replied, still glancing in their direction.

"C'mon make this your last one."

"Tre, I told you didn't even wanna drink tonight and now I'm 5 in. I have to get ready to leave soon."

"Leave? It's only a little after 12 and your curfew isn't til 4."

"You know damn well it's at 2, not 4."

"Ok, but either way you don't need to leave soon. Take this last one with me and we're done, pleaseee." he begged.

Tre stuck out his bottom lip like a sad puppy. I rolled my eyes.

"Fine."

We took our shot, and I knew that one was gonna put me on my ass.

"That's my girl…. now let's go check on your friend like I know you want to."

We made our way through the crowded basement. Most of our classmates were there as usual. Tre had parties often, but this one was extra packed because it was his end of the school year party, we still had one more week left but this was the weekend that worked best for most of our classmates. Everyone was excited because this upcoming school year we were all gonna be seniors. When I got over to Tia, Chris was whispering something in her ear that made her laugh.

"Yeah, we'll see." I heard Tia say.

"You'll see about what?" I asked, as Tre pulled me down to the floor with him and into his lap.

"Damn, nosey." Tia snapped.

"I like your friend Keyarra, she mean as shit but that don't scare me." Chris voiced as he kept eye contact with Tia, who now looked like she was blushing, but it was hard to tell because of the dim lights.

"Boy, I'm not mean. I just don't fall for bullshit."

"I promise baby, I'm not on no bullshit. Now come dance with me." Chris said standing up, extending his hand to her.

"Well one, I'm not your baby, and two that doesn't sound like you're asking me."

"I wasn't, but whatever will make you get up." Chris smiled.

Tia smirked at him, then took his hand, leading her to the area where other couples were dancing.

"See, I told you she didn't need a babysitter; my boy Chris got her." Tre said in my ear as he wrapped his arms around my waist and kissed me on the cheek.

Tre was the first guy that I ever had any real interest in and that's mainly because he refused to take no for an answer. He literally followed me from class to class almost every day. He would also miss his bus sometimes so he could walk me home. At first, I was so mean to him because he was giving me stalker, and I just didn't want to be bothered. But he was always sweet, and he was extremely patient. When I finally decided to stop being a shut in, he was the one who convinced me to join the cheerleading team just so I can cheer him on during football season. Shortly after, he asked me to be his girlfriend. I was hesitant at first because I wasn't ready for all that came with a relationship, but we went slow. The last 7 months have been good with him, but I wasn't in love or anything. We would say it to each other, but deep down I think he thought that's what he was supposed to say, so in return I would say it back just so it wouldn't be awkward.

"You wanna go dance?" Tre asked me.

"No, I just wanna sit here." I replied laying my head back on his shoulder.

The last shot was starting to kick in.

"C'mon, I wanna see you move."

"I can move for you." I said seductively.

Since I was already in his lap, I started to wind my hips to the beat of, "No Letting Go". I reached my hand around and started to play in his thick hair. Tre leaned more into my neck and started to kiss me from my ear down to my shoulder. His hands were exploring all over my body.

"You are so sexy." Tre whispered in my ear, then kissed it again. The liquor mixed with his hands and lips all over me had me feeling hot and bothered, I turned my head and connected with his lips. I felt bad because my thoughts instantly went to Derek, and how it would feel to get a real kiss from him. The way he licked his bottom lip at dinner, every time he looked at me had me thinking about things that I shouldn't of. It didn't go unnoticed the way he would just blatantly stare at me; it was hard not to stare back. His eyes were hypnotizing. They were honey brown, but in the sun, they looked hazel. Derek reminded me of this singer from Jodeci. I think his name was, Devante Swing. Derek was 90s fine but finer than that if that's even possible. He had this beautiful caramel skin with deep dimples and don't get me started on his lips, they were full and looked soft as hell. It really should be a crime for any boy to be that perfect.

"Oh shiiit, look at Chrissy and Ti-Ti getting busy." Sharin damn near yelled for the whole party to hear. Her voice took me out of my inappropriate thoughts and stopped the kiss that I was still engaging in.

"Sharin, why the fuck you so loud?" Tre asked in irritation.

"My bad…. I'm just saying though look at them. They cute as shit." she said as she sat down in front of us.

I looked past her and saw that Tia and Chris were grinding slowly together to the music. Her back was to him, and his arms were secured tightly around her waist. I could tell that he was whispering in her ear again. If they could be in each other's skin right now I'm sure they would be. I smiled at the sight, I wanted Tia to like my friends so badly and so far, so good, I think.

"Read the room Sharin, its mostly couples down here. Take your ass back upstairs and play kings cup or something." Tre snapped. He clearly was annoyed that she interrupted our make-out session.

"Get your light bright ass out your feelings, Ke-Ke wasn't fucking you tonight anyway." Sharin said popping her gum.

She was absolutely right; I didn't feel like being humped on for all of 5 minutes. Me and Tre just started having sex about 2 months ago and it wasn't bad, but it just wasn't what I thought it would be. I didn't feel fireworks like I thought I would with the first boy that I gave my body willingly to. It was always so rushed and vulgar. Since Tre was sweet, I thought that's how the sex would be too, but I was wrong.

"Sharin, please go away." Tre said harshly.

"Well, I was gonna tell you how they upstairs breaking yo mama's shit, but since you wanna be so rude, I'm not telling you a damn thing."

"WHAT?" he yelled.

He suddenly got up and made his way to the steps, which caused me to fall back and hit my head on the wall.

"Ow Tre, thanks for the warning." I yelled to his back as I watched him disappear up the steps.

"Girl they not breaking shit, he just was acting like a bitch." Sharin laughed.

"Now you know you wrong." I said, joining in with her laughter.

"Girl, you should be thanking me. The way y'all was slobbing each other down, he was gonna drag you in the bathroom in a few minutes and give you some of his good lovin." Sharin tried to say that with a straight face but we both bust out laughing.

I shared with her about how lack luster Tre's sex was, so we joked about it sometimes, but she knew to never mention it in front of him because I know he would be pissed. We laughed and joked about our drunk ass classmates for a little while longer when, Tia joined us.

"Okayyy sis, I see you and Chris was getting all extra close." I teased, nudging her.

"That boy is crazy."

"Girl don't be all shy with me, what's up with y'all." I pried.

Tia kind of looked over at Sharin, who was all ears as well. I could tell she didn't want to talk about her personal business in front of her, considering they had just met a few hours ago.

"Oh Ti-Ti, don't do me like that, but I get it. I'll get up out your business...for now." Sharin said as she got up and sashayed away.

"Why that girl keep calling me Ti-Ti?"

"Oh, she has a nickname for literally everyone. I'm Ke-Ke...Tre is light bright, Chris is Chrissy, Matt is Boo, GG is G-mam...she be trying to call our teachers different names too, but they don't be having it. Everyone on the cheer squad has a nickname too.... Sharin is just fun like that." I explained.

"Why is Matt boo?"

"Oh, cause they be fucking." I stated, matter of factly.

Tia looked taken back by that. I mean I was too when I first found out, but whatever kept him out my face I didn't care.

"Oh wow, she doesn't seem like his type.... not that I would know what his type was...she is just a little...loud." I could tell Tia wasn't trying to talk negatively about Sharin.

"Naw, I understand. She is definitely loud, but he shuts her ass up for sure. Rin has a big personality but she's a nice girl and she don't take no shit either. I could see y'all really getting along once you get to know her."

Tia had a blank expression on her face, I wasn't sure what to make of it, so I decided to get back on subject.

"Anyway girl, what did Chris say?"

"He asked me out." Tia answered dryly. Her mood had changed for some reason.

"Well, don't sound so excited. Trust me, Chris is one of the good guys. All he wants to do is play football and basketball, go to class and try to stay out the mix."

"Yeah, he seems cool."

We talked for a little while longer when my phone alarm went off, it was 1:15 am, and it was time for us to get ready to go home.

"C'mon Ti, time to go."

We got off the floor and made our way upstairs. As I climbed the steps, I was still a little tipsy. I was ready to sit my ass back down somewhere.

When we reached the living room, there was a big game of beer pong going on. Tre was on one end and another classmate I wasn't familiar with was on the other end. Everyone was screaming and cheering.

"Tre, Tre, I'm about to leave." I yelled as I waved my hand trying to get his attention.

He looked up then handed the little ball to his partner.

"Babe, why are you leaving so early?" He asked glancing down at his watch.

"Um, I told you I have to be home at 2."

"Just stay 10 more minutes please, I feel like I haven't had any time with you." Tre begged, as he tried to wrap his arms around my waist until I stopped him.

"Maybe that's because you left me a half hour ago and never came back downstairs." I argued.

"It's my party, I had to make sure everything was good. You should have been come upstairs."

"I should have?" I questioned, with a confused look

"I mean yeah, you knew I was up here."

This was one of the things I disliked about him. He came off as entitled and sometimes kind of arrogant.

"Ok, before I get upset, I'm going to go." I turned on my heels and started to walk away when I felt him grab me by my arm and pull me back to him.

"You know I don't like when you walk away from me." He gritted.

"Aye, don't be grabbing on her like that." Tia intervened.

"Ti its cool…. Tre you're drunk so I'm going to let this slide. Let me go, then you can get back to your little game and I will call you tomorrow." I said calmly, but my tone dripped with seriousness.

We stared at each other for a few seconds before he let me go.

"I'm sorry Key, let me walk y'all outside."

"No we're good…c'mon Ti."

I grabbed Tia's hand and led her out the door. When we stepped outside, I checked my phone to see how far the uber was.

"Is he always like that?" Tia asked.

"Naw, he just acts like a bit of an asshole when he doesn't get his way, plus he been drinking. He wouldn't hurt a fly." I answered nonchalantly

"If you say so."

"Damn bitch, you wasn't going to say you was leaving." I heard Sharin say, as she was walking down the block with Chris behind her.

"I just text you goofy."

"Oh…my phone died." She replied, with a silly smile.

I looked between her and Chris, and I could tell they were high as hell.

"How y'all getting home?" Chris asked, placing himself closer to Tia.

"Are you high?" Tia interrogated with an attitude.

"Just a little baby."

"I already told you, I'm not your baby."

"And I already told your mean ass that you are going to be." Chris said stepping into her face.

Tia stared up at him and she didn't have anything to say. Chris got my girl speechless already.

"Now can you answer my question please?" He asked in a low voice that me and Rin could barely hear.

"Uber." she replied, in damn near a whisper.

Chris stepped back, then looked at me.

"Cancel that shit Key, I'll take all y'all home."

"And who the fuck said I was ready to go home?" Sharin protested.

"Says the boys who rolling down the street, that's about to shut this shit down." Chris pointed as he started walking towards his car.

Our heads snapped in the direction of his finger, there was about 4 cop cars cruising down the block, ready to catch all us underage drinkers. We shuffled to his car and started to pile in.

"Aht aht, my baby gets in the front." Chris said to Tia as she went for the back door.

"Boy...." Tia started.

"Ti, get in the front so we can leave, it's about to get hot." I said cutting her off. She rolled her eyes and got in the front seat.

Chris took off and headed to Sharin's house.

"Mick gonna be in troubleee...looks like you won't be seeing your man for a while, Ke-Ke. His parents gonna get in his ass." Sharin stated.

"That's his fault. His parents told him not to invite too many people and it looks like the whole school showed up...how the fuck did freshmen even find out about the party?"

"You know everyone finds out about these parties." Chris answered.

"Who is Mick?" Tia asked, confused.

"Oh that's, Tre." Sharin replied.

"I thought you called him light bright?"

"Mckenzie is his last name...so she calls him Mick as well." I clarified.

"I call him light bright when he's having a bitch fit." Sharin said.

"Which is often." I added.

"Aye, chill on my guy." Chris threw in.

"Oh shut up, you know he be bitchin and moanin. It's because he doesn't have his full dose of melanin." Sharin joked.

"Ard, let up off my man." I warned with amusement.

Tre was mixed. He had a white mother and a black father. He was light skin with thick reddish-brown hair that he often wore in gangstas or individual braids, that reached his shoulders. Sometimes he throws it up in a big bun like he had tonight. He also had reddish freckles across his nose and cheeks; he was unique but cute none the less. After we exchanged more banter for a few minutes, we arrived at Sharin's house.

"Ard boos, I'll see y'all in a few hours." Sharin stated.

"You still coming to church?" I asked.

"If I can get my ass up. You know GG and boo cooking, so I want to make sure I don't look like a free loader by showing up to dinner, and not church." Sharin laughed.

"Stop calling that man boo, he don't want your ass." Chris teased.

Sharin's response to that was slamming Chris's door as hard as she could.

"AYE SLAM MY GOT DAMN DOOR AGAIN AND WATCH WHAT HAPPEN!" Chris yelled.

"Goodnightttt, Chrissy." Sharin sang as she went into the house.

"How she go to a school in the county?" Tia asked.

Sharin lived in the city right by Morgan State's campus, so she wasn't too far from my house.

"She uses her aunt's address, but she is in the magnet program too; so, y'all will probably have classes together." I answered.

"Aww, my baby is smart?" Chris teased, trying to pinch Tia's cheek but

she smacked his hand away.

"Boy don't touch me." She snapped.

"Ahhhh, now it's don't touch me, but where was that energy when you was grinding on me back at the house?"

"We were dancing fool."

"Yeahhh ok. I see you wanna act a little funny now. I got you."

"Y'all are a mess." I laughed.
We pulled up to G's house and we started to get out of the car.
"Hang back for a few." Chris said to Tia.
"For what reason?" She questioned with her arms folded.
"Tia, stop being so mean. I'll leave the door cracked for you. GG doesn't really wake up until like 5 anyway."
"There is no way I will be out here that long with a stranger." Tia quipped.
"Now I'm a stranger." Chris chuckled lightly to himself.
"Be nice Ti. Ard Chris, take care of my girl and thank you for the ride."
"I got her mean ass and no problem sis…. check on your boy too."
"Yeah yeah." I waved him off.
I snuck into the house trying to make as little noise as possible. I crept up the steps and made it to my room. It was a few minutes after 2 and I knew I was gonna be tired as hell at church, so I decided to take my shower now so I could sleep a few more minutes extra in the morning. I texted Tre to see if he was good; by the time I got out the shower he still hadn't replied, so I called him.
"What?" He answered abruptly.
"Um hello to you too, I texted you, and you never replied."
"Well, I just got my ass chewed out by my parents, so I'm not in the best of moods."
"Ok, I get that, but you still could've just said you were ok."
"What do you care…you left remember?" He spat, with an attitude.
"Ok Tre, I see you are on some bullshit. I will talk to you whenever." I ended the call and climbed into bed, I heard my phone ringing, and I knew it was him. I ignored it and turned over. I don't have time for his pitiful ass apology.

"AAAAHHHH!" I yelled, as I jolted myself out of my sleep.
"Ow, what the hell girl…. you ok?" Tia asked.

I was in a cold sweat. I held my face in my hands; I just had one of my recurring nightmares. I thought they stopped, but of course I would have one when Tia was here.

"Keyarra, what's wrong?"

Tia had come to my bedside and was rubbing my back. I sucked the tears in that were threatening to fall. When I finally looked up at her, I gave her a light smile.

"Girl I'm sorry. Sometimes when I drink, I wake up all crazy like." I lied.

She eyed me suspiciously. One thing about Tia was that she could see through just about anybody's bullshit, especially the ones close to her.

"You sure you're ok?" she asked again.

I gave her a reassuring smile "Yes girl, I'm good. My bad."

"Uh huh…. you made me burn myself with those hot ass flat irons." She said, walking back over to my vanity.

"I'm sorry Ti, I didn't mean to scare you."

Tia picked the flat irons back up and continued to do her hair. I always loved Tia's hair; it was naturally curly and full. It reached a little past her shoulders, in its natural state, but when straightened, it was maybe a little above her bra straps.

"What time did you get in?"

"Maybe about an hour later."

I could see how happy she looked on her face.

"I didn't even feel you get in the bed."

"Girl you were knocked out." Tia laughed.

"So, what happened?" I asked, as I walked to my closet.

"I don't kiss and tell."

I turned around and made eye contact with her through the mirror.

"Y'all kissed?" I screeched excitedly.

"Keep your voice down before the whole house knows…. but yes, that boy…."

Tia sat the flat irons down and started to fan herself.

"Look at youuu, 1st day and you already got you a man."

"That doesn't make me a hoe, does it?" Tia asked with concern written all over her face.

She spun around in the chair to face me.

"Girl shut up, no...even if you hopped on his dick, y'all just havin fun."

"I thought about it." She mumbled.

"What?" I asked.

"Nothing...what are you wearing?"

"This pink maxi dress. The youth choir has to wear a shade of pink today."

"I can't wait to hear you sing, it's been a while."

"Yeah, you ain't missing nothing."

Before she could respond there was a knock at the door.

"Who is it?" Tia asked.

"It's me."

Just the sound of his voice gave me butterflies.

"Who the hell is me?"

"Man open the damn door." Derek urged.

"We not decent."

"Tia, stop playing." I said, opening the door.

When I opened it, the butterflies intensified, Derek stood there looking every bit of beautiful. He gave me a look over, and then I suddenly felt embarrassed. I had on a thin tank top and no bra, so he could probably see my breasts; I also had on short boy shorts. Derek bit down on his bottom lip.

"I see you slept well." He spoke.

"What do you mean?" I asked.

He pointed towards my face.

"Oh my God!" I instantly covered my face in my hands.

I probably had dried spit and eye crust everywhere, how fucking embarrassing. I heard Derek laugh.

"Naw, don't cover it now, I done seen it already." He teased.

"Derek, what do you want?" Tia asked.

"I was seeing how long y'all were gonna be. I didn't know if we should take 2 cars or not."

"We are all showered, we just have finish our hair and make-up, then get dressed."

"Y'all don't need that shit all over y'all faces." Derek argued.

"Boy get out, give us 20 minutes."

"Man whatever, make it 15. Y'all not gonna have GG fussing my ass out." He said walking away from the door. I closed it behind him.

"I can't believe he just saw me like that." I groaned.

"Don't nobody care about his ass."

"I mean, yeah but still; I didn't want him to see me like that. Derek looks a lot different....in a good way."

"Ugh please don't be like those thirsty girls in Cali, they would drool all over him."

"I mean for good reason."

Tia sucked her teeth. "If you say so, I mean yeah he handsome, but Derek is a hoe. So steer clear of his ass." Tia said starting on her make-up.

"Girl I'm not checking for him; I have a boyfriend and he got a girl."

"That bitch Katrina is not gonna stop Derek."

"Stop him from what?" I asked curiously.

"Getting pussy." She said blatantly.

"Oh."

I always overheard conversations about Derek and his love for women, but I wasn't sure how deep it ran.

"So, what's really up with your friend and boo, since we on the subject of brothers." She asked sarcastically.

"I told you; they be fucking. Of course, Sharin likes him a little more than he does her but that's just Matt. He doesn't like no damn body."

"How long they been doing that?"

"Probably about 6 months."

"Wow." I heard her say quietly.

"Wow is right. I'm honestly surprised he kept her around as long as he has, because the other girls he just got low on they asses."

"How many other girls?" She questioned.

I turned around and looked at Tia. I was trying to figure out why she was so interested in Matthew's business suddenly.

"Um 1 or 2...that I know of." I replied slowly "You like him or something? Because you real interested in what he got going on."

"Says the girl who was just fan girling all over my damn brother. Do you like him?" She snapped defensively.

"Calm down Ti, I ain't mean it like that."

The room filled with an awkward silence, as we just continued to get dressed. Once we were done, we started to go down the steps until I stopped Tia.

"Hey, I didn't mean to accuse you or anything earlier. I mean if you like him, you like him." I joked.

"I don't like Matthew, but it's all good. Sorry for the attitude, you know how I am." she smiled at me warmly, then gave me a hug.

We continued down the steps. Matthew and Derek were waiting on the couch. I still wasn't fucking with Matt after the bullshit he pulled yesterday. I'm not sure why he had an outburst the way he did, but he had me fucked up.

"Good morning." I said dryly, walking past them into the kitchen.

"Good morning." I heard Derek say, but Matthew didn't say anything, which was typical of him.

"Everyone is on time, I love it." GG beamed.

"Can you make me some tea G? I feel like my voice a little hoarse." I asked.

"I already made you some. If you would of came in at a decent time last night, then you could of gotten proper rest." she said while pouring some tea into a cup for me.

"I came in at a decent time." I smiled widely.

"Girl, I heard that damn door around 3am."

"GG its Sunday...stop cursing." I teased.

"Shut up, smart little girl. Hurry and drink this tea, grab a few of those egg bites, then we can leave."

She walked out of the kitchen then I started to sip my tea. My back was facing the entrance to the kitchen, but the aroma that hit my nostrils let me know who had just walked in.

"You gonna eat these?" Derek asked, pointing at the egg bites in the tray.

"No, but I'm not sure if Tia wants any."

"She rarely eats breakfast." He stated, as he popped one in his mouth.

I didn't say anything. I just continued to sip my tea, trying not to stare at his fine ass. Derek had on a black T-shirt that hugged his biceps with grey khaki pants and some black sneakers that I'm sure were by some expensive designer.

"You look nice." He finally spoke.

"As do you."

As do you? Why the fuck did I say that lame shit.

"Thank you. How was your night?"

"It was really fun. How was your date?"

I really didn't give a fuck because I hate Katrina, but I didn't want to be rude.

"Eventful."

"I'm sure."

"Mm hm." he said, as he looked me up and down.

There was more silence as we gazed at each other.

"You ready for church?" I asked.

"I'm ready to hear you sing."

"I'm not sure what you and, Tia expect because it's nothing special."

"I doubt that."

It was something about Derek's voice. It was always really calm and low in tone. Everything he said was smooth, I wanted to hear what he sounded like in my ear as he pushed in and out of me.

"It's Sunday." I said out loud, but I thought I said it in my head.

"I'm sorry?" Derek asked with a raised brow.

I cleared my throat, "Nothing, let's get ready to go". I said, quickly.

I finished my tea then rushed past him. I needed to get away from his intense gaze because it was becoming too much for me, and my intrusive thoughts were trying to come out.

Although I didn't want to get in Matt's truck, we all piled in and made our way to Stronghold A.M.E Church. We pulled up about 15 minutes later. It wasn't a big church, but it wasn't a mega church either, which I was thankful for. I liked it here; the people were nice, for the most part, and I did enjoy the choir even though I had just started coming back, not too long ago. I immediately went to the back and gathered with the rest of the choir. We all got along well, but I didn't really talk to any of them outside of church. They tried to include me in stuff, but at the time I just stayed to myself, and eventually they got the picture.

"Hey Keyarra." my chipper choir mate, Cay greeted.
"Hey Cay, how are you."
"I'm very good. Are you nervous for your solo?"
"Um a little, but I will be fine."
"You are going to do amazing." She assured me.
"Thank you."
"Who is that? He is fine." I overheard the girl, Faith say.
Cay ran over to peek out the curtain.
"Oh wow, I've never seen him before. Oh wait, who is that girl next to him? She is gorgeous." Cay asked.
I swear Cay is bi-sexual because she admires women a lot more than men. I walked over to the curtain and peeked out. In the 2nd row was everyone DW, GG, Derek, Tia, Matt, and Sharin.
"If yall talking about the 2 in the second row, that's my best friend, Tia and her brother, Derek."
"Whew chile, that Derek, is fine." Faith gushed.
"Since when do you have a best friend?" my other choir mate, Lanee asked.
"Since forever. They just moved back from Cali."
"Who is the man sitting next to, Derek? They look like twins?" Lanee questioned.
"That's their father, Derek Sr." I laughed.
"I got my eyes on him." She stated.
"You are 19, he not tryna catch a case."
"Ok, but I'm legal." She said seriously.

I couldn't help but laugh at the 3 of them. They were star struck by the 3 new faces in the crowd.

"Ok ok ladies and gentlemen, it's time to welcome everyone." our choir director, Ms. Danae, said as she came in.

We lined up and waited for our introduction.

"Today our beautiful youth choir will bless this house with their rendition of Good to be Home." Deacon Cyril, introduced.

We walked out and I suddenly got nervous. All eyes were on us, and my mouth started to water.

I better not throw up.

Why did I agree to this?

Look at Derek, why does he have to be here?

So many thoughts ran through my mind at one time. I stepped forward, and locked eyes with Derek; he winked at me. I smiled shyly, then looked over at GG, who gave me a thumbs up. She held her phone up to record then DW did the same.

Lord please get me through this!

I was given a mic, then I stepped forward. When the music started, I envisioned my mother and started to sing.

Ooh yeah ooh yeah
With reverence I enter into this holy place
A home that's like no other full of mercy, love and grace
I know it's been a long time, I've never felt that far
'Cause You were always on my mind, and You were always in my heart
It's so good to be home, where I know that I belong
Inside this house of love, with a family so strong
And I'm here to worship and pour out my offering
In the presence of His love, I'm never alone

It's so good to be (home, home) home (home, sweet home)
So good to be (home, home) home (home, sweet home)
I know I'm always welcome into these open arms

When all of us are gathered, He shot a light into the dark
This home is where my heart is and it's always been that way
'Cause you're forever by my side and I know I'm here to stay

So good to be home, where I know that I belong
Inside this house of love, with a family so strong
And I'm here to worship and pour out my offering
In the presence of His love, I'm never alone
It's so good to be (home, home) home (home, sweet home)

Mid song, I felt a tear slide down my face. I felt a wave of sadness and happiness, at the same time. I was sad because singing reminded me of my mother. She had a beautiful voice, and I would give anything in the world to hear it again. But I was happy to be able to look into the crowd and see my family together. I will never be the cause of us to divide again. I will do everything in my power to take my secret to the grave because if any of them found out, they will never talk to me again.

TIA

We stood outside after church and waited for Keyarra to come out.

"Ti-Ti, I love that dress on you girl." Sharin complimented.

"Thank you, I like yours too".

"This old thing." She joked.

She had on a spaghetti strapped peach dress that flared out once it went past her knees, but it didn't quite touch the ground. She had these taupe-colored chunky heeled sandals that were cute as hell. I really wanted to dislike Sharin, especially after I found out she was fucking Matt, but there was something about her that I liked. I mean she was loud as hell, but she seemed liked a genuinely nice person, so I wasn't trying to be a total bitch to her. Sharin was a gorgeous girl too. I found out she was Blasian; she had a Chinese/Black mother and a Chinese father. Her skin was a rich tawny color. Her face was blemish free and she had slightly slanted eyes. Her black silky hair was thick and long like that actress, Tae Heckard. Sharin's hair stopped right before her butt. She also had a tiny frame, but she wasn't too skinny.

"Ti-Ti?" Derek questioned, with amusement walking up to us.

"Yes, Ti-Ti...and you are?" Sharin asked, sticking her hand out to shake his.

"Derek, and you must be the famous Sharin." He said, as he shook her hand.

"Famous...who be talking about me?" Sharin asked excitedly, with a wide grin.

"I've heard your name a few times."

"I hope it's all been good. But honestly, y'all are both pretty as hell. Like how did y'all come out so perfect?" she asked circling around us, taking in our appearances

"Thank you, but our parents are to thank for that." Derek said, proudly.

He seemed amused by her.

"Where they at because they need a round of applause."

"Well, our mother is dead." I stated flatly.

I watched as the color drained from her face.

"Oh my god, I am so so so sorry. I totally forgot. How stupid of me. Please forgive me, that is totally my bad." Sharin rambled, fast as hell.

"It's all good, Shar." Derek chuckled.

And just like that, her face lit back up.

"Did you just give me a nick name? I loveeee nick names. Imma have to give you one now, but it's not coming to me at this moment. That's why I call her Ti-Ti; that's her nick name."

"Are you on Ritalin?" I asked, interrupting another rant she was about to go on.

She was hyper as hell, which I hadn't noticed last night, she may have been calmer because she was high. She also had a slight accent when she started talking fast; which made her a little hard to understand. This was throwing me off because how the hell did Matthew have the patience to deal with her? He was short tempered and easily annoyed.

"Naw girl, I just talk too damn much, my bad.... aaahhh Ke-Ke."
She yelled suddenly and took off sprinting.

I looked at Derek with bewilderment. He looked so tickled.

"I like her." He smiled.

"What in the hell was that?"

"I don't know man. But you better be nice Ti, I seen the way you were looking at her."

"Shut up, I wasn't looking at her no way. I'm just confused because her ass is hyped up like a 6-year-old on Christmas morning."

"She seems high off life." Derek laughed.

"Naw, she high off of something else for sure."

We watched as Sharin damn near knocked Keyarra over trying to hug her. Derek and I walked over and joined them.

"Ke-Ke, you did so well." Sharin said excitedly.

She was more so shouting.

"Thank you, Rin." Keyarra replied.

"So, it was nothing special huh?" Derek questioned her.

"Um yeah, it was just…. regular."

"It was nothing regular about the way you sang, Key." He complimented

"Yeah Key, you sang that shit better than the girl in the movie." I joined in

"Thanks, but CoCo ate that song up. I appreciate y'all though; it meant a lot that y'all came." She replied bashfully.

Keyarra never liked attention, and she had always been on the shyer side. But my girl needed to know that she had an amazing voice, and it could probably take her places, if she wanted it to.

"They are right, you did that girl." Sharin beamed.

As I was about to say something, three girls approached us; they were from the choir. One cleared her throat to make their presence known.

"Oh, hey guys. Ok, this is Cay, Lanee, and Faith." Keyarra introduced.

They were all beautiful, chocolate brown skinned girls.

"Nice to meet you, I'm Tia." I introduced kindly.

"I'm Derek, and yes nice to meet all of you." Derek added.

The Faith girl was trying her hardest not to gawk at Derek, which was typical. Women didn't know how to act around him. It used to annoy me but now I'm used to it.

"You are so beautiful, and I love your hair." the Cay girl complimented.

"Oh, thanks so much." I said, with a smile.

"They wanted to meet y'all so bad." Keyarra laughed.

"Keyarra shut up, we just like...new people." Faith said.

"Yeah, new people." Cay repeated, as she continued to stare at me.

"Where is that older guy, y'all was with earlier?" Lanee asked, looking around.

"Oh, our dad? He is inside being groped by some of the elders." Derek joked.

"Babyyyyyyyy." a voice from behind us sang.

We all turned in the direction it was coming from, and if my eyeballs could've come out my head, they would of because that's how hard I rolled them when I saw, Katrina's ass.

I slapped Derek's arm, "Why the hell did you invite her?"

"I didn't."

"Oh, let's go. Last time she was here I almost knocked her ass out." Lanee said, as she walked away; the other 2 girls followed.

"Bye, it was nice to meet you, Tia." Cay waved.

"Likewise." I smiled and waved back.

"Hi baby. Wait, am I late?" Katrina asked, as she linked arms with Derek.

"Yes Tri, it's almost 12. Church started at 9." Derek told her.

"Oh darn." She said sarcastically.

"Um, hello Katrina. You can't walk up to a group of people and only speak to one person." I voiced with an attitude.

"Oh...hello." she spoke dryly, as she looked around at the 3 of us. She rolled her eyes when they landed on Keyarra.

"I suggest that's the last time you roll your eyes at me." Keyarra warned

"Or what?" Katrina challenged.

"Ayo, cut it out. We outside of a church." Derek intervened, as he looked down at Katrina.

"Esa perra lo empezó." Katrina snarled.
(that bitch started it)

"I know what, perra means dumbass." Keyarra snapped.

Katrina went to step towards her but was stopped by Derek.

"Lleva tu tresero al auto ahora." Derek growled, as he pointed in the direction that she had come from.
(take your ass to the car now)

"BUT DEREK!" Katrina protested.

"NOW!" Derek urged, with an elevated voice; it drew a few stares from the church goers that were still outside.

Katrina stomped back to her car. I cannot stand her ass, and I didn't understand why Derek dealt with her. She was more trouble than what she was worth. Derek followed her with his eyes as he watched her get back into her car, then turned his attention back to us; Keyarra and Sharin's mouths were ajar, in shock.

"What?" He questioned.

"You speak Spanish?" Keyarra asked, still in shock.

"Yeah, a little."

Sharin started clapping her hands, all dramatic.

"Brava...Brava papi. You shut that girl up with a quickness; I loved every second of that." Sharin expressed.

"Papi?" Derek questioned.

"Yes, papi chulo. You speak Spanish and you fine as hell, that's a perfect nickname."

"Rin, you are not going around calling this man daddy." Keyarra said.

"Ugh, fine, I'll think of something else." She said, with an eye roll.

"Hey, I don't mind it." Derek smiled.

"I bet you don't." I chimed in.

"No no, Ke-Ke is right, cus if that hoe, Katrina heard that, then it would be war world 3."

"Watch that hoe word." Derek warned.

"Ok ok, defending your girl, I like that jefe."

It was like a light bulb went off in her head suddenly.

"AAAHHH THAT'S IT THAT'S IT…. JEFE…. THAT'S YOUR NICKNAME." Sharin screamed, as she jumped up and down.

"It's perfect, he gives boss vibes all day." she added.

"SHARIN!" a voice boomed through the crowd interrupting her.

My eyes landed on a clearly irritated Matthew, approaching us. Although I was pissed at him still, I couldn't help but get turned on. He had a slight scowl on his face that only he could make look sexy.

"Why are you out here making all this got damn noise, I can hear you from inside." He growled.

"Oh, I'm sorry boo, I didn't know."

"You didn't know you were yelling?" He asked, smartly.

"Don't come out here being mean Matthew." I spoke up.

"Man whatever."

"It's hot as hell out here, I'm about to go inside and wait for, G." Keyarra said as she started to walk off.

I guess she was still mad at him and didn't want to be in his presence.

"You can't be mad at me forever little sister." He yelled after her.

"What did you do now?" Sharin questioned.

"Nothing, she trippin as usual."

"I wouldn't say trippin…I mean you did call her friends weird." I said with a smirk.

Matthew eyed me, angrily.

"Weird…wow Matthew." Sharin said with an attitude, but there was some sadness in her tone.

Matt started to speak, but Sharin held up her hand and walked away from him.

"Sharin!" He called after her.

"C'mon Tia, why you have to go and say that shit. That just hurt that girl's feelings." Derek scolded.

"I wasn't trying to hurt her feelings; I just was repeating what was said."

I really didn't want to hurt her feelings, I just wanted to make Matthew mad.

"Ok, but it wasn't necessary to say that in front of her." Derek continued.

He was about to get in my ass when we heard the blaring of a car horn; it was Katrina.

"Ughhh fuck, let me go deal with this girl, and I'll see y'all at dinner." Derek said, as he started towards the car, leaving me and Matthew glaring at each other.

"What the fuck is wrong with you?" He spat, angrily.

The nerve of these niggas!

"What's wrong with me…nigga what's wrong with you?" I countered.

"What do you mean, Tia? First, you blow me off to go to some whack ass party, then I hit your phone up all night, which you didn't bother to respond to. Now you stand here and pull that bullshit…so yes what the actual fuck is wrong with you?

"Ain't shit wrong with me…. you just salty because I called you out in front of your girlfriend."

"She's not my girlfriend and you know that Tia, but like your brother just said, it was unnecessary for you to bring that shit up."

"That's Keyarra's close friend, you don't think she would've mentioned that to her?" I asked, with a mug.

"No, she wouldn't have because, Keyarra knows when to keep her got damn mouth shut." He gritted lowly.

"Well, maybe I did Sharin a favor, because I sure would like to know if the nigga I'm fucking, thought I was weird. I would love to hear what you say behind my back." I spat, as I mushed him in the head, but he caught my wrist.

"Aye, keep your hands to yourself, you making a scene out here, Tia."

There were still a few people lingering outside in the shade, but they weren't paying us any attention. I snatched my wrist away from his hand and proceeded to walk away. I was pissed off and couldn't stand to look at his face any longer.

"Tia please." Matthew pleaded, as he gently grabbed my arm to pull me back to face him.

I glared up at him angrily, he didn't look so mad anymore.

"I was gonna tell you about, Sharin." He admitted.

"Were you really?"

"I was Ti...I just didn't know how."

"So, what, y'all together?"

"No, we not, she just cool as hell. She is easy to talk to, and sometimes we just chill. We don't always have sex, I just…. like her company." He expressed, with a little nervousness.

"I know she loud and shit, but when she not hype, she cool...I think y'all would get along for real." He continued.

"You want us to get along so you can have a threesome or something?" I asked, sarcastically.

He cracked a smile.

"I meannnn…"

"Oh you got me fucked up." I spat pulling away from him.

I was about to slap the taste out his mouth.

"W-w-wait Tia…. I was playing." He laughed.

"Does it look like I'm fucking playing with you?" I asked angrily.

"C'mon Ti, calm down." He said, still laughing.

He stepped closer to me, looked behind me, then bent down and gently kissed my lips. For some reason I felt like I was about to cry; every part of me craved Matthew but I really wasn't sure if he felt the same. He stepped back from me and smiled.

"You're not cute Matthew." I stated.

"I am, but would you maybe have time for me tonight, Tia?" he asked.

Before I could answer my phone started to ring; Chris's name flashed across the phone, along with a picture of him giving me a kiss on the cheek from last night. I smiled because his ass had to have done that when he put his number in.

"Why the hell is he calling you and when the fuck did y'all take that picture?" Matthew seethed.

There goes that anger again. I didn't even realize he moved close enough to see my phone.

"You not the only one who enjoy other's company." I taunted, then I turned on my heels and left his bipolar ass standing there.

***

"I'm glad you decided to still come to dinner." I told Sharin, as we chilled in Keyarra's room.

"Yeah, I wasn't feeling up to it, but you and Ke-Ke wouldn't take no for an answer."

When it was finally time to leave church, she said that she just was going to take an uber back home, instead of riding with us back to the house; but me and Keyarra, begged her to still come. I could tell her feelings were really hurt about what Matthew said, and I felt horrible for saying it. I apologized multiple times, but she insisted that I didn't have to do that.

"Again, I apologize." I said sincerely.

"Girl shut up, it's cool. Matthew is just...him I guess." She shrugged lightly.

"You like him a lot huh?"

I wanted to get some more information out of her since Keyarra was downstairs in the kitchen helping with dinner. GG always made her and Matthew cook together after a big blow up between them. Which I never thought was a good idea because she might stab his ass one day.

"Um, yeah, I do, but it's my fault for catching feelings. He told me that nothing more would form between us, and I just should've believed him."

"Boys are erky as hell. They do all this extra stuff, then expect you to not catch feelings."

"Exactly. Like at first, we were just having sex, that was cool; then he would come over to just chill and watch tv. Or sometimes he would just want to kiss and not have sex at all." She explained.

"It's only been a few months, but he has showed more interest in me than other guys have, so I thought maybe he wanted more. But I guess I was wrong."

There was a slight pause, I watched as she wrung her hands.

"That girl he lost his virginity to really has his heart honestly." She then added

"What?" I asked quickly.

"I hate to tell his business but fuck it, this is girl talk. Matthew recently lost his virginity like a few years ago to some girl that he really liked, but he said it was complicated between them."

"Complicated?" I repeated.

"That's what he said but he never really elaborated on how. But I know he really might be stuck on her because every time he brings up her name it's like a little twinkle in his eye."

"What did he say her name was?" I asked, curiously.

"Nicole."

"Oh wow...he talks to you about her often?"

"At first, he did because we were just messing around but after a while he stopped. That's kind of what made me think he liked me more then he led on." She said in a sad tone.

"I'm sorry Sharin, like I said boys are weird as hell."

"True, but imma just continue to play my part and stay in my lane." "Oh, you still gonna mess with him?"

"Absolutely! The dick is bomb girl, and he has his moments but otherwise he is really nice to me most of the time. He has texted me like 6 times saying he was sorry and that he wasn't referring to me...blah blah blah."

"Have you responded?"

"Nope, imma make him sweat a little. He gotta make it up to me somehow...if you know what I mean." She said, while grinding her hips and sticking her tongue out.

I felt myself getting a little hot.

"But enough about me, I done told you all my business, now tell me about you and Chrissy...you were being shady last night."

I smiled at the thought of him, we had been texting all morning. He was coming to dinner tonight and I felt nervous for some reason. I didn't want Matthew to lose his head, but shit Sharin was gonna be there so he really shouldn't be mad.

"I wasn't being shady.... I'm just private." I stated.

"Yeah yeah, give me the deats." She waved off, giving me her full attention.

"Um we danced, he asked me out, we kissed and today we have been texting." I said, nonchalantly.

"Y'ALL KISSED?" She shrieked.

"Aye, you gotta chill with all that screaming."

"My bad Ti-Ti, I just get really, really excited."

"I see…. but yeah, we kissed after Key went in the house last night. He seems cool but I'm not trying to jump into anything. I literally just touched down less then 24 hours ago." I explained.

"That's understandable but listen, Chris not like other high school boys. He is mature and wants to mind his business. He has lived a life at such a young age."

"What do you mean?"

"I'll let him tell you but trust me he is a good guy."

"That's what Keyarra said…. have y'all um…" my voice trailed off. Her eyes got big.

"Me and Chrissy? Girl hell no. He is like the brother I never wanted but that's my guy. We look out for each other; that's it and that's all. He gives great advice; he isn't the biggest fan of me and Matt's situation."

"Why not?"

"Because he thinks Matt is playing with my feelings."

"Do you think that?"

"To be honest, I really don't know what to think but like I said, I'm not going anywhere unless he makes it clear that he doesn't want me around anymore."

"I get it."

I was feeling the same way as her. I didn't know what to think about Matthew. The fact that he has even brought me up to her threw me for a loop; he always told me that a long-distance relationship wasn't something he wanted. But now I'm here and not sure what I expected, but it wasn't that he had another girl head over heels for him too.

"What y'all up here talking about?" Keyarra asked, as she walked into the room.

"Boys." Sharin giggled.

"Ugh, I can do without them." Keyarra scoffed.

"Stop itttt, you talk to Mick?"

"Yeah, for a little bit. He was supposed to come to dinner, but he is grounded."

"Damn for how long? Summer vacation is about to start." Sharin said.

"Probably not long. You know he is a spoiled brat, and his parents give in easily." She laughed

"Did he get in trouble because they didn't know he was having the party?" I asked.

"No, they knew, but it was way too many people and there was alcohol." Keyarra answered.

"How do y'all get it?"

"Tre has older cousins that always cop for him, so we can get it pretty easily as long as he never snitches on them."

"How do they think he is getting it?" I questioned further.

"Damn, Ti-Ti what you undercover or something?" Sharin joked.

"I'm just asking cus shit don't make sense. He in trouble for having alcohol but you are implying that he always provides alcohol so what makes this party any different."

"The police showed up." Keyarra answered.

"I guess he won't be having anymore then."

"Maybe not this summer but we'll see." Keyarra shrugged

"Did you and boo talk?" Sharin asked.

"Yes, he apologized for yesterday then he told me how proud of me he was for singing today...we hugged it out."

"Aww, well I'm glad y'all are ok."

"For now." Keyarra laughed.

We laughed and talked for about another hour until GG announced that dinner was ready and that myself and Keyarra, had guests at the door. I knew Chris was coming but we didn't know who would be here for Keyarra. When we came downstairs, we saw Tre and Chris standing in the living room with small bouquets of flowers. I had never had a boy bring me flowers before. I approached him and he smiled.

"Hey beautiful." He spoke.

"Hello, Christopher."

"See you think you know everything, that's not even my name." He smiled.

"For real...what is it?"

"It's Christian baby."

"Why you ain't tell me that?"

"Because you never asked...you assumed, and you know what they say about assuming." He replied, with a wink.

"Boy...shut up." I laughed and pushed him playfully.

He handed me the flowers, but he pulled one out.

"Rin." He called out behind me.

He threw her the one and she caught it. She smiled widely. I thought that was sweet of him to do.

"Thank you, Chrissy." Sharin smiled.

"No problem."

His eyes traveled back down to me.

"These are beautiful." I said admiring the arrangement

"Just like you."

I couldn't help but blush. I hadn't even known this boy for a full day yet, and I liked his ass already.

"Aww look at these flowers, they are beautiful boys." GG admired.

"Thank you." they said in unison.

"And these are for you, GG." Tre said handing her a small bouquet.

"Aww boys, you didn't have to do this but thank you." GG said.
"Tre, I thought you were grounded? You didn't sneak over here
did you." She questioned with a side eye.
"No mam, I begged my mother to let me come over because my
girlfriend was mad at me, and I needed to see her.... I'll be doing
yardwork for the rest of the summer." Tre explained, as he
wrapped his arms around Keyarra. She had her face buried in his
chest.
"Ok, now don't let me find out otherwise; dinner is ready. Go
wash y'all hands, and girls I will take these and put them in
water."
G took our flowers, then disappeared into the kitchen. Suddenly,
Derek and his father walked through the door. I was not ready for
the interrogation that they were about to do on Chris or Tre.
"Well, we certainly have a full house." DW said, as he scanned the
room full of teenagers.
Christian, immediately walked up to him and stuck out his hand.
"Hello Mr. Williams, I believe we have met before, but I'm
Christian. A friend of Keyarra's."
"Hello son, nice to meet you again but call me, DW. I'm sure you
haven't met my boy yet; this is my son, Derek. My namesake." he
stated, proudly
"What's up Derek?" Christian greeted, has he dapped him up.
"What up, good to meet you."
"Um, DW, you met him last year too, but this is my boyfriend Tre,
and Tre, this is DW and his son, Derek." Keyarra introduced.
Tre shook both their hands.
"Aaahhh, I've heard about you; we'll have to talk later." DW said.
He kills me with that fake authority figure shit.
"Yes sir." Tre responded.
"Alright, the table is set. Let's get seated." GG announced.

We all gathered around the table and held hands as GG blessed the food.

"Thank you, Lord, for bringing us to another day and another Sunday dinner. Thank you for these young souls, Father. I pray that you continue to put a hedge of protection around them everywhere they go, Lord. Please bless this food and the hands that prepared it. In Jesus name we pray, amen."

"Amen." we all said in unison.

The men pulled out all the women's chairs and we sat down. There was a feast in front of us. Baked chicken, fried fish, white rice and gravy, mac and cheese, cabbage, string beans, and crescent rolls.

"Dang G, you and Matthew, out did y'all selves." Derek praised.

"Hey, I helped." Keyarra said.

"Yeah, you buttered the rolls." Matthew joked.

The table erupted in laughter. We continued to pass each other serving bowls and trays as we built our plates. All you could hear were the scrapings of plates and an occasional moan because of how good the food was. GG could always cook, she passed the torch down to our mothers, who would throw down almost every Sunday. After they passed, Keyarra and Matthew tried to keep up the tradition by helping GG cook but Keyarra just wasn't the best at it. Matthew could burn though. He enjoyed cooking; it was one of the only things that could keep him out of trouble. When he visited Cali, he cooked a lot so that we could have a home cooked meal since Aunt Pam didn't know how to do shit but finish a bottle. I would be his little guinea pig in the kitchen when he experimented; and it was very rare that I didn't like something. He was slated to go to culinary school, but he wanted to take some time after graduation before jumping into school again.

"Where is Katrina?" GG questioned.

"She had to pick-up her grandmother from the airport." Derek answered.

"Ok, well make them both a plate before I pack the extras up and take them down to the homes." GG said.

GG always cooked a shit ton of food, so she could take them down to the same group homes that she met my mother and aunt at. GG loved young people, which is why her house was always open to all of our friends. She wanted to make sure no one was in the streets getting in trouble. Almost 20 years ago, GG's husband was robbed and gunned down by a bunch of asshole teenagers. Instead of holding hate in her heart, she made it her life's work to make a difference in as many young people's lives as she could. Although my father wasn't in a home, he had absentee alcoholic parents who didn't care what he did, as long as he made money to help fund their drunken escapades; so, he turned to the streets to make quick cash to keep the lights on. When GG got wind about my father, she intervened and helped him as much as he would allow. I may not like my father very much, but I know GG saved his life because a large percentage of young black men in Baltimore City aren't making it to their 20's these days.

"DW, did you see the flowers the boys brought for my girls." GG gushed.

He looked across the table at Christian and I sitting next to each other.

"Christian how do you know my daughter? She just got here yesterday?" he asked immediately.

"DW." I said sternly.

"Dad." He corrected me.

"Father." I quipped.

"I'm just asking him a question, sweetheart."

"It's ok Tia. I met her last night, at Tre's party. We conversed for most of the night, and we really enjoyed each other's company." Christian explained.

"So that prompted you to buy her flowers?"

"Yes sir. I thought it would be a nice gesture and to make my intentions known."

"And what would that be?"

"That I would like to get to know her better and see more of her." he answered boldly.

Matthew started choking on his food which made, GG start patting him on his back.

"You ok boy?" she asked.

"I'm good, I just need some water." he replied hoarsely.

I rolled my eyes because I knew he was gonna be on some shit later.

My father eyed Christian, but he was silenced. I loved that Christian was not intimidated by him or his intense eye contact.

"Well alright Christian, I like that answer." GG said proudly, trying to break the awkward silence.

"So, you talked to my sister last night, and you came back the next day? She usually scares people away." Derek joked.

"Oh, she definitely gave me some push back but I'm not the type to back down easily." Christian reassured.

"So, you don't take no for an answer is what you're saying?" DW asked, trying to twist his words.

"You know that's not what he meant." I interjected, eyeing him angrily.

Christian placed his hand on my knee under the table.

"I believe wholeheartedly that if you want something, you need to put in effort to acquire it." Christian said.

"But you're talking about my daughter, not a job opportunity."

"GG!" I called out as I stood up.

I had enough, my father acted like he was talking to a grown man and not a teenage boy. He was going to find something wrong with everything he said, and frankly, if this continued, he would be the next one with water thrown in their face.

"Derek chill out on the 3rd degree ok....it was just flowers. He's not asking for her hand in marriage." GG said seriously. "Tia sit down, and let's continue to enjoy dinner together."

I sat down but I had lost my appetite. Christian continued to squeeze on my knee gently. We were having a decent time until that asshole sperm donor decided to ruin it.

"So, Keyarra what are doing for your birthday?" Derek asked. I'm sure he was trying to change the mood in the room.

"Oh, um probably nothing." she answered.

"You didn't do anything last year; we need to figure something out." GG added.

"Yeah, it's only a few weeks away." Tre added, as well.

"Derek and I went to Seattle for mine last month, maybe we can go somewhere fun." I threw in.

"Uh yeah maybe." Keyarra replied meekly

"We'll figure it out." Derek smiled, with a wink that I'm sure no one else saw.

I noticed that Keyarra shied away from his eyes. Derek was a natural flirt; his ass can't help himself. The rest of dinner was mainly silent with a few conversations here and there. I still had an attitude and was ready to leave.

"I apologize everyone, I totally forgot about dessert, but I think I have some ice-cream in the freezer." GG announced.

"Oh, Mrs. Adams you have done enough...thank you so much. I have to get Tre home before his curfew." Christian joked.

"Oh, thank you for coming, and everyone calls me G or GG; whichever is fine." she said, as she hugged Tre and Christian goodbye.

"Rin, you need me take to you home?" Christian asked.

Before she could answer, Matthew came out of nowhere.

"Naw bruh, she good. I'll take her home."

Christian just stared at him, with a blank expression for a few seconds.

"No problem." he finally spoke.

"C'mon guys, we will walk y'all out." Keyarra said, leading the way

"I'm really sorry about my sperm donor." I said sincerely, once we got to his car.

"Aw, it's nothing Ti-baby, he just making sure his little girl is in good hands. Which I promise you are." he said, with his million-dollar smile.

"You are a trip. And what is with you guys and nicknames? What the hell is Ti-baby?" I asked.

"Stop playing like you don't like it."

"Boy whatever."

"Come give me a hug, so I can get outta here."

I walked into his arms, and he wrapped them around me.

Christian was skinny, but solid so I felt nice and secure in his embrace.

"Now, I'm not gonna tongue you down like last night because I'm sure your father is watching."

"Nobody is worried about him." I mugged.

"True, but I like to be respectful."

Christian leaned down and kissed me on my cheek. I wanted to grab his face and make him kiss me like he did last night. He had me feeling like I was ready to strip down and let him take me right then and there. When our eyes met again, we just stared at each other.

"I don't know what it is, but it's something about you, Ti-baby. You're gonna be mine." he said, in a low voice that was turning me on.

"Like I said last night, we'll see." I said, matching his tone.

He cracked a smile. "Yeah ok, I will call you later."

Him and Tre got into the car and drove off.

"Tiaaaa, omg you and Chris, are so cute together." Keyarra squealed.

"Keyarra, I like him." I admitted nervously.

I wasn't even going to front with her, Christian gave me a feeling that I never felt before with any guy, not even Matthew.

"Awww Ti that's a good thing. I'm telling you; Chris is the best guy and he doesn't take interest in just anybody either."

As we continued to talk, a black pick-up truck pulled up and parked.

A familiar face approached us.

"Well well, aren't you looking just like your mother, Tia." he spoke.

"Mr. Mark?" I questioned.

"Yes, I know it's been some years since I've last seen you."

"Yeah, it has been. How are you?" I asked, kindly.

Mark and Matthew shared similar facial features, but it was something about his eyes that I didn't like. They were dark and just seemed…. devious.

"I'm well Tia, thank you. Welcome back to the east coast."

He turned his attention to Keyarra and gave her a half smile.

"Hello, Keyarra."

"Hi Mark." Keyarra said, flatly.

Her demeanor had changed, and I noticed she held on to my arm a little tighter.

"Is everyone still inside? I just got off work; I tried to make it in time for dinner."

"Oh, there is still plenty left and yes everyone is still inside." I answered.

99

"Thanks, see you girls later." He smiled, then disappeared into the house.

Keyarra let out a breath as if she had been holding it the entire time.

"You good girl?"

"Oh yeah, I'm cool, Mark just…. gets on my nerves. He's annoying like his son." she answered quickly.

"For real? I always remembered him to be cool, I mean the few times he actually came around."

"Let's go walk this food off Ti, while it's still some light out." she suggested, changing the subject.

"Ok but what about Rin?"

"Rin always helps GG clean after dinner, then she's going to leave with Matt after, I'll call her later."

"Ok."

We walked around for about 20 minutes and talked about Christian mostly. I was happy that this weekend went well. I wasn't sure what I was gonna do if Keyarra still hated me for whatever reason, but I still was going to get to the bottom of her little disappearing act.

MATTHEW

"Oh my God, Matt." Sharin moaned, as she held on to my head.
I was trying to suck the soul out of her, so she knew how sorry I
was.

"I'm about to cum." she yelled.

I continued to suck mercilessly. I held her legs still as she tried to
scoot away from the attack, I was putting on her. We had just
finished having sex and I was little rough with her because I was
angry. This whole Tia thing had me messed up. I know I didn't
have a right to be mad about someone else showing interest in
her but got damn she just came back. I was even more annoyed
because it was that slinky ass nigga, Chris. I didn't like him, and he
didn't like me, which is cool. We avoided each other as much as
possible but that was about to become harder if he was going to
be around Tia more.

"You ok, Sharin?" I asked as I came up for air after she came hard.

"Yes." she answered, breathlessly.

I got up and went to the bathroom to get a wet rag. I washed my
face off then went and cleaned her up. I started to get dressed

and noticed she was sitting there wrapped up in the covers
looking all sad.

"What's wrong, Rin?"

"I thought maybe you were spending the night." she said, in a
small voice.

"I never told you I was."

"I know, I just thought...since my mom had an overnight
shift...that you." her voice trailed off, the expression on her face
was killing me.

"Don't do this, I wanted to take you home so we could talk."

"But we barely talked, you fucked me."

"Ok, but did we not talk on the way over here? I told you I'm
sorry. I was not referring to you, by any means, when I said that
dumb shit."

I went over and sat on the edge of the bed. Sharin was looking
down and fidgeting with her fingers. I lifted her face by her chin to
look at me. Sharin was pretty as hell and I liked her a lot. When
she wasn't screaming at the top of her lungs, she was really funny.
She was a sweet girl who I knew would be good for me, but
something wouldn't let me fully commit to just her. If I ever had
to really choose between her and Tia, then I would be stuck. I
liked them both for similar reasons, they could calm me down
when I was angry by just touching me, and they were cool to be
around, no matter if sex was involved or not.

"I promise I will spend the night with you soon...ok." I voiced
sincerely.

I felt like shit because honestly, I could've spent the night, but I
wanted to catch up with Tia and see what the hell was going on
with her and Chris.

"Ok." she simply said.

I kissed her lips, then went to leave out.

"Matthew." she called out before I could leave the room. "Am I the only girl you are having sex with?"

I let out a deep breath, I wanted to answer honestly but I knew she would be pissed.

"Yes, Sharin." I lied.

The look on her face told me that she didn't believe me.

"Ok Matthew, get home safe." she said, softly.

"Goodnight Rin."

I left her house and raced home. I couldn't talk to Tia while everyone was in the house, so I decided to wait until a little later.

As I was coming in, my pop was leaving out.

"I thought you said you were coming right back." he asked.

"My bad, I had to handle something real quick."

"Staying out of trouble?"

"For sure."

"My man.... I'm out though, I'll catch up with you later."

He dapped me up with his free hand. In the other hand looked like some leftovers that G sent him home with.

"Ard Pop, love you. Be safe."

"Love you too boy, be good. And I may hit you up for a few jobs I will probably need help with."

"Bet."

I walked in the house and almost everyone was in the family room, better known as the living room, but that's what GG always called it. Derek, Keyarra, and GG were playing skip-bo, one our favorite child-hood card games.

"Derek, did you forget how to play the game?" Keyarra laughed.

"Imma be honest, this not as fun as it used to be."

"You are only saying that because you are losing." GG chimed in.

"Man whatever, y'all cheating." Derek claimed.

"Don't nobody gotta cheat." Keyarra said, in between laughs.

It made me happy to see my little sister laughing and having a good time. I almost forgot what it sounded like.

"Yeah Derek, make sure you watch them. They be hiding skip-bos behind they back." I joined in.

"Matthew stop lying. I used to whip your tail in this all the time, y'all both just bad at it, and it's the easiest game ever." Keyarra said.

"I knew y'all was cheating." Derek said, shaking his head while he rearranged his cards.

"Boy, ain't nothing gonna change in your hand." GG teased.

"It's my first day back, y'all should just let me win for real."

We all bust out laughing. Derek was smart as hell but for whatever reason, he was bad at games. I walked into the kitchen and DW was face timing with some lady that he was sweet talking to. I just shook my head and laughed. I was wondering where Tia was so I checked the back deck, and she wasn't there. I didn't want to ask anyone because it might look weird, so I went upstairs, and Keyarra's door was cracked. Tia was on Keyarra's bed lying on her stomach with her feet kicking back and forth. She was faced towards the door giving me the perfect view of her pretty face.

"Boy, how you eating again and you just left here." I heard Tia say.

"I'm a growing boy, I need to eat every few hours."

I assumed she was talking to that nigga, Chris on Facetime. I ear hustled for a little while longer.

"You so skinny though, where all of it go?" she laughed.

"It goes to my heart."

Did this nigga really just say that...corny as hell!

Tia bust out laughing, "No you didn't just say that...you so corny."

"I'm serious though, Ti-baby, you gonna have to handle this big heart with care."

I heard enough; I knocked quickly, then opened the door. Tia's facial expression went blank, as we just stared at each other.

"Chris, can I call you back?"

"Imma head to bed love, I'll see you tomorrow."

"Goodnight Chris."

"Goodnight Ti-baby."

Tia put down her phone and continued to stare at me.

"Who the hell is Ti-baby?" I questioned.

"None of your concern." she replied smartly.

Tia rarely gave me attitude because she knew I had a low tolerance for it, so she must've forgotten that I wasn't the one to play with.

"Tia, I'm trying to have a conversation with you, so your attitude is not necessary." I said lowly.

"You asking questions about my personal business isn't necessary either."

I blew out a deep breath and quietly closed the door behind me. I approached Tia, and that hard expression on her face dissipated. I reached down and grabbed her hand to stand her up and I held her close to me.

"What are you doing?" she asked.

I leaned down and kissed her deeply. I knew I wasn't shit for kissing her and I was just face deep in Sharin, but I couldn't help myself. We made out for a few seconds before I brought my hand up and cupped her chin tightly, breaking our kiss. My four fingers were placed on one side of her cheek, while my thumb was on the opposite. I applied a little more pressure.

"Matthew stop...that hurts." she tried to mumble as best as she could.

I wasn't trying to hurt her, but more so to get my point across.

"Tia, stop talking to me like you're crazy. You know I don't play that shit...you understand?" I asked, calmly.

She nodded her head slowly. I pecked her pursed out lips and let her face go, but I kept my arm secure around her waist so she couldn't step away from me.

"For you to want this to remain a secret, you sure like to do this bullshit when our whole family is in the house." she fussed.

I chuckled. "I just can't seem to get you alone, so this is what I have to do."

"What took you so long to come back?"

"I had to talk to Sharin."

"That's it?"

Tia could spot bullshit a mile away. It was easy to lie to Sharin, but not her.

"Yes. Now answer my question, what's up with you and that skinny nigga?" I asked quickly, so she wouldn't question me further.

"That wasn't your 1st question."

"Ok...who is Ti-baby, and what's up with you and that skinny nigga?" I repeated.

"Matthew, I just met him, so I don't know yet, but he seems cool, and he calls me Ti-baby, because Keyarra's "weird" friends all have nicknames for each other."

"Tia, you don't know that nigga, so don't be getting all close to him and shit."

"I can get close to whomever I so please." she said, as she pushed herself out of my arm.

"I know that but I'm just saying be careful. I don't want you getting hurt."

"Matthew please, just say you don't want me fucking anyone else. And you don't even know him, so what makes you think he would hurt me?".

"You don't know him either, so how do you know he won't." I stated, firmly.

"Listen, I'm not going back and forth with you about this." she
said, attempting to walk past me, but I stopped her.
"Where are you going?" I questioned.
"Back downstairs."
"Tia, we not done."
"I am, Matthew."
"So, you can give that nigga your time but not me?"
"What do you want from me Matt? I come here thinking maybe
we could finally work on being together, but clearly you are
involved with someone else; and now you tryna cock block me. I
don't understand!"
I twisted my face up. "What you mean cock block? I know you not
thinking about fucking him and you have only known him for a
damn day?" I spat, angrily.
"Did you not hear anything else I just said?" She yelled slightly.
"Keep your damn voice down" I gritted.
"See that's what I'm talking about. I've been this big fucking
secret for the past 2 years and I'M DONE."
"Tia please, I'm just not ready for a relationship. We have talked
about this."
"No nigga, you told me you weren't ready for a long-distance
relationship...I'm here now, so what's up?" she argued, with her
arms folded.
I was silent because I wasn't sure what to say next.
"That's what I thought, miss me with your bullshit." she said,
going for the doorknob.
I pulled her arm back and spun her towards me, crashing into her
lips. I put everything into this kiss. I can't lose Tia, she had a
special place in my heart, and I wasn't letting her walk away from
me so easily, no matter how selfish it was. I got down on my
knees and lifted her dress up.

"What are you doing? Everyone is downstairs." She spoke breathlessly.

"Then that means cum fast and keep your voice down." I said, as I ripped her thong.

I threw her one leg over my shoulder and latched on to her clit.

"Oh my God!"

I licked and sucked up and down her slit. I paid most of my attention to her clit.

"Ssssss" She hissed.

I continued for a few minutes until I felt Tia's leg start to shake.

"Aaahhh…" she started to say out loud, but my free hand flew to her mouth and covered it. She bit down into the palm of my hand to help muffle her moans as she came. I licked up her juices then came up for air.

"Don't give my pussy away to anyone else." I warned.

"Ok." She whispered.

I wiped my mouth, then kissed her lips quickly, before leaving the room. I could hear DW's roar of laughter; I know that alone saved our asses because his voice could be thunderous. I went into the bathroom to once again, wash my face. As I came out, Keyarra was coming up the steps. I was happy as hell I slipped out of the room when I did.

"Matthew…what did you do to Sharin?" She asked.

"I didn't do anything to her, why you say that?"

"She is on Snapchat playing I Wish You Loved Me."

"What makes you think that's about me?"

I knew damn well it was.

"Matt please, if you don't want Rin, just leave her alone."

"She knows our situation Key, but I will talk to her later…I promise." I assured her.

I wanted this conversation to end quickly because I didn't want Tia to overhear.

"Ok." She sighed. "Is Tia still on the phone?"

"Um, I'm not sure. I was in my room." I lied.

"Ok, I'll check. Come downstairs, we are about to play monopoly."

"That long ass game." I fussed.

"Shut up, you don't have nothing to do."

"How you know?"

"Because I know. I'm the car, so pick something else." she said, heading towards her room.

I made my way downstairs and joined everyone else.

"What were you up there doing boy?" GG asked.

"I was chillin G." I laughed.

"He was probably playing with himself." Derek joked.

"Man shut up."

"Yes, Derek shut up. I don't wanna hear that mess." GG said, with a look of disgust.

"Would you rather hear about a girl playing with me than." I joked trying to push her buttons.

GG threw the stack of skip-bo cards at me that she was putting away.

"Now clean them up and be quiet!" She ordered, sharply.

Me and Derek bust out laughing. Getting on her and our sister's nerves was the funniest thing to us.

"At least you got the cards thrown, back in the day, G would go upside all our heads in a New York minute. She got soft when y'all came around." DW chimed in.

"I would like the hands because now she just throws whatever is close to her." I said.

"Boy hush, I'm too old now to be putting my hands on y'all but if y'all acted like y'all was raised with some sense, then I wouldn't have to throw things."

"She only throws things at you Matt, she still hits me." Keyarra added, descending the steps.

"Like I said, if y'all had some sense, then that wouldn't be an option, now would it."

We all laughed and started the set up for monopoly.

"Where is Tia?" DW asked.

"She is going to take a shower, she not pressed to play she said."

"Figures, she always the difficult one." Derek added.

"That's because your hardheaded father made her upset." GG scolded.

"Listen, I just questioned the boy." DW defended.

"You can't scare the first boy off that she showed real interest in."

I was secretly hoping that DW stayed on Chris's ass because I don't want him around.

"Yeah yeah, well if I see him again, then I'll be a little more...."

"Nicer." GG said, finishing his statement.

"G, I was nice."

"No you weren't! Now shut up and stop talking to me." She said, with finality.

I couldn't help but laugh because this entire weekend, GG had been fed up with us and our shenanigans. We started playing the game and about a half hour in, Tia came down the steps. She had on a cropped tee and leggings with some slides. I could tell she just got out the shower because her skin was shiny, which was probably from her baby oil. Tia was never ashamed of her body, and she shouldn't be because it was perfect. My dick got hard instantly; I can't wait to get her alone for real so I can do what I want with her.

"Coming to play baby girl?" DW asked.

"Um no." she answered quickly

Tia was never going to give her father a break. She was so fixated on making him pay for his past mistakes.

"Don't be a jerk, Tia." Derek warned.

"Listen I can go back upstairs if it's a problem."

"No Ti, sit down." Keyarra said.

Tia sat down next to her and was on her phone. She was trying her hardest to avoid my eyes. I decided to text her.

I can still taste you...

I watched her eyes get bigger. She looked up slightly and made eye contact with me. I smirked at her, and in return she bit down on her bottom lip.

Nicole: When can I taste you?

My dick twitched a little bit. I know, Derek would kill me if he knew that I let his sister deep throat my dick, but she was so good at it.

I didn't care how he viewed it. If she wanted to, I would let her.

You gotta sneak out later tonight and meet me down the street at my truck.

Nicole: How am I gonna do that?

Tell Key, you going to meet that nigga.

Nicole: Ugh ok.

I couldn't wait to get this family night over with now. About an hour later, Keyarra bankrupted everyone. Derek was salty as shit.

"Man, I'm out. Ain't no way she done won every game we played." Derek complained.

"Aww Derek, are you a sore loser?" Keyarra teased.

She went and pinched his cheek causing Derek to get this look in his eye. A look I've seen many times before. It makes women drop their panties without him even having to say a word.

"Naw, I ain't a sore loser." he responded coolly.

"Sure seems like it." she laughed walking away from him.

His eyes followed her. We made eye contact for a few seconds. I know that nigga like the back of my hand, and vice versa, so he knew what I was thinking.

"You don't gotta look at me like that bro." He voiced, low enough for me to hear.

"I didn't say anything."

"You didn't have to; it was written all over your face."

"I just don't want any problems."

"I'm done causing problems, plus I wouldn't cross that line." He said, seriously.

I felt like shit for a second because I couldn't say the same, but it was different. Derek was a womanizer who had little to no regard for women's feelings. That wasn't me. I cared for Tia deeply, but I also cared for Sharin, too. So, I was just stuck between a rock and a hard place.

"You good bro, I know."

"Derek, do you want me to take you to Katrina's house?" DW asked him.

"Yeah, we still getting my truck this week before you leave?"

"Yes son, we can go tomorrow."

"I don't know why you didn't just ship your old one here." Tia interjected.

"Because I wanted a new one nosey…. Matt's new truck is better than that one. I gotta catch up with my boy."

"Man, I was in a whole accident. I loved my old baby." I voiced.

"That's why I pray and put my seat belt on twice when I get in the car with any of y'all." GG spoke.

"G, my brakes went out. That wasn't my fault."

"Don't remind me of that horrible day." GG said getting up.

"Yeah…it was the worst day." Keyarra said, putting her head down.

About 2 years ago I got into a car accident, it was bad. I had a concussion, a broken leg, and a little brain swelling, which made me go into a coma for a few days. To this day, I have no recollection of the accident. The only thing that they could tell me was that it looked like I never hit my brakes. My car was totaled, and GG says it was by the grace of God that I survived. I came out of the coma totally fine, and you would've never thought I was in such a horrible accident. Now that I think about it, that was the last time we were all in the same room together.

"Keyarra, make sure you go to bed. You still have school tomorrow." GG said, as she made her rounds to say goodnight to everyone.

"But G, it's the last week, and I passed everything. Can't I just stay home?" Keyarra whined.

"No, you missed enough days last school year. And you have a half day Thursday and Friday, so you will be fine."

"But, what about Tia?"

"Girl hush up, she don't need you to babysit her."

"Yeah girl, you ain't been worried about me." Tia said playfully.

Keyarra put her head down slightly until Tia nudged her.

"I'm just playing, plus I'll be moving in all week."

"Ok fine." Keyarra pouted.

I forgot all about Keyarra still having school this week, that meant Sharin and Chris did too. That works in my favor, so it will be easier for me to spend some more time with Tia.

"Ok family, we gonna get up outta here." DW announced.

We all said our goodbyes and I went to my room to impatiently wait for Tia to tell me that she was able to leave out; then she would come meet me shortly after. I decided to get on Snapchat and see what, Keyarra was talking about and sure enough, Sharin was on there playing all these sad ass songs on her story. I plugged in my earphones and facetimed her. I knew she had school in the morning, but it was only 10, so she should still be up.

"Yes, Matthew." She answered, but she said it as if I was bothering her.

The room was pitch black, so I couldn't see her face.

"Why you sitting in the dark?" I questioned.

"Because I'm trying to go to bed." she answered, with sarcasm.

"Yo, cut the attitude and turn on the light."

"Why?"

"Because I wanna see your face."

I heard her mumble something, then suddenly the light came on. And just like I expected, it looked like she had been crying. Her eyes were a little puffy and her face was flushed red.

"What's wrong with you Sharin?"

"Nothing."

"So, you gonna lie? Why you online acting all depressed and shit?"

"Just leave it alone.".

"Naw, tell me." I persisted.

I was met with silence.

"If I have to get out of my bed and come to you, then it's not gonna be a nice conversation."

"Why the fuck do you even care?" She shouted.

It took me off guard because we have never argued before. She has pressed me a few times about furthering our situation, but it always ended civilly. She wasn't like Tia; she rarely gave me any problems, and I thought she understood what we were doing.

"First...stop yelling and what you mean why I care? Cus we friends and I wanna know why you upset all of a sudden....is it because I didn't spend the night?"

"Matthew, I'm just emotional. Can we please talk about this another time?"

I blew out a deep breath, I don't have time for this shit.

"Ard man, if that's what you want."

"You never cared about what I wanted before." She mumbled, but I heard her ass.

"I heard you. What the fuck does that mean?"

"Goodnight Matthew."

And before I could say anything, she ended the call.

"Ughhhhhhhh." I groaned

Sharin hasn't been trippin and now she wanna do all this extra shit. I would have to catch up with her sometime this week. I wasn't sure how to handle that just yet, but I know I didn't want her to go anywhere.

I must have dozed off because the ringing of my phone woke me up, it was Tia, but when I went to answer she hung up. Then I realized she had texted me about 15 minutes ago saying that I could go outside. I threw on my basketball shorts, a shirt, and my Nike slides, then headed out. I called GG and told her that I would be back a little later. She didn't trip over me being out late like she did with Keyarra, sometimes. I hopped in my truck and drove a few blocks down. I texted Tia where I was and waited for her outside so she could see me. About 10 minutes later, I saw her making her way down the street.

"Hey." she said, shyly.

"Naw, don't act shy now."

I leaned down to give her a hug and she wrapped her arms around my neck. I picked her up and our lips found each other, we stood there kissing for forever, it felt like.

"Mm, it seems like you needed to get that off your chest." She purred.

"It's a few other things I need get off my chest too."

I put her down and walked over to the passenger side to open the door for her. Once I got in, we drove around for a few minutes until I found an apartment parking lot. It was late, so people should be in the house, plus I had tinted windows, so I wasn't worried about anybody seeing us. Before I could barely put it in park, Tia was pulling at my shorts.

"Damn Ti, I was gonna ask you how your day was." I joked.

"Boy shut up."

When she released my dick from my shorts, she flicked her tongue against the tip. She wasn't playing when she said she wanted to taste me. Tia slowly filled her mouth up with me and went to work.

"Damn." I whispered and tilted my head back and closed my eyes. I had the radio playing for a little background noise, but all I could hear were the slurping sounds.

"Fuck Ti." I whispered.

After a few minutes I felt my nut building up and she didn't like it when I came in her mouth.

"I'm about to nut, let up." I told her.

She sucked for a few more seconds, then continued to jerk me until my cum spewed up.

"Mmmmmm." I hummed.

Tia got some napkins out of the glove box and wiped the mess up.

"You not done right?" She asked sensually.

"Stop playing, you know I didn't bring you out here just for that. Hop in the back."

I slipped out of my shorts and boxers then followed Ti to the 3rd row of my Expedition. The back seats could tilt back a little. She removed her shorts, then positioned herself so that way her ass was faced towards me, as she held onto the back of the seats. I was putting my condom on when I smacked her ass hard.

"Ow Matt, that hurt."

"No it didn't."

Before she could reply, I slipped my dick right inside her and I heard her gasp, and that shut her ass up immediately. This shit was tight and warm like always. I started to pick up my pace a little, and Tia was throwing it back.

"Yeah Tia, give me that shit." I said, as I smacked her ass again.

"Mmmmm, Matt this feel so good." She moaned.

I know I just had sex with her yesterday, but that was rushed. Even though we were in my truck we were still alone finally, and I could really enjoy it. I leaned forward, so I could be in Tia's ear.

"I meant what I said about not giving my pussy away." I whispered.

"Mm hmmm."

I reached my hand around and started playing with her clit, as I continued to pump in and out of her.

"Oh fuck." She cried out.

"You understand what I'm saying to you?"

"Yes Matthew…. Oh God."

Tia was getting wetter, which meant she was about to cum soon.

"Yes what?" I gritted.

"I won't…. I won't give it away….mmmm…I'm about to cum." She stammered.

I smacked her ass again and, Tia came all over my dick.

"Matt, stop smacking my ass like that." She complained almost immediately.

Tia's the only girl I knew that could still talk shit after having an orgasm.

"Tia cut it out and turn around."

"What?" She questioned, confused.

"You thought I was done with you?" I chuckled

"I…um…I thought so."

"Naw, now turn around."

She did as she was told and I dove right back into her. For the next hour we had sex on and off. I couldn't get enough of Tia. I wasn't sure how this summer was about to play out with her, but I knew that neither she or Sharin were about to play my games but for so much longer. I will just have to cross that bridge when it gets here. But until then, I was going to continue to try and juggle the two of them, to the best of my abilities.

DEREK

"Okay Derek, that finishes up our session for this week.... anything you wanna add?" my therapist, Carmen asked me.
"Yeah…. you miss me yet?" I flirted.
She gave me one of her infamous disapproving looks, and I couldn't help but laugh. I flirted with her almost every session and just because we had to do it on Skype now, doesn't mean it was going to change. Carmen was a beautiful woman with the prettiest cocoa smooth skin. She became me and Tia's therapist when we moved out Cali 4 years ago, so we were close. I enjoyed our in persons a lot, but there were a few times that she had to warn me about my behavior. I couldn't help it though, if she ever gave my young ass a chance, I would be all over that. She was heavy set but that didn't mean shit to me. I would show her the time of her life.
"Derek…if you mean do I miss our in persons, then yes. But this Skype session wasn't bad at all." she said, knowing that's not what I meant.
"Yeah ok, I'll talk to you later love."
"It's Carmen, Derek." She corrected me.
"Ok, Carmen." I said, with a wide smile.

She rolled her eyes and disconnected the call. She always tried to remain professional as possible, but I know I got on her damn nerves. Over the years she has done things that I know she isn't supposed to, legally. She saw me off to prom, attended my graduation, and we even had lunches on occasions, but only if Tia was there. So, no matter what she says, I know she loves my ass; more like a nephew or something but still, she loved me. She has been there for me through all the bullshit; I could call her anytime and she would answer. Even though I would hit if she ever let me, I appreciated her more than I could express. And I'm not sure how I would've gotten through my grieving process without her.

I unpacked a few more boxes before I got ready to leave. We have been back in Baltimore for almost a week, and everything was cool so far. Once the rest of our stuff shipped from Cali, we moved into our spot out Towson and I liked it for real. It was a 3-bedroom, luxury apartment not far from the Towson mall. I had to fight with Tia about who got the master bedroom that had the connecting bathroom. But I won that because at the end of the day, I was older, and I would be keeping food in the fridge and taking care of the little stuff that we would need. My dad didn't mind having the smaller room of the remaining, since he wouldn't be present during the week. He wanted to pay me to let Tia have the big room so he could win some brownie points with her, but I refused. Plus, I got tired of him trying to buy her off all the time. Tia would come around eventually…. maybe…her ass probably won't but whatever.

I was on my way to G's house to see her, since I hadn't been there since Sunday. I missed her a lot while in Cali. She was the closest thing that I had to a grandmother, and I adored her. I had asked, Tia if she wanted to come but her response was that she still was trying to figure out how she was going to fit her clothes in that small ass closet. So, I left her whiny ass right there. I rode through the county and made my way to the neighborhood. I was happy as hell to have my new whip. It wasn't the one that we had originally looked at, but once I had seen how clean this all black 2015 Escalade was, I had to have it. If I had waited a few months, I could've gotten a 2016, but I needed something now. It came with a pretty price tag, and it took some convincing because my dad said it was a better car than what he was currently pushing. But eventually he agreed, as long as I continued to watch out for Tia, when he was away, which is what I had been doing since we moved to Cali. I was also responsible for paying the full coverage insurance, which damn near was the monthly payment for the car.

I hit the block and was almost at G's. I just so happened to glance at the park, as I passed it and someone on the swing caught my eye. It was 10 in the morning, so she should have been in school. I parked on the damn near empty street and walked over to the park. Keyarra couldn't see me, so I snuck up behind her.

"What yo ass doing out here?" I said, in a deep voice scaring the hell out of her, causing her to almost fall off the swing.

"Derek, what the hell, you scared the shit out of me." She yelled.

"Good, what you doing out here? Shouldn't you be in school?"

"It was a half day, so I figured it wouldn't be bad to skip."

"That's the day you shouldn't skip honestly. So, you just been out here in the hot ass sun all morning?"

"No, I just came out here like 15 minutes ago. I came back in the house after, G left to go to the homes."

"Came out here to do what?"

"To just sit here Derek...damn you ask a lot of questions." She snapped, sounding a little irritated.

"Damn killa, my bad." I joked.

"I'm sorry, I didn't mean for it to come out like that."

"It's cool." I said, looking around.

Not much has changed about this park, it was still yellow and green with a double slide, a bouncy bridge, and monkey bars. We used to come out here and play with neighborhood kids all the time when we were younger.

"Bringing back old memories?" Keyarra asked.

I brought my attention back to her and that beautiful face.

"Yeah, a little.... listen, am I disturbing you? I don't wanna intrude if you just wanted some time alone."

"Oh no, you good. Sit on the swing." she motioned towards the empty swing next to her.

I sat down and we just sat in silence for a few minutes.

"May I ask you something personal?" she asked, breaking the silence.

"What's up?"

"Did you get arrested for real?"

"Yeah, I got booked but I was just in a room for like 4 hours, then I was let go when my lawyer came."

"I wasn't sure how true it was. Matthew and GG were pretty tight lipped about it."

"Well, if you had called Tia, she would've told you everything."

She gave me a somber look; I wasn't trying to make her feel bad but, Tia needed her best friend at the time; but Keyarra, had gone full MIA on her at that point.

"I know, I treated her like shit. I think she forgave me, but I'm not sure."

"Between you and me, she has. But she just might have her guard up a little because she is scared it could happen again."

"It won't.... like ever."

"Better not....so let me get this straight you knew a nigga was booked, and you STILL ain't call to check in.... damn, Key...you cold. I thought we was better than that?" I said, playfully.

"I'm sorryyyyy, I'm a jerk." she whined.

"Yeah, you are." I laughed

"Sooooo...".

"Sooooo?" I repeated.

"Stop playing...what happened?"

I looked at her seriously and contemplated if I wanted to tell her, but she would find out anyway now, so fuck it.

"I um got...accused...of rape."

I watched her expression change, that's the exact reason why I didn't like talking about this shit. It was awkward and made people look at you differently.

"Maybe I should have said wrongly accused of rape." I added.

"What happened?"

"It's a long story, Key."

"I'm listening." she said, giving me her full attention.

I was still a little hesitant.

"I mean, if you don't really want to then it's cool."

"Naw, its fine. So um, I was messing with this white girl."

"You like white girls?" she interrupted.

"Naw, I like pussy. And at the time whatever girl was giving it up at my school then, that's who I was fucking."

She looked a little taken back by my statement, but I continued my story.

"So yeah, it was this white girl who I was messing with for a few weeks. She was DTF all the time and that's exactly what I needed. So, after a little while, I noticed she was a little clingy, but I was used to that for real. But this one night after we had sex, she was pressing me hard for us to be exclusive, but I had told her from jump that I wasn't looking for a girlfriend and she had got really upset. Like crying and all this dramatic shit, so right then and there, I decided to end it with her. Ard, so boom, fast forward to maybe 2 weeks later, I had flew Katrina out for the weekend and we had hit the mall to go shopping, and we ran into shorty."

"Oh shit." Keyarra said, she was tuned all the way into the story.

"So the white girl..." I started to say.

"What's her name?"

"I don't say that bitch's name." I said seriously.

Keyarra chuckled, "Ard, go head."

"So, the white girl starts wylin, talking about I just promised her that we would be together, and all this other bullshit that was straight lies. So, her and Katrina get to scrappin...like right in the middle of the mall."

"Katrina better had beat her ass."

"She did, but the shit was crazy. Now Tri knows that, at the time I was doing my thing, and she was doing hers. And I flew her out once a month so we could just spend a little time together, but of course her ass was all mad and start tryna fight me talking about I lied to her."

"In the mall? she questioned.

"In the mall."

Keyarra started shaking her head.

"So yeah, she starts spazzin on me. She said she was done with me and all that goofy shit, but that is beside the point. Back to the white bitch."

"Yeah, back to her ass." Keyarra added.

"So, a few days after the fight, the white girl keep calling me from blocked numbers and shit but I'm not answering. She leaving voicemails and telling me how sorry she is and just wants us to go back to how it was. So, one day she caught me coming home from school, she had this little ass dress on, and just kept rubbing all on my dick and my ass ain't have no self-control back then; so, we drove to a spot, and I fucked her in my car."

"Derek, noooo." Keyarra groaned.

"I know I messed up but listen, so later that night cops show up at my house, talking about I need to come down to the station for questioning, but my dad wasn't home. Only Aunt Pam was and thank God, this was the one day she wasn't drunk. So, she came with me to the station. I'm wondering why they are asking me questions about what I did after school. I told them I came straight home. I wasn't even thinking about the white girl because that had already left my mind for real. Next thing I know they showing me pictures of her all bruised up and shit." I continued.

"What?" Keyarra screeched.

"Yeah shit was crazy, I told them I had nothing to do with that. But of course, they thought I was lying because I did admit to seeing her after school, when initially I told them I went straight home. My Aunt Pam, had questioned was she saying that I had assaulted her, the cops said yes she was; but not only was she saying that but she was saying that I raped her."

"What...the...fuck." Keyarra said, in shock.

"I lost my shit Key; I never been so damn scared in my life. So, my Aunt told me don't say anything else until she calls my father and can get me a lawyer. Tia had already called my dad and he was busy trying to catch a flight home when he got the news that I had been taken to the station. So, when My Aunt called him, she was given the numbers to a few good ass lawyers that would hopefully, be available as soon as possible and let me tell you, he dropped some bands."

"Damn right." Keyarra said. Her ass was clinging to every word.

"So about an hour later, my lawyer comes, and after his back and forth with the detectives, they let me go. They wanted me to take a DNA test, which my lawyer refused. I wanted to because I strapped up with her, so I knew I was good there, but I listened to what he told me to do. So a few days go by and I'm on pins and needles. My lawyer not saying much and my dad wasn't either."

"Was DW mad?"

"He was, but not at me. More so at the situation, I guess. But honestly, I wasn't fucking with him like that, so I was avoiding him."

"Why?"

"He asked me if I had I done it." I replied.

"What the hell?"

"Right, and I just couldn't believe he asked me that shit."

"What did Tia, say?"

"Tia was ready to fight as always, but she showed up for me for real, Matt, and G too. They flew out often, just so I could just have more people to lean on because I was going through it."

"Again Derek, I'm sorry I wasn't there. I should have been."

"Its' cool Key, I'm sure you'll find a way to make it up to me."

There I was flirting again. She smiled at me.

"I'm sure I will." she said, flirting right back.

We stared at each other for a few seconds before I continued my story.

"Ard, so basically it was her word against mine since there was no real evidence because I eventually did give a DNA test, but they couldn't find anything on her to compare it to."

"Well, that was a good thing, right?"

"Yes, it was but the worst part of the whole thing were the looks I got at school. Everyone knew about the situation, and they judged me. I had this cloud hanging over me and it depressed the shit outta me. I was advised not to have any more female interactions and at the time, sex was the only stress reliever I had, so that was a big adjustment."

"Damn, so how did it all clear up?"

"About 3 weeks after everything started, one night I kept getting these blocked calls again, so when I finally answered, it's the white girl and she was drunk as shit. I was with Tia, and she told me to just listen to what she was saying, which at the time I didn't understand why. This girl starts crying and apologizing saying she didn't mean to lie on me, she just wanted to be with me. So, Tia recorded the conversation. But then she asked could we meet."

"You better not had." Keyarra said, seriously.

"Listen Key….so me and Tia got this plan together to meet her. Tia hid in the back of my truck and video recorded us, so it was solid evidence that she lied. And just like on the phone she said the same shit, she was just mad at me and wanted to get my attention. She even said she will go down to the police station and tell them it was all a lie, if I agreed to be with her."

"What a dumb bitch." Keyarra said, shaking her head.

"I even asked her how she got the bruises, and her ass admitted that she got her friend to beat her up. After that I walked away, hopped in my truck and left. We turned that into my lawyer and the rest is history. My case was dismissed, and we sued her ass for defamation, emotional stress, and a bunch of other shit."

"That's what I'm talking about, did y'all win?"

"Hell yeah, her parents are loaded. They wanted to settle out of court, but I said fuck that. I wanted to put her through the same embarrassment I went through. We got 1.2…"

"Million?" She screeched.

"Yeah. I repaid my dad for the lawyer fees, which he really didn't want, but I insisted. I gave damn near half to Tia, and I paid for me and her to go on a vacation to Hawaii. We just needed to get away and relax. I blew through a good amount of it honestly, but I saved some too."

"Y'all deserved it, Tia came through for her big bro."

"Yeah, she did for sure...but the damage was done. People still looked at me strangely because at the end of the day, I was a black boy, who was accused of raping a white girl. I was still guilty in most of my classmates' heads no matter what. I wasn't pressed for prom, but Tri really wanted to go then I took a gap year after I graduated because I was just depressed. I was going through a lot, and I felt like people stared at me wherever I went. When I finally did attend classes on campus, I swore it was like everyone knew what had happened. Girls were still on my dick, but a few had mentioned the situation, and I was just fed up at that point."

"I'm sorry that you went through that, it was fucked up.... um when did Katrina come back around?"

"A few days after the fight, I called her, and we were cool. She was there for me too, honestly. She never questioned if I did it and she called every day, not to nag, but just to check on me. I didn't fly her out or anything like I normally did because I was trying to stay abstinent for a while. And having her around wasn't going to help with that, and she didn't bitch and complain. She understood which I appreciated for real."

"Is that why you made her your girl?"

"Yeah, I'm trying to do the one-woman thing."

"And how is that working out for you?" She questioned, with a raised brow.

I laughed a little. "I haven't cheated, if that's what you're asking me." "Ok good.... may I ask you another personal question?" "Yeah."

"How many girls have you slept with?" she asked, curiously.

I squinted slightly at her. "Why?"

"Because you said you liked pussy, and you have insinuated that you have been with a lot of girls."

"I'm probably around that 25ish mark."

Her eyes got big, and her mouth dropped open a little.

"25? ...wow. Derek you're so young."

"I know, that's why I'm chillin now."

"Have you ever been burnt?"

My face dropped. "No, Keyarra I have never been burnt.... Tri, is the only girl I've gone raw with plus I get tested regularly, I just did before I got out here." I answered.

"Well that's good.... I do too. Do you not trust Katrina?"

"Do you not trust Tre?"

"Not really."

"Why?"

"I don't trust men."

"Why?"

"I just don't, now do you trust Katrina?"

"I just like to be careful."

"I see, so sex is like your thing.... like shopping is Tia's thing and cooking is Matt's?"

"I guess you can put it that way."

"What age did you lose your virginity?"

"14." I answered, quickly.

"Wow, how old was the girl?"

I pondered if I should tell her. I haven't told one person her real age. Not even Tia or Matt, but I felt like I could trust Keyarra with this secret.

"21." I finally replied.

Keyarra, looked at me with confused eyes, then suddenly she stood up.

"What do you mean 21? That's a fucking adult." she stated, with an elevated voice.

"I know, it just kind of happened. If it makes you feel any better, I was taller than her." I joked, trying to make light of the situation but her angry expression didn't change.

"Derek, that's not funny, that's like...rape."

"C'mon, I wouldn't put it that way, Key."

"No seriously, she took advantage of you......that's not ok. Does your Dad know? What happened to her? Did she go to jail?" Keyarra rattled off question after question and by this time, she was pacing back and forth. She had fire in her eyes, and it was turning me on for some reason.

"You are sounding like your friend, Sharin now, it's not that deep, Key. She taught me a lot, how to put a condom on, what women liked and didn't like, a bunch of shit it wasn't all sexual." I stated. She stopped pacing, and stared at me with glossy eyes now, like she was about to cry.

"I'm serious Derek, that's not ok it sounds like she was grooming you. Who was she?"

"Our tutor."

"So, she preyed on you...she's a pedophile."

"Stop, you're being dramatic."

"No I am not, people don't know the statistics of a female pedophile. They happen a lot more than people think, but for some reason it's not taken as seriously as a male pedophile."

"You sound very passionate about this."

"I am, I hate that it happened to you, Derek." she stated, as her voice cracked.

"Hey hey, come here. Don't cry." I said, as I pulled her by her hand gently. I was still sitting on the swing, so I pulled her between my legs.

"I appreciate your concern, but listen it was like a 50/50 thing. I was really interested in sex and in her defense, she tried her hardest to shut down all my advances. And eventually she just gave in."

"That still doesn't make it right, Derek." She voiced, softly.

"I know, but she felt really bad about it, and it only happened a few times before she quit tutoring us."

"Really Derek? A few times?" she asked with an eye roll.

"Listen, I can be very convincing." I flirted, with a wink.

She laughed a little. I still had her hand in mine and I was caressing it lightly with my thumb, it felt good to be this close to her.

Damn I want to kiss her right now.
I needed to get that thought out of my head before I acted on it.
"Look, you done had me spill all my dark secrets and shit to you in this damn park. Let's go take a walk." I said, releasing her hand and standing up.
Keyarra stepped back and looked up at me like I was crazy.
"Derek, it's hot as shit out here. I don't wanna walk anywhere. Plus school will be getting out soon and I don't want any of the buses riding past seeing me and shit." She fussed.
"I wanted to go get a snowball or something. We can take the alleys." I suggested.
"It's definitely gonna be hella school kids there at the snowball stand. They skip periods and go down there."
"C'mon Key, it's close to 11, and what time they get out? Like 12?" I asked.
"12:15."
"Its 10-minute walk, let's go." I urged.
"Ughhhh." She groaned but started towards the exit of the park.
"Thank youuu." I sang, as I walked behind her, zeroing in on her ass.
"Yeah yeah, whatever."
We made our way through the alleys and back yards to the snowball stand, until we hit a main street.
"So can I ask you a question now?"
"It would be kind of wrong if I said no, so I guess so."
We both laughed.
"Yeah it would be." I replied.
Before I asked, I walked behind her then ended up on her left side, so that way she wasn't walking on the street side anymore.
"Wow, I've only seen that done in movies." She chuckled.
"That means you messing with the wrong boys then, so speaking of…. what's up with you and your boyfriend?" I asked.
"What you mean?"
"Like how did y'all come about out of nowhere

"It wasn't really out of nowhere. We have had classes together since freshman year, and he has always had a crush on me. To be honest, I was a little mean to him, but he never gave up."

"Persistence is always good I guess."

"Yeah, it worked for sure. He has been patient with me."

"So, you love him?" I asked.

"Mmmm, do we really know what love is at this age?"

"I feel like we could."

"Do you love Katrina?"

"I have a lot of love for her, but I don't think I'm in love with her. If that makes sense."

"It does, I think I feel the same way about Tre…. I do think Katrina is in love with you though."

"She says that shit, but I don't know." I shrugged.

"Why you say that?"

"Just a feeling…back to you, so how did you convince your boyfriend not to go to Jr prom?"

"Oh he went, just by himself. To be honest, we almost broke up over it."

"Why didn't you wanna go?"

"Because I just didn't wanna do the whole dress up shit, but I promised him that I will go to homecoming and senior prom." She answered dryly.

"Don't sound so excited…. you and, Tia are hardheaded, we had to beg her to go."

"I saw the pics, her and Matthew looked nice…you and Katrina looked good too."

"Yeah it was cool. But I am happy, Matt offered to take Tia, she seemed a little more at ease when he said he would go…why didn't you bring your ass out there last month to see her off, since you decided to come out of hiding?"

"Because I didn't want her to kick my ass in her dress."

"She wouldn't have, but if looks could kill, she might've taken you out that way." I joked.

"I believe that…. so may I ask you another personal question?" she asked, with a nervous tone.

"You are 3 for 3 Key, let me hear it."

"What is it about sex that entices you so much?"

That question surprised me more than the others.

"Um, it's gonna sound weird, but it's one of the few things that distracts me from the thoughts of our mothers." I answered truthfully.

"So, that's why you have so much of it?"

"Yeah, it sounds bad, but it gives me this high that I can't explain. It relaxes my mind."

"Ok I understand um I know the number of girls isn't the best, but what makes it so bad?"

"My need for it, as opposed to my want for it."

"Like an addiction?" she questioned.

"Yes, my therapist calls it compulsive sexual behavior, but in other words a sex addiction."

"Oh wow, I um..." Keyarra, was trying to come up with what to say.

"It's cool Key, I'm dealing with it. That was another reason I made things official with Katrina. My therapist didn't think that was the best decision because she wanted me to practice abstinence more, but that shit wasn't working for me. If I had an actual girlfriend, then I could just get sex from her plus, that whole rape thing scared me straight a little. I really didn't trust anyone else besides her."

"But at the time, she lived across the country."

"That's what made sense to me. I was practicing controlling my urges when she wasn't around. I wouldn't cheat because that's a form of lying in my eyes and I try my best not to lie. Real shit though, I thought about sex everyday...so I spent a lot of bread flying her out, damn near every weekend."

"Yeah, her ass almost got kicked off the cheer squad because she was missing weekend practices."

"Yeah, I know." I laughed.

"You would've done me a favor." she mumbled.

"Chill on my girl Key. What's the deal with y'all anyway? What's the beef?"

"She's a bitch." she answered, bluntly.

I tried not to laugh because I didn't like anyone talking about Tri in a bad way. I know she wasn't the nicest, but she still was my girl. "Watch it, Key."

"At least I didn't say hoe" She joked.

"Uh huh."

"But seriously, I'm glad you are doing better….do you have to go to classes or anything?"

"I tried that a few times, but they are wild in there. They were paying for sex from hookers and shit. They were too far gone for me…. I wasn't on that type of time and never will be."

"Oh yeah, that is wild."

We approached the small snowball stand that sat in the corner of the Putty Hill Shopping Center. This was another staple in our childhood, the little stand was owned by an older couple, and they had the most unique flavors. They would be busy all summer long. We stood in line behind 5 or 6 people and waited until it was our turn.

"You getting the superman? They added a lot more combinations I see." I stated viewing the menu.

"How'd you remember that?".

"I remember everything about you Keyarra, plus that's the only kind you got every time we came here."

"You remember everything about me huh?" she questioned.

"Yeah, I do."

"What's my favorite food?"

"Pizza when we were younger, but I noticed how you tore that chicken up on Sunday, and at Kobe's you got chicken, while everyone else got steak and shrimp; so imma say chicken now." She just stared at me blankly, so I was going to assume I was correct.

"What's my favorite color?" She asked next.

"Silver or grey. I figured that hasn't changed because I saw you painted your room grey, and you still wear silver jewelry."

Again, she didn't say anything.

"Do you remember our first kiss?" She immediately looked embarrassed, like she didn't mean to say it.

I fully turned to her and sunk my teeth into my bottom lip.

"If I don't remember anything about you Keyarra, it would be that for sure." I said lowly.

"I-i-i don't know why I asked that." She stammered, shyly.

"Because clearly, it's been on your mind, like it's been on mine."

"Why has it been on your mind?"

"Why do you think?"

Before she could answer, we heard a man call us up.

"Come on up kids...what can I get for ya?" The old man asked.

Keyarra looked a little flustered. I wasn't sure if it was because of the heat outside or the heat between us.

"She will have a medium superman, and I think I'll have the same." I answered.

"Great choice, that will be 6.50."

I pulled out a 50 and handed it to him.

"Oh son, I'm not sure if I have that much change yet. We just opened not too long ago.".

"Don't worry about it, keep the change." I said, coolly.

"Oh, I couldn't possibly.".

"I promise its fine sir." I insisted.

"What's your name son?"

"Derek."

"Tell ya what, your next 2 snowballs for you and your girlfriend are on the house."

"Yes sir." I didn't even bother to correct him about the girlfriend part.

A few minutes passed and we were handed our snowballs.

"I made them a large for you 2." he smiled.

"Thank you, sir."

"Thank you so much, we appreciate it." Keyarra said, sweetly. She slowly started to walk away.

"Hey son", the old man whispered, "she's beautiful."

"Isn't she?" I smiled, "Thank you."

We started to make our way back home.

"Why'd you get quiet on me?" I asked.

"I'm hot." she responded, but I knew her ass was lying.

"That didn't stop you from talking before."

"Why didn't you tell that man I wasn't your girlfriend?"

"Because you are my friend, who's a girl."

"Derek, you know that's not how he meant it."

"Yeah so, it's none of his business."

She remained quiet.

"I don't think, Katrina, would have liked that." she finally voiced.

"Are you gonna tell her?"

"No."

"Ok, then shut up." I joked.

"No, you shut up." she laughed, as she pushed me slightly.

We laughed and talked a little more when we finally made it back to the block. We stopped at the bottom, finishing our snowballs.

"I wanted to run something past you." I spoke.

"What is it?"

"Your birthday."

"What about it?"

"What if we got a beach house in OC, and stayed a few days?"

"Just me and you?" she asked, confused.

"I mean if you want it to be" I said, just trying to see what she would say.

"Um, I'm not sure how we would explain that."

"But you would be open to it?"

She looked like her wheels were spinning in her head.

"I'm messing with you Key; you can invite whoever you want. Of course, Matt and Tia would come."

"Derek, I don't think G will pay for that."

"Who said she was? I would be."

"Oh no, I don't want you to spend your money on me."

"I'm gonna do it anyway." I said, walking away from her and heading up the block.

"Derek, wait." I heard her footsteps rushing behind me. "Why do you want to do that?"

"Because I think it would be fun; I also remember how much you love the beach."
"You really don't have to do this."
"I know I don't have to; I want to."
"I don't know what to say."
"Say thank you."
"Thank you, Derek." she gave me a half hug, since we were both still holding our cups.
"But wait....is Katrina coming?" She asked.
"So, you and your friends can bank my girl? No."
"Nobody gonna touch her ass. If you want her to come, then I promise to be on my best behavior." she assured me.
"Can you say the same for, Tia?"
"That, I cannot." she answered, quickly.
"Exactly, but I appreciate you."

"You wanna know what I can't seem to figure out?" a voice called out ahead of us.
Me and Keyarra looked a few houses up to see a pissed off, GG walking towards us.
"Shit." Keyarra hissed.
"Oh yeah, don't look all scared now. Why aren't you in school, Keyarra?" GG questioned.
"I um...I w-was but I did leave early." Keyarra stuttered.
"Were you? Where is your book bag then?" G asked, suspiciously. She was not about to buy into her bullshit.
"I left it in the house. It's a half day G, I didn't need to bring anything." Keyarra said, trying to sound convincing.
She eyed me next, and I hated to lie, but I couldn't let Keyarra drown especially, since I'm part of the reason why she got caught.
"She's telling the truth; I saw her walking home and picked her up, then we got snowballs, then we just took a walk."
"Why would you be driving from that direction Derek?" GG asked.
"I was leaving Katrina's."

"So, did Katrina skip school too, because why the hell would you be there, and she wasn't there."

I had to say the only thing that I knew would get her to end her line of questioning because our story wasn't making any sense.

"To be real G, she really put it on me between last night and this morning, and I was dead tired...."

"AHT AHT AHT STOP STOP!" GG yelled, interrupting me. She threw her hands up in a stopping motion.

I heard Keyarra, snickering; she was trying her hardest to hold in her laugh and I was trying to keep my straight face.

"I don't wanna hear that, Derek! Keyarra, I don't believe you because it doesn't make sense that you would leave early on a half day when you have what." she held her arm out to look at her gold watch, "when you have 20 minutes left, but you know what, I will be dropping you off tomorrow and picking you up, since you can't be trusted." GG fussed.

"And you Derek, don't be covering for this child. Her ass just getting back on track and you lying for her not helping." she continued.

"But G...I really was with..." I tried to tell her.

"AHT SHUT UP.... I don't wanna hear anything about your escapades."

And with that said, she stomped back up the street into the house. Keyarra, and I couldn't hold our laughter in anymore.

"G is so sick of our shit." Keyarra said, once we finally gained our composure.

"She is." I agreed.

"Were you coming to see her today, is that why you were in the neighborhood?"

"Yes."

"Oh, she goes to the homes most mornings, so you would of missed her anyway."

"Well, I'm glad I found something else to pre-occupy my time then."

She smiled at me. "Derek, I really enjoyed your company today."

"I enjoyed yours as well...I hope we can do that more."

"I would like that, and I promise not to repeat anything we talked about today as well."

"I know, I trust you."

I stared at Keyarra's lips, it was becoming harder and harder to resist the urge to kiss her.

"Derek, you have to stop staring at me like that." she whispered.

"Like what?" I questioned.

"Like you wanna kiss me."

"Would that be a bad thing?"

"Yes, because I think I will like kissing you more than my boyfriend."

Before I could say anything else, she walked away from me. I watched her as she made her way in the house. Did she just admit to wanting to kiss me too?

"Shit." I said to myself.

My mind was screaming to stay away from her because I knew it would be trouble, but just being in Keyarra's presence made me feel good. I for sure wanted to be inside of her, but it was more than that. I wasn't sure what it was yet, but it was something. I was about to go in the house but the way I was feeling had me ready to relieve some pressure. Just as I was about to text Katrina, she was calling me.

"What's up Tri?" I answered.

"Hiiii baby, can you come over I miss you and my grandmother wants to see you."

"Yeah, why are you home already?"

"What do you mean?"

"School not out yet.... did you not go today?"

"Oh um no, I thought I told you I wasn't."

"No you didn't, so all y'all just skipping today I see."

"Who else didn't go?"

I didn't mean to say that because she would lose her shit if she knew I was alone with Keyarra.

"I saw a bunch of kids walking down G's block." I lied.

I hate lying about dumb shit!

"Yeah nobody goes on the last 2 days, and yay you're close. Hurry up we miss you."

"Who is we?"

"You know." she purred seductively.

"I'm on my way."

I ended the call then went over to my truck; I was going to stop past G's on my way back home. In less than 5 minutes I was pulling into Katrina's driveway. I walked up and knocked on the door; almost immediately her grandma opened the door.

"Derekkkk, look at you boy." Grandma Bev beamed, as she pulled me into the house.

"Hey Granny B, how are you?"

She suddenly hit me in my chest.

"Ow, Granny." I said holding my chest like it really hurt.

"You been here how long and just getting around to coming to see me?"

"When I came Sunday and dropped the food off you were sleep and when I woke up in the morning you were gone, and Katrina been coming over to my place after school." I explained.

"Yeah, I had to go play my numbers that morning chile, but still it's Thursday. Katrina, don't have to be here for you to come by."

"I'm sorry granny, it won't happen again."

"Yeah whatever and stop calling me granny, you know I liked to be called the, Big B.".

"Granny B, you know I'm not calling you that."

"Whatever boy, did you tell Virginia thank you for the food?"

"You know you can call her and tell her, right?"

"And You know that lady don't like me."

"That's not true."

GG, and Granny B used to go the same church, and they were good friends at one point; they are how me and Katrina got introduced a few years ago. Granny B was a little rough around the edges though. She cursed, drank, gambled religiously, and she also had no type of filter; and for whatever reason she thought that GG, judged her for that, which was not true. G just didn't want to be around it often, so she distanced herself, but there was no beef.

"Yeah whatever." Granny sat down and unmuted her tv.
"Where is Tri?"
"In the shower."
"It's a little late for her to be doing that."
"Mmmm, I agree."
Granny gave me this odd look and I wasn't sure what to make of it.
I started to make my way upstairs when Granny stopped me.
"You know Derek, the apple doesn't fall far from the tree."
"What does that mean?"
"You'll see." She said, with a sly smile.
I was confused as shit but left it alone and went into Katrina's room. I sat on the bed and took out my phone to look at beach houses.
"Hiii baby." Katrina beamed when she walked into the room and closed the door behind her.
"Hi." I said, putting my phone down to look at her.
"I missed you." She leaned down to kiss me.
She removed her hair from her shower cap and stood in front of me in her robe. Water was still dripping from her legs.
"Yeah you've said that a few times, why are you taking another shower?"
"I'm not sure what you mean."
"You either take showers at the ass crack of dawn or at night...but not in the middle of the day. And last night when you got off the phone with me you said you were about to take a shower."
"I didn't know it was a crime for me to take another shower."
"It's not, I'm just asking is there a reason why?"
"No." she answered quickly.
"Another question, if you knew you weren't going to school today why wouldn't you call me, so I could of came over earlier or even last night?"

"Because Derek, I didn't know until this morning that I wasn't going."

Katrina was looking everywhere except at me. I just stared at her, she was fidgeting and looked nervous. I wasn't sure what the hell was going on, but the energy was weird. Plus, my head was still stuck on what Grandma Bev just said to me.

"Any other questions?" she asked.

"Naw."

"Good, because..."

"You missed me?" I said completing her sentence. Katrina was being weird, she never told me she missed me this damn much. *Maybe I'm over thinking this.*

"Yes.".

She sauntered over to me and climbed in my lap, she started kissing and sucking on my neck. I knew I was thrown off because my dick wasn't even getting hard.

"Chill out Katrina, I just wanted to see you."

"But earlier on the phone, you seemed happy to come over when I told you that WE missed you."

Katrina opened her legs slightly and trailed her finger along her wet thigh.

"I know, but we have had sex every day since I've been here, and I'm not even supposed to be doing all that."

"I know, but we were just making up for lost time." she said, as she nibbled on my ear.

"Mmmm." I moaned lowly.

"See, you saying one thing but he is saying another."

She must of felt my dick finally getting hard underneath her but I still wasn't feeling right.

"C'mon Katrina, get up for me. We can do that later, I just wanna chill with you plus your grandmother downstairs."

"You know she doesn't care Derek." She snapped.

I just ignored her while I peered around her room, I'm not sure what I was looking for but I had an odd feeling.

"What are you looking at?"

"Nothing Katrina." I replied, my eyes landing back on her.

We stared at each for a few seconds and she visibly became tense.

"Ugh fine Derek and stop calling me by my full name. I like when you call me Tri, or you could actually call me baby, like I call you." she said, as she got up and sat next to me. I can tell she was going to have an attitude.

"I don't like pet names."

"Whatever, I don't know why you came over here just to be an asshole."

"I'm being an asshole because I don't wanna have sex right now? How does that even sound?"

She didn't reply, she just got up and began to rummage through her drawers, I assume looking for something to wear. I shook my head and started my search again for a beach house. Keyarra's birthday was less than a month away and a lot of places were booked already. I was getting frustrated until I found one that sat on the beach; it had 5 bedrooms and a pool. It was a little above what I wanted to pay but fuck it. I was trying to convince myself that maybe a lot of people hadn't stayed in it since it was so expensive, but either way, I was bringing my own sheets. I was almost done booking the place when Katrina took my phone out of my hands.

"Yo, what are you doing?" I asked.

"Are we going to the beach?" she asked, looking at my phone.

I snatched it back. "No, WE are not."

"Well, who is going?"

"Tia and her friends."

"That bitch doesn't have any friends." she snarled.

"Ayo, watch your fucking mouth when you talking about my sister, you know I don't play that shit." I spat, angrily.

"She calls me names all the time and you never say anything."

"You talking out your ass right now because I defend you all the time, from everybody, so stop talking about shit you don't know about."

"Are you going with her and these so-called friends?"

"Yeah."

"Well, why can't I come?"

"Because I don't feel like breaking up fights."

"Ain't nobody gonna touch me."

"Katrina...you are giving me a headache already, and I haven't even been here for 10 minutes yet."

"I don't care." she huffed, standing in front of me with folded arms.

I blew out a deep breath. "Fine, Katrina you can come."

"There is no way I'm staying with them."

I couldn't help but laugh.

"Oh, so I'm funny now?" she asked, angrily.

"Of course not." I answered sarcastically. "How about this, we can get our own place."

"How about no, you still gonna want to hang out with them while we are there."

I didn't have anything else to say; I put my focus back to my phone. I was not about to play these games with her spoiled ass.

"Derek...is Keyarra going?"

"That would be one of her friends." I stated, not even bothering to look up at her.

"You can't go."

This girl is tripping.

"Yeah, imma head out."

I proceeded to get up.

"No, you aren't." she said, pushing me back onto the bed.

"Katrina, please don't touch me again." I told her calmly. I tried to get up again but before I could, she got on top of me and pushed me until I was flat on my back.

"Derek, you can't go. I don't trust Keyarra."

"Why don't you trust her?"

"Because she's...she's sneaky.".

"Sneaky how?"

"She just is...you have to trust me."

Her eyes got watery.

"Why are you about to cry?"

She didn't say anything as the tears started to cascade down her face. Katrina didn't cry often, so I wasn't sure what was going on with her. She still hadn't said anything, she just leaned forward and cried into the crook of my neck. I rubbed her back until she calmed down a little.

"She is going to try and take you from me." she whispered.

"Katrina, me and Keyarra, are like siblings. Nothing is going to happen between us. Where is all this coming from?"

"Promise me!"

"I promise that you have nothing to worry about, Tri."

Katrina dried her eyes, then kissed me deeply, while removing her robe and was now completely naked. Before I knew it, we were fucking.

"Derek, I'm sorry for being a brat earlier." Katrina apologized, as she laid on my chest.

I was silent because my head was still fucked up. Why did Katrina think that Keyarra was sneaky? Why did she think something would happen between us, and that whole apple from the tree thing was still in the back of my mind.

"Did you hear me baby?" she asked.

"Yeah Tri, it's cool. I'm tired. Let's take a nap."

"Ok baby, I love you."

Again, I was silent; my mind was going into overdrive. Suddenly, my thoughts floated to Keyarra, and the morning we had together, and that alone settled me enough, so that way sleep could find me.

TIA

The past few weeks have flown by. We were fully unpacked and moved in. I finally got my room the way I liked, after struggling with it. Even with unpacking, I had seen Christian, damn near every day since we first met, and it drove Matthew insane; especially since Sharin, had placed him on ice for a while. I mean me and him were still having sex when we could, but I was starting to feel bad because I really liked, Chris. I had learned a lot about him, he was the oldest of 4. He adored his 2 sisters and brother, but only his brother lived in the house with him and his hard-working mother. The 2 other siblings lived with their mothers. I had already met his mother and younger brother Devin, and they were nice. Devin told Chris that when he got older that I would be his first girlfriend; he was the cutest 9-year-old, who looked just like his older brother. I had been with Chris and sneaking around with Matt so much that I barely saw Keyarra. I hadn't talked to her in like a day, so I facetimed her.

"Hey girl, long time no see." Keyarra joked, when she answered.

"Stop it, I just seen you a few days ago."

"So, I thought we would be joined at the hip again, but you done went and got you a boyfriend and said forget me."

"I could say the same about you."

"Ughh, you are never gonna let me live this down."

"I am, but no time soon." I teased.

"Whatever, well since you called, I was thinking we could have a best friend day."

"Today?"

"Yes, it's still early."

It was only like 11, but I was hesitant because Matthew was supposed to come over in like an hour. Derek took Katrina to DC for the day, and they would be gone all day.

"Um, I kind of had plans already."

"Oh...ok, no problem." she said, but I could hear the disappointment in her voice.

"You know what, forget it. Where did you wanna go?" I said instantly, changing my mind.

"Are you sure? We can do another day."

"Naw girl, its fine."

"I was thinking we could go out Arundel Mills."

"Why the hell you wanna go all the way out there?"

"Because it's hella stores and since, Derek, refused to cancel that big ass beach house, I wanted to get some clothes for that weekend."

"Ok, we gonna take an uber out there?" I asked.

"No, G gonna take us and I was going to ask Matt, to pick us up. He been extra nice to me lately for some reason, so I'm trying to soak it up while I can." she laughed.

"What time you gonna be here?"

"In like an hour, G should be back from the homes soon."

"Ok cool, let me shower and get dressed."

"See you soon."

I hung up then immediately facetimed Matt.

"What's up beauty?" he answered.

I admired his handsome face.

"Nothing, I um have to re-schedule with you today."

"Why, Tia?"

"Because I have something to do."

"Like what?"

"Matthew, I will see you another time." I said, sternly.

"Just tell me you gonna see that nigga, Chris."

"Imma go see him."

"Ok Tia, have fun."

He hung up right after that. I was about to call him right back, but I decided against it. I shouldn't have lied but he jumped to conclusions, so imma just let him run with it, I mean since he was picking us up, he was gonna find out that I lied anyway. I got ready in record time. I decided on a pink Nike crop top, jean shorts and my matching pink prestos. I was putting on my lip gloss when Keyarra let me know that they were outside. I made my way through the apartment and out the door.

"Hiiii GG." I said, once I got in the backseat.

"Hi my baby, you look pretty as always." she complimented.

"Thanks G, hey Key."

"Hey Ti, we matching; I have my prestos on too." she laughed.

Me and Keyarra used to dress alike all the time when we were younger, not because we were forced to but because we wanted to. That's why it hurt so much when she left me; she was my sister in every sense of the word.

"You wanna be my son so bad." I joked.

"Girl bye, I'm sure I was dressed before you."

"Don't matter."

"Y'all have inadvertently been dressing alike for the past few years." GG chimed in.

"Huh?" I questioned.

"I would see Keyarra leave for school in a blue shirt and jeans, then I would Facetime with you, Tia after school, and you would have on a blue shirt and jeans." GG replied.

"How many times has that happened?" Keyarra asked.

"Enough times that I took notice, and I didn't talk to Tia, every single day, so I'm sure it has been a lot of times that I just didn't see it." GG said.

I locked eyes with Keyarra, in the mirror and she gave me a small smile, I didn't return it though. I was still angry with her, but today I was going get to the bottom of it. It may not have been the right setting, but I needed to know something. We pulled up to the

146

mall half an hour later. I hadn't been here probably since before our mothers died; this mall was far out, so we rarely came here. I think the last time was for one of our classmates' birthday parties, at Dave and Busters.

"Matthew, is coming right?" GG asked Keyarra.
"Yes, he said to text him when we were almost ready to go."
"Ok, y'all be safe and don't be talking to strangers."
"Yes, Mother May I." me and Keyarra, said in unison.
We really are in sync still, we both bust out laughing.
"Smart mouth little girls, bye." GG said, as she pulled off.
"Where you wanna go first?" Keyarra asked me.
"Girl, I don't even know what's in this mall anymore…. when did they put a casino out here?"
"Oh, maybe right after y'all left, so a few years ago…but come on, we can just hit whatever we see."

We went into the mall, and it was like a mad house; even though it was a Thursday afternoon, it was filled with kids running around. Keyarra and I hit the ground running; we went everywhere, Forever 21, H&M, Victoria's Secret, Steve Madden, Saks, Michael Kors, and other little boutiques in between. I had to stop Keyarra from going into every damn sneaker store with her tom boy ass.

"Your father is going to kill me." Keyarra said, as we got seated at Chevys.
We were exhausted, we had so many bags that our arms hurt.
"Why?"
"You had me use that credit card he gave me, at all those expensive stores."
"Girl shut up, I already told you I overheard, DW say that you barely use it…and you said yourself he told you to get whatever for your birthday."
"Yeah, I know but I might've over did it."

"How? G gave you cash, and you used the card, so it's not like everything was on it."

"I guess you're right." she agreed.

"I know, now let's eat. I'm starving."

After a few minutes, the server came over and placed our orders. We got appetizers to share, and we each got an entrée. We talked a little, but it did feel a little awkward. This was the first time that we were actually alone.

"I have to ask you something." I said.

She looked at me with worried eyes; she knew what I was going to ask, I'm sure.

"Ok, what is it?"

"What happened?"

She stared at me for a few seconds, then started to shift in her seat uncomfortably.

"Um, like why I went ghost?"

"Yes, and please, Key...no bullshit." I said, seriously.

"Tia, I just got depressed...I don't know what from, but it overcame me. I couldn't get out of bed yet, I barely slept. I went days without eating, then I would just eat non-stop. It was a really scary time for me, and I just didn't want to put my shit on anyone else." she explained.

I believed her somewhat, but I couldn't shake the feeling that it was something else.

"What are your nightmares about?"

"I don't have nightmares."

"Yes, you do. I witnessed one, and G told me that you do."

"Why are you asking G about me?" she asked, defensively.

"I didn't ask, she told me. But what does that matter?"

"I finally got her off my back, I just don't want her to start worrying about me or breathing down my back again."

"She's our family and your guardian Keyarra, so of course she is going to worry about you, especially when you started treating everyone like shit.... now what are your nightmares about?" I repeated.

"Tia, its nothing."

AGE IS JUST A NUMBER

"Oh, but I thought you didn't have any?" I quipped, catching her in a lie.

"JUST DROP IT." she yelled.

She startled me and a few others around us. I looked at her with hurt in my eyes because how dare she yell at me, when I'm trying to figure out what the hell was wrong with her. In my opinion, everyone just left Keyarra alone when they should've intervened more. That's why I got my ass on that plane to see her, but that Keyarra I fought with wasn't the same girl I grew up with, and it wasn't the one that was sitting in front of me right now, either. I felt bad for leaving her alone after that, but that fight hurt me way more emotionally than it did physically, so I had to lick my wounds and try to carry on without her.

"Fine." I said, getting up to leave to go to the bathroom.

"Tia wait..." Keyarra said, with a cracked voice.

The hell was she crying for, she was the one who was sitting in my face lying, and she just embarrassed us in the middle of this got damn restaurant. I stood in the bathroom and started to cry, so I called the only person that I knew could calm me down.

"What's up little sister?" Derek said, when he answered my Facetime.

"Derek." I sobbed.

"Whoa whoa, what's wrong?" he asked, voice filled with concern.

"I just...tried...to talk to...Key...arra...and it just went bad." I stammered, in between trying to get my sentence out.

I felt myself breathing heavily and I was on the verge of a panic attack.

"First off, calm down I can barely understand you; just breathe through your nose and out your mouth."

I did what he said and felt my breathing going back to normal.

"Better?" he asked.

"A little yes."

"Ok good, so what went bad with Keyarra?"

"I pressed her about why she disappeared, and she just got upset. I can tell she didn't want to talk but Derek I need to know. Then I caught her in a lie, so that's when I got upset. I really tried not have an attitude, Derek, I swear, but then she yelled at me, and I didn't even go off like I wanted to; so I just left and came into the bathroom." I rambled, quickly.

"I told you she can't be trusted." I overheard Katrina say.

"Derek, why you got that hoe listening to my conversation?" I yelled.

"Who you calling a hoe?" she yelled back.

"Aye man, go over there Katrina." Derek said, clearly agitated by our bickering.

"But, Derek that's what I'm talking about, she called me a hoe and you didn't say shit."

"I'm going to handle it, now go back inside the store."
He moved his hard glare back to me.

"Tia, STOP calling her out her name. How many times I have to tell you that." he said seriously, as he turned his attention back to me.

Derek's eyes got a little darker, which meant he was angry.

"Derek, nobody told you to have that h..." I started.

"I dare you!" he challenged, as he squinted his eyes at me.

"I'm sorry, ok...damn."

"Ard, now listen, Ti. Personally, I think in the middle of the mall wasn't the best time to do this, but I know it's been bothering you...now did she answer any of your questions before shit went left?"

"Yes, when I asked her what happened she said she got depressed or some bullshit like that. She couldn't eat or sleep blah blah blah."

"Cut it out Ti, it's not bullshit. That shit ain't no joke. I told you how I felt after that whole thing back in Cali."

"Ok, but that's because you were actually going through something."

"So...that can hit you out of anywhere; you don't have to be traumatized, and you know Carmen taught us that."

"Derek, we are too young for that, for it just to be coming out of nowhere for no reason." I countered.

"What does that even mean? Age is just a number Tia, it can happen to anyone, at any age, at any stage in their life....and I'm not sure if you forgot, but she lost her mother. That finally setting in could of broke her...you just don't know. So, don't write her off."

I hated to, but I started to see his point.

"You didn't have to throw in the mother part, Derek." I said, rolling my eyes.

"Clearly, I did because you talking about she wasn't going through anything, at the moment.... that shit gonna affect us the rest of our lives, no matter how good we got it; we just gonna deal with it in our own way. You use excessive shopping and asshole-isms to deal with your emotions. Keyarra maybe just had to figure her shit out."

"And what is exactly is an asshole-ism?"

"Asshole shit that you do."

"I really wish you weren't so damn annoying."

"I'm only annoying when I'm right." he laughed. "Now go back out there and try to enjoy the rest of y'all day."

"Thank you, big brother, I love you."

"I love you too Ti, and you better had got me something.".

"Bye, Derek"

I ended the call and laughed to myself because I did get him a few fits, I loved dressing, Derek. He could pull off any look effortlessly. I looked in the mirror to make sure I didn't look crazy. I didn't put any make up on besides a little eye liner and gloss so, I looked fine.

"Ok girl, we got this." I talked myself up in the mirror.

I walked out of the bathroom and back to the table; our food was there, and I could see Keyarra trying to wipe her eyes.

"I'm really sorry that I yelled at you." Keyarra apologized soon as I sat down.

"It's ok..." I started to say, but she interrupted me.

"No, no it wasn't. You have been worried about me and I get it…. I just want to put the past behind us. There are certain things that I just can't explain, and I don't want to lie to you."

"I can't say I understand fully but I want you to know that you hurt me, deeply…. you are my sister, and you cut me off with no explanation, whatsoever."

She started to talk but I needed to get this off my chest.

"Please let me finish…. I never wanna feel how you made me feel again; it nearly broke me. Without Derek, and my therapist, I'm not sure how I would've gotten through. I was still grieving our mothers and then I started to feel like I had to grieve our friendship. I forgive you Keyarra, but you have to promise me that you will never do this again because I will beat your ass this time."

Keyarra laughed a little at the last part, which I was hoping she would. She had tears streaming down her face, which also caused mine to sting again.

"Tia, I promise I will never ever hurt you like that again; I put that on my mother. I'm sorry from the bottom of my heart."

I stood up and held out my arms so we could hug; she got up and we embraced.

"Keyarra, just know I'm here for you. You don't have to go through anything alone."

"I know Ti, I love you."

"I love you too girl. Now let's eat and leave because people are staring at us again."

Keyarra laughed. We sat down and enjoyed our meal.

"Our manager wanted you guys to have a little dessert on us." the waitress said, as she sat down what looked to be a brownie sundae.

"Aww, thank you." we again, said in unison.

We ate our dessert and started to gather our things.

"I texted Matthew like 20 minutes ago, so he should be almost here." Keyarra said.

"Ok good, I'm beat."

"Looks like him and Rin, are officially back on good terms" she said looking at her phone.
"Why you say that?"

She turned her phone to me and there was a video of Sharin and Matt riding around. She was singing the words to Usher and Alicia Keys' song My Boo. Matthew actually looked happy; I thought he would be annoyed by something like that but clearly, he wasn't. I knew I blew him off today, but I was mad.
We waited near the movie theater entrance since that was where we got dropped off at, and it was the easiest to find, about 10 minutes later, Matthew pulled up and Sharin was in the front seat.
"Hey boos." Sharin yelled out the window.
"Sharin, please don't start with the yelling." Matthew said, calmly.
"Sorry. Ke-Ke I just know you better have something in one of those bags for me"
"I actually do."
"For real?" she shrieked.
"Yes, girl"
Keyarra had a got a whole outfit, including shoes for her. She told me today how Sharin really was a good friend to her, even though Keyarra was really stand offish to her in the very beginning; but Sharin, always brushed it off. I thought I would feel jealous about that, but it made me happy that Keyarra had someone outside of me. I never made friends back in Cali; partly because of my attitude but also because those bitches were fake.
"I can't wait to see." Sharin said, excitedly.
"And what about me sister?" Matthew inquired.
"You too Matt, but Tia, actually picked it out; I'm bad with boy clothes."
"Is that right?" Matthew asked, as he looked at me through his mirror.
"Yup." I said, being short.

He had an amused look, and I wanted to smack it off him. We pulled off, and for most of the ride Keyarra and Sharin talked; I didn't have much to say. I'm not sure why I was mad because I wanted to chill on Matt, but that video got to me. Besides my Jr prom, we didn't have any pictures together, and here he goes on snapchat with Sharin, like they were a couple.

"Boo can we go to your house, so I can see everything they got instead of you taking me home right now?" Sharin asked.

"That's a lot of back-and-forth Rin, I gotta take Tia, home still."

"Chris can get me from the house" I said, immediately.

Matthew looked at me quickly then back to the road.

"That's cool." he answered.

When we pulled up to the house, Matthew got out and opened all our doors. He barely looked at me when he opened mine. He just took a bunch of bags and headed into the house.

"He is being so nice; I can't handle it." Keyarra said.

"I told you he has turned over a new leaf." Sharin expressed.

"How so?" I questioned.

"I can just feel it."

"Girl bye." I said, walking past them and into the house.

I walked upstairs and Matthew was leaving Keyarra's room; he had just sat the bags down in there. He attempted to walk right past me.

"What, you mad at me?" I asked.

"Yeah, I am"

"Why?"

"Because you lied to me, Tia. Like why you didn't just say you wanted to go out with, Keyarra. I wouldn't have been upset at that, y'all haven't had too much time together."

Now he had me feeling bad.

"I don't know...I just...."

"You just what...wanted to make me jealous?"

I heard the door open, and the laughter from Sharin and Keyarra.

"That's kind of fucked up, Tia." Matthew said, before he started down the steps. I couldn't even defend myself.

"Ard Rin, I'll be back in like an hour." I watched Matthew through the mirror, as he pecked her lips and left out the door. Tears stung to my eyes, because what the hell.

Sharin even looked shocked that he just did that; if he was trying to make me jealous, then that worked because I was feeling hot all over.

Sharin slowly turned towards Keyarra and started squealing in excitement.

"We really about to be sisters for real, because I'm marrying him!"

I went into the bathroom, slamming the door; I had to calm myself down.

"Tia, make up your mind. Either you gonna let Matthew go or not." I said, talking to myself in mirror. I let my stinging tears fall freely.

"Ughhh, what the fuck." I groaned, drying my tears.

"Ti-Ti, you ok girl?" I heard Sharin say from the other side of the door.

"Uh yes, I'm coming out

I wiped my face, then swung the door open, and to my surprise, she was still standing there.

"You good? I thought I heard you crying." she asked, sincerely.

I smiled at her warmly, I really couldn't dislike Sharin. Over the past few weeks, I had gotten to know her as well, and I could tell she was a genuine person. Christian, also talked very highly of her. The two of them were best friends and like Sharin had also told me they looked out for each other. Sharin was an only child, and her mother was always working doubles, so she was home alone a lot, which she hated. I also learned that her and Matthew, had been flirting heavy for well over a year before they started having sex; she told me how he would stay the nights when her mom wasn't home, so that way, she wouldn't be alone all the time. Overall, I didn't view her as my competition for Matthew, he had just made both of us feel as though we had a chance at being his girlfriend.

155

"Yes, I'm fine. Let's go see what Keyarra got you. I'm sure you will love it."

"I don't care if its rags, I'd be happy." she joked.

"Shut up." I laughed.

We went through all our bags and showed Sharin all our purchases.

"Y'all dropped a few racks." Sharin said, in awe.

"No, Tia did. I stuck to the lower price stuff."

"Puh-lease, it's really not that much." I said, shrugging it off.

"Yeah ok, we not even halfway through your bags." Keyarra said.

"Chill on me, I gave a lot of stuff to G to take down to the homes, so I needed replacements. Now show Rin, what you got her."

"Aww, you called me Rin." Sharin beamed.

"Don't start."

Keyarra pulled out these dresses from one of the boutiques that we went to. The 1st one was lavender, it was knee length and stretchy. It had thin spaghetti straps and with ruched fabric.

"Oh Ke-Ke, this is so pretty...it's mine?"

"Yes girl, I saw it and thought it would look good on you." Keyarra said, as she handed it to her. "I also got these gold sandals too." she added, as she went to find the shoe box.

"Oh no, you didn't have to get me all this."

"I know I didn't have to, I wanted to. You have really helped me this past year, trying to get me to come out of my shell and I appreciate you." Keyarra said, then turned to me.

"Ti, I don't think I told you but all those times I called you was because every time I said out loud that I wanted to, Rin pushed me to. She didn't even know the details about everything, but she just knew I missed my best friend, and she wanted me to make it right."

I smiled, then she turned back to Rin.

"I also got one more thing." Keyarra said.

I rolled my eyes because I knew what was next. She pulled out the big Victoria's secret bag and pulled out 3 bathing suits. One powder blue, one light pink, and one green.

"WE GOT MATCHING BIKINIS FOR THE BEACH!" Keyarra squealed, with excitement.

"THE THREE OF US?" Sharin yelled, matching Keyarra's energy.

"Yes, we are gonna look like the got damn powerpuff girls." I said, unenthused.

"Omg that is sooo cute, which one am I?" Sharin asked.

Me and Keyarra gave her a knowing look.

"Bubbles." we said, together.

Sharin burst out laughing. "I figured."

"You wanna guess which one Ti, is?" Keyarra asked.

"Mean ass buttercup." Sharin laughed.

"I'm not even mean, and green isn't my color either. I only agreed because it's for her birthday." I said, snatching mine.

"Yeah, not a mean bone in your body." Keyarra said, sarcastically.

I threw up my middle finger and started to put my clothes back in their bags. A little while later, Chris finally returned my text about him taking me home and said he would be there in 15 minutes.

"Chris, be taking a long time to return my messages sometimes." I complained.

"He was probably at the library, reading." Sharin said.

"But it's summertime now."

"Yeah, he's an odd ball, so he still likes to challenge himself or some shit like that; but he be looking up all that police academy stuff too."

"Police academy?" I questioned.

"Oh...yeah. I thought maybe he mentioned that to you...if he didn't then don't say I told you." Sharin said, nervously.

"I thought he wanted to go to college when we graduated?" Keyarra asked.

"He does, I think both; but listen, just forget I said it." Sharin insisted.

Chris and I talked a lot, and he has never mentioned the police academy to me, which I thought was odd because he joked with me about going to whatever school I was thinking about attending.

I know Sharin said drop it, but I was going to try and see what that was about when he came to get me.

"Sharin!" Matthew yelled from downstairs.

"And he always talks about me yelling." she said, as she rolled her eyes.

"Coming boo." she yelled back.

Keyarra emptied one of her bags so Sharin could put her things in it.

"Thank you again, Ke-Ke, I love everything. I guess I will see y'all next weekend." she said hugging us bye.

"You're welcome, I can't wait to see you next week." Keyarra said.

"Bye girl." I waved.

Sharin disappeared out the room; I heard the front door close. I told Key I was going to the bathroom. Once I shut the door I went over to the window and peaked out the blinds. I don't know why but I just wanted to see them leave. The window was right above the porch, and it was cracked so I could hear them talking.

"Let me get on your back." I heard Sharin say.

"Rin, the car right there; it's like 10 steps away."

"Pleaseee, boo." she begged.

"Ughhh come on."

I couldn't see them all the way, since they were directly under the window. A few seconds went past, and they were walking across the porch and down the steps. Sharin had her legs wrapped around his waist and her arms were draped around his shoulders and interlocked. I saw her head tilt into his neck.

"Mmmm, you better stop that shit, Rin."

"Or what?"

"I can show you better than I can tell you." he replied.

"Like you did this morning?" she laughed.

"Chill, you caught me off guard, get down" he said, as they approached the car.

Sharin hopped off his back and he opened the car door for her; but before she got in he pulled her in for a kiss. I couldn't hear what they were saying, but I know he said something in her ear, and it made her burst out in laughter. After he closed the door and went to walk over to his side, he looked up at the window. It's like he knew I was watching them. I wasn't sure if he could see me or not because it looked like the sun was in his eyes, but I saw the slight smile on his face and I didn't like that shit, at all. If he was putting on that show to make me jealous, then that meant he was playing with Sharin's feelings and that wasn't ok with me. I made my decision right then and there that I was done with Matthew. I texted him.

As far as me and you are concerned.... we're done!
I saw the little bubbles pop up immediately.
NWA: Yeah we'll see.
He also put a smiling face at the end of it.

"UGHHHHHHH!" I yelled.
Next thing I know, Keyarra, walked through the bathroom door.
"Damn girl, what if I was using the bathroom?" I asked.
"Well, we were gonna have to call the police or something because you screaming like that ain't normal.... what's going on?" she asked.
"I hit my nail" I lied.
"Did you break it?"
"No."
"Then, what the hell you scream for?"
"Because that shit hurt, inspector gadget."
Keyarra, bust out laughing. "Girl go to hell." she joked.
We exited the bathroom and back into her room. I must have had my irritation written all over my face.
"You sure you okay?"
"Yeah, I'm fine. Are you seeing Tre this weekend?" I asked, changing the subject.
"Um maybe. He has been acting strange."
"Strange how?"

"Almost like he doesn't want to be bothered. One minute he's up my ass, then the next he can't return a message, and I don't hear from him for days." she explained.

"Damn, I hate when boys act a certain way in the beginning, then change it up later."

"Right! It's so dumb...like I rather he just breaks up with me."

"For real? You wouldn't miss him?"

"I would, but if he doesn't want to be with me anymore then, oh well.... maybe I'm thinking too much into it."

"Naw, you not. Boys are wishy washy as hell." I said, really speaking of my own situation.

"Very true. So how are you and Chris, coming along?"

"Pretty good, I think but...he hasn't tried to have sex with me yet." I admitted.

"Is that a problem horn ball? It's only been a month." she laughed.

"No, but isn't that what all boys think about? It makes me feel like he isn't attracted to me in that way."

"So, nothing else has happened besides kissing?"

"Nope, we just make out.... heavy."

"Well like I said, Christian is different...I haven't known him to sleep around."

"He's not a virgin right?"

"No, he was with this one girl for a little while before me and him became friends, but she was drama."

"How long ago?"

"Last year, but like I said, it was before me and him were tight. Sharin, told me about it."

"Oh."

"When is the last time you've had sex?" She asked me, out of nowhere.

I was about to lie but then my phone dinged.

"It's Chris, he's outside." I said, relieved.

"Damn, we were just getting to the good part." she laughed.

"I know right, you going to be okay by yourself?"

"Oh, for sure, G will be home soon. I think imma follow your lead and go through my clothes to give some away."

"Good, then we can go shopping again."

"Girl no, I can't keep up with you."

We gathered my bags and made our way outside to meet Chris.

"Why didn't you tell me you had bags?" He asked when he met us halfway to grab them.

"Because I'm big girl and can carry them myself."

"Well, clearly you can't if Key, is helping you." he said, smartly.

"Touché." I responded.

"Hey Chris." Keyarra greeted.

"Hey Key, you ready for your birthday weekend?"

"I guess, I'm just happy that all y'all could make it."

"Hell yeah I was, I seen that dope house and told them people at Giant, I'll see them when I get back." he laughed.

Chris, had a part-time job at Giant to try and help with bills at home, but his mother really wanted him to focus on his studies. Since it was summer, he wanted to work as much as he could.

"It'll be fun" she said.

"Sure will, but I'll see you later Key. I have to spend some time with my future wife."

Keyarra laughed, while I rolled my eyes.

"Bye, Tia." she said hugging me.

"Bye, Key."

"What's up with you, Ti-baby? How was your day?" Chris asked me as we pulled off the block.

"It was really good, how was yours?"

"It's so much better, now that I've seen you." he said, trying to be cute.

"Boy shut up, why you be taking so long to answer my texts?" I asked, bluntly.

He laughed. "I be studying."

"For what?".

He didn't answer immediately.

"Helloooo." I said, impatiently.

"I want to go into the police academy."

"Ok, so why you have to be secretive about that?"

"It's not really a secret, I just don't like to divulge every part of my life to everyone."

"I'm not everyone."

He took his eyes off the road for a second, to glance over at me.

"You are right about that, Ti-baby." He smiled. "You hungry...we can go eat if you want?"

"No, I ate not too long ago, but I still want to chill with you."

"Where you wanna go?"

"My house." I answered, immediately.

He glanced over at me again. Whenever he dropped me off he would never come in, and whenever I went to his house, his mother or brother were home.

"To your place we go."

We rode the rest of the way in silence. When we arrived, I got out and tried to grab some bags from the back.

"I got it, Ti."

"I can grab one or two."

"No, what you can do is give me a kiss, though."

I walked over to him and kissed him quickly.

"I'll get the rest of that when we get inside."

"Oh, you will."

I couldn't fully read his facial expression. We got up to the apartment and he followed me to my room, so he could place the bags in there.

"I like your room, it's very…. legally blonde." he joked, admiring my decorations.

I was a girly girl, so naturally, pink was my color. We couldn't paint the walls but that was fine. Most of my furnishings were pink, with some white accents.

"That's my 2nd favorite movie." I laughed.

"Save the Last Dance is your first, right?"

"Look at you remembering shit."

"Yeah I remember you saying that corny shit…. you got an attitude like that light skin girl in there."

"Hey, don't do that. That's a good movie and who Nikki? I'm not that bad."

"Whatever you say, Ti-baby."

"Can I get you anything, like water or chips?"

"Naw, I'm straight. You wanna go out to the living room?"

"No, I don't." I said walking over to my bed and sitting down. I patted next to me, for him to come over.

He looked at me apprehensively.

"Maybe we should go out to the living room." He suggested.

"Chris, I'm not going to bite you."

"I know...I just uh don't want your pops or brother to bust my ass for being in here."

"You know my sperm donor is in New York and the last time I checked Derek's location; he was still in DC...so it's fine...please sit down."

He walked slowly over to the bed and sat next to me. I was feeling bold, so I turned his face towards me and connected our lips. For some reason he resisted a little but that ended quickly. As our kiss intensified, I leaned back pulling him with me and he ended up in between my legs. We went at it for a few minutes, and I was horny as hell. I started to trail my hand in between us so I could massage his dick through his pants, but he stopped me, right as I put my hand on it.

"We gotta stop." he said, breaking our kiss and getting up.

I propped myself up on my elbows.

"What's the problem?" I questioned irritated.

"It's no problem, I just..." he began to say.

"You just what.... you don't like me in that way?"

"Hell no Tia, that's not it. I want you, believe me."

"Then what is it?"

He just stared at me.

"Are you a virgin?" I asked.

He twisted his face up.

"No Tia, I'm not a virgin."

"Ok, then what is it?" I said, louder than I should have.

"I'm abstinent." he blurted out.

"What?"

"I said, I'm abstinent." he repeated, almost sounding embarrassed.

"Like celibate?"

"Yeah, they are the same thing, I guess."

"So, you've had sex but just don't want to anymore?"

"Yeah."

"Why?"

"Because I just want to be in love with the next girl that I have sex with."

"So, you wanna be married?"

"Not necessarily, I mean it would be nice, but I know that might be a stretch. I just want it to be different, so the next time I experience sex, I want to be with a girl that I love."

"Christian, we are so young, how will you even know if you are really in love?"

"I just would know."

"When was the last time you had sex?"

"Last year."

"Oh."

"I'm sorry Tia, maybe I should've told you before we went any further...I didn't mean to lead you on."

"No, don't apologize, I'm sorry if I have been putting pressure on you."

"You haven't, you didn't know. But I admit Ti, you make me want to break it so bad. I usually steer clear of girls now because of the temptation, but I was drawn to you that night at the party and after kissing you, I can't stay away."

"I tend to have that effect on people." I joked, trying to lighten the mood.

I got up, walked over to him and wrapped my arms around him.

"Thank you for telling me, I will never kiss you again." I said, with a playful smile.

"Naw, don't do that to me." he leaned down, and we locked lips again.

"We can go to the living room, if that would make you more comfortable." I suggested.

"It would."

"Ok, make yourself at home. I'll be out in a few minutes."

"Bet."

I went to grab some new shorts and a t-shirt, then went into the bathroom to freshen up. I returned to my room to grab what I purchased for Christian, from the mall. I walked into the living room and saw Chris on the couch drinking a bottle of water.

"You got thirsty?" I asked.

"I got a little hot."

"I bet." I smirked, "Here, this is for you and your brother."

I tossed t-shirts at him, as I sat down.

"What's this?"

"Look at it."

When he unfolded them, I could tell he was reading what the shirts said. His shirt said I have the best little brother and his brother's said I have the best big brother.

"I know they are a little corny, but I thought they were cute."

"Tia, I love it. His bad ass is going to as well…. thank you."

"You're welcome, but just don't wear them around your sisters. I don't want them to hate me before I meet them."

"They could never hate you." Chris said, as he leaned over and started to kiss me again. I loved kissing him; it was passionate, and it gave me butterflies.

"You better stop, before I really say forget your morals." I mumbled, against his lips.

He laughed. "Ti-baby, I think it would be worth it. But imma chill." he said, leaning back. "How did you know our sizes?"

"I can guess sizes pretty well."

"I see, you were dead on."

"Good, that's what I want to do."

"You wanna guess sizes?".

"No silly, remember I told you I wanna be a designer, but I also want a degree in fashion merchandising. I wanna be a stylist to celebrities too though, and a buyer for Nordstrom or for a big

name like that." I rambled, excitedly. I was excited about getting
any type of career in the fashion industry, I wanted to do it all.
"You will be great at all that shit, Ti.".
"Thank you, so why the police academy?" I asked.
"I wanna be a cop.".
"Well duh…. why do you wanna be a cop?"
"I want to eventually be a detective."
"Ok, that's different."
"Yeah, I don't tell people because they associate being a cop with
being a snitch."
"That stigma is dumb; I feel like you would be a good detective.
Are you trying to solve murders or something else?"
"Maybe, but I want to try and do missing persons."
I felt like there was a bigger picture.
"Why?" I asked.
He looked at me and I could tell he was contemplating on telling
me his real reasons.
"Only Sharin and my mom know this." He finally spoke.
"I'm listening."
"My irresponsible father has another child, but she is missing."
"How old is she?"
"She would be 13 now."
"How long has she been missing?"
"7 years."
"Oh wow, that's a long time."
"I know what you're thinking, I'm probably insane for thinking I
could find her, but I just want answers on what happened to
her."
"What does your father or her mother say?"
"My father doesn't know shit and he acts like he cares but he
doesn't, he is barely around, and that's why I don't fuck with him.
He is an abusive rolling stone, who impregnated half this city. I'm
sure I have many siblings out there that I don't know about. But
Mina is different, we were close. My mom looked out for her
because her mom was a drug addict. Then one day we just
stopped hearing from them. A week went by and that's when my

mother went past the house, then she broke in when no one answered the door. She found Mina's mother dead, she died from a drug overdose."

"Oh God." I gasped, in disbelief.

"But the worst part was, Mina, was nowhere to be found." he continued.

"What?"

"Yeah, she was gone."

"What did the police say?"

"They barely said shit, there was an amber alert out but nothing came out of it. Her mom had to have been dead for at least a week, so they assumed that's how long she had been gone, so there wasn't much to go on. They supposedly investigated but truth is they didn't give a shit about a little black girl with a crack addicted mom."

I was too shocked to say anything.

"Her mom was known to have men in and out that damn house…. I don't give a fuck what no one says, but someone kidnapped my little sister…. she was only 6 Tia. I need to find out what happened to her."

By this time, Christian was emotional, a tear slid down his face and I wiped it a way gently.

"Have you ever thought about a private investigator?" I asked.

His face contorted.

"Tia, I know you come from money, but I don't. I can't even imagine how much something like that would cost. My mother, brother and I just got onto solid ground a few years ago. We were homeless; in and out of shelters for many years, so no, I never thought about a private investigator. I want to find my sister but we gotta keep the lights on first." Chris snapped.

"I'm sorry Christian, that was very tone-deaf of me." I apologized.

"No, I'm sorry for snapping like that, Ti. That's my fault." He said, after a few seconds.

It was an awkward silence, for a minute or two.

"You said your father was abusive?"

"Yeah, he was. He used to hit me and my mom, when he would get drunk...then her dumbass went and got pregnant by him again."

I felt like I was on the brink of tears, but I didn't want him to think I was taking pity on him.

"Did he ever hit your brother?"

"Yeah, once when he was like 4 or 5.... I was 13 at the time. I was still skinny like now, but I fought that nigga like I weighed 300 pounds. I put all my anger into every single hit, and I beat his ass.... he hasn't touched any of us since because he left but with him out the picture my mother couldn't afford the bills and that's how we ended up in the shelter."

"When did he start coming back around?"

"A few years ago, he wanted to introduce us to my sisters and their moms. He wanted to come back home because he got help and stopped drinking, but the damage was done. He still tries to get back with my mom, but she promised me she wouldn't let him back in the house. Now that lame ass nigga just uses the excuse of trying to have a relationship with my brother as a way to be around and spend the night and shit...if he does spend the night, I just go to Rin's because I can't stand to be around his ass."

"Christian, I'm so sorry. You've been through a lot."

"I'm not telling you all this because I want you to feel sorry for me. It's life, shit happens. I'm telling you because even though it's been a short time, I feel comfortable around you. And that doesn't come easy to me."

"Well, I'm happy that I make you comfortable, I feel comfortable around you too." I admitted.

"Good, now tell me something." he said, fully turning to face me.

"What?" I asked.

"What's up with you and your dad?"

"Nothing is up with us."

"Really, Tia? .... you look at that man like you hate him."

"I do." I admitted, honestly.

"Why?"

"Many reasons."

168

"Ok, well tell me one."

"He's an asshole."

"How so?"

"Christian!"

"Tia!" He said, coolly.

I let out a deep breath. I explained everything to Christian that happened with me and my father. How he disowned me, how he favored my brother, how he used to yell at our mother, and how he just overall treated me like shit for so many years.

"So, after your mother passed is when he tried to be a part of your life?" He asked, after I finished my story.

"About a year or so before; I don't know what suddenly changed his mind. I just remember him buying me this bracelet, and it had 9 pink rhinestones; he told me that they represented each year that he had missed out on my life and one day they would be 9 diamonds."

"How did you feel about that?"

"I refused to take it, but it ended up in my jewelry box anyway."

"Do you still have it?" He asked.

"Hell no."

"Damn Ti, yeah that's rough. I can see why you would still be upset with him."

"I wouldn't say I'm upset with him…. he's dead to me." I said, bluntly.

"Tia, that's a little extreme."

"It's not."

"It is. It seems like he's trying to make things right."

"I don't care."

"Tia, don't be cold."

"If I'm cold, it's because he helped make me that way. And to be very honest with you, I don't wanna talk about this anymore." I snapped, with an attitude.

I felt myself getting hot. I don't like talking about that sorry ass excuse for a father, and I really don't like when people try to make me feel like shit because of the way HE treated me. The only person who ever fully had my back, was my mother; she told me that I don't ever have to forgive him if I didn't want to and I sure as hell would never. Nobody knows how he made me feel. I was a little girl who just wanted the love and attention from her father, and he gave me his ass to kiss, time and time again; so therefore, I was giving him mine. Fuck him! I was about to get up and leave Christian's ass sitting right there, but he pulled me back by my waist and I landed on his lap.

"Listen Ti-baby, I didn't mean to offend you. I get it! I just told you my father is back around, just to fuck my mother, he's ungenuine. It's just that, in my opinion, your father seems like he is, but at the same time, I don't know the extent of the damage he has done. I would never invalidate your feelings on purpose, I'm sorry." He apologized.
Just hearing him say that last part made my eyes water. Not even my brother has said something like that to me.
"Thank you." I said, in a cracked voice.
I wrapped my arms around his neck, hugging him while my tears fell freely.
"I didn't mean to make you cry." he said, as he hugged me back.
"It's a good cry."
We sat there for a few minutes, until we heard the key turning in the door. I felt Christian's body tense up under me.
"Get up, Tia." he said, trying to gently lift me up.
"It's just Derek, you're fine."
"I know, but his sister is sitting on my hard dick, and I don't want no problems."
"Well, then that would be more of a reason for me to stay where I'm at then." I laughed, as I tightened my grip around him.
"Stop playing, Tia."
Derek entered the room and stopped when he saw us.
"Hi brother." I beamed.
"What's up, Tia."
"I'm trying to get up, but your sister is holding me hostage."
Christian said.

"It's no problem bro." Derek said, as he walked around the couch and dapped Chris up.

"Where's your…" I started to say.

"Get embarrassed in front of your company." Derek warned.

"I was going to say girlfriend Derek." I lied.

I was definitely about to call her a hoe again.

"Yeah ok; I took her ass home. I spent the whole day with her, and she was starting to get on my nerves." Derek said, clearly annoyed.

Me and Christian couldn't help but chuckle.

"I bet."

Derek eyed me, suspiciously.

"You been crying?"

"A little."

He then zoomed in on, Christian.

"You making my sister cry already?" he asked, with a raised brow.

"Naw bruh, it's not like that…"

"Derek, he validates my feelings and I'm going to marry him." I teased, as I squeezed, Chris, harder and made us cheek to cheek.

"Yeah, whatever. Ard I'm going to bed." he said, walking away.

"And don't be out here fucking my sister either."

"DEREK!" I yelled.

I could hear him laughing as we walked down the hall.

"He is so embarrassing." I said, rolling my eyes.

"That's what you get for not getting your ass up, but for real Ti, I gotta go."

"Why?" I asked, in a small voice.

"I gotta get my mother's car back, so she can go to work tonight."

I poked out my bottom lip, I didn't want him to leave yet.

"I wanted you to stay a little longer."

"I want to too, but she gotta get to work and I have to get my brother ready for camp tomorrow."

"Ok." I said, sadly.

"Don't be like that, next weekend you'll have me for 4 days." he said kissing my lips, gently.

I got up and walked him to the door.

"I might not see you as much until next Friday because I got as many shifts as they let me and since me and my mom are sharing her car, it's gonna be a little tight." Chris explained.

My facial expression hardened.

"That mean face doesn't scare me Ti-baby."

"I guess, I'll see you when I see you." I said, as I opened the door wider for him.

"Oh wow, you'll see me when you see me? A few minutes ago you were going to marry me."

"I only said that to get on my brother's nerves." I said, flatly.

"Yeah, ok Tia, you meant that. Keep playing and you gonna get what you want, a lot sooner than you think." He teased.

"I won't hold my breath." I teased back.

"Wow." he said, fake hurt.

"Shut up, I'm joking."

I held my arms out; he pulled me into a hug and lifted me off the floor.

"Thank you for being a great listener." he whispered.

"Thank you for sharing and for being a good listener as well."

We said our goodbyes and soon as I closed the door, I melted right on to the floor. If I didn't like Christian before, I 100% did now. I loved how transparent he was, I loved how mature he was, I loved that he had goals, and he also isn't letting his past define his future, in a negative way. Sharin was right when she said he has lived a life already. The no sex thing did take me by surprise, but I respect it and I'm going to try my hardest to not cross any boundaries with his fine, skinny ass.

"Tia, why are you on the floor?" Derek asked.

I didn't even hear him walk out here.

"Because I'm in love." I answered, in a breathy voice.

"Shut up, don't let that nigga sweet talk you out your pants, Tia."

"He would never."

"I'm serious, and when we go on this trip, y'all not sleeping in the same room. So, you can get that shit out your head."

I hopped up and ran towards Derek who was now walking back to his room.

"Derek, you can't do that." I whined.

"Like hell I can't, y'all not gonna be fucking on this trip. I'm cool, but not that damn cool."

"He's not even like that."

"Tia, you was just sitting on this nigga's lap and you expect me to let you spend 3 nights in the bed with him?"

"He doesn't have hoe tendencies like yourself."

"All niggas think about is getting their dick wet. Now that I'm thinking about it, Keyarra not sleeping with that light skin nigga either."

"Derek, that's her boyfriend."

"And what part of that am I supposed to give a fuck about, exactly?"

"I haven't heard you say anything about Matthew, not being able to room with, Sharin." I said, folding my arms.

"That's a grown man, I can't control what he does."

"Derek, you're not being fair."

"And guess what, Tia, I don't give a fuck." he said, as he went into his bathroom and shut the door.

I yelled out in frustration.

"Aye, do that brat shit in your room." He yelled.

I plopped down on his bed, and I waited for him to come out. A little while later he walked out.

"What were you doing in there?" I asked.

"Taking a shit, get out, Tia. I'm tired as hell."

"I hope you washed your hands."

"TIA.... get...out." he yelled, pointing towards his door.

"No, I have to tell you something."

"Ughhhhh, you females are pissing me off today." He groaned.

"Derek if I tell you this, you have to promise not to say anything." I said, ignoring his outburst.

"Why don't you tell Keyarra, or something?"

"Because I'm not sure if I can trust her with secrets yet."

"You can Tia, she's your best friend...wait, how did the rest of the day with her go?"

"It was fine, can you focus please?"

"What is it Tia, damn." he said, frustrated.

"Do you promise?"

"I'm 10 seconds from losing my shit. I promise.... now tell me, so you can get the hell out."

"Christian, is abstinent."

"Try again." he said, not believing me.

"I'm serious, he told me tonight. We were in my room, and I was trying to..." my voice trailed off, because I was about to tell on myself.

I watched Derek's eyes transition.

"You were trying to do what Tia?" he gritted his teeth, walking up on me.

My voice got caught in my throat. Like most big brothers, Derek was a little over-protective. He knew I wasn't a virgin, but he just liked to pretend that I still was, for some odd reason. Him and his father loved sex, so why did they think that trait stopped with me?

"Tia, please don't make me fuck you up in here. Don't have him in your room anymore." He scolded.

"Ok, but Derek listen I'm not lying to you. I did try ok, but he stopped me, and that's when he told me. He hasn't tried anything the past few weeks we've been chillen."

Derek was massaging his temples.

"This parenting shit ain't for me man." he said, out loud.

"Well, good thing you are not my parent." I responded, folding my arms.

"Tia, you are giving me a headache. Can we talk about this later?" Derek asked, calmly as he started to usher me out of his room.

"Yes, we can but let me just say one more thing." I asked, as I made it outside his door frame.

He leaned his head against his door and closed his eyes.

"What is it?"

"I really do think that's your future brother-in-law."

And with that, Derek slammed the door in my face. I loved getting on his nerves.

"I love you brother." I yelled.

I didn't wait for a reply because I'm sure I wasn't going to get one. I just skipped to my room. I went to put my new clothes away, when I heard my phone ring with a Facetime call; I saw it was Matthew, and debated if I should pick it up. Before it ended, I answered.

"I told you we were done."

"Come outside, let me talk to you for a second."

"Absolutely not.".

"Tia, I'm not playing. We gotta talk."

"Matthew, it looks as if things between you and Sharin, are getting serious, which is fine. Let's just end whatever this is between us."

"No thank you." he said, seriously.

"It wasn't a request."

"Come outside!" he demanded.

"No, thank you. Goodnight." I said, throwing his words back at him, right before hanging up.

He called me 3 more times, back-to-back, and sent a bunch of text messages.

"I might have to block this nigga." I said out loud.

I heard my phone go off once again and now I was pissed off.

"STOP CALLING ME!" I yelled, when I answered.

"Damn Ti-baby, you changed your mind about me already." Chris said, with a confused look on his face.

"Oh my God, Chris, I'm so sorry. I thought you were someone else." I apologized.

"Who?"

"Those damn bill collectors. I told them 1000 times that they have the wrong phone number." I lied.

"On Facetime?"

"I wasn't really thinking."

"Yeahhh ok...... I was just calling because someone wants to talk to you."

"HI, TI-BABY!" Chris's little brother yelled into the phone, excitedly.

"It's Facetime, back up so she can see you and stop yelling and don't call her Ti-baby."

I couldn't help but laugh.

"Hi Devin, how are you?"

"I'm great, can you see my shirt?"

"Yes, I can see it. It looks nice on you."

"Thank you! I like it a lot...how did you know blue was my favorite color?"

"I really didn't know, but now I do."

"Oh wow, you might be psychic. I'm going to make Chris, wear his shirt everyday with me."

"I told you I'm not wearing this every day."

"Yes, you are, but I'm going to go play my game. I'll see you later, Ti-Baby." Devin said, then blew me a kiss and ran away.

"Aye, don't be blowing kisses at my girl and you got 10 minutes left on that game little nigga." Chris yelled.

I was cracking up. "Your girl?" I questioned.

"You know what I meant."

"Mmmm, I guess."

"Is it crazy to say, I miss you already?"

"I told you I have that effect on people."

"See, I can't say nice shit to you."

"I'm playing." I laughed. "I miss you too."

"Yeah whatever, mean ass."

"You like my mean ass, though."

"Something like that."

I admired Chris's handsome face, with his bright sepia colored skin, which made his pretty white smile pop; they complimented each other well. Chris had a curly top fade that was full of these thick and soft curls. You can tell he had been growing it out for a while. My eyes landed on his thick lips, whenever he ran his tongue against them, it reminded me of the character, Malcolm, from the movie, "Soul Food".

"What you over there thinking about?" He asked.

"What I can't have...yet." I replied in a seductive tone.

Chris looked away and started to shake his head.

"I see you not gonna make this easy for me."

"I promise, I will; I'll respect your boundaries and try my best to behave." I smiled.

"Yeah, we'll see Ti-baby. Imma go get my brother ready for bed, then take a cold shower. Can I call you back in a few?"

I burst out laughing. "Of course."

"Aight bet."

Chris hung up, and again I melted, but on my bed this time. I laid down and impatiently waited for him to call me back.

MATTHEW

It was finally the weekend of Keyarra's birthday, and we were on our way to the beach. Derek, myself, and Rin, were in my truck while Tia, Key, Tre, and that nigga Chris were in Tre's car. Sharin opted to ride with us, so she could have the back seat to herself, plus she said that was the couple's car, or some bullshit like that. I corrected her the few times she said it because only my sister and Tre were in a relationship. I tried to get some information out of Sharin about Tia and Chris without it being weird, but she was tight lipped. Chris was her best friend, and she knew we didn't like each other, so she never said too much about him around me. Tia really has avoided me the past week and she was really starting to piss me off. I know she fucking Chris, and just the thought of that has me ready to knock that nigga down.

"So, you about to be around all this ass and titties out here and not gonna look at nothing?" I asked Derek to get out of my thoughts.
"Who said I wasn't looking?"
"You did...you told Katrina, that you weren't even gonna look another girl's way."
"Damn nigga, you was all up in my conversation." he joked.
"You was loud as shit."

He laughed. "I told her that shit, so she would shut the hell up; she was whining about how I was going to cheat on her."

"Why she think that?"

"I don't know man. She been acting real insecure lately, and it's been rubbing me the wrong way."

"Well jefe, every girl needs a little reassurance." Sharin, chimed in.

"I thought you were sleep." I said.

"I was but now I'm not....so what do you mean by, insecure?" she asked Derek.

"Rin, stay out that man business." I fussed staring at her from my rear view.

"It's cool man, I don't really have a female to talk to about it because Tia don't wanna hear shit about, Katrina."

"See boo, he needs my help." she said, proudly.

I just shook my head.

"She just been real.... different. Like one minute she clingy as hell and she misses me every 30 seconds, but then does weird shit, like disappearing for hours at a time. And when she pops up, she argues with me about why I don't love her." he explained.

"Hmmm...what else?"

She looked like she was trying to be a detective or something; she was loving every second of it, with her nosey ass.

"For example, we been in the car for 2 hours and I just knew I would've heard from her within the first 30 minutes. She hasn't texted me once. But yesterday, she begged me not to leave, damn near on the floor, in tears. Katrina doesn't act like that, when I lived in Cali, she was cool as shit; of course, when she visited she didn't wanna leave but she never acted like this."

"And how long y'all been together?"

"Shit.... I don't even know. We've been messing around for at least 3 years, but I made it official last year; may be right before Christmas, so 6 or 7 months."

"Interesting."

Derek turned around and looked at her.

"What's interesting?"

"Derek..." Sharin, sat back and pulled her shades up. "She's cheating." she said, coolly.

Derek looked over at me and I locked eyes with him for a second before I looked back at the road.

"Nah." he and I said, at the same time shaking our heads.

Sharin kept the same knowing expression on her face.

"Did you and Katrina have a conversation about ending whatever situations y'all had going?" she asked.

"Not really."

"So, what makes you so sure that she cut them off when y'all finally got together?"

"I-I just assumed that she would do so."

"Hm."

"Sharin, you can't come to that conclusion and not tell us why." I jumped in.

"Katrina sounds guilty as shit. She picking fights with you and trying to make you feel bad, and everyone knows that you start pointing fingers when you doing something that you have no business doing.... aka, cheating." Sharin explained.

Derek was silent; he was still staring at her, but I could see her face through the mirror, and she looked a little nervous now.

"Bro...you good?" I asked.

Derek faced forward and I got a glimpse of his eyes, and they were dark. I know that scared the shit out of Rin because it used to scare the shit out of us when it first started happening after our moms had died.

"I'm straight." he replied

"Derek, I'm sorry. I didn't mean to sound so insensitive." Sharin apologized.

"Naw Shar, you good; I appreciate you." he said, before he put in his earphones; he had the music turned up loud as hell.

"You right, I should have stayed out his business. I'm so stupid." she said, sadly.

"Aye don't do that.... It's ok Rin, he asked. If what you are saying is true...Katrina is going to see a side of Derek, no one should see."

Derek has always been mild mannered but when he was angry, he
damn near turned into the hulk. His eyes would get dark as the
night sky, and I swear he would go up a size. I remember one
time, a boy said something about his mom after she died, and it
took myself and 2 other boys to pull Derek off him. But the crazy
part was that it's like Derek, would black out, so he would be
extremely regretful after. The same boy he beat up, he walked
him home, told his mom what happened, and apologized
profusely. She was livid until she met with DW, and I'm willing to
bet money that he fucked her and that's why all was forgiven,
magically. Ever since then, Derek tries his hardest to remain calm
but if Katrina ass is cheating, that is going to be all she wrote.

"He looked mad…. did you see his eyes?" she said, nervously.
"That happens sometimes but he's not mad at you."
Sharin was fidgeting with her fingers again.
"Rin, look at me."
She looked at me through the mirror.
"You good. Ok?" I reassured her.
She nodded her head.
"Ok." she said, softly.

Sharin could sometimes be a little hard on herself, but I always
made sure she didn't do it around me. As beautiful as she was
inside and out, she had her own insecurities that she let show
sometimes. For the remainder of the ride, we made conversation,
and she snapped back to her loud self, which was welcomed; I
didn't want her stuck in her feelings. I was looking forward to this
weekend and I was going to try my hardest to just steer clear of
Tia and Chris. I would have to address that situation back home.
We finally arrived at this beach house, but it looked more like a
mini mansion that Derek rented out. I asked him why he randomly
did this and he just stated because he had the money, but I wasn't
too convinced. I saw Keyarra and Derek a few weeks ago walking
back to the house but I didn't see anything too alarming. I just
didn't want Derek to fall back into his old ways and I especially

didn't want my sister to fall victim to that either. We all hopped out of the car and admired the big house in front of us.

"This weekend just what I need." I said out loud.
"Me too, boo." Sharin said, as she linked arms with me.
I put my arm around her and pulled her close, it's like when I'm with her I feel like I want to make her my girlfriend, but Tia, has this hold on me that I can't shake; if I had it my way, they both would be my girl but hell would freeze over before that happens.

"Where the hell slow ass at?" Derek asked.
"I don't know man; he couldn't keep up."
We walked into the house, and it was something out of that old ass show, "MTV Cribs"; there was a huge foyer that had marble flooring. It had an open floor plan, so you could pretty much see every room downstairs.
"Bro, let me give you something towards this." I offered to Derek.
"I already told you it's cool; to be honest, the shit is a steal because I didn't expect it to look like this. The pictures don't do it justice." he replied.
I had offered him money several times, but he refused. I wasn't stacked like Derek was, but my pockets were good. When I turned 18, GG gave me the life insurance policy money that my mother had, so I had a good portion of that left, plus GG frequently gave me "allowance". I also had the credit card that DW gave me and Keyarra, I recently found out it had $5000 limit on it; he tells us all the time to utilize it, but myself and Keyarra, rarely did. We never wanted to seem like free loaders or some shit. DW brought me not one, but 2 trucks, so I'm grateful for that and I never want to take advantage of his kindness, no matter what he says. I worked with my dad part-time as well; he worked as a mechanic, and HVAC tech, so he taught me a lot.

"I don't care what room y'all get, but that big one upstairs is mine." Derek stated.
"Bet, c'mon Rin. I'll get your bags in a few minutes."

"Am I staying in a room with you?"

"Yes, who else would you room with?"

"Um, I thought with the girls."

"Is that what you want to do?"

"No."

"Ok then, let's go." I held my hand out to her, and she took it. We went upstairs and went from room to room until we decided on the one at the end of the hallway.

"This house is huge." she said, as she looked out the window.

"It is, call Keyarra, and see how far they are."

I heard the ringing from the Facetime call.

"Hey Rin." Keyarra answered.

"Hey Ke-Ke, where y'all at?"

"Um, about a half hour way...y'all there?"

"Yes girl, this house nice as shit. Me and boo picked our room already."

"Hey, it's my birthday, I should get the first pick." she whined.

I took the phone from her.

"Well, you snooze you lose. Why Tre, taking so damn long?"

"It's not my fault man, these damn girls have a bladder the size of a pea." Tre complained.

"Whatever Tre, it's not our fault." Keyarra argued.

I caught a glimpse of Tia and Chris in the back seat, and he had his head in her lap, and she was playing in his hair; his eyes were closed, so I guess he was sleep. I was trying to not let it bother me, but it did.

"Man whatever, hurry up and get my sister here...safe."

"I got you bro." he replied.

I ended the call and handed Sharin her phone back.

"You, ok?" Rin asked.

Sharin was good at sensing when I was upset but I wasn't going to get mad about shit this weekend. It was about my sister, and I was going to enjoy this mini vacation.

"I'm good."

I closed the door and walked back over to her.

"I thought you were getting the bags?"

"I will."

I leaned down and started to kiss her neck.

"Mmm." she moaned, "boo we can't...they will be here soon."

"I'll make it quick." I said lowly, as I continued to place kisses up her neck until I connected with her lips. We kissed and made our way to the bed; I removed my tee, and I helped her remove her cropped shirt. Sharin's breasts were on the smaller side, but they were perky, so she rarely wore a bra. I pinched her nipples slightly, which always caused a small chill to go through her body.

"Lay down." I told her.

She did as she was told and removed her spandex shorts as well, Sharin also rarely wore underwear, too. She was easy access, which I loved. I took my shorts and briefs off; I went in my wallet for a condom and put it on. I climbed on top of her and found her lips again, as we engaged, I slowly entered her.

"Shit boo." she moaned.

"You feel so good Rin."

I picked up my pace and pumped in and out of her. She wrapped her legs around my waist and pulled me in tighter.

"Damn, you so deep boo." she whimpered.

"And you wet as shit"

She started to match me stroke for stroke and that's something I loved about her ass; she just didn't lay there.

We went at it for a few more minutes, when I started to feel my nut build up.

"Cum on this dick Rin."

"I'm cumming" she shrieked.

"Uhhhhh...shit." I grunted.

I pumped a few more times as I emptied my seeds into the condom.

"Got damn." Sharin said, breathlessly.

"You never disappoint me girl." I joked.

"Boy, go to hell" she laughed, as she tried to push me off her.

"Chill, let's take a nap." I yawned.

"Shut up, everyone is about to be here."

"So."

"Matt stoppp, get up" She whined.

"Ugh, fine."

I pulled out, pulled off the condom and disposed of it in the trash can next to the bed.

We threw on our clothes and I went to get our bags while Rin went to explore the rest of the house. When I came back in, Derek was leaving the kitchen.

"Damn nigga, we here 15 minutes and you getting pussy already."

"Listen, I had to do what I had to do…. was we loud?"

"Naw, but I'm the only person in here, so of course I heard y'all."

"I would say my bad but it's gonna happen again, so no point" I laughed.

"You ain't shit, but she gonna be the only one moaning this weekend, I'm not playing with those 2 little niggas and imma make that shit known." Derek said, seriously.

"Damn right." I agreed.

If I had to hear either Tia or my sister having sex, I was going to lose it for sure.

"THEY'RE HERE, THEY'RE HERE!" Sharin screamed, racing to the door.

"Stop screaming Rin, damn." I scolded.

"Matthew shut up."

"Keep talking shit."

She just rolled her eyes and went out the door.

"You got your hands full with that one for sure." Derek laughed.

"Tell me about it; let me take this shit upstairs."

I put the bags down and sat on the bed, I just needed a few minutes alone before I joined everyone. I was ready for the weekend, but I wasn't the most social person. I didn't like being around a bunch of people for too long, whether I knew them or not. I sat with my thoughts for a little bit, when I heard everyone start to come inside.

"Damn this house big as shit." I heard Chris say.

I blew out a deep breath and tried to prepare myself to be around his ass for the next 4 days. Chris hadn't really done anything to me, it's just this vibe that he gives off, is what I don't like; he comes off as an asshole. He also be in Sharin ear telling her all types of bullshit about how I don't really care about her. If you ask me, I think he wants to hit for real, but Sharin swears up and down that's not the case. I'm just going to try my best to avoid his ass and I hope this weekend goes smooth as can be.

"Ard hold up, before yall start running around and shit." I heard Derek announce.

I got up off the bed and went to the top of the stairs, where I could look down at everyone. I saw Tia on Chris's back and I couldn't help but laugh to myself; she was trying to beat me at my own game. That day I made up with Sharin, I wasn't trying to make Tia jealous, with the videos and shit, I just didn't want to kill Rin's mood. I did know Tia ass would be looking out that window though, so the little scene I did outside was just pay back for her lying to me, for no damn reason.

"My sister has spent the last week trying to convince me that y'all 2." Derek said, pointing at Tre and Chris. "won't be on no funny shit this weekend, because so help me God, if I hear so much as a laugh that is too loud out one of those rooms."

"Derek…. they get it!" Tia interrupted.

"I'm just saying man, I will shut all this shit down!" he continued.

"I got you bro; ain't gonna be no baby making." Tre said, as he dapped Derek up.

"Better not be, because I wouldn't be the only one you have to worry about; GG would be on that ass."

"And that's smoke I don't want." Tre joked.

"That's for sure; ard there are 5 rooms. I got the master, Matt and Shar got the room at the end of the hall upstairs; there is one down here and the other 2 are upstairs."

"We can take the one downstairs." Tre volunteered, immediately.

"See, I don't even like how fast you said that shit." Derek said shaking his head.

We all laughed, Tia must have heard me because she turned around and looked up at me. I winked at her, and she rolled her eyes. She couldn't avoid me this weekend, but I wasn't going to mess with her for real; she'll have to face me eventually, so I wasn't sweating it.

"Let me go get the bags, and you go pick a room, Ti." I heard Chris say.

"Okay." Tia replied.

She hopped off his back and started to make her way upstairs.

"Hello, Princess."

"Hi, Matthew." she replied, dryly.

"You look nice." I said eyeing her lustfully.

Tia had on these thin leggings with a fitted t shirt that came right above her pierced belly button. The outfit was casual and simple, but it hugged her curves in the right places.

"Thanks. Rooming with your girl?"

"Something like that."

If Tia wanted to play we could play; she scuffed then proceeded to walk in the direction of the room I was in.

"Not sure if you want the room right next to me." I said, as I followed her.

"Well, I really don't want to be next to Derek either."

"Why? He just told you there better not be any bullshit going on, so there's no reason why you can't."

"And? What makes you think I'll listen to Derek?"

"So, you fucking Chris, is what you're telling me?"

"What I do is my business, thank you very much. And you're right, I don't want a room next to you. As a matter of fact, I don't wanna be anywhere near you."

She walked away in the other direction and went into one of the other rooms. I was about to follow her, when I saw Chris walking up the steps. I decided to be the bigger person and speak first.

"What's up?" I greeted.

"What up, where did Tia go?"

"One of the rooms down there." I pointed.

"Bet"

"Did you need help with those bags?"
He was carrying 4 of them, Tia always over packed.
"I'm straight."
That's the shit I'm talking about, Chris was an asshole.
"Cool."
"Listen, I know we not the biggest fans of each other, so I guess we can just try our best to stay out of each other's way this weekend."
I really wanted to say, fuck him.
"Great minds think alike." I responded.
He nodded his head slightly, then proceeded down the hall.
"TI-baby, where you at?" He called out.
"In the last one." she yelled from the room.
I hated that dumb ass name, Ti-baby. I stood there for a second to get my anger in check because I felt it rising.
"Boo!" Sharin yelled as she climbed up the steps.
"I'm right here, you don't have to yell."
"I'm sorry, I thought you were in the room."
"What's up?"
"We were gonna get in the pool, you wanna come?"
"Yeah, let's go change."
"Ok." she said, excitedly.
She grabbed my hand and led me back to the room, before we reached the doorway, I looked behind me and I saw Tia, standing in the hallway. She had a hint of sadness in her eyes, I know she was cursing me out in her head, but I also know seeing me with someone else bothered her just as much as me seeing her with someone else. Tia wasn't done with me, no matter how much she tried to convince herself otherwise. We were each other's first, so we had a special bond, and she can't just throw that away.

A few hours had passed, and everyone was drunk, thanks to Tre's ass, who decided to bring a suitcase full of liquor. If that boy wasn't going to do shit else, he was going to have a drink but shit,

I wasn't complaining. We were supposed to go the boardwalk tonight but since we all started drinking, I just ordered hella food, so we chilled and played games in the pool. Throughout the night I watched Tia's and Chris's interactions, and I could tell that they were really feeling one another. On top of watching them, I also took notice to Keyarra and Derek too, they were very playful towards each other. Tre's drunk ass was barely paying attention, between him on his phone or him pouring another drink, but I saw them, and I can't say that I liked it. The way he looked at her was lust filled and the shit wasn't happening on my watch; he wasn't going to hurt my sister like all those other girls.

"Hey boo, come over here with us." Sharin said, as she swam over to me.
This pool was big; it was in the ground and maybe about 20 to 25 ft long. I was sitting on the deep end with my feet in the water, while everyone stayed on the other side, since it was shallower.
"Didn't I tell you to stay on that end, so your drunk ass won't drown." I fussed.
"I'm not really drunk, so shut up. Stop being anti-social and come to the other side."
"I played chicken with your ass earlier and now my shoulders hurt. I'm down here relaxing."
"Oh my God, you are so dramatic." She laughed.
"I'm not, you was being extra."
"We won, didn't we?"
"Whatever, you been in this pool for hours. Let's go to bed."
"Stop acting like an old man, ain't nobody going to bed. We about go hit the boardwalk."
"It's almost 1 am, no y'all are not."
"I didn't realize my father was here."
"Come here." I motioned.
She swam closer to me until she was between my legs. I leaned down and kissed her.
"Stop playing, come upstairs with me, so we can finish what we started earlier." I whispered against her lips.

"You know boo, I would really consider that IF you were my boyfriend but you're not, so I'm gonna go to the boardwalk to go find one." She stated boldly.

She kissed me one more time then proceeded to swim backwards.

"I see that liquor got you feeling yourself."

"Don't worry boo, you can feel me too.... later though." she winked.

I just shook my head. I watched everyone get out of the pool and go inside except Derek. He went to sit on the patio furniture, I got up and joined him.

"You good?" I asked him.

He was texting what looked like a paragraph.

"You know I still haven't heard from, Katrina? Like all fucking day bro and I texted her ass when I got here...no reply. She got me fucked up for real, she must've forgot what type of nigga I am." He said, angrily.

"What you telling her?"

"That I'm good on her, she can go ahead and stay with whatever nigga she fucking with for real."

"Don't let that shit Rin said get to you; you don't know if that's true."

"It would make sense though. She been sketchy as hell, and I'm not for the shit. I can dive in some other pussy."

"I thought you was laying off randoms, bro?"

Derek blew out a breath. As far as I knew he was doing good with just having sex with one girl, but I know that if him and Katrina break up, then he was only going to be able to control himself but for so long.

"FUCK!" He yelled out in frustration.

"Chill D, just wait until you get back and talk to her."

"Yeah ard, I'll wait." He agreed, sitting his phone down and sitting back in the chair.

"You think it's a good idea that we let their drunk asses go to the boardwalk this late?"

"Chris ass just high as shit, he gonna look out; they'll be fine. I fuck with him for real. I'm not sure about Tre. You know I don't trust light skins like that."

"Nigga, you damn near light skin." I laughed.

"The hell I am, I am a subtle, brown skin nigga."

"Bro, you were getting sun burnt earlier." I joked.

"Fuck you, Matt." He laughed.

"For real though, I don't know about Chris though. He a little arrogant."

"You think so? I mean, you know him better than me. He been at the house nonstop; he just seems cool, like he not into no shit."

"He spends the night?"

Here I go, trying to get information from the last person that I want to find out about me and, Tia.

"I suspect he has a few times, but I don't bust in Tia room. I trust her, she said they not fucking, so it's cool."

"And you believe her?"

"Tia don't have no reason to lie to me. You need to be worried about your sister and not mine. That light skin don't be paying her no mind and that shit ain't cool."

"Seems like you worried about her enough for the both of us."

"What's that supposed to mean?" Derek asked, sitting up.

"It means I see you nigga, the way you look at her. Y'all was all touchy, feely earlier. You probably don't see it, but I think she has a crush on you, and I just don't want shit to get out of hand." I explained.

"What you mean, get out of hand?"

"Bro, c'mon, you know how you used to run through girls, like it was a sport for you."

"Why would you think that I would dog your sister like that?" Derek was looking at me with squinted eyes, and he was leaning on the rail of his chair, with his hand cupping the side of his face. I noticed his eyes were flashing. I wasn't trying to make him mad, just aware.

"I'm just saying...."

"Saying what?" he asked, firmly.

"Saying that I don't want you lying and seducing my sister like those other girls." I said bluntly.

"First of all nigga, I don't need to lie to get pussy; never have and never will. They knew what it was; I needed to get my nut off and that was it. If they got other ideas in their head later, then that was on them. And the fact that you think I would dog Keyarra like that, is wild as fuck to me. But just so you know…. ain't shit going on between us but imma make sure to keep my distance, so you, or nobody else thinks otherwise."

Derek got up and made his way into the house; I got up and followed him. I wasn't trying to start any shit.

"Bro wait…. that's my bad. I didn't mean for shit to sound like that."

"It's cool." He replied, nonchalantly.

"It's not, we bros and I know you wouldn't intentionally do no grimy shit. I don't even know why I said that."

"It's all good, imma head to bed. I'll see you in the morning."

I watched as he climbed the steps and disappeared into his room.

"Fuck." I whispered to myself.

I don't even know why I pressed Derek like that, knowing I'm sleeping with Tia. I paced around the house for a little while, just stuck in my thoughts. It was damn near 3 and they still weren't back, so I facetimed Keyarra.

"Matt why you still up old man?" she questioned when she answered.

"Why you still out?"

"We are at the boardwalk, it's live out here. You and Derek should come."

"Derek went to bed, what time you coming back?"

"Um, I don't know."

It was hella noise in the background, but I could still hear Sharin loud ass screaming.

"What the fuck is Rin doing?"

"Um…" Keyarra hesitated.

"Don't lie either." I warned.

"She just being Rin, I gotta go, my phone gonna die." she said quickly, then hung up.

"I'm gonna fuck them up." I growled.

I facetimed Rin next.

She picked up the phone, but she wasn't in the camera.

"Bitch, didn't I just say don't pick up the phone." I heard Keyarra say.

"Aye, I can hear y'all!" I said loudly.

I could see they were shuffling the phone around and I could hear Rin laughing, I could tell her ass was drunk now, but what pissed me off was I heard some other niggas too, that didn't sound like Chris or Tre, bitch asses. I was about to say something then the call disconnected. I almost threw my shit against the wall. I was about to call again, when I got a text from Tia.

Nicole: I know how you get; everyone is fine. We just having fun. We'll be back soon.

Thank you, be careful. We need to talk soon, I miss you

She looked like she was typing, then it stopped, which was fine. This is why I can't let Tia go, she knew me better than anyone, and she had a way of knowing what I was thinking. I decided to just take my ass to bed, and I'll deal with Rin's ass in the morning.

"Who was all those guys I heard last night?" I asked Sharin, as I watched her get dressed.

"We met them on the boardwalk, and they wanted to hang."

"Well, why the hell you didn't just say that? Instead of hanging up on me last night."

"I don't know."

Sharin had been short with me since we woke up this morning. I felt her get in bed maybe an hour after I talked to them on the phone.

"What's your problem?"

"I don't have one, Matthew."

"You do, because you only call me by my name when you're mad at me."

She sighed, lightly. "I'm sorry boo, I don't have a problem. I think I just over did it last night."

"I don't believe you."

"Well, now it sounds like you have the problem. Can we just enjoy this weekend?"

"Okay Rin."

I didn't want to argue with her; I walked over and kissed her quickly and left the room. I joined everyone downstairs, they were all eating cereal. I made a mental note to go to the store later, so I could cook breakfast in the morning, since it would be Keyarra's birthday.

"How were you the first one to bed but the last one down here?" Tre asked me.

"I was trying to wait for y'all slow ass friend, but she is moving like a turtle this morning"

"I don't even know how she is up; she was done last night." Keyarra said.

I pulled up a stool next to Derek.

"Morning bro."

"Good morning, how'd you sleep?" he asked, with a mouth full of frosted flakes.

I was thankful that he wasn't holding on to the dumb shit I said last night, but that's just how he was; never let little shit get to him. I always admired that about him.

"It was cool, until Rin drunk ass stumbled in."

"Yeah, I heard all of their loud asses. But Katrina ass finally decided to call me at 3am, so that kept me up for an hour."

"Y'all talk?"

"Yeah, her grandmother sick, so she said she been trying to take care of her."

"How you feel about that?"

"Like that's bullshit, but it what it is." He shrugged.

"Well, still see where her head at when you get back."

"For sure."

"Ard y'all, what's the moves?" Chris asked everyone when he entered the room; I didn't even notice that he wasn't in here. I also noticed Rin followed in after him and once again, I could see it looked like she had been crying. She was trying to avoid eye contact with me.
"BEACH!" Keyarra responded, eagerly.
"LEGGO THEN." he said, matching her energy.
We all got ready to hit the beach, I tried to talk to Rin, but she kept insisting that's she was fine, and I was getting fed up; so, I left the shit alone before it turned into an argument. We had got the idea to hit the boardwalk first, so we could get some stuff for beach games.

"Do you think I can see you tonight, before I leave in the morning?" I overheard this girl say to Derek.
This was like the 4th girl that had approached him, he was like a magnet. And they came with friends, but I wouldn't even give them the time of day. I already had enough on my plate, no one was holding a match to Rin or Tia.
"I already told you; I have a girlfriend." he said, smoothly eyeing her up and down.
"Lucky girl, but make sure you use that number if things don't work out." she said seductively, finally walking away.
Derek had put on his shades, but I know he watched as she walked away because she had an ass on her!
"Bro, you got these girls swarming." I said.
"Naw nigga don't just blame me, they drooling over you too. I seen that shorty pay for your shit at the beach bar."
"She wouldn't take no for an answer, then she slid her number on the receipt too."
"See, they bold out here."
"Y'all ready to play? I got those 3 dudes over there to play as well." Tre pointed out.
We had played a bunch of shit with girls but now we wanted to play touch football, while they stayed in the water, but we needed a few more heads.

"Bet." Derek said.

We got up and started our game. Since myself, Derek, and Tre were a little more solid, Chris volunteered to be on the other guys' team to even it out a little bit; so, it was 4 on 3.

Everything was cool, but the other team was up by 1 and that's only because Chris slinky ass, was fast as shit. We were about to make another play, and it was Chris's turn to try and block me. Before the ball could even come down, this nigga knocked the shit outta me and I damn near hit the ground.

"Ayo, this touch nigga, not tackle!" I yelled.

"Stop acting pussy, I barely touched you." He spat.

I cocked my head back.

"I'm not sure who you talking to, but you need to watch that shit." I warned, as I walked up on him.

"And I think you need to back the fuck up." He barked.

"Or what, nigga?"

We were face to face at this point, he had to be about 6'3, so he had about an inch or so on me, but I didn't give a fuck.

"Yo yo, let's chill." Derek said, as he made some space between us.

At this point the girls had gathered around, and Tre was also trying to ease Chris back. Our eyes were dead locked on each other, still.

"Matt let's go man, we not doing this out here." Derek urged, as he continued to push me back.

"Listen to your boy." Chris said.

"You talking like you want this work, little nigga."

"Chris, stop!" Sharin said, as she also helped to create distance between us.

"Don't be checking me, when you was just up at the house crying over this nigga again Rin. I keep telling you he a fuck boy and he don't give a shit about you!" he yelled.

"Christian, don't yell at her!" Keyarra fussed.

I stared over at Sharin, who looked at me with watery eyes. I just shook my head because I asked her multiple times what was wrong, but she goes ahead and cry to this bean pole ass nigga.

"You know what, I'm out." Chris said, as he walked away angrily towards the house.

"Imma go with him." Tre said.

The little crowd that had gathered dispersed as well.

"You good?" Derek asked.

"I'm always good, fuck that nigga. They might as well go the fuck home."

"Matthew chill out, it's not that serious." Keyarra fussed.

"Go tell him that, he tripping over nothing."

"It's not nothing."

"And who side you on exactly, because last time I checked, you were my damn sister, even though you don't act like it."

"I'm not sure what that means but it's not the place, nor time for that."

"It means you always have everybody back but mine."

Anger formed in her eyes.

"You have no idea how much I have your back so miss me with that shit. How about you grow up and fix your fucked up attitude."

"You know what, Keyarra; I'm cool on you." I said walking away.

"I BEEN cool on you." She yelled at my back.

"Man, what the fuck ever." I said out loud.

I walked towards the boardwalk because if I had gone to the house and seen Chris, I would've trashed his ass, so I decided to settle down before I go back there.

"Matthew, wait!" I heard a voice behind me say.

"Please leave me alone." I said without turning around.

"I just want to make sure you're ok."

"What do you think Sharin? Everyone making me out to be the bad guy because of you!" I yelled, turning around to face her.

"I'm sorry…. I didn't mean for all that to happen." she said, sadly.

"What the hell did you think was going to happen? Why is it that I asked you 50 times what was wrong with you, and you said nothing all 50 fucking times! Then you turned right around to go and cry to that bitch boy, KNOWING we don't fuck with each other." I fussed loudly.

Tears started to stream down her face, and I instantly felt like shit. I hated to yell at her, but I was pissed off.
"Stop crying, Rin." I pulled her to me and let her cry in my chest.
"Matthew, I'm sorry, it wasn't like that. I was in the room and about to come down and Chris came in and asked how I was feeling from last night. I had got all in my feelings about everyone being boo'd up, so I started drinking more with guys on the boardwalk. The next thing I knew I was crying; I don't even know why. I just like you so much and I want to be with you but that's not what you want; and I want to be ok with what we have going on, but I don't know if I can." She rambled, fast as hell.
"Rin, slow down."
At this point she was crying hysterically; I wrapped her in my arms tighter, hoping that would calm her down some.
"I'm sorry boo, I really am. Chris is my best friend, and he just doesn't like to see me upset....it was dumb for me to think that he wouldn't blow up about it." She explained.
"Aye stop talking like that, you're not dumb.... I don't like to see you upset either, so maybe after this weekend we should just cool it for a while. I can't give you what you want right now and..."
"No, Matthew, I don't..."
"Stop." I said, cutting her off. "I care about you a lot Sharin, I really do, but I can't fully commit to a relationship with you or anyone for that matter. So, don't think I'm trying to be with someone else. Let's get through the rest of the weekend, then we can discuss this when we get back if you want, ok?"
She just nodded her head slowly. Her eyes welled up with tears again.
"Stop crying Rin, even though Keyarra, and I not fucking with each other like that, I want her to still try and enjoy the rest of the weekend and she needs her friend for that. So, I need you stop

crying and be that crazy ass Sharin, that everyone loves…. Can you do that for me?

"Yes." she said lowly, as she dried her tears.

I leaned down and kissed her deeply. "Do you need me to walk you back to the house?" I asked.

"No, it's not far."

"Ard, I'll see you later."

"Where are you going?"

"Imma just go chill somewhere for a little bit and let everything cool off."

"Ok, I'm sorry again boo."

"It's all good, Rin."

I watched as she walked back down the beach and towards the house.

I wasn't sure what I was about to do but damn, did I need a drink.

KEYARRA

It had been a few hours since the whole blow up between Chris and Matt and I was just ready to go home at this point. Sharin was trying to be ok, but I could tell all she wanted to do was cry. Chris came and apologized but I was really annoyed with him because I saw that he pushed Matt first, and it was just uncalled for.

"You ok, Key?" Tia asked, as she came outside.
I had been in the pool for the past hour, water had always been my happy place.
"Yeah, I'm just over it."
"I understand, Matt thinks everyone is pissed at him, when really everyone is mad at, Chris."
"You talked to him?" I asked, surprisingly.
"Uh …. yeah, I just texted to see if he was good."
"I guess I should check too."
"You should."
"I know, he just makes me so crazy sometimes. He can be hard to talk to."
"I don't think so."
"You two have always had a good relationship, it's different with us for some reason…. maybe I'm the problem." I said, sadly.
"I'm sure that isn't it."
I wanted to change the subject, talking about Matthew, and our issues was a sore topic for me.

"Did you talk to, Chris?"

"A little, but I didn't have much to say. I think they are thinking about leaving."

"I don't want them to, but I don't want Matt to be uncomfortable either."

"Yeah, Chris feels bad. He said he is willing to apologize to him when he comes back."

"I think they should just stay away from each other, honestly."

"Yeah, me too, but what we are not about to do is sit around this house sulking. The plan is still to go to H2O tonight."

"I don't know, Ti."

"What you mean? We are finally able to go to one of those foam parties."

"I know...but I don't think Rin is up for anything."

"I don't wanna sound like a bitch, but it's really not about her, she'll be fine. Matthew isn't leaving her alone." she said, with an eye roll.

"I guess you're right."

"Duh, and we have to put those bathing suits to use too, I know you would hate to waste DW's money."

She was trying to guilt trip me.

"Ugh, fine."

I heard the back door open, and Derek stepped out. Since we've been here, he hasn't worn a shirt, and I couldn't help but to gawk at him. He was toned from his shoulders down to his stomach, but he swore up and down he doesn't work out much. The tattoos that adorned his body only added to his sexiness. He had a half of sleeve on his left arm and GG's favorite scripture, Proverbs 3:5-6, tatted on the right side, near his rib cage. On the back of his left shoulder, he had a portrait of our mothers. He got a dope tattoo artist to do it for his 16th birthday and it looked exactly like the picture that he had given them. I remember, GG was up in arms about DW, not only giving Derek a car, but spending close to $1000 on a tattoo for him.

"Y'all good out here?" he asked, sitting down on the chair close to the pool.

"Yes, I finally got Keyarra, to agree to come out tonight."
"Why weren't you?" He asked me.
"I just felt like it was a lot going on."
"Shit happens. Chris was tryna leave but I told him to chill."
"Really?" I asked.
"Yeah, after he apologized, he told me that him and Tre were gonna dip but I said if he was gonna be around Tia, then he probably gotta be around Matt eventually; so just get the shit over with now."
"Have you talked to Matt?"
"Yeah, I called him, he cool. He'll be back later."
"I guess I'm the only one who hasn't checked in on him."
"Don't sweat it Key, he good."
"Yes, Matthew is fine, everything is fine! Keyarra, hurry up out the pool, so I can do your make-up; imma go start mine." Tia said.
"You're going to a foam party, why do you need make-up?" Derek questioned.
"I'll yell when I'm ready, Keyarra." Tia said, as she went in the house, totally ignoring Derks's question.
I couldn't help but laugh.
"Don't laugh at her, she's ridiculous."
"Besides the obvious, are you having a good time?" I asked.
"It's not really about me. Question is, are you?" He said, while looking down at his phone.
Whenever we had conversations, he gave me direct eye contact, but I noticed for most of today he barely looked at me.
"I am."
"Good, I'm about to go chill until it's time to go." He said, getting up.
"Oh, I didn't think that would be your type of scene."
"I don't have shit else to do."
And without another word he went inside. I felt weird like my feelings were hurt or something. I looked forward to when me and Derek would have a few minutes alone, and now it was like he couldn't wait to get away from me.

"Are you feeling better, Rin?" I asked, as we waited in line to get into H2O.

"Yeah, I'm fine, but don't worry about me. We are going to party until dawn for your birthday."

"This place closes at like 1." Tre said, smartly.

"You know what I meant, light bright." Sharin snapped, rolling her eyes.

As they continued to bicker, I looked back at Chris and Tia. Chris looked like a sad puppy, as he tried to talk to her and she looked as if she wasn't listening, at all. Chris was talking quietly, so I couldn't really hear what they were saying, but what I could hear was this girl who was trying to talk to, Derek. She was extremely close to him, and he looked as if he was entertaining her. Earlier at the beach and boardwalk the girls flocked to Matthew and Derek. Matt, I was kind of used to, but every 5 seconds a girl was eye-fucking Derek, which I understood because I did the same; but I still didn't like it. When we finally made it inside it was like a mad house; people were everywhere.

"C'mon y'all, before it gets too crazy; let's take one more pic." Sharin said.

"Y'all took like 50 back at the house." Tre complained.

"Oh my God, do you ever shut up!" Sharin argued.

The 3 of us gathered and one pic my ass. Rin made us do hella poses; Charlie's Angels, Hear No Evil, See No Evil, Speak No Evil, jail poses, and all this goofy shit.

"Ohhhh, The Powerpuff Girls; just call me, Mojojo." some horny white guy said to us.

"SEE, he gets it." I yelled, excitedly.

I really wanted our matching suits to make people think of The Powerpuff Girls. He could only see our tops because we had shorts on, but he got the picture.

"You can take that one but these 2 off limits." Chris said, pointing to me and Tia.

"Christian!" Sharin yelled.

"What? You single.".

"So am I." Tia countered.

"Yeah ard." Christian said.

Tia seemed to be really upset with him. One thing about Tia was that she was loyal as hell, and Matt was family; so that's something she didn't play about.

"Let's go danceeeee." Sharin shrieked.

We all danced and partied for what felt like hours. I went to go take a break and went over to where Derek was posted.

"You don't look like you're having fun." I said.

"It's cool." He responded, simply.

"Are you ok?"

"Yeah, why I wouldn't be?"

"Because you..."

Before I could finish my sentence, this girl walked up to me.

"Um excuse me, is this your boyfriend?" she asked, kindly.

"No."

"Oh good" she said, as she introduced herself to Derek.

I expected him to brush her off like he had the others previously, but he didn't. She asked him to dance, and he agreed. I watched as she led him onto the dance floor and grinded all on him. I knew I was blatantly staring at them, but I couldn't help it.

"HAPPY BIRTHDAYYYYYYY!" Sharin and Tia screamed.

I'm sure they could be heard over the blaring music. I didn't even realize it was 12 already.

"Thanks guys."

We were joined by Chris and Tre who also showered me with happy birthdays and hugs. Tre rained kisses all over my lips and face. It felt good to be surrounded by them because the last 2 birthdays I hadn't done anything; I stayed in my room and cried damn near all day.

"Happy Birthday, Key." Derek said, re-joining us.

"Thank you." I smiled.

That stare was back but only for a few seconds.

"I think imma go back to the house, y'all have fun." He announced.

"Awww jefe, it looked like you were having a good time." Sharin said.

"Yeah, it was cool, I just wanted to wish Key happy birthday, then I was gonna dip."

I got a few butterflies when he said that because the thought of him only coming out for me, made me feel special.

"This place is about to close soon anyway, let's go to the boardwalk." Tre suggested.

We all agreed! We were out until at least 3 in the morning. When we finally got in, I let Tre give me birthday dick, which just consisted of him doing me from the back for 10 minutes or so, I was definitely tired of faking it. After he was done, I begged him to see the sun rise with me, but he was also drunk, so he fell asleep. But he promised that we would tomorrow morning.

"Ayo it's 11, wake y'all asses up." I heard Derek say, as he banged on the door.

I heard Tre groan; I'm sure he was hung over.

"We're up." I yelled. "I'm going to hop in the shower real quick." I said to Tre.

"Can I join you?"

"You know my brother and Derek, would kill us."

"They don't have to know."

"They're not stupid."

"That's your problem now, you're scared of everything." He snapped at me.

I was a little taken back because it came out of nowhere.

"What are you talking about?"

"Nevermind, go take your shower."

I watched as he reached over and took a swig from his vodka; I was starting to think that he had a drinking problem. Instead of pressing the issue, I went in the bathroom, took my shower and got ready for the day. I styled my braids into a half up half down, I wore acid washed jean shorts, and a cropped fringe shirt that read, "Birthday Princess".

When I came out the bathroom, Tre was on the phone; but when he saw me, he ended the call.

"Who was that?" I asked.

"My mother, she said happy birthday. I'm sorry I snapped at you earlier." He said walking over to me trying to kiss me, but I could smell the liquor on his breath. I turned my head and stepped back.

"I think you should go wash up and I will see you out there."

He looked at me funny; then he walked past me into the bathroom, slamming the door behind him. I looked over at the bed and picked up his phone, I had never gone through it before, but something in me was telling me to. I unlocked it and looked through his call logs, the call that he had ended was from a private number, so it wasn't his mother. There were a lot of phone calls with a private caller.

"If I walk in this room and see some shit I don't wanna see, it's gonna be a shitty birthday." Derek shouted, from the other side.

"Open the door." I giggled.

I put Tre's phone down and met Derek at the door. He looked around, suspiciously.

"What are you looking for?"

"You and Tre showered together?"

I burst out laughing.

"I'm serious Key, y'all been in here a long ass time."

"He was waiting for me to come out the bathroom."

"Yeah ok, close your eyes."

"What?" I asked, confused.

"Take my hand and close your eyes."

I was hesitant at first but did it. He led me out into the living room and when he let my hand go, he told me to open my eyes.

"SURPRISE!" everyone yelled.

I looked around in amazement, there were tons and tons of balloons everywhere, and a big Happy Birthday banner.

"How...when..." I couldn't get my words together. "When did y'all do this?" I finally said.

"We've been hiding everything in that extra room, hoping you wouldn't go in there." Tia said.

"We blew up most of the balloons last night though." Rin added.

"Y'all didn't have to do all this." I said, with my voice cracking.

"Here come the water works." Matthew said, as he rounded the corner.

I poked my bottom lip out and walked towards him. I hated our blow up yesterday, I didn't like the fact that he thought that I didn't have his back. Me and him fight but at the end of the day, he's my brother and I love him more than he knows; I would do anything to protect him.

"I'm sorry." I said, as I wrapped my arms around his waist.

"Nothing to be sorry about, Happy Birthday kid."

"Thank you, thanks to all of y'all for real." I said, turning to everyone.

"We're just happy you let us celebrate with you this year." Derek said.

"Say that again; she was a mean little bitch last year when I tried to surprise her with a cake." Rin joked.

"Shut up; I wasn't that bad."

"I don't know man; you gave Tre hell for a while." Chris added.

"Ard, settle down. Don't be ganging up on my bestie." Tia defended.

"Thank you, Tia." I smiled

"Let's go eat before the food gets too cold." Matt said.

"What did you make?"

"Go see."

I went into the kitchen and at the breakfast bar there was a feast. Shrimp and grits, waffles, bacon, sausage, and fresh fruit.

"Imma scramble these eggs quickly; I didn't want them to get cold." Matt said, as he walked over to the stove.

"What the hell?" I heard Tre say; I guess he just saw all the decorations.

"Isn't it pretty?" Sharin asked him.

"Why didn't y'all tell me about this? I would've helped."

"Because your drunk ass can't keep a secret." Chris laughed.

"That's what you think, but yeah this shit's nice." He said as he came over and sat next to me.

I didn't really know how to feel about that first comment, but I wasn't going to worry about it now. Everyone started to make their plates, then we sat and ate.

"What all do you wanna do today?" Tia asked me.

"I'm not sure about after breakfast, but I want dinner at Hooters and for us all to go to the amusement park, at the end of the boardwalk

"Hooters?" Derek questioned.

"Yes, I love it there."

"Girl we could do a steak house or something." Tia suggested.

"Everyone is not high maintenance like you Tia." Matthew teased.

"I'm not high maintenance, I'm just saying, we could do something better than Hooters."

"She wanna do Hooters, then that's what we'll do." Derek said.

I smiled at him, but he didn't return it; he just focused back on his food. I wondered if he was mad at me, he seemed fine a few minutes ago.

"Ok, what about the beach?" Sharin asked, absent-mindedly.

We were silent for a few seconds.

"I think we are beached out." Matthew laughed.

"Oh right..." Sharin said.

I texted Tia.

Did Chris and Matt talk?
My bestie: Chris apologized, Matt just said it's cool but it's still some animosity there.
I bet.

"I'm fine with just hanging out around the pool until later." I suggested.

After breakfast we all went out to the pool and relaxed. Derek and Matthew stayed by the side, for the most part, though. A few hours later we went to the boardwalk, had dinner, then got on damn near every ride at the amusement park. It was around 2am when we got back, finally. We were leaving in the afternoon, and I was sad. I had a great weekend and wasn't ready to leave. Everyone had finished the liquor and went to bed; I was tossing and turning until my alarm went off at 4:30, so I could go watch the sunrise. I shook Tre a little to wake him up.

"Tre, Tre. Wake up so we can go."

"Go where?" He groaned.

"To see the sunrise."

"Key, I'm too fucked up." he slurred. "We can go tomorrow."

"Are you joking? We leave today...wake up." I shook him some more.

"Go ahead and go with the girls." He said, pulling the covers over his head.

"You're an asshole!"

I got out of bed, threw on my thin boy shorts and a sports bra, then I grabbed a beach blanket. I made it outside and went to close the door behind me, when I turned around I collided straight into, Derek.

"Shit, I'm sorry." I apologized.

He took out his earphones and stared at me while breathing heavily. He was shirtless and was dripping sweat, even though it was early in the morning, it was still humid as hell outside.

"Where are you going?" he asked me, curiously.

"T-to the beach to watch the sunrise." I replied nervously.

"By yourself?"

"Yes, Tre was supposed to come but he's passed out."

Derek continued to stare at me then he looked over at the beach, which was only a few feet away. He looked as if he was contemplating something. I took the time to admire him, sweaty and all, he was still fine as hell. He had on running shoes and black basketball shorts; I wanted to see what hid behind those shorts.

"Keyarra!"

"Huh." I said. I thought maybe my intrusive thoughts came out again.

"I said do you want some company?"

"Uh...yeah...yeah. That would be cool."

"Do I have time to change into my slides real quick?"

"Yeah, the sunrise isn't for like another half hour, or so."

"Cool, I'll be right back."

I waited outside, nervous as hell. The last time I was with Derek alone, it took everything in me not to tongue him down. He got me horny as hell without doing much. A few minutes had passed, and he came back outside, still shirtless, but with his Nike slides on and a pair of green Nike basketball shorts.

"Ready?" he asked.

"Yes."

We walked down to the beach; it was still a little dark out, but we could still make out where to go.

"May I ask you something?" I said, after a few minutes of just walking in silence.

"Here you go with the questions." He laughed. "You can ask me whatever you want but stop asking me can you ask.... just ask, ok?"

"Ok, sorry.... but um, are you mad at me?"

He looked over at me.

"Naw, why would I be mad at you?"

"I don't know, you've just been a little stand offish towards me; so I thought maybe I did something."

"That's my bad, I wasn't trying to come off that way. I just wanted you to enjoy your friends."

"But you're my friend too."

"True, true. Again, that's my bad."

We walked a little more, until I said we could stop; we were out of eyesight from the house. Further down the beach were less people; I guess a lot of people had the same idea of watching the sunrise.

I laid the blanket out, then we sat down; we just stared out into the ocean for a few minutes, each in our own thoughts. I took my phone out my bra and put on Pandora, to the 90's R&B station. "One More Day," by New Edition, started to play.

"What you know about this song?" he asked.

"Boy bye, this is all I listen to. You act like you so much older than me."

"So, Chris Brown not the best artist of all time anymore?"

"I love him, but 90s R&B has my heart. It's what I think love should feel like."

"Okay okay, I respect it." he said, nodding his head in agreement.

"Is Monica, still end game for you?"

"Oh yeah, I was in the same room with her a few years ago and I almost lost my shit. My dad had to tell me to calm the hell down."

"You was fan girling?" I laughed.

"Chill on me; I was just excited."

"Yeah ok."

"Man whatever. So, if you not on Chris like that anymore, who you fan girling over lately?"

"Michael B. Jordan."

He looked like he was thinking for a few moments about who I was referring to.

"The little nigga from, "The Wire"? he finally asked.

"Yes, but he fine fine now; I seen him in this movie, "The Awkward Moment", and I've been in love ever since. He has a boxing movie coming out later this year and I'm finna be front row."

Derek took his phone out and googled him.

"You know I look better than him, right?"

"You don't." I protested.

"Keep telling yourself that."

"I'll tell you one thing; you have nice feet." I said, pointing towards his toes.

"Ayo chill." he said, trying to dig his feet into the sand, trying to hide them.

I couldn't help but laugh.

"Ain't nothing wrong with having nice feet, that's very attractive on a man."

"Next topic; did you have a good birthday?"

"I had the best birthday, thank you again, Derek. I really appreciate it."

"I told you, stop thanking me, it's cool. It seems like we all needed a little get-away."

"I agree."

"What made you want to see the sun rise?"

"I've always wanted to, on a beach; they make it look so good in movies." I answered.

"True. You know, you should really be out here with your nigga."

"He didn't want to come, and I wasn't missing it." I shrugged.

"Thank you for coming with me, though."

"No problem, I was up."

"I didn't know you run."

"I don't usually. Only if I have a lot on my mind and can't sleep."

"Care to share with the class?"

"It's nothing worth sharing."

"Ok...is there anything else you do to clear your mind?"

He looked over at me and gave me a knowing look.

"Ok, besides that."

"Mmmm to distract myself, I practice times tables sometimes."

"What, like 6x7 is 42?"

He laughed a little. "Naw, like 670x420 is..."

He squinted slightly, as he worked out the problem in his head for a few seconds.

"281,400."

"Oh wow, you a math genius?"

"Not at all; I just like numbers."

"Well, I may need your help in my college prep class this year." I smiled.

"You know I got you."

"Thanks. So, to be honest, I thought you were up because you were making sure there was no baby making going on." I joked.

"I'm not gonna hold you, I did the first night; I had to make sure y'all wasn't playing with me."

I cracked up.

AGE IS JUST A NUMBER

"You were outside our doors?" I laughed.

"Hell yeah. I damn near slept outside Tia's."

"What if you had heard something?"

"Man, Chris would have been done."

"Oh my God Derek, you know Tia's not a virgin." I said, while I continued to laugh.

"I don't like to think about that shit because if I ever was to catch her...it's over. She was supposed to wait til marriage."

I could not tell if Derek was serious or not, but I couldn't stop laughing.

"You didn't though."

"I was a lost cause, she supposed to be better than me."

"Shut upppp, I can't stand you."

"No, but for real, if I caught Tia having sex, yeah imma be mad; but if I ever catch her giving a nigga top.... both of them gotta see me."

"What? Head worse than sex?"

"To me it is. Like this gonna sound wild but getting on your knees and giving a man head seems a little demeaning to me." he explained.

"I'm confused, so you don't like head?"

"I do for sure but it's not a requirement in my relationship. Like I only let Katrina give me head, if I'm mad at her."

"Wow, I've never heard anyone say that before; so, you didn't let any of your past girls give you head?"

"They weren't my girlfriends, Keyarra. I usually hit them from the back because I didn't care to look them in the face. So, if they offered me head, I let them. It sounds harsh but I didn't care that much about them, to care if they disrespected themselves or not. But when it comes to Tia, and you too, don't let me find out." He spoke, seriously.

"Well, you don't have anything to worry about over here."

Me and Tre rarely did foreplay; the most we did was kissing. I wouldn't let him give me head and I could only give him head for no more than 30 seconds, before he came.

"I hear you. You and him don't seem to care for each other that much."

"Why do you say that?"

"He always in his phone and you seem to want to be with Tia and Sharin more than him."

"I'm not really the clingy type, and it can be either or with him."

"Ok Ok; so what else should I know about you, Keyarra?"

"What you mean?"

"Just what I said. You not clingy, you love R&B, you like nasty ass, Hooters, if you could live in a swimming pool you would, and you like dry ass food…. what else should I know?"

"First of all, Hooters is not nasty; you tore those wings up yesterday and I don't like dry food."

"Because the sauce on the wings were good. I watched you eat mozzarella sticks, no sauce…. DRY…. you ate shrimp, no sauce…. DRY…. you ate wings, no ranch, blue cheese or nothing…. DRY….so therefore, you like dry food." He argued, playfully.

"I just don't like condiments; I'm cutting a lot of calories by doing so."

Derek couldn't control his laughter.

"Shut your ass up. Just admit you like dry food."

"Go to hell Derek, why you watching me eat, anyway?"

"Maybe I liked what I saw." He flirted.

There go those eyes again, I could stare into them all day.

"You like watching me eat? That's not weird at all." I said, as I shied away from his piercing gaze.

"You know that's not what I meant."

I chose not to respond to that.

"I know something you don't know about me."

"What?"

"I smoke." I said, pulling a small tube from bra that contained a blunt.

"Naw, I didn't know that. You do that often?"

"No. Chris rolled this, plus like 5 more and gave them to me. I guess it was my birthday gift." I chuckled.

"I could never get into it heavy."

"That's surprising, since you were on the west coast for so long. I can't roll, so that's why I don't too much." I also took a lighter from my bra, lit the blunt and put it to my lips.
"You can hide a lot in there can't you?"
I started to choke on the smoke because I was laughing.
"Shut up...here." I said, passing it to him.
"Naw, I'm good."
"C'mon Derek, don't make me smoke alone."
"Your ass was going to anyway, if you came out here alone."
"Shut up and hit this."
"Ok bossy." he said, taking it. He hit it and immediately started to choke.
I started to laugh.
"See ...that's why I don't do... that shit." He choked out, in between coughing.
"Give it back."
I hit the blunt a few more times and started to feel its effects. The sun was starting to peak over the horizon, and it was as beautiful as I thought it would be.
"Here, hold this." I said, passing him the blunt again.
I picked up my phone and started to record the sunrise, there was the view of the waves crashing, along with the horizon. Promise by Jagged Edge was playing in background; it made for a great Instagram video for my profile. I ended the video and took the blunt back.

"This is dope." Derek nodded his head in appreciation of the view.
"It is, have you ever shot gun before?"
"Naw, what's that?"
"You did not take advantage of living in Cali." I said, shaking my head. I turned towards him. "Ok, so imma hit this, then blow the smoke into your mouth."
"What?"
"I know how it sounds but our lips don't have to touch."
"Okay?" he said, hesitantly.

"So just purse your lips but leave them open slightly, then inhale slowly."

He did as he was told. I hit the blunt and held the smoke in, I leaned forward and slowly blew it into his mouth. He inhaled it, then blew it out his nose.

"See, not as bad as you thought, right?"

"Yeah, I wasn't sure what you were trying to do."

"I do that with Rin, sometimes."

"You do anything else with Rin?" he asked, with a raised brow.

"What? Hell no!" I snapped, with an attitude.

A slick smile dressed his face. "Ard, I was just asking. She seems like she might be down with anything."

"Ok, but I'm not."

"Uh huh."

"Shut your ass up and come here." I said, as I hit the blunt and we shot gunned again.

Derek's eyes were naturally low, but they looked a little lower which meant he also was starting to feel the effects.

"You bossy as shit." he said, blowing the smoke out from his nose.

"No, I'm not."

"Yes, you are but I like it."

"I bet."

"Come here, let's do it one more time."

"Who's bossy now?"

He chuckled and leaned forward. I hit the blunt and leaned forward as well. I blew the smoke in his mouth, but I lost my balance a little causing our lips to touch. I felt something when that happened, like electricity or something but it made me want to feel it again. We stared at each other for a few seconds, I finally said fuck it and leaned in again to kiss him. Derek immediately parted his lips and engaged. The butterflies in my stomach started break dancing, but I also had a throbbing in between my legs that was intense and damn near painful. I slipped my tongue in, and he accepted. Derek's hands were exploring my body and when they tried to go in between my legs, that's when realization set in causing me to pull back,

"Oh my God, I'm so sorry." I panicked, covering my mouth.
"Sorry for what?" he asked, confused.
"For kissing you, that was totally my fault."
"You don't see me protesting, come here." He said, tugging at my boy shorts to pull me forward.
"Derek, we can't."
"Naw, you done lit the match now, Key. Now come here." He urged, with a little more aggression.
Derek reached around my waist and pulled me on top of him. He pulled his legs up, so I could have some support. We were forehead to forehead and his hand was trailing up and down my back.
"You didn't like it?" He asked, lowly.
"I did." I whispered.
"Then what's the problem?"
"You know what the problem is, Derek."
"It's just a kiss."
Before I could protest, he slipped his tongue in my mouth again. I didn't want to fight him because I was enjoying it so much. We were both moaning as we made out. When he flattened his legs, he wrapped his arms around my waist tightly; bringing us closer. When he did that, I got a better feel of his erection, it made my throbbing intensify. I started to grind my hips against it and after a few seconds, I got a familiar feeling. It was starting to feel good, and I wanted more of it. I pressed my hips down a little more and started to grind a little harder; the pressure was driving me insane. Derek stopped kissing me, then tilted my head to the side and started sucking on my neck; it felt so damn good. Between that and the grinding, the feeling was intensifying, and I heard myself moan out loud.
"Mm hm, get that shit off, Key." He whispered, as he continued his attack.

Derek knew what was happening and I felt a little embarrassed, but not enough for me to stop. After a few seconds, I was ready. "Oh my God...." I moaned in a hushed voice.

Derek started to kiss me again and I moaned into his mouth loudly, as my body started to shudder. This euphoric feeling washed over me, and I damn near wanted to scream. I had only felt that a few times, but I hated it every time it happened; but this time it was different, I welcomed it, and I would give anything to feel it again. Derek slowly stopped kissing me and we were touching foreheads again. I was breathing heavily, with my eyes closed. I was embarrassed that I just made myself cum on him.

"Look at me." He said, softly.

My eyes fluttered opened and stared into his beautiful set.

"You good?"

I nodded my head yes and he smiled.

"Seems like you needed that."

"Derek I-I.... I'm..."

"Don't say you're sorry. It's fine."

"It's not, you have a girlfriend, and I have a boyfriend."

"Who's going to tell them?"

I didn't say anything.

"Exactly, so it's fine. I just wanna make sure you're good."

"I'm fine. I want to go back to the house now."

"Ok."

I was about to get up then I froze.

"Did anyone see us?"

The sun was still rising but it still lit the beach up.

"A couple walked past, but it just looked like we were kissing."

"Ok."

I got up and I immediately felt all the wetness between my legs, and if I felt it, he felt it. I was mortified. He got the blanket, then we walked back to the house in silence; before we hit the pathway, he grabbed my hand and pulled me to him.

"You sure you, ok?"

"Yes."

"I've been wanting to kiss you since I seen you at the airport. So don't feel bad, we both wanted it." He reassured me.

Derek kissed my lips again gently, and I savored it. They felt like pillows, making me feel all types of things.

"And don't let shit change between us." He added.

"What you mean?"

"Like don't start acting weird around me and shit. We still friends and we can kick it."

"We never kicked it before."

"You know what I mean, Keyarra."

"Ok."

"Ard, good."

He let me go and I walked to the door, I entered the code and went in.

"I'll see you in a few hours Key."

"Ok."

I walked in the room and Tre was still sleep, thank God. I headed into the bathroom and turned on the shower; I stayed in there for almost an hour; my thoughts were all over the place. Kissing Derek was a mistake, and it couldn't happen again. What if our siblings found out? But I'm not sure how I would be able to stay away. The attraction I had to him was bigger than ever and that was just after kissing. What would happen if things escalated? I brushed that thought out of my head and got out the shower. I was going to try my best to stay away from Derek, that would cause more problems than what I was ready for.

DEREK

It had been almost a month since we came back from the beach and Keyarra, was going to make me bust her ass. She was avoiding the fuck outta me and if she keeps it up, she was gonna see a side of me that she didn't wanna see. My texts were going unanswered and when I would call, she wouldn't pick up. I get that she may have been embarrassed or whatever, but I told her not to act weird around me, and that's exactly what she was doing.

"Derek."

"Yes." I answered, annoyed.

"You zoned out on me, what's going on? Our past few sessions you've seemed bothered." Carmen stated.

I blew out a frustrated breath and held my face in my hands. I was avoiding telling her this, but she was right, I am bothered.

"I have to tell you something."

"I'm listening, but I would like for you to look at me." she said, calmly.

I removed my hands and sat back in my chair.

"Well, really it's 2 things; I kissed someone." I admitted.

"Ok, and by that, I guess you mean someone other than your girlfriend."

"Clearly." I said, smartly.

She raised her brow at me, then started to write something down. I hated it when she did that.

"I didn't mean to get smart."

"It's fine; what's the 2nd?"

"I think Katrina....is cheating on me."

"Would the two have any correlation?"

"No.... I mean I don't think so."

"So, did you suspect you were being cheated on before or after you kissed this girl?"

"Before." I mumbled.

"Hm."

"Ok but listen, I been wanting to kiss this girl like before the subject of cheating got put in my head.... I mean technically, I already kissed her but that was a long time ago. That's beside the point though; I'm extremely attracted to this girl, so it wasn't just a get back thing because I don't even know for sure, if Katrina is cheating." I explained.

"Who is this girl?"

"I don't want to disclose that yet."

"Ok, what makes you think you're being cheated on?"

"It's just a lot of shady shit going on. Like she not returning my calls, disappearing, saying she one place, when she not and I'm just tired of it for real."

"Have you had a conversation with her?"

"I have and it turns into an argument, or she throws ass at me."

"That sounds like deflecting."

"For sure. But you know I can't be single."

"Why?"

"You know why, I don't want to fall back into my old ways. I've admitted to you that I'm not strong enough to go without sex, so if I was single, we both know what would happen."

"Derek, I believe you are stronger than you think. You've told me yourself you have stopped your own girlfriend from trying to have sex with you every day, and I'm sure you've done that while certain parts of you were screaming for you to oblige. You also informed me of many women who approached you while you were away. So, what makes you think you can't stop yourself?

That's only one fight and that's the most important one. That's who I want you to put all your focus into...yourself."

I let her words soak in; I don't feel strong enough to stop myself. I think about sex every single day, but I guess she has a point because I try to limit myself to 4 days a week with, Katrina.

"I want you to think about that and we will continue this next week, ok?"

"Ok."

"How are you feeling?"

"I'm good, I'm enjoying being back."

"Good. Have a good week."

"You too."

"And, Derek."

"Yes?"

"Stay away from that girl that you kissed."

"Got you."

I closed my laptop and put it away.

"Yeah, that's not happening." I said out loud.

I couldn't shake the thought of Keyarra's lips. I also kept hearing her moan, every time I closed my eyes. The way she made herself cum on me will live rent free in my head, forever. I felt how loose she got after that, she needed that, and I would allow her to do that as many times as she wanted. Shit, I wanted her to cum on my dick, but I knew that was wishful thinking. I just needed to see her again and explain to her that she can't keep avoiding me. I took my phone out and Facetimed, G.

"Hi baby boy." She answered.

"Hi G, where you at?"

"I'm at the homes still, we had some new girls come in, so I helped get them settled. I'll be leaving soon."

"Ok, I wanted to take you to dinner. Can I meet you at the house?"

"Aww, thank you baby. Sure! You can head over now; Keyarra should be home, and I'll leave here in a few."

I smiled inwardly when I heard Keyarra's name.

"Take your time G, it's still early."

"Ok, I'll see you soon."

We ended the call, and I rushed out the door. Keyarra was going to have to face my ass today. I made it to the house in record time. I put my key in the door and opened it, quietly. I thought she would be in her room, but I heard Tevin Campbell's song, "Can We Talk", coming from the kitchen, so that meant she was in there; and I smelled food cooking as well. As I crept closer, I heard Keyarra singing along with the song. She had a beautiful voice and I wanted to hear more. But I knew I was on limited time because the homes were only 20 minutes away and I wasn't sure if G had left yet. I made it to the doorway and her back was to me. I admired her ass, in these grey leggings and once again, she had on a sports bra.

"Matt, if you're trying to scare me, it's not going to work. I heard you come in." She said turning around.

The look on her face was priceless.

"I guess, I wasn't as quiet as I thought." I said, as I leaned against the door frame.

'Wh-what are you doing here?" She stuttered, nervously.

"I came by to see G, but she's not here...but you are."

"Um-um, she's at the homes."

"I figured. Now question for you. Didn't I tell your hardheaded ass not to be weird around me?"

"I-I..." she started to stutter again.

That was starting to get on my nerves.

"Do you usually have a stutter?" I asked sharply, interrupting her.

"No."

"Ok, then stop doing that and talk to me."

She inhaled deeply then started to speak again. "I'm not being weird, I'm just embarrassed. What happened wasn't supposed to and I just feel bad."

"So, you walking out of a room when I walk in, or not answering when I call, is you feeling bad?"

"Yes."

"Interesting." I walked into the kitchen to get closer to her but she stepped back until she was against the counter.

"Keyarra, stop playing with me."

I reached for waist and pulled her towards me.

"That shit you're doing hurts my feelings. We cool. You are thinking too much into it." I said, as I stared down at her; I cupped her chin with my thumb and pointer finger.

"I'm sorry."

"Make it up to me."

"What?"

"You heard me."

"How?"

"I wanna feel your lips again."

"Derek, I-I…"

"Stop…stuttering." I said, slowly.

I leaned down and without hesitation, she met me the rest of the way and our lips connected. She wanted to kiss me again, just as bad as I wanted to kiss her. We moved back until she hit the counter again, then I abruptly picked her up and sat her on top of it. We never broke our kiss; I was now in between her legs and her hands were placed at my side. Our kiss intensified, as we started to moan again. I was getting rock hard, and she must have been feeling a way too because she suddenly pushed me back.

"Derek, we have to stop."

"Why?"

"Because it's just a lot…. I don't want things to escalate."

I went back in between her legs again and started to kiss her neck gently.

"Do you want them to?"

"No." she answered, quickly.

"Ok…then they won't…. You don't like my lips on you?" I asked, as I trailed kisses along her neck.

"I do." She whispered.

"Ok then, stop fighting it." I latched on to her skin and was about suck hard, when she pushed me again but this time, I didn't move.

"Derek, you can't do that. You gave me a hickey last time and I had to convince Tre that he did it when he was drunk."

"My bad." I turned my face back to hers. "I got you something."

"Where is it?" She asked.

"It's in my car."

"Well, what is it?"

"I guess you gonna have to come and find out."

"Why didn't you bring it in?"

"I wasn't sure if you still deserved it."

"Derek, really?"

"I'm serious."

"Whatever. Move, I have to stir my soup."

"Why are you making soup in August?"

"Because I like soup."

"Hm, let me taste it."

"The soup?"

I cracked a smile. "I mean I can taste whatever you want me to, but yes, the soup."

She rolled her eyes and moved me back a little, so she could hop off the counter. She went to the stove and stirred the pot. She took a little onto a spoon and blew on it gently, then brought it to my mouth.

"It's not bad." I said, after I swallowed it.

"I can't follow a recipe for shit." She frowned, as she turned back to the stove.

I came behind her and wrapped my arms around her waist.

"I told you, it's not bad."

"You're just being nice."

"I'm not gonna lie to you, Key."

She was about to respond, when we heard the screen door open. Keyarra stiffened and tried to get out of my arms, but I had tightened my grip.

"I will hit you, let me go." she panicked.

"I might like that, but you gonna stop being an asshole around me?"

"Derek, let me go." she demanded, struggling to get out of my hold.

"Answer my question."

"Yes, yes."

"You sure?"

We heard the front door open.

"Keyarra, what are you in here burning?" GG yelled.

Keyarra was in a panic.

"I said yes, now let me the hell go!" She urged, as quietly as she could.

I turned her face back towards me and kissed her, then let her go. I backed up and leaned against the wall. Keyarra turned towards me with an angry expression. I blew a kiss at her; she threw up her middle finger.

Eventually!

"Did you hear me girl?" GG asked, as she entered the kitchen.

"I'm not burning anything."

"Smells like it, hi my boy." GG said to me.

"Hi G. Yeah, she definitely burned it."

Keyarra's mouth dropped.

"But you just said it wasn't bad." She whined.

"I was just being nice." I said, throwing her words back at her.

"Derek, go to hell."

"Hush your mouth little girl. Derek, I'm going change, then I'll be ready." GG said.

"Where y'all going?" Keyarra asked.

"Pappas."

"Oooo, bring me back a crab cake." she begged.

"Or you just could come with us." I suggested. "I mean, if it's ok with G."

"Of course."

"Oh no, I don't want to impose."

"Girl you've been in this house all week, go put some clothes on." GG fussed, as she went downstairs.

"You heard what she said." I said to Keyarra, who was just staring at me.

"You're trouble." she stated, pointing at me as she exited out the kitchen.

"I told you…. you lit the match."

I spent the rest of the evening with Keyarra and GG, and we had a good time. I couldn't keep my eyes off Keyarra all night. She was radiant and her personality made me want to be around her more; she's sweet, with an infectious laugh, and surprisingly funny.

"Ok my boy, I'm going to go to bed. I had fun with the both of you. Thank you." GG said to Keyarra and I.

"No problem, G; I had a good time too. Have a good sleep, I love you."

"I love you too." she replied.

GG really was the light of my life next to Tia. She kept me grounded and she was always there, whenever we needed her. I don't talk to God often but when I do, I thank him for, GG, every time.

"Goodnight, Keyarra. Don't be up on that phone all night."

"It's summertime, G." Keyarra replied.

"I know but only a few more weeks left."

"Goodnight, G. I love you."

"I love you too, goodnight."

We watched as GG disappeared into the kitchen and we heard her make her way down the steps, to her room.

"Walk me to my car."

"Are you asking or telling?"

I squinted at her slightly.

"Telling!"

I walked out the door and I heard her follow me.

"Get in." I said, as I rolled down the passenger side window.

"To go where?"

"Around the corner."

"Derek, I didn't even lock the door."

"It'll only be a few minutes; I mean we could talk out here, but Matt might pull up on us."

227

With that said she hopped in, and I drove around the corner. I killed the engine, then looked at her.

"So, who you been on the phone with all night?"

"Why?"

"Because it's not me, so who is it?"

"You kiss a guy one time, and he thinks he owns you after that." she shook her head.

"It was a little more than kissing."

She eyed me. "Don't bring that up."

"You be on the phone with, Tre?"

"Yes, Derek. He is my boyfriend; now what do you want?"

"I'm just making conversation with you, since you've been treating me like shit for the past few weeks."

"I thought I made that up to you?" she asked, with a raised brow.

"I mean, I'm always down for more making up." I said, leaning towards her.

She leaned back and shook her head, no. "Derek, this can't become a thing."

"And why is that?"

"Because of obvious reasons."

"Keyarra, I know you felt what I felt when our lips first touched. I saw it in your eyes. I can't stay away from you, nor do I want to; so please don't fight me on this. I promise it won't go anywhere that you don't want it to." I said, honestly.

I was laying it on thick because I wanted her...bad. I know I can't have her the way I want, so I will settle for this...for now.

"That's all you wanna do, is kiss?" She asked.

I bit down on my bottom lip and nodded my head slowly. I can tell she was thinking.

"Has anyone ever told you, that you give really intense eye contact?"

I smiled. "No, but I do believe that you should look a person in their eyes when you're speaking with them...especially, when persuading."

"Is that what you're doing...persuading?"

"Trying, damn near begging, which is something I'm not particularly accustomed to."

"Right, because girls just do what you say?"

"Sometimes. You're not though."

"Derek, I want to but...I just feel bad...it's cheating."

"You've already done it, plus some."

"I told you don't bring that up."

I leaned towards her again, gently grabbing her by the back of her neck, pulling her towards me.

"It'll be our little secret."

Our lips met and we made out until we finally decided to come up for air.

"I have to get back in the house now." she said in a small voice.

"You sound like you don't want to."

"Um-um Tre...h-he is calling me...." She stuttered, as she looked everywhere but at me.

"Do I make you nervous, Keyarra?"

"Sometimes." She admitted.

"I see. There's no need to be nervous around me though."

I started my car and crept up the block to see if Matt's car was anywhere in sight. The conversation that I had with him kept replaying in my head. I had every intention of staying away from Keyarra, since he felt so strongly about it. I'm not the type to lie and sneak around but that seemed like the best option for right now.

"Before you go."

I reached in the back, pulled out the shoe box and sat it on her lap.

"I heard you were a sneaker head." I said.

"Derek, you didn't have to get me anything. You have done enough."

"Open the box, Keyarra."

She opened it and removed the tissue paper, revealing the shadow grey Js. Her mouth dropped. She had the same look in her eyes, like when I get a new pair of shoes.

"Derek.... how the hell did you get these? They came out like 2 years ago."

"I have my ways."

"Thank you so much, I love them."

"I thought you might."

She sat the box on the dash and leaned over to kiss me, which turned into us making out again. I loved her lips, and I liked the way she made me feel when I was kissing her.

"Damn, I'll buy you whatever shoes you want, if you gonna kiss me like that every time."

She smiled, shyly.

"I think I should go now, before Tre pulls up on me. He's blowing my phone up."

"Ain't nobody worried about him pulling up."

"Goodnight, Derek." she said, with an eye roll.

"Quick question?"

"What?"

"You like kissing me than your boyfriend?"

"U-um..."

"Keyarra!" I said in warning.

She sighed. "Yes." she replied with her head down.

I hated that!

I grabbed her by her chin and pecked her lips twice.

"I don't like when your head is down." I whispered peering into her eyes.

"Um ok.... Derek?"

"Yes?"

"You have some really soft lips."

I chuckled. "Back at you."

She smiled shyly then leaned back from me. She grabbed her box and got out of the car but before she could close the door.

"So, you gonna sit on the phone with me tonight?"

"I guess you'll have to call, and we'll see." she said, as she winked and closed the door.

That nervousness must of went out the window.

"Bet."

I watched as she disappeared into the house. I had a message from Katrina earlier that she wanted me to come over. I know I ain't shit for this, but I was about to go fuck her with the thoughts of Keyarra on my mind. That's the only way I was going to be able to keep my promise of not escalating things between us. I hope Keyarra wasn't waiting for that phone call.

TIA

"So, you just gonna spend the night during the weekdays, so you don't have to take the bus?" Keyarra asked me.

"Maybe. Unless you start getting on my nerves." I responded, as I laid out my clothes.

It was the Sunday before school started and I decided to spend the night with Keyarra, so we could get dropped off together. There was a bus that would get magnet students and take them to school, but the hell I look like getting on a school bus.

"You know I walk to school sometimes, too."

"I'm not doing that either."

"Tia!"

"What girl? GG can take me or my man."

"Now Chris your man? You been putting that boy through the ringer the pass for weeks."

"Because that shit he did at the beach was lame."

I had put Chris on ice, and he was not happy about it. No matter what me and Matt have, he is like my family, which is a weird way to look at it. But either way, I don't play about family and Chris needed to understand that. Even though I was mad at Chris, I still tried to avoid Matt but that didn't work long. He played the sympathy card then, he guilt tripped me and my ass folded like a lawn chair, so we were having sex again. I do feel like Chris is going to ask me to be his girlfriend soon and I wasn't sure how that would play out because I wasn't ready to give up sex, altogether. But I also wouldn't cheat, so I hope I don't have to cross that bridge any time soon.

"You know Chris takes the bus too; he doesn't always drive."

"Or how about this, you can go get your license. DW will buy you a car, then YOU can take me to school every day."

"I'm working on it, Tia; you know you can do the same."

"I'm not doing that."

After the death of our mothers, Keyarra and myself developed the same fear of driving. Keyarra was coming around to the idea of driving but not me. The thought of me behind the wheel and getting on a highway terrified me.

"Tia, it's really not that bad. Tre been giving me lessons and it's not as scary as I thought."

"I'm sure. I can take an uber, if need be. I wear heels damn near every day, so you won't catch me walking or on a bus."

"You're going to wear heels…. everyday…to Parkville?" she questioned.

"Not like stilettos or anything but my wedges or something like that"

"Mmmm, good luck with that girl."

"Let me guess, you're wearing sneakers?"

"Uh duh, Derek got me the shadow grey Retro 1's…. I wanted those bad when they released. I don't even know how he got another pair for me."

"He has a very expensive plug; I'm glad he is able to share his sneaker fetish with someone because myself or hoe ass, aren't sneaker girls."

"I'm really surprised you and Katrina don't get along, y'all both are a little…high maintenance."

"The difference is, she's a mean girl…. I'm not. And she's a hoe, which I also am not."

"Do you really think she is a hoe or you just like calling her that?"

"I really think that. I can smell it on her." I said, seriously.

Keyarra burst out laughing.

"Girl shut up."

"I'm for real but Derek a hoe too, so birds of a feather."

"Yeah, I guess. So, are you excited or nervous for tomorrow?"

"Neither. I've been the new girl 3 times already. You get used to it."

"Oh, right. Well Parkville is probably not as nice as your other schools but it's decent."

"I'm sure it'll be fine...so the Js and what else?"

Keyarra walked to her closet and pulled out some new stuff she recently bought. I had been able to convince her to go to the mall with me a few more times, so she damn near had whole new wardrobe. She pulled out a black high waisted spandex skirt, that probably would stop right above her knees, once she filled it out.

"This skirt, for sure, and between these shirts"

She had a few crop tops, but they wouldn't really look like it since her skirt would be covering her stomach.

"I like the grey one." I pointed out.

"That's what I was thinking."

"Do you plan on wearing anything else besides sneakers?"

"Yes, Tia. I have sandals and stuff, but I am not on your level."

"Such a tomboy."

"I am not, you see I'm wearing a damn skirt...you could wear one with me and we can match." she said, with a hint of excitement.

"I was planning on it anyway."

"We'll be matching."

"Oh joy." I said, sarcastically.

"Girl, fuck you."

We both burst out laughing.

"But for real, I'm so happy we have the same lunches. And you have most of your classes with Rin, too."

"Yeah, I am thankful for that. I'm not really interested in making friends"

"Why?"

"Because I'm here for one year, there is no need."

"True."

"Plus, I've met your friends, and they are a handful, but I like them." I laughed.

"I agree."

"Giiiiiirls." GG sang, as she poked her head in the room. "Dinner is ready."

We joined GG, Matthew, Derek, DW, and to my un liking Katrina, at the dinner table.

GG made baked ziti, with a big Caesar salad and garlic cheese knots.

Keyarra and I were quiet. Neither one of us liked when Katrina was around. She does this fake ass nice girl act around GG and DW and they always ate that phony shit up.

"So, are you girls excited to be seniors?" GG asked the 3 of us.

"So excited." I said, dryly.

"Ecstatic." Keyarra said, just as dry.

Derek gave us both the eye, but we just continued eating our food.

"Well GG, I am very excited. Bittersweet for sure but excited none the less." Katrina stated, cheerfully.

What a fake bitch!

"I'm sure it is bittersweet for you; you have been cheering since your freshman year. I know your final game will be emotional." GG expressed.

"It will be for sure, won't it, Keyarra? I mean I know you just joined the team last year, but you have improved tremendously." Katrina said, with a fake smile.

Keyarra just stared at her.

"Keyarra, she is talking to you." GG said.

"Why yes, Katrina, it will be quite emotional. I don't know how I'm gonna manage without the joys of shoving pom-poms in people's faces." Keyarra stated, in the same fake tone as Katrina.

I snickered a little, along with Matthew.

"I can smell your enthusiasm." Katrina responded, staring Keyarra down with a raised brow.

The tension was thick in the room. I wasn't 100% sure what their beef was but all I know is, they have almost exchanged blows, on more than one occasion; but it was always someone there to separate them. How they have managed to be on a team together and not beat the shit out of each other, is beyond me.

"When is that last home game, by the way, so I can make sure to attend?" my sperm donor asked.

"Oh, I'll double check the date and get that to you Mr. Williams." Katrina answered.

"You must be overwhelmed Katrina, that date is Oct 24th. Which also happens to be our homecoming." Keyarra said, with a sarcastic smile.

"Oh great, I can kill 2 birds with one stone." DW voiced.

"You are such a good side-kick Keyarra. You remember all the little things that I can't be bothered with." Katrina remarked, clearly, throwing daggers.

Keyarra dropped her fork and looked at her angrily.

"Sidekick?"

"Precisely." she smiled.

"Ok, that's enough. Let's go Katrina." Derek announced.

Keyarra looked over at Derek, and ever so calmly said.

"I think you need to get a muzzle on your bitch."

DW spit his water out, while the sounds of forks clattering against plate filled the room.

"KEYARRA!" GG gasped.

Suddenly Katrina stood up as well as Keyarra.

"I got your bitch." Katrina spat, as she tried to reach across the table to get at her but was stopped by, Derek.

"Ayo chill!" Derek yelled, as he attempted to drag Katrina away from the table.

Keyarra just stood with an amused look on her face, as she waved bye to her. Katrina struggled to get out of Derek's grasp. She shouted in Spanish, as she was pulled out the door.

"Now that is out the way." Keyarra said calmly, as she sat back down.

I was tickled pink.

"Keyarra, you are going make me knock all 32 of your teeth out!" GG threatened.

"G, why would you invite her to dinner anyway? You know we can't stand each other; you saw she tried to attack me."

"Because I can invite whoever I want to my damn house!" GG responded, angrily.

"You heard her call me a sidekick but I'm the one getting yelled at."

"How many times do I have to tell you, you can't let people get the best of you. She wanted to get under your skin, and you fed right into it. That is Derek's girlfriend, so she is going to be around…. you all need to cut the shit and act civilized."

Keyarra just continued to eat her food. I'm sure GG's words went in one ear and out the other. I wouldn't wanna hear that bullshit either.

"G, I understand what you're saying but you can't expect her to sit there and be belittled by someone in her own house." DW spoke.

Finally, he says something important.

"THANK YOU, DW!" Keyarra said.

"BUT, at the same time, Keyarra, you can't disrespect G, in her house either. There are a million other things you could've said, besides that."

"Yeah, I guess. I'm sorry G."

"I'm teaching these kids that you have to think before you react, Derek. But yes, I see your point." GG stated.

"You gotta admit…that was funny." Matthew said, as tried to hold in his laughter.

"I almost lost it." I added.

The table erupted into laughter except for GG, of course.

"What y'all laughing at?" Derek asked, as he walked back in the house.

"How you need to keep your girlfriend on a leash." I answered.

"I told G that this was a bad idea." Derek said, shaking his head.

"How you get her to leave so fast?" Matthew asked.

"She knows I don't play those type of games with her."

"I don't know why you're with someone who constantly disrespects your family." I fussed.

"Kill the noise, Tia; I just won't bring her around. It wasn't my idea anyway."

"What kind of relationship is that? You can't bring her around your family because of what?" GG asked, concerned.

"I don't know G, and quite frankly, I don't care."

"Well, you should!" GG replied.

"I'm sorry you can't bring your beloved girlfriend around because of me." Keyarra said sincerely, but with a hint of sarcasm.

Derek smiled.

"It's cool Key, it's for the best."

I noticed the eye contact that they held for a few seconds. Derek's eyes gave him away every time. They'll tell you how he is feeling, and I've seen these eyes before; they were flirty eyes.

"What time are we taking pictures tomorrow?" DW asked.

"Do we really have to do that, still?" I groaned.

"Hush your mouth. Tina and Kiara took your pictures every 1st day of school and every last day of school. We've kept that up the entire time and we surely aren't stopping now." GG fussed.

I just rolled my eyes.

"It's the last time, Ti. It'll be fine." Matthew said.

"I'm not sure about all that. My 1st day of college, my dad took pictures of me because GG made him." Derek laughed.

"You damn right." GG confirmed.

We all laughed and continued our dinner with no issues.

"Last one I promise." GG said, as she continued to take pictures. For the last 15 minutes GG made us take group shots, single shots, and whatever else she could think of. She was just as bad as Sharin was when we were in OC.

We were in an apartment parking lot, directly across the street from the school.

"G, my feet are starting to hurt, and the bell is ringing in a few minutes." I lied.

They really weren't but I was tired of this photoshoot.

"Well princess Tia, nobody told you to wear stilettos to school."
Matthew teased.
"They aren't stilettos dummy, they're wedges."
"Same thing." he shrugged.
"No, they're not." I fussed.
I had on a pair of, "Alaïa", black strapped wedges. I also had on a
pink skater skirt with a black shirt that read, "She doesn't even go
here", in pink. "Mean Girls", was my 3rd favorite movie.
"Stop that back and forth." GG said. "Ok babies, have a great 1st
day." she continued.
"We will." Keyarra and I said, in unison.
She hugged us both, but she held on to Keyarra and whispered
something in her ear. Keyarra smiled and said, "I promise", then
kissed GG on the cheek. I walked over to Derek, and grabbed my
tote bag that will be one of my many bookbags.
"You sure you don't need me to walk you class to class?" he asked
jokingly.
"No, I think I'll be fine."
"Ard, you know big bro got you." he said, as he stuck his fist out.
I cracked up laughing.
"Stop it, we haven't done that in forever." I laughed.
"Don't leave me hanging."
I bumped fists with him, and we blew it up, like we did when were
kids. It was supposed to be our, "secret", handshake.
"Have a good day, baby sister."
"Thank you," I said, with an eye roll.
"You not gonna be happy until they fall out your big ass head."
"Shut up."
"You ready?" Keyarra asked when she came and stood next to
me.
"Yup."
"Have a good day Keyarra." Derek said.
He was giving her those eyes again.
"Thank you." she said, shyly.
She was trying to avoid looking at him.

"Keyarra, I forgot to give you your physical paperwork from the doctors." GG called out from the car.

Keyarra walked away towards the car. Derek followed her with his eyes; he looked almost like he was in a trance. I snapped in front of his face.

"Helloooo. earth to Derek."

"What?" he said, as he turned his attention back to me.

"What the fuck is up with you and the way you been looking at her." I asked, quietly.

"I'm not looking at her no specific way."

"That's bullshit. You be winking at her and giving her those damn sex eyes that you give bitches."

"Sex eyes? That's a new one." He laughed.

"I'm serious, Derek. You like her or something?"

"Naw, you know I'm just a natural flirt. And in case you haven't noticed, Keyarra fine as hell. So, I'm just admiring her." he said, with a smile.

I didn't believe him, but I don't have time to press the issue any further.

"Ok, I'm ready." Keyarra said, as she re-joined us. "Derek, what are you looking at?" she laughed.

I looked back at him, and he was staring straight up into the sky. *I can't stand his ass.*

"Tia said I can't look at you, so I'm looking at the clouds instead."

"You are such a clown." I sneered.

I grabbed Keyarra's hand, and we made our way across the street to the school.

"Ok, so what do you usually do before the bell rings?" I asked her.

"To be real...I'm never here this early."

"Girl...so, what we just gonna stand here?"

"We only have 10 minutes; I can walk you to your homeroom." she suggested.

"Fine."

We made our way through the crowded halls. A lot of people said, "hey", and gave hugs to Keyarra on our way; mostly guys though.

"Well, aren't you popular among the boys." I teased.

240

"Not really. Those are mainly football and basketball players, so I know them from the games and stuff."

"I thought you only did football cheerleading?"

"I do, but Rin does year-round; so, I went to most of the games last winter, just to support her and Chris."

"Well, I'll be right next to you this year."

"I didn't think you'd be caught dead at a school event."

"Stop trying to make me out to be stuck up. I'm not. I wanted to but at my other schools I didn't have any friends, so that's why I never went."

I really did try to make friends in Cali, but the shit never worked out, so I just stayed to myself.

"I'm sorry Ti, I wasn't trying to make it sound that way. We'll have a lot of fun this year. You're gonna do everything you wanted to do here, that you couldn't do out there…. maybe you can try out for cheerleading."

"Alright now, slow your roll. I wouldn't go that far." I laughed.

"You don't wanna be my little cheerleader?"

I felt an arm go around my waist and the weight of a person on my shoulders, but I knew exactly who it was. I turned around and saw the boy who already has me in a chokehold, and I haven't even had the dick yet. He had on a pink Ralph Lauren tee, blue skinny jeans, and a pair of high-top white dunks. His defined curls and perfect shape-up made him look good enough to eat.

"I can from the side lines." I responded.

"As long as you're there. Whats up, Key."

"Hey Chris, I like your shirt. Pink looks good on you."

"Ahh thanks, I got this for my baby. It's her favorite color." he said, as he looked down at me with a boyish grin.

I felt myself blushing.

"Did you decide to surprise me at my homeroom?" I asked.

"Naw, I'm in this homeroom." he smiled.

I pushed him slightly and he laughed.

"You lied to me!"

"I was trying to surprise your mean ass."

"Awww, at least you know someone in your homeroom now." Keyarra smiled.

"I can hardly contain myself." I said, sarcastically.

"Tia, don't be a jerk. My homeroom is down the hall. I'll see you at lunch."

"Bye." I replied.

I looked back at Chris who was still smiling.

"I want to kiss you so bad right now." he admitted.

"Well, I guess you'll just have to do that after school now, won't you."

"That's a little too long." he said, slowly leaning down.

"Hi Christian." this girl greeted appearing out of nowhere beside us.

Chris closed his eyes and dropped his head, I heard him mutter "shit" under his breath.

"What's up Lisa?" he replied, dryly.

"How's your brother?" she asked, totally ignoring the fact that I was standing there.

"You know he is fine. Lisa this is Tia, Tia this is Lisa."

"Ohhhh, so this is the IG girl." she said, smartly.

Lord, I know this a test; I don't want to beat this girl's ass. Give me the strength.

"Nice to meet you." I said, as nicely as I could muster up.

"Likewise; thank you for the other day, Chris. I really needed that. See you in homeroom." she remarked slyly and walked into the class.

I cocked my head to the side and looked at him, indignantly.

"I know how that sounds but it's not what you think." He tried to explain but the bell rang.

I walked past him, not even waiting to hear the rest of what he had to say. I heard him groan as he followed behind me.

"Alright roomies find a seat, then I will take roll." the energetic teacher exclaimed.

Students scrambled to find a free seat.

"Yo Legs, over here." a boy called to Chris, from across the room.

"My boys saved us a seat." he said.

Although I really didn't want to sit next to him anymore, I didn't have a choice. Chris pulled my seat out and I reluctantly sat down.

"Look at Legs, pulling girls' seats out and shit." This one skinny boy teased; he was cute but not my type.

"Tia, this is Fatman and Nelly. I play football with them." Chris introduced.

"Hi." I said, sweetly.

"You the girl that is about to get Chris kicked off the team for missing practices." Fatman pointed, as he snacked on some chips at 8 in the morning.

I looked over at Christian and he was trying to avoid my eye contact.

"I've been working bitch boy, mind your business." He snapped.

"You are just full of surprises today, aren't you."

"Chill Ti, I'll talk to you about it later." He responded.

"Whatever…. why do they call you Fatman?" I asked, as I turned my attention back to him.

"You see why, he a big ass man baby." Nelly joked.

Fatman was a little chubby, but I wouldn't say fat.

"But I'm a tank, you not getting shit past me when I'm on the line."

"Yous a mutha fucking lie. Legs just scored on your ass the other day." Nelly argued.

"That's cus he a tall ass, freak of nature."

I couldn't help but laugh at their banter.

"I would feel more comfortable calling you by your name."

"You can call me, Rae, but ONLY you." He said.

"Nice to meet you, Rae and you too, Nelly." I smiled.

"Yeah, I would be missing practice for this one too." Nelly said, nodding his head in approval, throwing up the "ok" signal towards Chris.

"Shut the fuck up." Chris spat.

"Tia Williams?" the teacher called out.

"Here." I said.

I heard snickering and I looked over at Lisa and some other girls who were looking in my direction. I breathed in my nose and out my mouth slowly. Chris leaned over and whispered in my ear.

"Ignore them, Tia."

"Who is she?"

"I'll tell you later."

"Tell me now." I demanded.

Chris just shook his head in defeat.

"My ex-girlfriend, we broke up last year. We've barely spoken until she saw all of us hanging out this summer; then she started blowing me up." he explained, quietly.

"What did she need the other day?"

"She needed me to change her tire. That's all; so, what she said was just to get under your skin. She does shit like that."

"She's the last girl you've had sex with?"

"Yeah."

I rolled my eyes and shook my head. I wanted to have a good year; I don't want any beef with anyone, especially over a boy.

"Don't worry, she won't be a problem, Ti-baby." Chris reassured. He quickly kissed the tip of my nose and I smiled.

"She better not be."

I looked over at her and she looked every bit of pissed. I smirked at her and leaned back in my seat.

Game on bitch!

I was finally halfway through my day, and it wasn't as bad as I thought it would be. I was waiting outside the cafeteria for Keyarra. Katrina walked past me and rolled her eyes.

"I'll tell my brother about that." I called out after her.

She looked over her shoulder and threw up her middle finger. I just laughed at her miserable ass.

"Heyyy Ti, how's it going?" Keyarra asked.

"So far so good." I shrugged.

"Well, that's better than bad. C'mon, I think Rin in here already."

"KE-KE!" Sharin yelled.

The cafeteria was noisy, but you could hear her loud and clear.
"I think that's her over there." I joked.
"You think?" she laughed.
We made our way over to the table, where Rin had already had her lunch. It looked like a taco salad or something.
"Hey Rin." Keyarra spoke.
"Hey girl. Ti-Ti, how's your first day so far?"
"Not terrible." I replied.
"Oh good, we have our next 2 classes together." she reminded me, enthusiastically.
We had gone over our schedules several times and she was more excited than the last, every time she thought about us having classes together.
"Are you getting lunch?" Keyarra asked.
"Mmmm, I think imma just get snacks or something."
"That's what I usually do."
"Yeah, Keyarra is too uppity to eat lunch." Sharin teased.
"No, I'm not. Just eating home cooked meals like G's and Matt's, makes you want to pass on anything else."
"Very true." I agreed.
I followed Keyarra over to the vending machines. There was an assortment of snacks to pick from.
"That yellow machine in the hallway, was that candy?" I asked.
"Yeah, they have M&Ms and shit."
"Ok, can you get me a water. I really want chocolate."
"I can walk you."
"Girl I'm fine. I'll meet you at the table."
"Ok."
I walked out into the hallway and made my way through the sea of students, until I got to the vending machines.
"Well, you look like you need someone to show you around." I heard a male voice say behind me.
I turned around and a brown skinned boy, with a low cut and 2 "diamond" earrings in his ear was standing there. He had locs in that didn't touch his neck yet; he was taller than me, but I could tell he wasn't quite 6 feet.

"I'm Darren, and you are?"

"Tia."

"Hello Tia, are you new?"

"ish." I simply replied.

"It's nice to meet you. I would love for you to take me up on my offer and show you around."

"Around the school? Naw, I'm good. I came to the open house." I said, as I proceeded to walk away.

I heard his footsteps behind me still.

"Well, I um can show you around my room one day."

I turned around quickly.

"Excuse me?" I said, with an attitude.

"Aye, everything ok?" Nelly asked, coming out of nowhere.

"Yeah, everything good. I just was offering to show the new girl around." Darren said, with a menacing smile.

"She good. This Legs' girl."

Darren's expression changed.

"His girl? Since when Mr. Holier than thou, have a girl?"

"He got a new one after you fucked his last one. C'mon Tia, let's go." Nelly sneered, as he guided me back towards the cafeteria.

"Stay away from him. He's a fucking weirdo."

"Thank you, I'll keep that in mind."

"Tell Legs he owes me one."

"I will."

I was looking at my phone on my way to the table, when I bumped shoulders with someone.

"Oh, I'm sorry, I wasn't looking." I apologized.

"Well next time, maybe you should." Lisa hissed, with a mug.

I took the chance to really look at her, she was going for a preppy look with her spiral curled ponytail and pleated skirt. Her cropped denim blazer and knee-high socks were out of season but cute. Overall, she was pretty with her copper-colored skin, slightly slanted eyes, and button nose, but her attitude stank as hell.

"Girl bye, how about you watch where you're going next time."

She looked me up and down and laughed.

"There is no way Christian is really into your cheap looking ass."

"Cheap? Girl, my nails cost more than your entire fit. Let's try again."

"Yeah whatever, I'm only gonna tell you this once. Stay away from Christian. We are getting back together, so just move along. He's a good boy and doesn't need some ghetto ass barbie distracting him."

I stepped a little closer to her.

"That was cute…. Now you listen to me. What myself and Christian do, is none of your concern. If he decides to lower his standards again, then you will hear from him. But until then, I highly suggest you stay the fuck away from me. And this is me being nice; I promise you don't want to see me when I'm mean."

We just stared at each other.

"Well Lisa I see you've met, Tia." Rin said, as she stood next to me, propping her forearm up on my shoulder.

Lisa peered over at her and rolled her eyes.

"I think you should keep it moving cousin, Chrissy not playing about this one." Rin pointed.

Cousin?

I wasn't familiar with this Sharin; this was the most serious I've heard her sound since I've met her.

"Fuck you, Sharin." Lisa hissed.

She turned around and walked out of the cafeteria.

"You good? I thought we was gonna have to beat her ass in here." Sharin laughed.

She went right back to her silly self.

"Cousin?" I questioned.

"Yeah girl, we share the same amah. Our moms are sisters. But to be real, we have never been cool. She acts like Hillary Banks, and I can't stand that bougie shit."

"I guess Chris likes it, if they were together."

"He was blinded by pussy." she joked.

We went back over to the table and joined, Keyarra.

"Girllll, I was about to be on that ass when I seen her in your face." Keyarra said.

I laughed.

"I had Ti-Ti back." Sharin bragged.

"I appreciate y'all. It's some bold ass kids in here because the one boy just offered to take me to his room, when I went the vending machine."

"Who??" they asked in unison.

"I think he said his name was, Darren."

"Ain't that about a bitch." Sharin said, shaking her head.

"What?"

"Lil miss innocent Lisa, cheated on Chris with Darren." Keyarra revealed.

"Straight up hoe." Sharin said out loud.

She had a look of disgust on her face.

"Is that why they broke up?" I asked.

"Yeah, but Chris was trying to work it out with her; but the rumor is her and Darren were still sneaking around." Keyarra explained.

"She broke my best friend's heart." Sharin stated.

Her face was getting a little red, I can tell it was still a sensitive topic.

"Well, is he over her?" I asked.

"Yeah, once Darren screwed Lisa over, she tried to come crawling back, but Chris wasn't having it." Sharin said.

"I really don't want to be involved in this fucked up love triangle or whatever it is." I voiced.

"Trust me, Ti-Ti, Chris not sweating that girl."

"Yeah, he not. And Darren probably just got wind that you and Chris might be together, so he just trying his hand. He's a creep, he will stick his little dick in anything." Keyarra said.

"How you know it's little?" I asked, with a raised brow.

"He showed me on the bus one day, on our way to a game. I'm so glad he got kicked off the team last year."

"He has showed every girl that damn half of a pinky." Sharin laughed.

We all burst out in laughter. The bell rang and we gathered our things to get ready for our next period.

"Let's go Ti-Ti. Off to the wonderful world of AP calculus." Sharin said.

We linked arms and made our way to class.

I was outside waiting for Chris to come out. He had texted me before school was over to meet him out front. He wanted to see me before he went to practice.

"Hi Ti-baby, how was the rest of your day?" he asked when he approached me.

He was in his practice football uniform, and I instantly got turned on. I had never seen him in it before and he looked damn good. I was gawking at him.

"Tia, did you hear me?"

"Um yeah, it was good. I like seeing you in uniform."

He smiled, bashfully.

"For real? This not even the real one, wait until you see the official one."

"I won't, if you are missing practices. What's up with that? I hope what Rae said wasn't true. I don't want you missing practices because of me."

"It's not all the way true, Ti. Yeah, I skipped out on some to chill with you but mainly because I had to work. We have two a day practices and the coach knows I work to help my mom. So, he don't be on my ass like that." he explained.

"Well, don't miss any more because of me; the word around the school is, Legs is a beast on the football field and basketball court."

"Naw, they bluffing. I'm just alright." he smiled.

"I'll just have to see for myself then. But I do have to ask you something else." I said, nervously.

"What is it?"

"Lisa told me y'all are getting back together. Why did she say that?"

Chris sucked his teeth.

"Man, that girl is crazy. I'm not worried about her, Ti. To be real, at one point I would've done just about anything for her, but she did me grimy. So, fuck her. I told you she won't be a problem."

"Chris, I really don't want to be in any shit with anybody."

"And I promise you, you won't be."

"Ok I'm trusting you; one more thing."

"What?"

"Nelly, said you owe him one."

"For what?" he asked, as he furrowed his brows.

"That guy, Darren, approached me today."

"And said what?"

Christian instantly got angry, he clenched his jaw and narrowed his eyes.

"He offered to show me around school, but Nelly stepped in and took me back to the cafeteria."

I decided to leave out the bedroom part.

"Listen Tia, try to avoid him. We don't fuck with each other."

"Because of Lisa?" I questioned.

He looked at me like he was trying to figure out how I knew that.

"Yes. But I'm not mad because I still want her or anything like that. We were boys since middle school, and he got with my girl. So, it's fuck him too."

"I understand."

"I gotta go Ti, I'll call you when I get out of practice."

He seemed a little down now. I reached for his arm before he could walk away.

"What about that kiss?"

He smiled at me, put his helmet down, then wrapped me in his arms and kissed me.

"Aye, cut that shit out." Nelly called out from the parking lot.

Him and some other players were making their way across the lot, down to the field for practice.

"Stop being a hater." Chris yelled back.

Nelly just shook his head and continued with the rest of his team.

"Have a good practice, Legs." I teased.

"You don't have to call me that, Tia." He laughed.

"Everyone else does."

"Didn't you tell me, you're not everyone?" he said with a slight tilt of his head.

I couldn't help but laugh.

"Still stands."

"You know what I rather you call me?"

"What?"

"Your boyfriend."

My heart started beating fast and I think my stomach dropped a little. I've never actually had a boyfriend before, so I was taken by surprise.

"You don't have to answer right now."

He leaned down and kissed me again.

"Bye, Ti-baby."

"Bye, Chris." I smiled, shyly.

I watched as he walked away; I felt a hint of sadness. I knew he wouldn't have as much free time like he did over the summer, between school, work, and practices. Chris, was also an honor student, so he took his schoolwork pretty seriously. I wasn't sure where I would fit into his world. I can't see where he would have time for a relationship.

"Chris and Tia sitting in a tree, k-i-s-s-i-n-g." Sharin and Keyarra sang behind me.

They were coming from turning in their paperwork for cheerleading.

"Y'all have to grow up." I said shaking my head.

"You and Chrissy are just so cute; y'all will win cutest couple for sure." Sharin gushed.

"We are not even a couple."

"Well, why aren't y'all yet, it's been a few months." Keyarra asked.

I wasn't ready to tell them that Chris just asked me to be his girlfriend because then the questions about why I didn't answer would follow. I was about to give them some bullshit, when my real answer pulled up. Matthew was blasting Jay Z's, "Glory"; he was the biggest HOV fan.

"Get y'all non-walking asses in here." he yelled, from the window.

Sharin got in the front seat, while me and Keyarra climbed in the back.

Sharin turned the music down.

"Hey boo."

"What's up. How was y'all 1st day?" he asked.

"Good." we all said in unison.

We all giggled after; we were really becoming 3 peas in a pod.

"That's what's up."

"Tia and Chris are going to win cutest couple." Sharin boasted with excitement.

"I didn't realize they were a couple."

"Not yet, but they will be."

"Hm." Matt hummed.

"Sharin, shut up; Matt don't care about that." Keyarra fussed.

He looked at me through his rearview mirror and I could see the irritation in his eyes. Matthew and I weren't seeing each other as much as he would have liked because I opted to spend my free time with Chris, when he had it. I was also starting to feel a little guilty about this entire situation. I know Matthew and Sharin were sleeping together and for me to sit here and call her my friend, but sleeping with him as well, was not cool, no matter if I had him first or not. Chris just asked me to be his girlfriend, but if I did that, then sex would be out of the picture for a while; and I'm not sure if I was ready to give that up yet. Ugh, I need to talk to Carmen!

MATTHEW

Tia was sleeping peacefully on my chest, after yet another disappearing act from her ass, but I finally convinced her to let me come over last night. Derek took Katrina to NY for the weekend to go to some upscale events with DW. Sharin, Keyarra, and Chris had a game around 12 today so Tia was planning to attend that later. Since Chris was at work last night, she decided not to attend the sleepover that Rin and Keyarra had because she had a project due on Monday, so she wanted one night to focus on that, but when I heard she was alone, I called her and slid right over here. She got some work done but not much. She stirred a little in her sleep until her eyes opened, I smiled at her, but she didn't return it.

"Good morning beautiful."
"Good morning. What time is it?"
"A little past 8."
"Ok, I'm going to start getting ready." she said, as she got up. She wrapped herself up in the sheets and sat on the side of the bed.
"Why so early? The game doesn't start til 12."

"JV starts at 10. Keyarra and Sharin are going to be there, so I wanna sit with them before they go cheer. Sharin is leading since hoe ass is away and she needs support."

"I may stop pass later."

"Hm ok, I know she would like that."

"Chris sitting in the stands with yall before the game?"

"I don't see why that matters."

Tia was being a little distant with me, the sex didn't even feel the same last night. It's like physically she was there, but her mind was somewhere else.

"It doesn't. I'm just saying."

She didn't say anything, she just walked to her closet and looked through her clothes. I sat up and looked at my phone. Rin Facetimed me twice and I had a message from my dad asking me to stop by the shop at some point today.

"I was thinking I could take you to breakfast, then I can drop you off at the school." I offered.

"No thank you, I can just take an uber."

"Tia, what's going on?"

"Nothing is going on." she responded, nonchalantly.

She was still rummaging through her closet.

"That's bullshit because you have still been ducking and dodging me. I know you dealing with Chris, but y'all not together; so, I'm not sure why you are acting shady towards me."

Tia took a deep breath and turned around.

"Matthew, do you ever plan to make me your girlfriend?"

"Tia, you know..."

"I'm not ready for a relationship." she said, finishing my sentence. "Well, I am. Chris asked me to be his girlfriend a couple weeks ago and I haven't given him an answer yet." she continued.

"Why?"

"Because of you. I needed to figure out my shit with you, first."

"Sounds like you have it figured out."

"I have, now I'm asking for you to let me go."

"I can't do that, Tia."

"Yes, you can! Matthew, you don't want a relationship and that's fine. I'm done begging you. To be honest with you, if you asked me now, I wouldn't even say yes because that's how much I like, Christian."

I was silent; I wasn't sure what the fuck to say next. The thought of Tia leaving me alone completely, was fucking my mind up right now.

"Now, I'm begging you to let me go. I want to be with Christian, but it's not fair to him or me that you still have me in your back pocket."

At this point she had tears coming down her face. My intention was to never hurt Tia, but I guess I could see how I was. I got up to put on my clothes. I walked over to her and kissed her, for what might be the last time.

"I'm sorry if I hurt you, Tia. I didn't mean to."

Tia just smiled slightly and dried her eyes; she looked a little relieved and that shit broke me, even more.

"It's ok, thank you. You'll always a special place in my heart, Matt. That won't ever change." she said, sincerely.

I just nodded my head and left the room. I felt like I just lost my best friend, and I would be lying if I said this shit didn't hurt. I got in my car and started banging at my steering wheel, until my hands hurt; I'm surprised the airbag didn't pop out. My head was resting on my steering wheel, when my phone started ringing with a FT. I did not feel like picking that shit up, but it was Rin, and she gets worried when people don't answer her calls after a few times.

"Yeah Rin." I answered.

"Are you ok?" she asked, concerned.

"Yeah, I'm cool." I said, dryly.

"You sure?"

"I just said yes."

"Um ok. I guess I'll see you later tonight?"

"I'll let you know."
I was in a bad mood, and I didn't see myself being out of it any time soon. I didn't want to take my anger out on Sharin, by lashing out. We had just got back on good terms a few weeks ago, after the beach incident. Everything was going good; it felt like when we first started messing around, without the pressure of a relationship and shit. I had to admit, I missed her crazy ass.

"Did I do something?" she asked, in a sad voice.
I swiped my hand down my face.
"No Sharin, you did not. I just want some time alone."
I tried my best to say it as nicely as possible but the look on her face let me know her feelings were hurt.
"Ok, I understand. Um, just call me whenever."
"Ard, have a good game and good luck with the squad, you're gonna do well."
"Thank you."
I didn't even say bye, before I hung up. I just sat in my car for a little while; I wasn't sure what to do or where to go. Then it popped into my head that my dad wanted me to stop by the shop. Work would keep my mind busy. I started my truck and made my way to the west side of the city.

"What up boy." My pop greeted, as he dapped me up.
"Nothing much."
"You good?" he asked, as he looked at me curiously.
I was never good at hiding how I was feeling.
"Yeah. Did you need help with something?"
"I was putting an engine together, and I thought maybe you might want to watch. I remember you telling me to let you know if I ever got another job like this."
"Cool. Yeah, I want to help, if I can."
"Bet."
For the next hour, my dad taught me the ins and outs of this engine. Tia was still on my mind heavy, but this helped.
"Son, have you been fighting?"

"No, why you say that?"

He nodded towards my now swollen and bruised knuckles.

"Oh um, naw, I wasn't fighting."

I flexed my hand and tried to make a fist, but I winced at the pain.

"What happened then?"

"I hit something...a few times."

"What was it?"

"My steering wheel." I revealed apprehensively.

My dad was big on me controlling my anger.

"You gonna fuck that car up like you did the first one, and imma tell Derek's ass don't get you shit else." He fussed.

"I got in an accident, and you know that."

"Yeah whatever!"

I just stood silently, trying to settle my rising anger.

"Why were you hitting the steering wheel, Matt?"

"I was mad."

"No shit sherlock! Why were you mad?"

"Tia...she ended things with me today."

My father chuckled. I told him about Tia when I first lost my virginity. I couldn't tell Derek, so he was the next best thing.

"I told your hardheaded ass that she was going to do that. She is just like her mother, doesn't put up with bullshit. I'm surprised she dealt with you as long she did but that's only because you popped her cherry."

I just listened to him talk, I can tell he was about to give me an earful.

"You sitting around here sulking and in your feelings. Bitches come and go, that's just how it is."

"Aye man, don't be calling her no bitch." I fumed.

"Shut your sensitive ass up. Unless you about to go get her back, which I know your stubborn ass not, so shut the hell up."

Mark was hard up and said what was on his mind most of the time. He was in juvie, then prison, throughout his life. A year after I was born, he got locked up again; he got out when I was around

5, but my mom didn't let him around much. He didn't try too hard either, in my opinion. When I moved in with him for a while, we got close but there were certain traits about him that I didn't like. For one he could be insensitive and if I ever had kids, I didn't want them to have an angry or inconsiderate father.

"If you want Tia back, go get her and don't take no for a got damn answer. I don't like the word no and neither should you! But don't bullshit around this time; and if not, stick with that rice eating girl, she's cute."

I sighed and shook my head.

"Stop calling Sharin, the rice eating girl."

"She Asian, ain't she?"

He could be ignorant as fuck too. I felt my phone ringing again, it was Keyarra.

"What's up, Key?"

"Nothing, I was just seeing if you were ok. Rin mentioned that you didn't look well earlier."

I could hear and see all the people in the background, cheering and yelling. I couldn't help but wonder if Tia was nearby.

"Aww, look at you caring about me and shit." I joked.

"Boy shut up; I'm about get on the track, but I just wanted to check in real quick."

"Hello, Keyarra." my dad said, coming behind me and into the frame.

Keyarra's face dropped a little but that wasn't anything out the ordinary. She only liked DW, she didn't want any other father figures in her life.

"Hey." she said.

"I hope you're being a good girl, unlike your brother."

"Mm hm, ok Matt, I gotta go. I'll talk to you later."

"Ard Key, love you."

"Love you too."

We ended the call and I put my phone back in my pocket.

"How is she doing?" Mark asked.

"She cool. A lot better this past year than the past 2 years. She was the damn devil child."

"That's good. I bet it's the dick she is getting from that mulatto boy."

"Aye aye, I don't want to hear about my sister getting dick from anyone." I said annoyed.

"I'm just saying." he shrugged.

I shook my head.

"I'm done with this shit for today, we can go back to my house and get drunk but if you cry imma bust you in the head." he said, as he cleaned off his tools and packed them up.

"I'm not gonna cry asshole but yeah that's a bet; I need a drink."

I was going to drink my pain away for the rest of the weekend and try my hardest to forget about Tia. I fumbled her and I'll just have to live with that.

HOMECOMING
KEYARRA

It was almost 7 in the morning, and I was around the corner with Derek, in his truck. I was straddling him, while we tongued each other down. Since we kissed that day in the kitchen, we saw each other at least 3-4 times a week but we talked or texted every day.
"Matthew, Tia, and Rin are going to wake up and wonder where the hell I am."
"And I told you to tell them you took a walk."
"It's the end of October, they're not gonna believe that."
"You the one who came out here in these little ass shorts, like you was ready to get some dick or something; so yeah, they might not." he said, as he caressed my bare thigh.
"Shut up. I didn't know you were gonna come this early, so I grabbed the first thing I saw."
"You said G went to go help set up for homecoming, so it was the perfect time."
"Mm hm, I'm about to get ready to go back."
"Why you acting like you in a rush to get away from me?"
His grip around my waist became tighter.

"I'm not, I just don't wanna get caught up."

"Yeah, whatever. How you feel about this being your last home game?"

"I don't feel any way." I shrugged, as I played with his short curly ringlets.

"Why?"

"Because I don't."

"C'mon Key, it's your senior year! Your last homecoming and you're a cheerleader. You gotta be excited or sad or something." he pushed.

I was starting to get uncomfortable; if I could forget the last few years, then I would in a heartbeat.

"Derek you're trying to get in my head again, and I told you, I don't like that. I'm about to dip." I voiced, trying to get off his lap.

The past few weeks, Derek and I really got to know each other a lot better but there were a few times that I could tell he was trying to pick my brain. He would ask questions but in a certain type of way, like he was trying to catch me in a lie or discover new information about me.

"Chill chill, I'm not trying to get in your head. I just…. feel like you kind of cold. You act like you don't care about anything."

"I care about my family, that's it."

"Ok, but what about you? You gotta care about yourself too."

I felt like I was about to break down and cry; he can see right through my bullshit wall, that I was trying to keep up. The truth is, I don't care about myself and that's because I hate myself. I can barely look in a mirror without the thought of smashing it into a million pieces; that's how disgusted I am with my own reflection. Derek made me feel safe though, I wanted to throw my arms around him and tell him everything, but I can't, so I needed to get his mind on something else.

"You seem to care about me enough." I whispered in his ear, before I nibbled on his lobe.

He inhaled deeply and I felt his manhood grow under me once again.

"Mmmm, I've heard that before." he said lowly.

"From who?"

"Doesn't matter."

I turned to face him, and he was biting his bottom lip again.

"You bite that a lot."

I used my thumb to gently pull it from under his teeth.

"I wanna try." I said, slowly getting closer to his lips.

I bit down on his bottom lip, and I watched as his eyes flashed. When they did that, it turned me on but made me nervous at the same time, I was never sure if that was a good or bad thing. I sucked on his lip while I returned his heated gaze. Derek moved his hands to my hips and started to move me back and forth slowly. I haven't made myself cum on him again since the beach, but I wanted to so bad because I got that throbbing feeling every time, I was around him. I started moving a little faster as those tingles started to creep up again. Derek and I were still staring at each other, our foreheads touching, and our lips were close.

"When you gonna let me taste how wet you are?" he asked, huskily.

"Never." I teased.

"Never say never, Key."

I felt the vibration of his phone in his pocket against my inner thigh.

"You wanna get that?" I whimpered lowly.

I was close.

"Naw." he said, right before his mouth covered mine again.

I moaned a little louder as I started to cum; I felt the vibration on my thigh once again and the sensation was adding to my pleasure. As I came hard, I broke our kiss and bit down on Derek's bottom lip again, but with some more pressure; he groaned at the slight pain that I inflicted. I released his lip and connected our lips again. I couldn't get enough of kissing him, there was a lot of sparks every time we kissed, and I would always be in such a good mood after spending time with him; even if it was just for a little bit. I felt the vibration from his pocket, yet again.

"I think someone is trying to reach you." I said, as I leaned back.

Derek just stared at me; I couldn't really tell what he was thinking.

Soon as the vibrating stopped, it started right back again. He still didn't move, so I dug in his pocket and retrieved his phone; it was Katrina, facetiming him.

"It's Katrina, you want me to answer it?" I asked, sarcastically.

"Go ahead." He answered, coolly.

"Derek, answer this damn phone."

He took the phone.

"Yes?" he said, as he lazily took his eyes off me and brought them to the screen.

"Where the fuck did you go?" She yelled.

"First, lower your fucking voice and didn't you tell me to leave? So that's what I did." He spoke, seriously.

"Derek, I didn't mean it." She whined.

"Well, you shouldn't have said it then."

"Please come back, I want you at the game."

"I will be there."

"Nooo, I want you to arrive with me." She continued to whine.

I rolled my eyes; Katrina, was a spoiled little bitch, and I can't stand the sound of her voice.

"I'll think about it, let me call you back."

"DEREK!" She protested loudly.

"What did I just say about your voice?" He asked, calmly.

Derek has this subtle dominance about him; he didn't have to yell to get his point across. It was all in his tone; it made you listen to him. It could make you scared, nervous or even horny, in some cases.

"I'm sorry, why are still in your car?"

"I'll call you back." he said, before he ended the call.

Jefe was indeed a good nickname for him!

"Are you happy that I answered the phone?"

"Didn't make me a difference." I shrugged.

"Uh huh, come here." he said as he tried to pull me forward, but I pulled back.

"What's wrong?"

"So, that's why you came to see me? Because y'all got in a fight?" Derek squinted at me.

"No, I was going to anyway, but she started tripping; so, I didn't have to lie to leave, I just left." He clarified.

"What was she tripping about?"

"A watch."

"A watch?"

"Yes, a watch."

"What…. she wanted a new one or something?"

"Naw. For someone who doesn't like to be asked questions, you sure are asking a lot."

"I'm just curious at what she could have done, that made you leave at 6 in the morning."

"I just told you; she was tripping."

"You going to go back?"

"I can't right now, since you came all over me."

I just rolled my eyes.

"I need to get ready for the game and you should go clean up before you go back to her." I spat, with a hint of an attitude.

I tried to get off him, but he grabbed me by my waist and pulled me forward with some force, I was still a little sensitive down there so the friction made me whimper lowly.

"What's wrong with you?"

"Nothing."

"It is, because your whole demeanor changed."

"It hasn't. May I go now?"

Derek smiled slightly, then released my waist. I got off him and went to open the door.

"I can drop you off, Keyarra."

"It's fine. I'd rather walk."

Before he could say anything else, I opened the door and hopped out. I made my way up the street; I folded my arms to try and warm myself up a little. These shorts and t-shirt were not a good idea for a chilly Oct morning, even though I preferred the colder months. I sped up a little and made it into the house. I walked into the kitchen to make some hot chocolate. I heard someone coming up the steps from G's room, but her car wasn't outside, so I was confused.

"And where the hell did you go?" Tia questioned, once she entered the kitchen.

"I went for a walk."

"A walk?" she asked, with a raised brow.

"Yeah. What you doing up?"

"I was making sure our dresses were still hanging."

"Girl, you have been obsessing over these dresses since school started." I said, as I started to prepare my hot chocolate.

"Because they need to look perfect."

"What needs to look perfect?" Sharin yawned, as she joined us in the kitchen.

"Our homecoming dresses." I answered.

A few weeks ago, we all went shopping for homecoming. Rin and I found our dresses at the Bloomingdale's outlet in Philly. Tia found hers in Saks, her favorite store. Mine was spaghetti strapped and silver, with glitter everywhere; I probably would be cleaning glitter off for weeks. It was tight and showcased my breast a lot, which GG was not a fan of at all. But I begged her for it, she only agreed to it if I wore a shawl. I said whatever I needed to, but I wasn't wearing that shit. Rin had a strapless fit and flare dress; the corset part was black, then kind of ombred into a reddish-purple color. It was really pretty and something about it just fit her personality; it was fun! Tia had a crimson red dress; it was also strapless and was made with satin material. It hugged her in all the right places; she gave off a very classic look, and she looked good as hell in it.

"She just wants to make sure our dresses shit on everyone else's." Sharin said.

"Exactly." Tia agreed.

Tia and Sharin liked attention, me on the other hand I was never a
fan. I didn't like all eyes on me. I really stepped out of my comfort
zone last year by re-joining the choir and taking on solos, also
becoming a cheerleader was never something I thought about,
but I wanted to try and enjoy life again. I wanted to feel like a
normal teenager, at least for my last year of high school.

"Are you making hot chocolate? I want some." Sharin asked.
"Yes."
"Y'all little family recipe is the best." she said, excitedly.
Our mothers used to make us this crock pot hot chocolate. They
would use milk and melt whole Hershey's chocolate bars. And the
secret ingredient was a dash of cinnamon; it was the best. GG
shared it with us after they passed. I made it the most, so GG
always kept Hershey's in the house.
"I haven't had that in forever." Tia said.
"I can make enough for you too." I smiled.
Tia smiled at me, but I could see the sadness in her eyes. We
missed our mothers terribly, and I knew something small like
making their hot chocolate would flood her with memories.
"Ke-Ke, where were you earlier?" Sharin asked.
"She went for a walk." Tia answered for me.
She squinted her eyes at me a little. A habit that her and her
brother clearly shared.
"Girl, it's cold as hell outside, and you went for a walk?" Sharin
questioned.
"Yup." I replied, keeping it short.
"I know you like the cold but going for a walk this early is insane."
Sharin continued.
Tia, just had her arms folded and continued to stare me down. I
prepared our cups and handed one to her and Rin.
"Are you ready to tell us what you were really doing?" Tia
questioned, as she blew on her hot chocolate.
Tia wasn't going to let this go so easily, so I had to think of
something. I don't think she would have a problem with whatever

Derek, and I were doing but it was a weird situation to explain; so, I preferred to keep it on the low for now.

"Ughh, fine. Tre and I were having sex in the car." I lied.

"WHAT?" Sharin screeched.

"Yeah, he wanted to have good luck sex for the game."

"Okayyyy, I'm here for it. Was it piss poor as usual?"

"Sharin!" I hollered.

I hadn't really shared with Tia too many details about Tre and I's relationship. To be honest, I don't think she likes him very much.

"Piss poor?" Tia questioned.

"You didn't tell her?" Sharin asked.

"No, she didn't, but she tends to keep secrets from me." Tia stated, seriously.

She could hold eye contact just like her brother as well, and the shit was making me nervous. I knew the keep secret's part held some more weight behind it. But it also had me thinking if Derek told her about us, since they are so close.

"Um, Tre isn't the best at...." I hesitated.

I was trying to find the right words, so it wouldn't sound so embarrassing.

"He not good with his dick girl." Sharin blurted out.

I rolled my eyes.

"You was beating around the bush." she shrugged.

"Why don't you teach him what you like? That's what me and my 1st did." Tia suggested.

"Yeah I tried, and it's just awkward."

"Try harder; no one deserves bad sex, certainly not us. We're too young for that."

Tia sipped her hot chocolate, and she closed her eyes for a quick second; when she re-opened, they were glossed over.

"This is really good, Key. I'm gonna go see what I can do about your glitter falling all over the damn place."

Before I could say anything, she disappeared downstairs.

"She ok?" Rin asked.

"I don't know, imma go check. I'll be upstairs in a few"

"Ok."

I went downstairs and stepped into GG's mini apartment. It was gold and white everywhere. Her sofa was white with gold pillows; she had gold lamps with white shades. It looked like a celebrity lived here; that's how upscale and classy it looked. Her bedroom was no different. It was luxurious. I entered the bedroom and heard sniffling. I rounded the corner and saw Tia, staring at the picture on the wall. It was the last family picture we all took together before the accident; all 7 of us were in it. We were only able to do that a few times, but each time was special.

"You ok, Ti?" I asked.

She jumped a little, so I guess she didn't hear me come down. She dried her eyes and turned her back to me a little.

"Oh, yeah yeah. I'm fine." she sniffled.

"No you're not." I said, as I approached her.

I turned her around to face me and she had tears running down her cheeks.

"Aw Ti, what's wrong?"

Her bottom lip trembled, she threw her arms around my neck, and I lost my balance; so, we collapsed onto the floor but that didn't stop her from sobbing.

"I miss them so much, Keyarra. They're supposed to be here. It's not fair." she cried.

I rubbed her back and let her cry for a little longer.

"I know Ti, I understand. It's hard and you're right, it's not fair. But you know, G tells us all the time that they are still here with us. I feel my mom's presence all the time."

"That's because you're living here. I feel like my memories are fading; we just didn't have enough time." she cried harder.

I felt like she was starting to hyperventilate.

"Tia, just breathe ok? I don't want you to pass out on me. You did that to me before, and my ass passed out too."

Tia started to laugh a little.

"Girl shut up; we were like 6."

"So what, that scared the shit outta me."

One day DW and my aunt Tina were arguing, of course about Tia. The boys were gone with GG, and we were in our rooms peeping out the door. I remember my aunt hitting DW, and him trying to, I guess restrain her. But it looked like they were fighting. Tia and I were both crying, but Tia said she felt like she couldn't breathe. Then she closed her eyes and fell to the floor. I ran to get help and when they were trying to help her, I passed right the hell out too. Tia and I really were like one person back then.

"We were so dramatic." Tia laughed.
"Yeah, but are you feeling a little better now."
"Yes, thank you. I'm still a little dramatic, if you haven't noticed." she joked.
"You're not, you miss your mom. But you know what I do? Just talk to her."
"Like out loud?"
"Yeah, I started doing that a while back and it helps. Yeah I don't get a reply the way I would like, but you don't get a direct response from God, right? But He still shows up. I like to believe it's the same with our mothers."
"I think I'll try it." she smiled.
"Good. Now Ti, I gotta go take a shower. I feel sticky."
"You're gross, get out my face." she laughed.
I got up and made my way out the room.
"Hey Key." she called out.
"Yeah?" I said, turning around.
"Thank you."
"Anytime. I told you Ti, I'm not going anywhere again. I got you." I smiled.

Two hours later, I was preparing to walk onto the field to sing the national anthem before the start of the homecoming games. I really didn't want to do this, but some ass clown told my cheer coach that I could sing, and she was married to whoever put all this game shit together. Next thing I know, I was begged to sing. If I find out it was Sharin, then that would be her ass.

"Are you ready?" my energetic cheer coach Courtney asked.

"Um, do I have a choice?" I asked, sarcastically.

"Nope, may I touch your hair." she smiled.

"Yes." I said, rolling my eyes.

Courtney was this perky, mid 20s, white woman, who graduated from Parkville. She was always really polite and would ask could she touch anyone's hair before she did it. She made some adjustments to this goofy ass, clip-on ponytail that I had on.

"Ok perf. Let me go see if they're ready for you."

I watched her literally skip off onto the field. I was talking myself down because I was nervous; I sang in church, not in front of half of the damn school.

"Nervous?" Derek asked.

He came out of nowhere, leaned up against the fence facing the field, like I was. He had on a black hoodie, jeans, and some black huaraches; even in casual wear, he oozed sex appeal. I could smell his cologne, and I was instantly turned on; even though I had been spending more time with him, his presence still made me nervous.

"Um, yeah a little."

"You know the words?"

"Yeah." I laughed.

"Ard then. You'll be fine."

"Thanks."

"So, what was up with your attitude earlier?" He asked looking over at me.

"I didn't have one."

"Keyarra, we lying to everyone else, but we don't have to lie to each other."

He was right. I don't even know what I had an attitude about. It's just something about him being with Katrina, that rubbed me the wrong way.

"I mean if you love a nigga already, then that's all you have to say." he joked.

"Oh shut up." I said, pushing his shoulder and laughing.

"But for real though, just be honest with me. Did I do something to make you upset?"

"No, you didn't."

"Then what was it?"

"I really don't know."

Derek sucked his teeth.

"This shit not gonna work Key, if you can't be real with me."

"I am, I really don't know."

"Yeah ok. I know you used to hiding how you feel but you don't have to do that with me, but imma leave it alone, for now."

Derek turned to face me fully and looked me up and down.

"I've said this before, but I like you in your uniform.... a lot." he stated, then running his tongue across his bottom lip.

"Thank you." I replied, avoiding eye contact.

"Yeah, you giving off different vibes than you were this morning. Biting my lip and shit."

"I think you liked it though." I quipped, finally looking up at him.

Derek just smiled but his eyes told me everything I needed to know.

"They're ready for you Keyarra." Courtney announced.

"Ok. Courtney this is Derek, Derek this is Courtney, my cheer coach."

He stuck his hand out to shake hers.

"Very nice to meet you."

"Nice to meet you as well. Let's go, Keyarra."

I went through the opening of the gate and walked with her.

"Good luck, Key." Derek called out.

I looked behind me and he winked. That will forever give me butterflies.

"Oh my God, Keyarra, he is so cute." she gushed, as she put her arm around my shoulder.

"You better stop, before I tell your wife."

"So, she would agree with me." she laughed.

"I'm sure."

"And you better not let Tre catch that boy looking at you like that; he looks like he wanna eat you up."

"Is it that obvious?"

"I mean, I only saw that small exchange but its clear you guys are feeling each other…. That's what y'all kids say, right? Feeling each other."

"Courtney please, you act like you so old." I laughed.

"I feel old but y'all keep my lively…. Ok, here."

She handed me a mic and gave me a thumbs up.

"You're gonna do amazing sweetie." she quoted, mimicking her favorite reality star, Kris.

"Girl byeeeee."

"Now would everyone stand for the singing of our National Anthem, by senior, Keyarra Devore." the announcer said.

I took the middle of the field and belted out the anthem. I got nervous as hell because it was eerily silent for a few seconds, so I thought I messed it up; then there was a sudden roar of applause and screams.

"KEYARRA, THAT WAS BEAUTIFUL, YOU REALLY DID DO AMAZING" Courtney yelled excitedly.

"Thank you."

I started to walk back to the sidelines, but Courtney stopped me because all the senior players and cheerleaders were being called to the field.

"Ke-Ke, you did so good, like so so good. You're going to go viral; everyone was recording." Rin said, in her usual loud tone. She nearly knocked me over, hugging me.

"I told y'all my baby gonna be famous." Tre boasted, as he picked me up and spun me around before kissing me.

"MCKENZIE, put her down!" Coach Brown yelled.

"I wish y'all stop acting like a bunch of children and chill the fuck out. Hype over nothing." Katrina said, nastily.

"Shut your hating ass up. Who the hell was even talking to you?" I spat.

"Hating? On what? Puh-lease, you wish bitch."

"Aye, chill out, Trina." Tre interjected.

"Call me another bitch." I warned.

"Have y'all lost y'all minds? Keyarra and Katrina, separate!"
Courtney gritted.

"But, Courtney." Katrina whined.

"NOW!... Y'all about to get some senior recognition but acting like
middle schoolers." She scolded.

I just rolled my eyes and stood on the other side of, Chris.

"It's all good sis. Want me to dump the bucket of Gatorade on
her, instead of coach after we win." Chris whispered.

"Yes." I laughed.

We waited one by one, as the principal called our names.
Courtney gave out the little plaques to the cheerleaders, and
Coach Brown gave them to his players.

"My baby, my baby, you sounded just like your mother. I'm so
proud of you." GG gushed, as she pulled me in for a hug.

My family was waiting on the sidelines after the little ceremony
was over.

"You did great little sis." Matt complimented.

"Yes, you did." DW added.

"Yess. I told you I'm coming on tour with you as your stylist, when
you start selling out stadiums." Tia said, proudly.

"Thanks y'all, I really appreciate it, but Tia, ain't nobody going on
a tour."

"I don't know, baby girl may be right. I already have a few people
inquiring about who was singing when I was live." DW expressed.

"Cut it out. I'm about to go get something to drink real quick." I
said, brushing his statements off.

DW was making a name for himself in the music industry, and I
really think he could put me on, if that's what I wanted; but I'm
not too sure of anything right now, though. I just want to get
through my senior year. I made my way out of the small crowd
and over to the concession stand. Several people complimented
me on my singing voice while I stood in line. I'm glad I won't ever
do that shit again because I wasn't a fan of the attention. I stood

in line for a few minutes, grabbed my Gatorade and stood over to the side.

"Katrina, I'm not about to fucking argue with you in front of all these people man."
"You're the one that is arguing; all I asked is why you felt the need to be that close to her."
I could hear Derek and Katrina's voices behind the sports shed, which was directly next to the concession stand. They were kind of loud if you were close to them, but you couldn't really hear them above the noise of the crowd. I peeped around the corner to try and get a look at them.
"And I just told your ass we were having a conversation. You the one who been acting funny lately, and the shit really not sitting right with me."
"Derek, I don't care. My boyfriend doesn't need to be booed up with some other girl, especially her, after I specifically told you how I feel about her! How does that make me look?"
Derek just laughed.
"You are absolutely ridiculous, and I think I'm good on you."
"Excuse me?"
"You heard me."
"Derek, you can't break up with me, I love you." she cried, on the brink of tears.
"You love me but can't even answer a question about that watch. So, save the bullshit."
"ALL VARSITY CHEER, TO THE STANDS. ALL VARSITY CHEER TEAM TO THE STANDS!" Courtney called out, through the megaphone. Whenever the JV cheer team went on, we were expected to sit in the stands altogether and show them, "support".
"Derek, I'm sorry ok. We can talk later; I have to go." She got on her tip toes and kissed him, which he didn't return.
She walked away and Derek just shook his head; he looked frustrated. I wanted to go say something to him, but I decided not to. Looks like I was causing enough issues. I joined Rin on the bleachers, and we sat through the JV game.

Butterfly: Can I see you tonight?
I don't know. Tre is having that party after the dance.
Butterfly: Sneak away for a little bit...please
I will try
Butterfly: I'll take that as a yes
I didn't bother to reply because I knew my ass was going to but I was going to tell him that we should chill and just be friends without all the extra shit. I have been lying so much lately that I can barely keep up.
"Ok ladies, let's hit the field." Courtney announced.
JV had won their game, so hopefully varsity could do the same. Every time we would face the crowd and do a routine, Derek's eyes were dead locked on me. Katrina glanced over her shoulder and gave me a death stare.
"EYES ON THE CROWD!" Courtney yelled.
Courtney was fun and easy going but when it came to our routines, and how we conducted ourselves at games or on the mat, she didn't play. We finished up one of our final cheers and some of the seniors got a little emotional. Rin and a few others still did winter and spring cheer but for the ones who didn't, like me, it would be our last home game. I didn't feel too sad about it, but I would miss it a little; cheerleading was a good distraction for me. The girls quickly got themselves together at the request of Courtney. We had 13 seconds left on the clock and we were one touchdown away from winning the game. We were playing our rival, Perry Hall, so we had to win; they couldn't beat us at home and on our homecoming day. They snapped and Tre was looking to see who was open, Chris was flying through the players and was finally open. Tre whizzed the ball through the air, and it's like the stands went silent. We were all holding our breath to see if Chris was going to catch it. The sounds of Tia screaming made the rest of the crowd start roaring again as Chris caught the ball and was rushing to the end zone. I watched Fatman catch the legs of a player, who was on Chris's wheels. Chris used his long legs to jump over another one.

"GO LEGS GO!" Tia shouted.

I've never seen her so excited. I started chanting, "LEGS LEGS LEGS",

Rin joined me and before we knew it, the crowd was chanting as well.

Chris was nearly at the line when he was tackled from behind. He stretched his arms out as he went down, but we couldn't tell if the ball had crossed or not. The chanting had halted, as we all went back to holding our breath. The ref held up his 2 arms signaling, touchdown, and everyone erupted with cheers; we had won! Rin and I hugged each other as we yelled with excitement. The players had picked Chris up and put him on their shoulders as they celebrated.

"You see your man?" I said to Tia, as she came off the stands.

"Yes, yes, he was so amazing! Omg, I loved it. The whole experience!" she said, excitedly.

She was smiling from ear to ear, and she was more so looking behind me. I assume, waiting to see when Chris was going to come over. Tia told me this was only her 2nd high school football game and her 1st homecoming. I'm so glad she enjoyed it.

"Babe, babe!" I heard Tre call out.

I ran over to him, jumped in his arms and kissed him.

"You did so good Tre, I'm so proud of you."

"Thank you, thank you! Homecoming about to be so lit tonight!" he beamed.

"I guess that good luck you had this morning worked, light bright!" Rin said when she approached us.

"Good luck?" he questioned.

"The kiss I gave you right before the game." I said, thinking fast.

"Oh, yeah that was good luck. Let me go find my parents. If I don't see you before you leave, I'll see you at homecoming." he said, before kissing me again and running off.

"Kiss?" Rin asked curiously.

"Girl, you know Tre likes to be private, you almost got my ass in trouble!"

"Oh right, my bad." she responded, but I can tell she wasn't fully believing me.

"Keyarra and Sharin let's go. Y'all gonna be late for your hair appointment!" GG called out to us.

Rin and I went to the same stylist. She was an Asian lady, who did well with thick, natural hair, and I had a lot of that. My hair used to remind everyone of, Rudy Huxtable's; it was crazy thick and long. It's gotten a little shorter since then because of me not taking care of it, but it was still thick and came down to my bra strap.

"Coming, let's go Rin."

We linked arms as we made our way over to G; she was having a conversation with Courtney.

"Yes, she is our little superstar and I want her to do winter cheer." I heard her say.

"I would like that too, she's a natural." G smiled.

"Yes, do winter cheer with me. It's our last year." Sharin begged, as she poked her bottom lip out.

I rolled my eyes.

"I'll think about it."

"Keyarra, can I talk to you for a quick sec? It won't be long." Courtney asked.

"Sure. G, I'll come to the car when I'm done."

"Bye Cori, I'll see you at the dance. Maybe I'll see you let loose a little." Rin said.

"We'll see, great job today Sharin." she replied.

When they disappeared into the crowd, Courtney once again put her arm over my shoulder as we walked slowly towards the parking lot.

"2 things... I am very proud of you, Keyarra. You have come a long way, in the short year you've been on the squad. When you joined last year, I'm not sure what you were going through, but you seemed very down. I'm happy you turned that around and I know you already know I'm only a phone call away, if you ever feel like you need an ear."

"Thank you, Courtney, I really appreciate you more than I can express. But we still have a few games left, why are you telling me this now?"

"I just felt like the timing was right; but 2nd thing."

She pointed towards a black truck that I recognized as Derek's. I saw that he and Katrina were making out in front of it.

What the fuck? A few hours ago, he was trying to break up with her.

"Katrina's boyfriend? The one who flew her ass all over the damn country? The one who she can never shut up about? That's who you were making googly eyes at earlier?" she asked, letting me go and folding her arms.

"It's just a mutual crush, nothing more." I lied.

"That boy seems like trouble Keyarra, and messing with Katrina's boyfriend, will certainly not end well. I don't want either of you getting suspended because of some dumbass boy. And any senior that gets suspended is restricted from all senior activities. That includes prom and graduation."

"Yes, I know I know." I groaned.

"I'm just letting you know; and Tre seems like a good guy to you. He helped bring you out of that bubble you were in. Don't do anything to hurt his feelings, ok?"

"Yes." I replied, sadly.

Why did I never consider how Tre would feel if he found out about Derek and I? I mean, Derek said it's just kissing so it's not that bad, but I would be really upset if Tre was just kissing some other girl.

"Alright Key, can't wait to see you later." she smiled and gave me a warm hug.

"Bye, see you later."

I felt like shit now. This just gave me more of a reason to end things with him. He clearly likes putting up with Katrina's bullshit and I'm just going to leave him right where he was.... with her.

DEREK

"Aw, don't you two look good." Katrina's mother, Maria cooed as she snapped more pictures of us.

Katrina had begged for me to escort her to homecoming. I finally gave in a few days before. She had already brought 2 tickets, without even asking me if I wanted to go.

"Don't we." Katrina smiled, as we changed positions for another photo.

I was high as fuck and didn't feel like doing this shit anymore. I had smoked with Chris pothead ass, about an hour before. I really grew to like him over the past few months, even if Matt didn't; he treated my sister well, so I don't have a problem with him.

"Oh shoot, I forgot my purse upstairs. Baby, can you go grab it for me, it's on my dresser?" Katrina asked.

"Yeah, no more pictures though. I'm ready to go."

"Aw Derek don't be in such a hurry to get away from me. You don't see me often." Maria purred.

"That's cus you're never around." I mumbled as I climbed the steps.

I looked around Katrina's room and grabbed her purse. I turned to leave and saw Maria standing in the doorway.

"Found it?"

"Yeah."

She just stared at me with seductive eyes.

This lady wants some dick so bad.

"So, you just gonna stand in the doorway?" I questioned.

"You have enough room to get pass."

I just shook my head and attempted to squeeze past her, but of course, her hand found its way on my dick as usual. Ever since I turned 18 a couple years ago, she has made it very known to me that she wants to fuck. I mean, the old me would've gave her some, but I guess she wanted to wait until I was of age; which to me, there wasn't much of a difference between me at 17 and 18, but whatever. But now, I wouldn't touch her with a 10-foot pole, whether me and Katrina were together, or not. She moves funny, and she is rubbing off on her daughter for real.

"You treacherous as fuck, you know that right?"

"Some may say."

"One day your daughter gonna catch your ass, then what?"

"She will cut ties with me, before you, so it would be a little easier for us to....do whatever."

She eyed me up and down then gripped my dick a little more.

"Even on soft you feel like a monster."

"You foul, let my mans go, so I can go take your DAUGHTER to her dance."

"You just let me know when you're ready to get in the ring with the big girls."

"So what, you tried to fuck my pop and he swerved you, so you moved on to me?"

Maria had met my dad a few times and her ass saw dollar signs, but I had already put him on game with her. He was not interested and avoided her, as much as he could.

"Please, your father begged for this but missed out."

"Yeah ok, keep telling yourself that."

I removed her hand and headed downstairs.

"What the hell took you so long?"

"I was talking to your mom."

"About what?"

"She wanna fuck my dad. Let's go."

I opened the door for her and we went outside to my truck.

"Baby, I don't know if I can step up."

Katrina had on this tight ass black dress, that she looked damn good in; but she could barely breathe in it, let alone walk.

"You're blowing me today Tri, you really are."

I swooped her up and placed her in the passenger seat.

"Thank you, baby." she said, dismally.

She knew I wasn't fucking with her like that after this morning. I tried to have another conversation about that watch I had found a while back and she blew up on me. We had a screaming match until she told me to leave, so I dipped. I wanted to go see Keyarra, anyway. I was feeling the fuck outta her; I just liked being in her presence. I was really attracted to her in more ways than one.

"Derek, I know you're still mad at me, but thank you for coming."

"Mm hm."

"What else do you want me to do?"

"I want you to be honest with me."

"I don't know who's watch that was, I can ask my mom again, but she said she didn't know either."

"Ard Katrina."

"Please believe me, Derek."

"You sound like you're trying to convince yourself, more than me."

I was met with silence.

"That's what I thought."

We made it to the school in 5 minutes. We pulled up and I took a deep breath. I did not feel like going in there, but then I saw her. Keyarra was walking with Tre. I could only see her from the side, but she looked beautiful. I opened my door and hopped out; I went to Katrina's side and scooped her ass out.

"I know I said it already, but you look really good Derek. Thank you for coming."

"No problem." I gave her a fake smile.

Suddenly, I was ready to go inside, but I had to play it cool. I was never pressed over a female, but Keyarra had my ass open; and I haven't even slid in her yet. I grabbed Katrina's hand, and we walked in. She was rather popular I guess, because hella people complimented her as she walked past. I caught the eyes of several girls and watched how they ogled me.

"Hi Katrina, you look amazing." the lady, Courtney, I met earlier said.

Katrina had on this black spandex dress that had horizontal slits, that went from her thighs and stopped a little above her waist. Her thick black hair was dressed in fresh curls, and she had these metallic gold heels, with matching gold jewelry, including the bracelet I got her.

"Thank you, coach. This is my boyfriend, Derek, Derek this is Courtney, my cheer coach."

"It's nice to meet you, again." I said.

"Again?" Katrina questioned.

"Yeah, we met earlier at the game. Keyarra introduced us." I smiled.

I knew that shit would burn her up, but I couldn't help myself. Katrina looked annoyed, immediately.

"Um yeah, we did meet but this introduction is not so rushed. I've heard so many great things about you, Derek." Courtney said, trying to cool Katrina off.

"I'm sure. She has also said great things about you as well."

"Well, I'm glad to hear that; you both look divine."

"Divine? Really Courtney?" Katrina questioned.

"I have to use my big girl words, Katrina; I've been mistaken for one of y'all kids tonight, already."

Courtney was petite. She was the size of a student, so I can see why she would get confused for one. But from what I hear, she could be tough, so she was well respected by the students.

"But anyway, the 2 of you have fun, and fingers crossed on you getting the crown." Courtney said.

"It's in the bag." Katrina stated, confidently.

She was running for homecoming queen. She had won homecoming court for her freshman and sophomore year as well as princess for her jr year so, naturally she felt like she should get queen. I pray she did win because I did not feel like hearing her mouth about it, if she was to lose. We made our way through a sea of students all excited for homecoming night.

"Hi jefe." an excited Sharin greeted.
"Hi Shar, you look nice."
Sharin was a beautiful girl, with a beautiful personality to match. I had also grown to like her a lot and I didn't mind her hyper outbursts.
"Thanks. Wow, you clean up very well…. Hi, Katrina."
"Hi." Katrina spoke, dryly.
Sharin smirked at her and continued, as if she wasn't there.
"We are all in the gym, close to the back, if you want to come back there."
"I will come by in a few."
"Ok, bye Jefe." she smiled.
She turned on her heels and sashayed away.
"I don't like that she calls you that." Katrina gritted when she looked up at me, with malice in her eyes.
"Please don't start your shit. Go find your friends and have a good time."
"I don't have any friends Derek, you know that."
"So what the fuck are we doing here, Katrina?"
"Um, I need my picture taken for the yearbook when I win the crown, duh."
I couldn't even come up with what to say next; I was so over her. We stood there in silence for a few minutes. More people came past and spoke to her; whenever they walked away, she had a nasty remark to say about them. She was like a real-life mean girl, and I can't believe it took me this long to really see it.
"I'm going to go find Ti, to get a picture with her."
"I don't want to go mingle with that group."
"Nobody said you had to."

I walked away before she could say anything. At this rate, I wouldn't even be staying long enough for them to announce who won anything.

I entered the gym and I saw a horde of students all dancing and having a good time. Parkville was a decent looking school from what I've seen the few times I've been here to pick up Tia and Katrina. The gym looked nice and spacious. There were a few bleachers pushed out for people to sit on, I walked off to the side close to them, to avoid the crowds in the middle of the gym. I heard a few girls question to each other who I was, and if I went to the school. I was too busy looking for the bright red dress that I knew Tia had on, that's when I spotted Keyarra again. She had on this glittery silver dress, and it just made her stand out among everyone, as she danced with some girls.

"What's up, Key?" I yelled over the music.

"Hi, wh-what are you doing here?" she asked, confused.

"Tri dragged me along."

"Oh, wow, I'm happy to see you." She smiled brightly, but her eyes looked a little glassy.

"Are you really?"

"I am, you look good as shit." she complimented, as she looked me up and down, which is unusual for her. She is usually shy around me, unless we are alone, then she opens up a little more.

"Have you been drinking?"

"Yup...are you high? Your eyes are extra low." she laughed.

"A little. You can barely see my eyes. It's dark in here."

"Your eyes are one my favorite things about you."

"Mmm I thought it was my lips?" I questioned, stepping closer to her.

"Derek don't, I will get glitter all over you."

"If that's your only concern, then I can live with that."

"Stop it. When did you get bottoms?"

"I've always had them." I said, coolly.

I had two silver caps over my bottom canines. I rarely wore them, but I thought it would add something to this basic ass fit. I had on a long sleeve, black button up; I tucked it in some black, slim fit khakis, and I had a pair of, Common Projects, black leather sneakers. Tia added a black leather belt, a silver Movado watch, and she pushed me to wear my white gold, thin rope chain. Which was something else I rarely wore because I didn't want to break or lose it. It peaked through my shirt, since I hadn't buttoned my top two buttons.

"I like them…. a lot." Keyarra purred.

I see liquor makes her bold, she was looking at me like she wanted to eat me alive. I leaned down and brought my mouth to her ear and spoke just loud enough for her to hear me above the music.

"You better stop looking at me like that before we do whatever it is you are thinking about."

"I wouldn't protest." she responded immediately.

I couldn't help but chuckle.

"Yeah, you're drunk. Where's your boyfriend, Keyarra?"

She started to fake look around.

"Mmmm, probably somewhere drinking."

"Ok, where is Tia?"

"I don't know…. shit, I don't know where anybody is." she said, looking around confused.

I just stared at her for a few seconds. She was so cute to me; she was innocent but sexy looking, at the same time.

"Why are you looking at me like that? Is it my hair? I can feel it getting puffy." she panicked, as she started to finger comb through her bone straight hair.

I had never seen her hair straight like that before. Whether it was in its natural state or like that, it was beautiful, and I wanted it to be wrapped around my wrist, while I hit her from the back.

"Stop, it looks fine."

"You sure?"

"I told you; I don't lie to you." I said sincerely.

Keyarra started to blush, then stumbled a little. I held her steady.

"You good?"

"Yeah, I hate heels. Tia wouldn't let me wear sneakers." she joked.

"They look good on you though."

I admired the shiny black heels that graced her feet; my eyes traveled up her legs and landed on her breast. She was showing plenty of cleavage, and it was doing something to me; I was getting hard.

"Your dress is making feel some things, Key."

"Derek, we really have to talk." she said, nervously.

I hated those words.

"Talk."

"Not here."

"Ok, let's go to my truck."

"Are you crazy? Your girl is here and so is my boyfriend."

"Keyarra, I don't give a fuck about that, but fine we can talk later when you sneak out that party."

"I might be too fucked up by then."

"We can either go talk now or later, you choose."

She groaned. "Later, there's Tia." She pointed behind me.

I looked over my shoulder; Tia and Chris were hand in hand, as they came back from wherever.

"Ard. You good?"

"Yes sir." she laughed.

I was thinking she might be high too, since she couldn't stop laughing.

"I'll see you later."

I walked over to Tia, and she had this unreadable expression on her face. I'm not sure if she was angry, or what.

"What's up, Ti?"

"Hi Derek. See, your fit turned out nice." she smiled.

"Thanks. You look just like mommy."

The dress she had on looked great on her, although I didn't like how tight it was. Her hair was pinned up into this curly like ponytail; with pieces of hair trickling down from the sides and a little in the back. My dad paid for this hair stylist that Tia found from IG, to come do her hair at the house. My little sister looked all grown up, and I wasn't sure how to feel about it.

"Do I really?"

"Yeah, just like her." I assured her.

"Thanks."

"What's up, Chris?"

"What's up man, you still good I see." he laughed.

"My eyes really must be low as shit, cus I don't even really feel high anymore."

"Well, I got you later, if you wanna slide through the after party."

"I'm good. Don't get caught with that shit, especially with my sister around you."

"You can trust me."

"Bet. Listen, imma let y'all enjoy the rest of the dance, but I just wanted a few flicks with, Ti."

"Cool. I got you."

I gave Chris my phone, so he could take them for us. Keyarra and Rin came out of nowhere and photobombed us a few times. I was able to get a few with just Keyarra and Tia as well.

"Ti, let me talk to you for a sec." I said.

We walked into the hallway so we could hear each other.

"Everything ok...You seem a little off?" I asked.

"Um, it's Chris's ex."

"What she do?"

"She made a scene earlier, after Chris and I took pictures at the photo booth. It was embarrassing; I'm gonna beat her ass before the year is out. I can feel it."

Tia sounded more sad than angry; I know how important it was for her to stay out of trouble this year.

"Did Chris handle it?"

"Yeah, he did. But I have homeroom with her and it's just going to be more awkward now."

"Ok, well let him continue to handle it. Don't let that girl get to you and make you do something you gonna regret...ard?"

"Ok." she said, softly.

"I love you Ti, go have fun. And call me later, so I can pick you up. I know they going to be drinking and shit."

"I will. Love you, Derek."

"DEREK! I've been looking all over for you. Why would you leave me all that time, by myself." Katrina fussed as she walked up to us.

She drew a few stares, and I was about to dig in her ass.

"Katrina, I know you see us talking. Stop yelling at my brother like you've lost your fucking mind!" Tia said, sternly.

"I wasn't talking to you."

"But I'm talking to you!"

"Ti, go in the gym and enjoy yourself. I will talk to you later." I spoke.

She hesitated for a few seconds, before finally walking away. Her and Katrina nearly bumped shoulders when she walked past.

"Let me tell you something Katrina, you are skating on extremely thin ice with me. I'm trying to be patient with your spoiled ass, but I'm bout through man." I gritted.

I didn't want to bring any more attention to us, so I tried not to yell.

She stared up at me, with those sad ass eyes that she always gave me.

"You don't mean that."

"I really do. I'm about to go sit in the car and you can come outside whenever you are ready."

I attempted to walk past her, but she caught me by my arm.

"Derek don't, please stay. We can leave as soon as they announce the homecoming court."

"I'm good."

She pulled me back more, until we were face to face.

"Pretty please. I promise I will make it worth it." she said, sensually.

Her hand made her way to the middle of my pants; I was still semi-hard from speaking with Keyarra, earlier.

"See, I think a part of you likes fighting with me." She purred in my ear, then licked it softly, which caused my dick to stiffen more.

AGE IS JUST A NUMBER

I hated that she manipulated me with sex, as often as she did. It's like she was playing off my weaknesses and it didn't sit right with me.

"Chill, Katrina."

I stepped back away from her, and she looked puzzled.

"Homecoming court nominees, make your way inside the gym. Homecoming nominees, make your way inside the gym." A teacher announced in the hallway.

"See baby, it's time. Let me get my crown, take pics, then we can go home."

She grabbed my hand and pulled me along towards the gym. I just didn't feel like fighting anymore, so I went along.

"Wish me luck, even though I don't need it." she said, as she let my hand go and walked towards the center of the gym, where the court gathered.

I noticed Tre and Chris were standing in the middle as well. I didn't know they were nominated. I saw Sharin, Keyarra, and Tia standing off to the side; I decided to walk over and join them.

"Why y'all over here looking mean as fuck?" I asked.

They all had these mugs on their faces.

"Because, if Lisa and Chris win, I'm knocking the crown off that bitch's head." Tia seethed.

"She won't win, she's ran every year and hasn't won shit. She thought because she got with Chris, that she would be a shoo in last year." Keyarra said.

"Good." Tia replied, still mugging.

"I'm just confused on how Katrina has won every year. Her ass gotta be stuffing the ballot box." Sharin chimed in.

"These weak ass students be so stuck up her ass, that they be pressed to say they voted for her." Keyarra fussed.

I didn't even have the energy to get on them for talking shit, as far as I was concerned Katrina, and I probably wouldn't even make it to Christmas.

We watched as the underclassman winners were announced and crowned.

"And your homecoming king is…. your quarterback, Tre McKenzie!"
The crowd roared as Tre stepped up to take his crown; he was flushed red. Since being around him for a while, I noticed he turned red when he was drinking, they better hope they can't smell it on his ass.
"And up next, your homecoming queen, is none other than…. Katrina Vazquez!"
Once again, the crowd roared as she went and stood next to Tre. He pulled her close to him, as they posed cheek to cheek for pictures with their crowns and sashes. They looked very comfortable around each other. As far as I knew, Katrina didn't have close relationships with anyone at the school. Keyarra glanced over at me, and we made eye contact. I feel like we were thinking the same thing. The shit was weird.
"Ok, I'm ready for the real party. Ke-Ke, see if Tre is ready to go back to his house; we can pre-game again, before the crowd shows up." Sharin said.
"I feel like y'all have pre-gamed enough." I expressed.
I can tell that all 3 of them had been drinking, at this point. All their shoes were off, but they were still a little wobbly.
"Derek chill. We're just having fun." Tia whined.
Tia had never been to any parties or homecomings, so I didn't want to spoil her having fun, but I needed all of them to be safe.
"How y'all even get here?" I asked.
"G mam dropped us off. Chris drove Tre's car, so we are going to ride to the party with them" Sharin explained.
"Chris been drinking?" I asked.
"Naw, I knew I had to drive home." Chris answered, as he joined the group.
"Ard. Tia, call me" I said.
"Yes, I know."
I walked away, in search of Katrina. I immediately texted Keyarra first.
Let me know what time you want me to come through
My Songbird: I think I miss you already

I want you to miss me all the time, not just when you're drinking
My Songbird: *What makes you think I don't?*
The way you be trying to run from me....
I didn't see the bubbles pop up.
That's what I thought...hit me later
My Songbird: *K*
I walked into the hallway and started to search for Katrina. I was about to just text her and tell her to meet me at the truck, when I heard Tre talking.

"C'mon Trina, the party will be fun." I overheard Tre slur.
"So, I can watch you and our drunk classmates be all marveled by Keyarra, I think not." Katrina sneered.
"Cut it out, she's gonna be chillen, like everyone else."
"Tre you're drunk, back up and go to your little party."
When I heard her say back up, I rounded the corner. They weren't close or anything, but shit was just weird to me, that they were in a hall by themselves, talking.
"Hi baby, I was looking for you, we can go now. Be safe Tre."
"Ard Trina, you not coming past later, Derek?"
"No, he's not." she answered for me.
"I may. I have to pick Tia up anyway." I said, ignoring her.
"Derek!"
"I'll be in the truck." I said, walking away.
I heard the clicking of Katrina's heels behind me.
"Why are you acting like this?" she asked.
"I'm not acting like anything."
"You haven't even congratulated me." she said, sadly.
I stopped walking and took a deep breath. I turned around to face her.
"Congratulations Tri, my bad. I know how important this was to you."
I pulled her in for a hug and our lips met.
"Thank you, baby."
"Do you wanna go get something to eat?"
"Yes." she answered, excitedly.

We settled on Valentino's, because it wasn't too far, and it shouldn't be too busy, since it wasn't that late yet. That's where everyone liked to hang out, as an after-hours spot.

"Why does Tre call you, Trina?"

"Um, I'm not sure...why?"

"Just wondering."

"You know we've known each other since middle school, so that's probably why."

"Hm."

"Park back there." Katrina pointed to the smaller lot that was further away from the entrance.

"Why?"

"So, nobody will see us."

"See us do what?"

"Just do it please."

I shook my head and parked where she said; there were only 2 cars back here. Katrina undid her seatbelt and leaned over the armrest; she pulled me towards her and kissed me deeply. As we made out, I felt her start to undo my belt.

"What you doing?" I asked.

"Te deseo tanto" she whispered.

(I want you so bad)

"You gonna mess up your dress Tri, let's wait."

"I don't care, I'm never wearing it again."

She continued to undo my pants, once my dick was free, she covered him with her mouth.

"Shit." I hissed.

Katrina was giving it her all this time, around and I was shocked. My dick was barely at the back of her throat but shit still felt great. She finally came up for air then, hiked up her dress, as I finished pulling the rest of my pants down. She climbed over and I leaned my seat back a little. She moved her thong to the side and started to lower herself down, when I stopped her.

"Let me put a condom on."

"It'll be fine. I'll get up when you tell me to."

I was hesitant because I didn't want any slip ups, but my horny ass didn't stop her. I loved going in her raw. She lowered herself down and I lifted my pelvis to meet her the rest of the way.

"Oh God." she cried out.

Katrina started to bounce up and down.

"Asi como Asi"

(just like that)

"Me encanta esta polla" she yelled.

(I love this dick)

"el también te ama"

(he loves you too)

Katrina started to suck on my neck, as she continued to moan, loudly. I felt her juices on my lap, and it contributed to the slapping noises.

"Derek, I love you!" she whispered in my ear. "I love you so much, and I don't want to lose you.... I can't lose you."

"I know, Tri." I grunted.

I was close to busting; her moans, combined with the feel of tight slit wrapped around me, was about to be my undoing.

"Please tell me you love me, Derek." she whimpered.

Before I could even think about it, I said the one thing I knew I would regret sooner, rather than later.

"I love you, Tri."

FUCK!

It was like me saying that, sent her over the edge. She started to moan and shudder; she was cumming...hard.

"AAAHHH, YES, YES!" she screamed.

I know for a fact, if anyone was close by, they heard us.

"Let up Tri, I'm about to nut." I gritted.

Katrina continued to ride me, and my nut was at the tip.

"Yo, get up!"

I tried to lift her up but before I knew it, I bust inside her, grunting hard. I leaned back, as I came down from my euphoric high. All that could be heard now, was both of us trying to catch our breath. My head was spinning, as I thought about what I just did, and said. I had instant regret, on top of a bad feeling.

"That was amazing." Katrina smiled, as she sat up and looked me in my eyes.

"Why didn't you get up?"

"I didn't hear you baby."

"Katrina, you know damn well you heard me." I spat with anger. She seemed unphased by my anger.

"Sorry, it'll be ok. Let's go eat, I'm starving now."

She slowly lifted herself up and got back to the passenger side. I didn't even feel like going to go eat anymore, I was so pissed at her and myself. I feel like I just fell for a fucking trap or something! I tried to shake my thoughts, as I got myself together. I opened my console to get some napkins out to wipe myself off. I stuffed my dick back in my boxers and opened the car door. I didn't feel like redoing my belt, so I took it off and left my shirt untucked. I watched Katrina, as she freshened up her lip gloss.

"Ready." she chirped.

She hopped out of the truck with ease this time and met me on the other side; she grabbed my hand and we walked to the restaurant.

"Get us a booth. I'm going to go to the bathroom."

"Ard." I replied, dryly.

I watched as several men, damn near, broke their necks to watch her as she walked away. Once I got us a booth, I sat down and immediately started looking up Plan B's. I only had the need for it one other time, when I had condom break, and I didn't even buy it, my pops did. I read she had to take it, at least 72 hours, after unprotected sex.

"Shit, imma try to get that shit tonight." I mumbled.

"Did the waitress come yet?" she asked, when she sat down.

"Not yet"

"Do you know what you want?"

"Wings."

"BBQ?"

"Yup."

"Derek, stop being so short with me. We just had a special moment in the car, and now you're being an asshole."

"What special moment?"

"Um, you finally said you loved me!"

FUCK ME!

"Katrina, you know that I care about you, but that was a heat of the moment thing."

I didn't want to hurt her feelings, but I try my hardest not to lie. So, I wanted to be real with her.

"You still said it." she smiled.

She had this look in her eye, that made my stomach drop.

"You know you have to take a Plan B, right." I said calmly.

Her eyes instantly started to water.

"Hi guys, may I start you off with any drinks?" our waitress asked.

Katrina looked stuck, so I just ordered for her.

"Um yeah, may I have a coke and she'll have a lemonade. And we'll both take waters, as well."

"Great, be right back." she said, walking away.

"Why do I need to take a Plan B?"

"What do you mean? What if you get pregnant?"

"That was never a concern of yours before."

"It always has been. We started using condoms again, when you wanted to get off birth control. And the times I have slid in you raw, whether you were on birth control or not, I've always pulled out."

"I didn't want to get off birth control; I needed to!"

Katrina was on birth control when we first started messing around, but even after she was put on 2 different ones, she still had terrible side effects. Blinding headaches and abdominal pains were the main ones. She just decided to stop taking them, which of course I was fine with, but we just needed to be more careful, and so far, so good.

"I know that, but I'm just letting you know that I'm not ready to be a parent, so I would like for you to take a, Plan B."

Katrina just looked off into the distance.

"Whatever you want." she finally said.

We looked over our menus in silence, and it was just awkward now.

"Ready to order?" the waitress asked, returning with our drinks. We placed our orders and didn't say much to each other. A short time later, our food was sat in front of us. I ordered BBQ wings and seafood cups; Katrina ordered seafood lasagna. We ate in silence. In the middle of us eating, my phone went off.

My Songbird: Still wanna see me?

Always, be there in a few

"Are you done eating?" I asked.

She barely touched her food.

"Yeah."

"Want to take it with you?"

"Um, yeah that's fine."

Her mood had changed drastically, which I really don't understand because Katrina had plans to go to college and move to New York to be a model, and all this other shit. Not saying she can't do that with a baby, but why would you want to, if you really didn't have to. I paid the bill, and she packed up her food, then we left. I expected her to ask me to help her get in the truck, but she didn't; she got in with no problem. I didn't know if her dress was a little looser or she never needed my help, in the first place.

"Let me walk you to the door." I said, as I parked my truck in her driveway.

"You're not staying?"

"I told you I have to get, Tia."

"Don't worry about walking me to the door, I'm good." she spat.

"Yo, are you really that upset that I asked you to take a Plan B?"

"Yes, because that means you don't see a future with me. And after everything we've been through, that hurts my fucking feelings!" she yelled.

"First, stop yelling. Second, you act like I'm asking you to get an abortion, which you know I would never do. All I'm asking is that we take a preventative measure; if you happen to still become pregnant, then we'll deal with it." I argued.

"Fuck you Derek, I'm so over your bullshit. If you don't want to be with me, then that's all you have to say."

"If that's what you got from what I just said, then so be it." I shrugged.

"WHAT?" she screeched.

She instantly started to cry, her mood swings lately were throwing me for a loop, and there was no way I would be able to be around her, if she was pregnant. Any little outburst she had would be blamed on the child she was carrying.

"So, that's it, you wanna break up?"

"I told you earlier I was fed up, so maybe that's what's best." I said, nonchalantly.

"No."

"I'm sorry?"

"We're not breaking up. I'll let you go get your feelings together, then you come back."

She dried her eyes, leaned over to kiss my cheek, then hopped out of the car.

"What the fuck just happened?" I asked out loud.

I sat there for a few minutes and tried to process everything.

My Songbird: Hellooooo

On my way!

Keyarra, usually put me in a good mood, and I was hoping she would be able to do that again because my head was spinning. I pulled up to the address that Keyarra sent me; it was about 2 blocks down the street from where Tre lived. I pulled up and she was standing outside. She had on a long black sleeve crop top, with leggings, and a pair of tall black Ugg boots; her hair was now up in a messy bun.

"Hi." she greeted, energetically, when she jumped in the passenger seat.

"What's up. You not cold?"

"No."

"Hm. How's the party?"

"It's good, a lot of people as usual, so it will get shut down soon." she giggled.

"You been smoking?"

"Yeah, and drinking...more. You wanna hit this?"
She said pulling out a half of blunt, out of nowhere.
"Yeah...shot gun only though."
She burst out laughing; she was giddy with excitement. It was refreshing. Katrina and even Tia were always so angry and at times, it could be exhausting.
"Whatever you say boss."
Keyarra climbed over my console, and for the 2nd time that night, I had a girl in my lap. I was starting to feel like I was slipping back into my old ways, but Keyarra and I weren't having sex, so I guess it wasn't too bad...yet. I watched as she lit the blunt and inhaled; she leaned forward and pressed her lips against mine. I inhaled the smoke and almost instantly felt calmer. I leaned my head back and closed my eyes. I started to palm her ass and rub my hand up and down her exposed back.
"Everything ok, you seem a little off?"
"Yeah I'm cool, what did you want to talk about?" I answered.
"Mmm, I think you might get mad at me."
I opened my eyes and looked at her.
"What is it?" I asked.
"Um, I-I was th-thinking..."
"Stop stuttering."
She hit the blunt again, then inhaled deeply, and blew the smoke out.
"Ok, I was thinking that maybe we should stop.... whatever it is, that we are doing."
"You say that but you're in my lap right now."
She stared at me blankly, with her glossy eyes.
"I know, I just thought that would be the best way to shot gun."
"Yeah ok. Why you wanna stop?"
"Because I feel bad about Tre, and I don't want to cause anymore issues in your relationship."
"What makes you think you're causing issues in my relationship?"
"I um...kind of heard y'all arguing at the game earlier today. And I know it was about me."

I just stared at her for a few seconds. I took the blunt out of her hand and hit it. I was getting a headache; I understood what she was saying but to be real, I wasn't about to let Keyarra just walk away from me. I liked what we had going on and I didn't want it to end.

"I get that you feel like you cheating on your man or whatever, but Key, I think you enjoy our time together, as much as I do; so, why stop a good thing. And as far as Katrina is concerned, you aren't causing any more issues than what we already have. So don't worry about that."

"You tried to break up with her."

"Damn, I-spy." I joked.

"Shut up, y'all were loud."

"Mm hm. But we didn't break up, so there's that."

"Yeah I know. I saw yall tonguing each other down at your car later." she said, rolling her eyes.

"You just was watching me all day huh? And stop rolling your eyes at me, you starting to do it as much as, Tia."

"Whatever."

Keyarra had been acting like she was a little jealous lately. I let her rock when she caught that attitude earlier, but I was about to get to the bottom of it.

"You didn't like watching me kiss, Katrina?" I asked lowly.

She looked away from me and stared out the window.

"Naw, talk to me." I said gently, pushing her face back to me.

She took the almost gone blunt back and hit it. She held the smoke in, as she rolled down the window slightly, and threw it out. She leaned forward and blew the smoke in my mouth.

"No, I didn't." she finally spoke.

"Ok. And is Katrina also why you dipped out on me earlier?"

She just nodded her head.

"Say it!"

"Yes."

I smiled. "See, was that so hard?"

"No, but it's just confusing because I shouldn't care what you do with your girlfriend."

"You like me Keyarra, just like I like you. What's confusing about that?"

"You like me?" she asked, surprisingly.

"C'mon Key, let's not act like children."

I ran my thumb over her erect nipples, and I felt something odd. "What's that?"

"My nipple ring."

My dick instantly got hard.

"Why didn't I know you had your nipples pierced?"

"I barely wear the balls because that makes them more noticeable; so I just wear the bars. I also usually have these patches over them, so no one will ask questions."

"I'm assuming, GG, doesn't know."

"Of course not."

"How did you get them done?"

"I have my ways." she smiled with a wink.

"Mmmm, ok. Do you have a bra on?"

"No, I don't."

"And they sitting up like that? Naw, you gotta let me peek." I said, sitting up more.

"What?"

"You heard me...I wanna see them!"

"They are only sitting up because this is my old, rash gard top, from cheerleading. It got a little small, so its snug."

"I see that, now let me see." I insisted.

She wasn't protesting, so I took my thumbs and slid them under the tight material, on both sides. I slowly lifted it because I didn't want her bars to get caught and come out. When I finally freed them, they dropped a little and she immediately covered herself. "Derekkk." She whined.

"Chill, let me see."

I slowly removed her arms and replaced them with my hands, to hold them back up. They had to be at least a D cup, and they were pretty as fuck; my mouth started to water a little. Without a second thought, I flicked my tongue across the right one and ran my thumb over the left one. I heard Keyarra whimper a little; I bit down gently and started to suck on it. I heard her gasp, and she tilted her head back. Her eyes were closed, and she was biting on her bottom lip. I showed some love to the left one and went back and forth for a little bit.

"Mmm, that feels so good." she moaned softly.

I flattened my tongue and ran it up her breast, all the way up to her neck. I wrapped her up in my arms and she wrapped hers around my neck. Our mouths found their way to each other, and we made out.

"Derek." she whispered, breaking our kiss.

"Yeah?"

"I want you to fuck me."

"Huh?" I questioned, in shock.

"I want you to fuck me, please."

"Keyarra, that's the weed talking."

"No, it's not."

"It's the liquor or something."

Keyarra started sucking on my neck, and that shit had me about give in. I felt her go for my pants and I stopped her.

"Chill Key, we can't."

I couldn't have sex with her and I just had sex with Katrina, raw at that.

"Why?" she whined.

"We just can't...not here."

"Let's go to your place then." she suggested.

"My dad is town this weekend, so he's there."

She looked frustrated.

"Listen, if that ever happens, I don't want it to be in here." I voiced, sincerely.

"I guess."

"Don't do that." I said kissing her lips gently.

She smiled, then looked down for a few seconds. I saw her eyebrows furrow, then she lifted my shirt up a little.

"What?" I asked.

"Derek, where's your belt?" she questioned.

"I um.... I took it off."

"Why?"

"I just didn't feel like putting it back on."

I feel like I should've said, I didn't want to wear it anymore, but I really don't like to lie.

Keyarra cocked her head to the side and stared at me, suspiciously.

"Did you have sex with Katrina, in here before you came to see me?"

I didn't want to answer that question because she already looked mad, but I didn't have a choice.

"Yeah."

"Wow, ok."

Keyarra pulled her shirt down and adjusted it. She tried to get off me, but I held her still.

"What's the problem?" I asked.

"There isn't one."

"There clearly is. You did this shit earlier. Just talk to me, I'm not hard to talk to, Keyarra."

She just stared at me, with anger all over face.

"You mad because I had sex with my girlfriend?" I asked.

She knew if she said yes that shit would sound insane.

"No."

"Then what the fuck is it? I don't have time for guessing games and shit." I said, with irritation.

"Like I said earlier, we should just stop this before feelings get involved. I don't think I can handle this, like I thought I could."

"You can't handle what?"

"Whatever this is; it was a bad idea from jump."

"It's been a couple months; now it's a bad idea?"

"Derek, I still want to be cool, but I just don't want to do this anymore."

"You know what, that's fine. I'm not going beg you to do anything." I spat, angrily.

"Don't be mad." she said, sadly.

"You can't tell me not to be mad, when 30 seconds ago, you were about to leave pissed off because I had sex with my girl. You fuck your nigga, but you don't see me questioning you about that! But like you said, we cool. Let me drive you up the block a little, so you don't have to walk so far this late."

"It's fine, I can walk." she said, opening my door preparing to get out.

"It's like I'm having déjà vu all day today. Keyarra, you heard what the fuck I just said." I fussed.

I slammed the door back; I could feel my anger rising and I didn't want her to see that side of me.

"I will drive you around the corner, and please don't make me tell you again." I continued.

She stared at me, then finally got back in the passenger's seat. Between her and Katrina's temper tantrums today, I was ready to give this celibate and single shit a real shot. Because fuck this.

"I'm sorry I made you upset, Derek."

I stopped the car.

"It's fine. I will come back and pick y'all up when you're ready."

"We can take an uber, Derek. It's not far and I don't know what time we will be ready."

"Keyarra, I really don't like repeating myself." I said, as I looked over at her.

She had these sad eyes and I wanted to lean over and kiss her, but I just wanted to leave the situation alone, for now.

"Sorry, I'll make sure Tia, texts you."

"Ard."

She hesitated a little before she got out of the car. When she finally did, I watched her walk up the street and disappear into the house. Damn, I was gonna miss our little linkups, but something told me, Keyarra and I weren't finished. I just have to let her come to me because I'm not chasing her ass anymore.

Tri: Can you come back now? I miss you.
I'll be there in a little bit
And I was going to be right there with that, Plan B.

TIA

I was waiting in Chris's room while he walked his little brother to his aunt's car, so he could spend the weekend with her and his cousins. His mother was at work, so we would be alone until Chris had to work at 5, which gave us a few hours. I admired all the small trophies that he had in his room. Some were football and basketball, but a lot were for academics; my man was smart. A lot of our time together was spent studying and doing our homework. Which I didn't mind, at all, because it took my mind off of wanting to jump his bones. It had been a little over a month since I officially told Chris, I would be his girlfriend, and I loved every second of it; even without the sex. I expressed how I was worried about him not having enough time for me, since he had so much on his plate but I have no complaints. He balanced really well and I was just happy to be around him, even if it was us hanging with his little brother or me watching him at his football practices. Basketball season was starting soon and he gave me the idea to be a basketball manager, so that way I could go to all the games. He put a word in with his coach, and he said I was in. I was about to sit on his bed, when I bumped into his nightstand and knocked the binder over on top of it, and a bunch of papers fell out.

"Shit."

I kneeled and gathered the papers, when one caught my eye because it said, University of Utah, at the top. I started to scan it and it was an acceptance letter. It also stated he would receive a full academic scholarship and a sports scholarship for basketball.

"What the hell, why didn't he say anything?" I said out loud.

I heard the screen door close and I quickly stuffed the papers back in the binder, but I put the letter on top of the pile.

"Ard, now that's done, we can get some us time." Chris said, as he came in and laid on his bed.

He patted his thighs signaling for me to come sit on top of him. I came over and straddled him.

"Talk to me, Ti-baby. What's on your mind?"

"Why do you think I have something on my mind?"

"I don't, I'm just asking. I feel like we talk about me a lot. I wanna talk about you."

"You have a lot to talk about, your life is exciting."

"It's busy, not exciting."

"Whatever. Don't you want to take a nap for later?"

"No, I don't."

His eyes roamed my body as he rubbed his hands all up my thighs and waist; I could feel he was hard through his gym shorts. I admired his discipline because even though he would give me those looks, he never even brought up sex.

"Ok, so I do have a question." I voiced.

"Hit me."

"What's your dream job?"

"You know the answer to that question."

"No. To me, that is something that you just want to do, or maybe even feel obligated to do......what would you choose to do, that would really make you happy?"

He looked like he was contemplating his answer.

"Would it be corny to say that I want to work for a shelter?"

"Why would that be corny?"

"I don't know because be for real, who really wants to do that?"

"People who are passionate about it. What would you want to do?"

"I'm not sure. Maybe like an events coordinator or the person who helps get them funds. Just something that helps make it seem like it's not the worst place in the world to be." he explained.

"Is that how you felt when you were there?"

"Yeah. I would want to change that for others, especially kids."

"Ok great, so where would you start?"

"I don't know." he shrugged.

"You would probably need a degree in something like, community engagement, nonprofit-management, or maybe even in business finance."

Chris looked at me kind of funny. I reached over to the binder and opened it; I pulled out the letter and held it in front of me.

"Tia, why are going through my things?"

"I wasn't; I knocked it over. Now here's a better question. Have you accepted their offer yet?"

"No."

"And, why not?"

"You know why, Tia!"

"Christian, this is what my GG, would call "a blessing". You have a double scholarship. You can go to school and get your degree for free. It's simple."

"It's not that simple."

"How so?"

"It's just not!"

"Ok. Then why even go through the trouble of applying to this school and you have no intention of going?"

"Because they asked me to."

"Does your mother know?"

"No."

"Because she would tell your ass to go."

"Then who's going to help her with my brother? Who's going to help her with the bills? I can't do that shit all the way in, Utah!" he said, with an elevated voice.

"With all do respect Christian, that isn't your responsibility."

"You're sounding crazy right now."

Christian gently lifted me and moved me off of him. He swung his feet off the bed and held his face in his hands. I didn't want to upset him, but I just wanted to encourage him to do what he really wants to do. I scooted next to him and laid my head on his shoulder.

"I'm not going to apologize for saying that because I just want you to see the bigger picture here. You would make an amazing cop. I could see you making a difference in your community, but what happens after you solve Mina's disappearance? What if you don't have that same passion anymore? In the 30 seconds you talked about working in a shelter, your eyes lit up. I haven't seen that once, when you've talked about going to the academy."

"I understand what you're saying but I can't give up on my sister, I just can't."

Mina was a very touchy subject, so I had to tread lightly.

"No one is telling you to give up on her, but you can't give up on this opportunity either. You have a full ride. Imagine the things you can do after you graduate and start working wherever your heart's desire is. You can take care of your family. You'll also have other avenues to go down to help look for, Mina. And the academy will always be there if you so choose."

"They would want me to have a degree in criminal justice or some shit, Ti."

"Ok, but they won't turn you away if you don't. Listen, I'm just trying to put a bug in your ear; whatever you choose to do, I will support you 100%." I kissed his cheek and went to position myself at the head of his bed.

"Now come lay down. You're tired, I can see it in your eyes."

He turned around, and I had my arms stretched out; he gave me a half smile and cuddled up next to me. His face was nuzzled against my neck, he placed his left arm around my waist.

"How did we end up talking about me, again?" he asked, then kissed my neck.

"I told you, you have more to talk about."

"There were other offers." he admitted.

"Really? How many?"

"4, but I declined those already."

"All were offering the same scholarships?"

"2 were football ones; the others were similar to Utah."

"Ok, so what about Utah, hasn't made you decline it yet?"

"It's the coach. He seemed genuinely interested in me, but not like in a money hungry way, like the others. He really wanted to know my story and I told you, I don't tell people shit often. But he made me feel like it was cool to talk to him. I don't know if my ass is vulnerable because I don't have a father figure in my life or what, but I told him all my shit. And he never once brought up how coming to the school would help change my situation. He just applauded me for coming this far; and how I was talented enough, academically and physically, to achieve whatever I wanted in life. He almost made a nigga bust a tear, like how your ass just tried to make me do."

I laughed a little.

"I wasn't trying to do that, but I just want you to see, what I see. You're amazing, in every sense of the word, and I want you to take advantage of all the blessings that come your way."

"Thank you, Ti-baby."

I kissed his forehead.

"You're welcome. Now get some rest."

The next morning was Sunday, and I was waiting for Carmen to join our skype call. She usually didn't do Sundays, but I've been so stuck-up Chris's ass, that I had re-scheduled our last few appointments. But she wanted to catch up with me, so she made an exception.

"Hi Carmen." I beamed when she came across my screen.

"Mmmm well hello, miss busy body. You're a hard person to catch up with these days."

"I know, I'm sorry. But being the best girlfriend in the world, to a star athlete, is hard work." I joked.

"I get it, but I want to make sure you're getting some you time in, as well."

"I am." I smiled.

"Mm hm. So, how are you?"

"I'm great. Besides that little run in with Chris's ex at homecoming, I don't have any issues, and that was almost a month ago."

It was 1 week before Thanksgiving, and everything had been calm with Lisa since homecoming. Whatever Chris had said to her, when he pulled her aside worked because, for the most part, she had left me alone. She gave me the occasional eye roll, but I just ignored her hating ass.

"That's good to hear. How are your grades looking?"

"They better be good, all this studying I'm doing."

I came from private schools, where our schoolwork load was heavy. I don't know why I thought coming back to a public school would be lighter, but these AP classes were wearing me out. I couldn't wait for the break.

"I'm sure you are still a star student. How are you and Keyarra, coming along?"

"Very good; it's almost like we never skipped a beat. She is still a little jumpy sometimes but we're in a good place."

"What do you mean by, jumpy?"

"I told you about the sleep thing, but it's like sometimes she just zones out, and when you try to get her attention she jumps; like she was scared or something."

"Hm." Carmen said.

"I'm still trying to convince her to see you."

"Well don't push too hard; sometimes that can have the opposite effect. It will make people not want to do something more, if they are pressured too much."

"I understand. So, how are you?"

"I'm very well thank you. But this is your time, that your father pays a lot of money for, so we need to talk about you."

"But there's nothing to talk about."

"I'm sure we can find something. Have you had any further interactions with Matthew?"

Carmen was the only person who knew about me and Matt. I called her on the phone when I lost my virginity to him. She talked to me for a few hours because I was so emotional.

"Um, a few; he has been a little more assertive. Saying shit like, he won't take no for an answer. I slapped the shit out of him, like a week ago."

"Now Tia, I told you about re-directing anger. Physical expression isn't always the 1st option you should come to."

"Um, it was this time. He tried to kiss me...again!"

She sighed, deeply. "What happened?"

"We were talking, and he started talking all crazy, like how can I throw what we had away, blah blah blah...a bunch of shit I didn't wanna hear. Then, I told him that I was happy where I was, and he got upset, then he tried to shove his tongue down my throat.... I think he was drunk. He's been hanging out with his weird ass father a lot, and he's just been...different." I explained.

I still cared about Matthew deeply, but I didn't like this version of him. He was coming off really entitled at times, and he was letting his dark side show more.

"I am all for you defending yourself. That's different but he didn't hurt you, right?"

"Oh, he knows I would kick his ass, then Derek would too. I think this is just an adjustment for him."

"Ok. So you have no interest in re-visiting that situation?"

"No. But, if I'm being honest, I miss him. We understood each other; I miss the friendship and that's all. I want to get back to that part, nothing else. I mean, I miss sex for sure, but Christian, makes me feels things I've never felt before. He is so sweet and caring. I don't know how he does all that he does, but still makes me feel like the most important person in his life. I love him!"

I covered my mouth because did I just say that shit?

Carmen smiled, wide.

"I really like this for you, Tia; this softer side. Christian has made you discover a side of you that is delicate, and he seems to be very nurturing to it. It's ok to say that you love him out loud; yes, you are young, but also very capable of feeling those feelings. You saying that doesn't mean you are in love, necessarily. It could mean you love the way he makes you feel, you love the time you spend together, etc. You held onto anger for so long, that it seems to be all you knew. So, don't fear these new emotions coming through. Welcome them."

I got a little teary eyed because she was right; all I know is anger. I was angry at God, I was angry at my father, I became angry with Keyarra, and at one point, I was angry at, Derek. I felt like he also abandoned me. But Carmen informed me that his strong need to satisfy his compulsions were also affecting him, and that I should try my best to give him support. Especially, when he had that rape accusation. Derek is my best friend, so I could never be mad at him, but for so long.

"Tell me how you are feeling right now?" Carmen said, softly.

"I don't know." I said, as I wiped my eyes.

"You do know, Tia."

"I um, I guess I just feel good...for the first time since I moved out Cali. I feel like everything will be ok, for once."

"That's good, that's really good. Remember how nervous you were coming back to Baltimore? You wanted to stay in Cali and be miserable, instead of trying to start fresh in Baltimore, and now look at you. You got your best friend back and you may be in love, for the first time. How exciting." she gushed.

"I don't think I'm in love, but this feeling is something special, for sure."

"Well, whatever it is, like I said, welcome it"

"I will."

Carmen and I talked until time was up. She said she wanted to see me in 2 weeks, and I better not re-schedule, or she will fly to Baltimore and see me, personally. I may miss it on purpose because I missed her hugs; they were very comforting and just her in person presence was needed.

I closed my laptop and thought to call Derek. He hadn't been in the best moods lately for some reason, but I feel like it had to do with that bitch, Katrina. She just had a way of making him crazy. He wasn't home per usual, so I decided to Facetime him.

"What's up Ti, I was just about call you." he answered.

"I just wanted to see what you were doing. Why were you about to call me?"

"See if you wanted breakfast."

"Yes, from where?"

"Um, I don't know. Ihop or something."

"Ok, I'm ready now. I can meet you there, if it's easier."

"Naw, I'll come scoop you."

"Ok"

I decided to keep on my simple fit because I was going to GG's after that, to catch up with Keyarra, and to help with Sunday dinner later. About half an hour later, Derek and I were seated at Ihop.

"I just knew I was going to call your ass and you was gonna be with Chris." Derek joked.

"I could say the same about you. Katrina seems like she has you on a tight leash these days."

"Stop playing. I can't bring her to the house cus y'all be ready to kill each other, so I just be at her crib. But I've been kicking it with, Matt a lot too; that nigga walking around like someone done broke his heart."

Derek gave me a look that I couldn't fully gage and it caused me to shift in my seat.

"Him and Sharin, not doing good? She hasn't mentioned anything."

He chuckled. "They cool from what I hear, but I don't know man. He just in his feelings or something, but he'll be ard."

We ordered our food and continued to catch up. He told me how he tried to break up with Katrina, but in the same night, he told her he loved her, and she's been on cloud 9 ever since. No matter how much he bitches and moans about her, he likes that back and forth with Katrina. He got off on it somehow. And that's why I barely liked to listen, when he talks about her.

"You and Chris fucking yet?"

"Why ask a question you don't really want to know the answer to?"

"Because I need to know these things."

"What if I said yes?"

"Then he can't spend the night anymore."

Surprisingly, Derek had let Chris spend the night with me a few times, but I couldn't spend the night at his house. The rule was that we had to leave the door open; I got away with it being cracked, though. Also, he couldn't spend the night when our sperm donor was in town because he didn't want to hear his mouth about it. Chris and Derek developed a tight friendship. They were both intellectual, so they had interesting conversations. And Chris got him smoking weed, so they did that sometimes, too.

"You're ridiculous, but no, we are not."

"I don't know how he does it. I feel like I can't even go a week."

"But you have before. If you really tried, you can again. Have you only been with, Katrina?"

"I told you, I wasn't going to deal with anyone else besides her."

"I know, I was just asking. I'm proud of you." I smiled.

"Thanks."

"How are your classes going?"

"They cool, learning a lot."

"Good, can't believe you're in your 2nd year already."

"I would be on my 3rd if I didn't take that year off but my mind wasn't right."

"That's ok, doesn't matter when you start, just how you finish."

"Yeah you right. The thought of you graduating next year has me feeling a way too, though. I remember walking you to your classes in the 9th grade because you were terrified."

"Look at me now, walking to class all by myself." I grinned, proudly.

"Proud of you kid." he laughed.

I loved spending time with my brother. I thought I would be attached to his hip when we came back, but it worked out better than I expected.

"Can we go to the mall?" I asked.

"Yeah, let's roll."

Derek and I left the restaurant and headed to Towson, where we spent the rest of the afternoon. I barely paid for anything because Derek pulled out his card every time I hit a register. It was fall time and I was ready to upgrade my closet, so I went a little overboard.

"You done yet, these bags getting a little heavy." Derek said.

"They're heavy because you got all those damn shoes."

"I needed shit, like you did."

"Mm hm. You can go to the car. I want to look at something in Francesca's, then I'll be out."

"Ard."

I made my way to the store and looked around for nothing specific. I was looking at a sweater that I thought, GG, would look nice in.

"I would recognize that backside from anywhere." I heard a familiar voice say, and a chill went up my spine.

I turned around and there was, Darren, standing there with that same creepy ass smile, that he always has. I had avoided him as much as possible, but I still had a few run-ins with him. I never told Chris because he would lose his shit. They have almost come to blows a few times, and I didn't want to add more fuel to the fire.

"Hey." I said.

I put the sweater down and attempted to walk around him, but he stepped in front of me.

"You in a rush?"

"Yeah, my brother is waiting for me."

I don't know why, but he made me nervous. And the last thing I wanted was to be alone with him. There was no one in the store but a salesclerk, who was behind her register, on her phone.

"Every time I see you in school, you have a posse around you, or you with that weak ass nigga."

"Please don't make me cuss you out. Now move out of my way before I get mad." I snapped.

"Ooohh, I heard you were a little bad ass." he said, rubbing his hands together.

"You have 2 seconds to get the fuck out of my face."

"I wanna see what happens when you get to 2." he challenged.

I was ready to go upside his head, when the conversation that Carmen and I just had popped into my head.

"You know what, you're not even worth it. Stay the hell away from me."

I stepped around him and stormed out of the store.

"I'll see you at school...Ti-baby." he yelled after me.

I stopped in my tracks; I had the thought to go back and go fuck him up, but I didn't. I just continued out the exit doors where Derek was waiting.

"You didn't get anything?" he asked.

"No, I saw one of my asshole classmates and I needed to get the fuck away from him."

"What he say?"

"A bunch of nothing; he always saying some dumb shit to me at school. I told him to stay away from me."

"Where he at?" Derek asked undoing his seatbelt.

"It's fine, he's just a clown. Don't worry about it."

"You can't tell me don't worry about it, and he's clearly bothering you. I can see it all over your face."

"I will tell Chris to handle it." I lied.

I wasn't going to tell him anything, Derek will forget about it, and I will continue to avoid Darren's ass, like I've been doing.

"You sure, Tia?"

"Yes."

Derek didn't say anything else. He just pulled off in the direction of GG's, where we would spend the rest of the evening.

"Can we have brother/sister day, at least once a month?" I asked.

"Is that what today was?" he chuckled.

"Yes!"

"Sure, you let me know when."

"Thank youuuu." I sang.

We walked towards the door and heard yelling inside. Derek put his key in, and it became clear that it was GG yelling.

"Matthew, I need you to leave!" she cried.

"I said I was sorry, G!" Matthew slurred.

"I told you that there was no drinking in my house, and you are clearly drunk. GET OUT!" GG yelled.

"Matt, let's take a walk man." Derek announced.

Matthew didn't move. You could tell he was trying to keep his balance. Derek walked over to them and stood in front of GG.

"Let's go." he said, motioning towards the door.

Matt hesitated for a few seconds before finally making his way past me and out the door. He gave me the coldest look before he walked out, then he slammed the door behind him.

"You good, G?" Derek asked.

"Yes my boy. I'm fine, thank you. He just needs to get himself together."

"Yeah, he does. I'll go check on him, then I'll be back."

Derek kissed her on her cheek and walked out the door.

"We might just have order some take-out." GG laughed.

I can tell she was upset but trying to hide it.

"What happened?" I asked, as I approached her.

"Matthew tried to help me cook but he knocked everything over. I know it was an accident, but I can tell he had been drinking; which he has been doing a lot lately. I know he's drinking with that dad of his. I'm calling him later to give him a piece of my mind."

We entered the kitchen and there was a pan of meatballs and sauce all over the floor.

"It was his idea to have meatball subs for dinner." GG said, as she went to clean up.

316

"Let me do it, GG."

"No, I can handle it. Matt picked a fight with Keyarra, and she's a little upset. Go check on her please."

"I can do that after I help you with this." I insisted.

"Tia please, I'm fine."

"Ok."

I made my way upstairs and I could hear Whitney Houston's, "I Have Nothing," blasting from Keyarra's room. I knocked, but she didn't answer; I slowly opened the door, and she was lying across her bed, writing in a book. I knocked a little louder to get her attention. She looked up and closed her book, then placed it under her pillow.

"Hey." I said, loud enough for her to hear me over the music. She used her phone to turn the volume down.

"Hey. I didn't know you were coming this early."

"We were out already."

"Who's we?"

"Derek and I."

"Oh, did you guys see Matt? He's a drunken mess."

"Yeah, him and Derek went to take a walk. He dropped all the food."

"Damn for real, I wanted those meatballs too. I rolled the shit out of them." she joked.

"Girl, shut up." I laughed.

"But GG asked me to come check on you. You and Matt got into it?"

"I wouldn't say that. He's just an asshole and I get sick of that shit. I mushed his ass."

"I'm sorry that happened."

"It's cool."

"What were you writing?"

"Oh it's just some school stuff."

I took note of not seeing her bookbag or anything school related out.

"Let's go help GG." she said, standing up.

We came downstairs and GG was mopping the floor.

"That was fast." I spoke.

"It was nothing. You ok, Keyarra?" she asked.

"Yes."

She went to hug GG, and it lasted a few seconds.

"I want a hug too." I whined, playfully.

They opened their arms, and I joined them.

"You kids are my pride and joy; your mothers would be so proud of all of you."

"Even Matt?" Keyarra joked.

"Girl hush; even Matthew crazy self." GG laughed.

We joined in her laughter, until we heard the door open.

"Yo." I heard my brother call out.

"Is Matthew ok?" GG asked concernedly when she met him in the living room.

"Yeah. He wanna go to his dad's, so imma take him there."

"You most certainly will not. That's where he started this little drinking habit." GG protested.

"G, you just kicked him out. Where he supposed to go?" Derek asked.

"I only said that because I was mad. He can come back in here and sit in the living room. I want to look through his room and find those bottles." she said, pushing past Derek to go upstairs.

"G, wait." Derek said, following her.

"It's such a shitshow here." Keyarra stated, shaking her head.

"It is. Um, if Derek is going to leave, imma go grab my purse out his car."

"Ok."

I went outside and approached Derek's truck; Matthew was in the passenger seat, with the door open.

"Hey." I said, softly.

"Hey."

"Are you ok?"

"Not really, but I'm hanging in there."

"What's wrong?"

"You-you know what's wrong, Tia. I miss you! If you want a relationship, then that's what I'll give you. I've felt like shit since you ended things." he stammered.

He was still intoxicated and was trying his hardest to sound sober.

"Matt stop, you didn't want a relationship, until you saw me in one. Think about how Sharin, would feel if out of nowhere, we started dating."

"I don't know man. I just liked things the way they were."

"What? When I lived across the country and you could fuck both of us, easily. That's so fucking selfish, Matthew." I snapped.

I reached across him and snatched my purse off the console; I turned to leave, until I felt compelled to go back. I didn't want to leave the conversation like that.

"Listen, I'm happy, and I know you don't want to hear that, but that's the truth. What's also the truth, is that I do miss you, but just as a friend. Like how we were, before sex got involved; we had fun, and I would like to get back to that."

"How am I supposed to just be your friend, Tia?"

"You can start, by not trying to kiss me anymore."

"I learned that lesson already because you smacked the shit out of me. You don't have to worry about that."

"That's what your ass gets." I laughed.

"Yeah. Ard Ti, imma try this friend shit with you."

"Thank you, because I don't like seeing you like this. It makes me feel bad."

"Shit, me either. Imma chill on the drinking."

"Good because GG, ransacking your room right now for bottles."

"What?!"

Matt hopped out of the car with the quickness; he stumbled but made it into the house. I really hoped he meant what he said because if he tried to kiss me again, his balls would have to meet my knee, next!

MATTHEW

"How the hell is it, December, already?" Sharin asked, as we walked through the crowded mall.

It was the first week of December, and she asked me to take her Christmas shopping, so she could get it out the way.

"I don't know man, this year flew."

"I know right. Ok, I just want to go to Macy's, then I'm done."

"No rush."

She smiled at me. Since Tia and I had that little talk, I just decided to give up. My dad's advice only got me a slap in the face, and a few blackouts. I miss Tia still, but I'm getting over it; I also have been trying to make it up to Sharin, because I was a real asshole to her, the past few weeks.

"Thank you boo. I already asked Keyarra, but what do you think I should get Tia? You know she's a little high maintenance, so I can't think of what to get her."

"Um, I don't know, maybe a gift card."

"Gift cards are so impersonal; she has been so nice to me, and I just want to get her something."

"I'm sure she will appreciate anything."

She picked up a silver bracelet that had a small Emerald on it.

"Her birthday is in May, right? This is cute."

"Yeah, but she doesn't really like her birthstone."

"Oh, ok. Maybe this silver bracelet, without the birthstone."

"She really prefers gold."

"Damn Matt, you seem to know her better than Ke-Ke. All she told me, was anything pink."

I really do know Tia, like the back of my hand. But I had to chill, so it wouldn't seem weird.

"I mean, we grew up together...kind of."

"Ke-Ke's your sister, and you didn't have any suggestions on her."

"Rin, I don't know what either one of them wants, honestly. They all getting gift cards from me"

"Even me?" she asked.

"We'll see." I winked.

We continued to shop for a little while longer.

"Are you coming over?"

"Would you like me to?"

"You know I do; my mom is away."

"Ok, what you want to eat? We can pick something up while we're out."

"Stokos."

"Ard, call it in."

We drove from White Marsh to Loch Raven, and parked in front of, Stokos. I went to get out the car.

"I can get it, Boo."

"Naw, I got it."

"Ok."

Our food still wasn't ready, so I waited for a few minutes. I looked outside and saw this nigga, who was talking to Sharin through the window; she was all smiling and shit. I took a deep breath and counted to 10. If this nigga wasn't away from my car by the time I got back, it was going to be a problem.

"Hey buddy, order is ready." the man behind the counter said, holding up the bag of food.

I grabbed it and was about to storm out the door.

"Aye buddy, don't forget drink." he called out, but I ignored him.

"I'm good but I promise I'll hit you up if I need any." Sharin said, cheerfully.

"I mean I can still take your number down, too." he pushed.

"She said she good bro." I boomed.

I watched as her face dropped. The nigga turned around and looked me up and down.

"What you say?" he asked.

"You heard me."

"I don't think I did." he said, stepping away from the window. Sharin stuck her hand out the window and grabbed him by his jacket preventing him from stepping any further.

"Uh, can we not. Matt can we go."

"This your nigga? You just said you didn't have one." he stated.

I narrowed my eyes at Sharin.

"I want you step away from my truck." I said, sternly.

"Ahh, it's the car you worried about, got ya."

He turned back to Sharin.

"Use that number baby girl and come fuck with a man who's more worried about you, instead of his ride."

I was about to drop his ass, but I decided against it. Sharin wouldn't even look at me. I opened the back door and placed the food in there. I hopped in the front seat and looked over at her; she was just looking down, fiddling with her fingers.

"That's what we doing now, Rin? Booking niggas, while you sitting in my shit?"

"Matthew, I wasn't booking anyone."

"Then why the fuck you have his number?" I seethed.

"Can we not do this here?"

"Bet."

I pulled off and made it to her house quickly; I pulled up and parked.

"You're still coming in?" she asked.

"Yeah, why wouldn't I? What you wanna call that nigga you just met?"

"Matthew, you're ridiculous." she said, hopping out the car. She opened the back door to get her bags.

"I don't know what the fuck you have an attitude for, after the shit you just pulled." I fumed, coming around the car.

I went to reach for her bags, and she moved them from my grasp. "Sharin, I'm really about to lose my patience. Give me the damn bags. You get the food, and let's go in the house."

She reluctantly gave me the bags and did what I asked her to do. We got inside and she immediately went upstairs. I thought to follow her, but I was going to give her a few minutes. When she returned, her eyes were red like she was crying; she walked past me and sat in the living room. I gathered our food and sat it on the table in front of her. I plopped down next to her.
"So, what exactly are you upset about? I should be upset. That's some disrespectful shit you just did!" I asked.
"I didn't do shit!" She screeched.
"Then what the fuck was that, huh? What you talking about hitting him up for, then?" I yelled back.
I usually try to keep my cool with her, but I was pissed the fuck off.
"He was trying to sell me some funky ass oils. I told him no, then he asked if he could get my number in case I changed my mind. I told him no, but I'll take his. But he was still pressing me for my number." She explained.
"Ok, but all that cheesin in the nigga face and shit; is unnecessary. It looked like you were flirting, that's why he wouldn't go away from my damn truck. And why the fuck you felt the need to tell him that you don't have a nigga?"
She scoffed. "Because I don't! And you really have some fucking nerve. Don't act like it's about the car, Matt. Even if we were in the mall and that shit happened, you would've still lost it. It's ok for you to flirt with bitches and shit, but if I even look like I'm in some else's face, it's a whole fucking problem." She fussed.
"Kill that shit Rin. You know damn well; I wouldn't disrespect you like that."
"Oh, shut the fuck up. You been disrespecting me, but I like your stupid ass so much, that I ignore it.... you've been begging, Nicole, to talk to you and shit. That's why you've been a jerk the past few

weeks. Now all of sudden, you're good again? What she forgave you? You back fucking her or something?"

Sharin was livid; she was screaming while tears ran down her face. I've never seen her this upset before, and I felt like shit. I know how much she likes me, and I've just been dragging her along, but I can't lose her and, Tia.

"Why you going through my phone?" I asked.

I was trying to buy time, to come up with something to say about Nicole.

"Really Matthew? That's all you care about? Well, if you must know, your drunk ass been sloppy as fuck, leaving your phone all out. I didn't read much, since she been leaving your ass on read most of the times. And to be honest, I didn't even want to read anymore because I was scared of what I might see."

"Rin listen..."

"No! I'm done fucking listening....do you hear us? We are fighting like a couple, and we aren't even that! You don't give a fuck about me, Matthew, and I don't know why. I try so hard to prove to you that I'm good enough. Why am I not good enough?" She wailed, as she paced back and forth, wringing her hands vigorously.

She then started to pull at her hair which I've never witnessed, but her mother has made me aware. Sharin had a habit of self-harming; she wasn't a cutter, but she did shit to inflict pain. Her whole life, she hasn't felt good enough; she feels like her grades aren't good enough. She feels like her mother is always at work, to get away from her. And she feels as though, her father moving back to China when she was young, was to also get away from her, even though she talks to him frequently. She also doesn't communicate with either grandparent, for some reason. The only family she associated with was her mother's sister, who lived here too. But she barely visited because Lisa and Rin would fight when they were little, and now they couldn't stand each other. She feels like her entire family isolated her because there was something wrong with her, so she talks down on herself often.

"Hey, hey stop, stop doing that." I said softly, as I gently released her hands from her hair.

"Matthew, just please leave, I don't feel well." she sniffled.

"You're out of your mind, if you think I'm leaving you alone. Sit down."

I pulled her gently onto my lap, pushing her hair out of her face. Even with her face being tear stained, she was beautiful. I laid her head on my shoulder and wrapped her in my arms.

"Rin, I'm sorry that I'm making you feel like you're not good enough. I know this is some cliché shit to say, but it's really me and not you. Nothing is wrong with you baby, I promise; I'm just a stupid ass nigga, that's all. And, as far as Nicole goes, yeah, she stopped talking to me and that fucked me up, but we talked and I got a little bit of closure; so that way, I can move on. I know it's selfish of me to do what I'm doing to you, but I promise imma do better."

I heard Sharin, start to cry softly again; I kissed the top of her head.

"Stop crying."

She looked up at me and kissed me. I took her upstairs and I made love to her. I wasn't going to contribute to her pain anymore. I'm not sure how to be in a relationship, but I was willing to try for, Rin.

KEYARRA

I walked down the corridor in search of the apartment number that belonged to Tia. When I finally found it, I knocked lightly. When no one came to the door, I knocked again, a little louder. I was about to walk away, when I heard the door unlock. I wasn't expecting to see Derek, because most weekends he was with Katrina.

"Keyarra?" he asked, with concern.

"U-um, h-h-hey." I shivered.

It was the day after Christmas, and it was freezing rain outside. All I had on were some jeans and this thin, long-sleeved shirt and a leather jacket, with my black Ugg boots, that were now ruined.

"I-is Tia, h-home?" I asked.

"Naw, come in. You're shivering."

"N-n-no, I don't want to disturb you. I-I was just looking for, Tia."

"Keyarra, come in!"

I didn't move. Derek hung his head, then pinched the bridge of his nose.

"Please don't make me tell you again." He said, in a calm tone, but I knew he was serious.

I slowly walked past him and stood in the middle of their apartment, still shivering. Derek walked towards the bedrooms and came back with a big towel and wrapped it around me.
"Why are you soaking wet?" he finally asked.
"I um, got caught in the rain."
"Did you walk here?"
"Partially."
"Why?"
"It's a long story."

Derek just shook his head, then went to the back again. I sat my phone down on the counter and took a seat at the breakfast bar. I wrapped the towel tighter around me, attempting to warm up. I was trying my best not to cry again because I didn't want Derek to see. I was going to warm up here for a little, then I was going to call an Uber and go back home, I guess. Sharin, and her mother took a much-needed trip to spend some time together for winter break, so her house was out of the question. I had been blowing Tia's phone up because I just needed someone to talk to, but she hadn't responded; I thought she would be here, but I was wrong.
"Here, put these on."
Derek had what looked like a pair of his gym shorts and a T-shirt in his hand.
"I promise I'm fine. I'm about to leave."
"Keyarra, you aren't going anywhere with wet clothes on. Just stay until I dry, them at least."
I reluctantly took the clothes because I was drained and didn't want to fight with him.
"Go use my bathroom. Tia knows when people been in her shit."

I hopped off the stool and went down the hall to his room. I stopped at the hall closet to hang my jacket. I reached Derek's room and looked around; I've never been in here before. I can tell Tia decorated because Derek doesn't take me as the type to be into interior design. It smelled like Hollister; I wondered how he got it to smell like that. I admired the brown décor and how neatly his bed was made. I walked into the giant bathroom and closed the door. My reflection damn near scared me; my eyes were puffy from crying, for the past 2 hours, and my hair was wild. Yesterday, I had in these big pretty curls, but now it was just a big ass mess. I finger combed through it, and wrapped it around into a huge bun, on top of my head. I'm glad I still had in my hoops because I always thought I looked crazy without earrings. I removed my clothes and started to put on the dry ones.

These clothes smell like him!

I shook my thoughts then contemplated on if I should take my bra off since that was wet too.

"Derek has already seen them, so fuck it." I said out loud, as I went to take it off. I winced at the pain that shot through my arm; it was a little sore.

I saw some Vaseline on the sink and put some on my lips and face. Then I decided to put some on my legs and arms, too because I didn't want to look ashy. Once I was done that, I wrapped the clothes in the towel that I had earlier and carried them into the hallway.

"Um, you want me to just throw all this in the dryer?"

Derek was sitting back in the living room, on the couch and he was typing on his laptop. I noticed on the coffee table, there were papers spiraled all over the place.

"Imma put them in the washer." He said, standing up.

I was about to faint; I had seen Derek like this at the beach, but I could never get use to it. He only had on some gym shorts, and the necklace that he wore at homecoming. He looked so damn good; I got that throbbing in between my legs almost instantly.

"I can do it." I spoke.

"Keyarra, go sit your ass in there." he demanded, taking everything and walking past me to the washroom.

I just sighed and went to sit on the end of the couch; further from where he was sitting. Derek returned in a few minutes and sat down; he closed his laptop and turned to face me.

"So, what's going on?" he asked.

"Derek, you look like you are working. I really don't want to
intrude. I promise I will sit here and not bother you."
He squinted at me and took a deep breath.
"You're extremely hardheaded, Keyarra. I told you before, I don't
like repeating myself, yet you constantly make me do it. I will ask
you one more time, what's going on?"

Derek and I haven't spoken much since homecoming night. I
mean, we spoke at like Sunday dinners or when we were in the
same space, but the texting and linkups had stopped. I missed him
so much, but he seemed done with me, so I didn't press him. I
know I was crazy for getting mad about him and Katrina that
night, but I couldn't help it. He was right when he said I liked him,
but I had just never said it out loud.
"So, um, GG, and I got into it."
"About what?"
"I don't want to visit their graves next week." I admitted, faintly.
"Ok, and she got upset?"
"Yes. I don't want to go back there. I can't."
One week from today will be the 5th anniversary of our mother's
passing; they died the day after New Year's Day. None of us really
celebrated the holiday because of it; it was too painful. I wasn't a
fan of visiting their graves, but I have in the past. For the last 2
years I haven't. I can't step foot near it, knowing the things I have
done.

"It's not bad that you don't want to Key, but I'm just curious as to
what changed."
"A lot."
"Like what?"
"Derek!" I warned.
"Ok, I'll drop that. So, I know you didn't partially walk from
there."
"No. Tre's house."
"That nigga let you leave his house in the rain?" He fumed.

"I ran out. I took an Uber there because I needed to go somewhere else. I said some really terrible things to GG, and I just had to leave." my voice cracked.

I felt so horrible at the way that I lashed out at her; she didn't deserve it. She doesn't deserve none of the shit that Matthew and I put her through.

"Don't cry. G has tough skin. I'm sure it's not as bad as you think."
"It is, and I don't want to repeat them."
"That's fine. You can always apologize. So, why did you run out of Tre's?"
"I got there, and he was just so mean; he called me spoiled and ungrateful, but he was drinking."
"That's not an excuse."
"I know. I tried to just let him chill, but he was a little belligerent."
"Did he touch you?"
I quickly shook my head no.
"Please don't lie."
"I'm not."
I couldn't tell Derek that he tried to physically stop me from leaving the house. He wasn't trying to hurt me, but he did in the process.
"Ok, so what happened after you left?"
"I just started walking up Loch Raven to clear my head. Then when I got to the big Mcdonalds on Taylor Ave, I called an uber. I tried to call Tia a few times, but she didn't answer."
"Why didn't you call me or, Matt?"
"I don't involve Matt in my shit. We always end up arguing, and you...I just assumed you wouldn't come."
"C'mon, Key! You have to know me better than that. I would never leave you assed out anywhere."
"I-I know...but..."
"But nothing man, don't do that shit again. It's dark and cold as fuck outside, and you alone walking in the rain." He fussed.
I put my head down.
"I thought you were with, Katrina." I said, in a low tone.

"Keyarra, look at me!" He demanded

I looked up and he was glowering at me; his eyes were dark.

"I don't give a fuck what you think I'm doing, call me! I'll always answer for you."

"Ok, I'm sorry." My voice cracked, again.

"Look, I'm sorry, I don't mean to make you upset. You've had a rough night and I'm not trying to add to that, but I just want you to understand that...ok?" his voice softened, along with his expression.

I nodded "Ok."

"Ard. Let me go call G real quick and let her know that you're here."

He took his phone off the table and went into the kitchen. He was talking in a hushed tone.

"Key, she wants to talk to you. Is that ok?" He asked.

"Yes."

"Ard, it's on mute. I'll come back out, in a minute."

He handed me the phone and he disappeared down the hall. I took a deep breath and took the phone off mute.

"Hi."

"Hello, my girl." GG said, sweetly.

I burst into tears; no matter what we do, she never stays mad at us.

"I'm so sorry." I sobbed.

"Calm down, it's ok. Things got a little heated. I'm sorry for pressuring you."

"I'm sorry for the things I said."

"It went in one ear and out the other; water under the bridge baby."

"It still doesn't make it right."

"It's fine. Do you want me to come get you or do you want to stay with Tia and Derek?"

I guess Derek didn't tell her that he was the only one here.

"Can I stay for a little while longer, then I can ask Derek to bring me home, so you don't have to come out in the rain?"

"Of course. I love you."

"I love you, GG…so much."

"I know. Can I speak to, Derek?"

"Derek." I called out.

He came walking from the back and I handed him the phone.

"Yeah G, I'll bring her home later. Don't worry about it. Go relax yourself, somewhere."

I heard him laugh. "Ard G, love you."

Derek came back and sat on the couch.

"You good?"

"Yes, thank you." I said, nodding my head and wiping my eyes again.

"Cool. Now, did you eat?"

"No."

"I was thinking about getting Chinese, you want that?"

"Yes, that's fine."

"Let me show you the menu."

After telling him what I wanted, he ordered, then he started to gather the papers on the table.

"Is that schoolwork?"

"Naw, I'm reviewing the credit card bills for this company. Making sure shit add up, for when it's time to prepare their taxes."

"Have you always done that?"

"Not really, I usually only do taxes. This is new. If I do well, they may have me do this shit every year, and the payday is beautiful."

"That's what's up. I remember Tia telling me you enjoyed doing taxes."

"Yeah it's cool, but when I graduate, I can charge twice of what I do now. That's what I'm really looking forward to; that will make me enjoy it even more."

"I bet. So, question."

"There it is, I knew they were coming." He laughed.

"Shut up. Why are you here by yourself on a weekend…. where's Katrina?"

"Doing shit that, Katrina, does."

"And what is that?"

"No clue. I wanted to get this work done, so I wasn't pressed to see her. I just was with her yesterday for, Christmas."

"Derek, are you sure it's ok that I'm here? I can go home, so you can get your work done."

"Keyarra, shut up."

He got up, walking away with the stack of papers in hand.

"Now I have a question for you." He said, when he returned.

"And that is?"

"You missed me?" he asked seriously, sitting back on the couch, but a little closer to me.

"Yes." I answered, without hesitation.

"Good, I missed you too. So, what are we going to do about that?"

"Mmm. I can stop questioning you about Katrina, so we can start doing our little meet ups again."

"I don't mind the questions about her, I just don't want you to get mad, when I give you a truthful answer.... I never want to lie to you."

"I understand."

"We'll see."

Derek just gave me his infamous stare.

"What do you think about when you stare at me like that? You've been doing that since the airport." I asked.

"To be real, at first, it was how good you would look on my dick, but over time, it's just admiring how beautiful you are."

I didn't know what to say to that. I was flustered. The doorbell rang.

"Saved by the bell." He smiled.

Derek got up and went to answer the door. I was still reeling over what Derek's admission, compliments from him whether raunchy or sweet made me feel things that I couldn't fully explain. He returned with the bags of food and started to take everything out. He ordered a lot; there was shrimp fried rice, egg foo young, house lo-mein, and a plethora of egg rolls.

"Why'd you get so much?" I asked.

"Tia likes to eat when she's upset, so I thought maybe you might be the same way."

"I am." I laughed.

"Cool, let me get plates."

"I can get them." I offered getting up.

I got up and went to the kitchen to get plates and utensils. I turned around and Derek was standing directly behind me. I almost dropped everything.

"I thought maybe you needed help." he said, lowly peering down at me.

"Um-um, no I got it.... thanks."

We just stared at each other, as the heat between us radiated. I moved to the side and walked around him. I sat the plates down and Derek came back in, with waters and 2 servings spoons.

"I have other stuff to drink if you don't want water."

"Oh no, water is fine." I said taking the bottle.

I got on my knees in front of the coffee table and started to make our plates.

"I could of done that, Key."

"It's the least I can do." I shot over my shoulder.

"Ard, what you want to watch?"

"I'm not picky."

"I don't watch TV like that, so you pick."

"Y'all have Netflix?"

"You wanna Netflix and chill with me?" he asked, with a raised brow.

"Do you have any other suggestions?"

"I can think of a few." He answered smoothly. His eyes quickly roamed my body.

I cleared my throat and took the remote from his hand. I scrolled through the horror section, until I just settled on, "Prom Night."

"You like scary movies?" I asked.

"They cool."

I turned it on and got comfortable on the couch, with my plate. We watched the movie until the end.

"That shit was weak, Keyarra."

"You didn't like it? I love that one."

"Naw. We can do better than that."

"I think I saw, "Scream", on-demand, but you have to pay for it. You might like that one more."

"That's cool, just order it. It gets added to the bill."

I found, "Scream", and turned it on. Suddenly, I had a chill go through my body.

"You cold?"

"No, it was just a chill."

"Let me get you a blanket, in case you need one."

Before I could say anything, he hopped up and went to the hall closet, he came back with a thick fleece blanket. He unfolded it and laid it across my legs. I pulled it over me; it was so soft and warm. Derek lifted my legs and sat them across his lap.

"You can join me under the blanket, if you want."

He looked over at me, with a blank stare.

"I-I mean, i-if you're cold." I said nervously.

"Stop stuttering."

He shifted to the side a little and I removed the cover, inviting him in. I opened my legs, so he can lay in between them. I felt myself craving to be closer to him; to be touched by him. No words were said, as he positioned himself on top of me. He laid his head just above my left breast, and his arms were curled under me. I placed the blanket around us and got comfortable. My left hand found its way, to his soft hair. Derek's short curls were fine, and they went well with his perfect fade.

"Hmmm, I like when you do that." He mumbled.

I used my right hand to trail my fingers up and down his bare back; I immediately felt his erection. I wondered if he could feel the heartbeat that was coming through my vagina now. We laid there and got halfway through the movie, when I heard his soft snores.

"Derek, are you sleep?" I laughed.

"No, I'm watching the movie." He answered, groggily.

"Liar."

"Chill."

"Derek, it's getting late. I can call an Uber, so you don't have to leave out."

"What I tell you about trying to run away from me?" He said, turning his head into the crook of my neck.

The feel of his breath against my neck tickled me, which caused me to squirm a little.

"You good?" He asked.

"Yeah, are you?"

"Yes, you soft as shit." I felt his arms tighten around me. "Spend the night with me."

"Huh?"

"You heard me."

"Derek…. I don't know."

"Why?"

"What if Tia comes home?"

"She's not."

"You talked to her?"

"Yeah. She's lying to me, for some reason, but yeah, I talked to her."

"Lying about what?"

"Don't worry about it."

I felt his lips against my neck, as he gently kissed it.

"Derekkk." I whined.

"What? Why don't you want to stay with me? Nothing is going to happen, if you don't want it to." he said, as he continued to gently suck and kiss on me.

"Mmmm." I moaned.

Fuck it!

I lifted his face and closed the space in between us, until our lips met. His hands went up the oversized shirt I was wearing, until it found my breast; he squeezed gently. His erection was right at my opening and pressed up against my clit. I started to press my body into it. He broke our kiss and went back to my neck.

"Make yourself cum again." He whispered, as he added more pressure in between my legs.

"No."

"Why not?"

Go for it!

"I want to cum…. when you're inside of me."

Derek stopped his movement and faced me. He was looking at me like he was looking for any uncertainty in my eyes.

"That's what you want?" He questioned.

I nodded my head up and down.

"Answer me!"

"Yes, that's what I want….and I'm not under the influence, either."

Derek cracked a smile and kissed me again, but this was intense. His tongue was damn near down my throat, and from that alone I felt like I was about to cum. Suddenly, he stood up, but he took me with him. I secured my legs around his waist as we kissed all the way to his room. He hit the lights and gently laid me on his bed; he made his way in between my legs again, but this time, he slowly took my shirt off.

I covered myself because I started to feel shy. He moved my hands, then ran his thumb over my nipple. I attached the balls to my piercings that morning.

"Did this hurt?" He asked.

"I barely felt it."

Derek's tone was a little different. It was deep and sensual, but very arousing, all at the same time. His lips covered my nipple, and I damn near yelled. His touch was doing something to me; I've never felt anything like it. He bit down gently, and I whimpered.

"Did you feel that?"

"Yes." I replied in a breathy tone.

He smiled before doing it to the other one, it caused me to squirm and try to move away.

"Stop moving, Key…. I don't like runners." he said, softly.

"I'm sorry."

Derek stopped and moved back up to kiss me some more. I felt the coolness of his chain on my chest.

"I like this." I said, breaking our kiss and gently touching the chain.

"Thank you, it was my mother's." He revealed, getting up and walking over to his dresser.

He took the chain from around his neck and placed it in a box, then he opened the drawer and took something out of it.

"Really?" I asked.

"Yeah, Tia let me have it. She kept the rest of her jewelry. I don't wear it often.... only when I want to feel close to her." he replied, walking back over to the bed.

Derek grabbed me by my ankle and slid me down to the end of the bed. He did it so fast, I didn't even have time to react.

"I felt your heart beating fast, are you nervous?"

"Yes."

"This still what you want to do? Because once it happens, we can't take it back.... I didn't ask you to stay the night, with this expectation; so I won't be mad, if you changed your mind."

"I haven't changed my mind."

Derek rubbed his lips together and slightly nodded his head. He leaned down to pull the string to the shorts I had on; once the tie was undone, he slowly pulled them down. I was completely naked and exposed; my breathing got a little shallow because Derek's eyes got dark. I thought they only did that when he got angry, so now I was even more nervous. Derek just stood over me and roamed my body with his intimidating eyes.

"Derek, you're making me extra nervous now, with the way you're looking at me."

His look was almost carnal like.

"Don't be nervous, I just really like what I see."

He took the gold foil packet in his hand, put it to his mouth, and ripped the top off with his teeth.

"Are you on birth control?"

What the fuck?

"Um, yes."

"Cool."

338

"Why?"

"Condoms tend to break with me, but I'll pull out…. don't worry." He winked.

He pulled his shorts down and my eyes nearly popped out of my head.

Where in the fuck was all that going to fit, surely not inside of me? He finna bust my shit open!

I knew Derek was big because of what I've felt. But I wasn't expecting that, by any means.

"Aye, eyes up here. Imma go slow…ok?" He comforted, as he rolled the condom down his 3rd leg.

Our eyes met but my voice was gone. Fuck being nervous. I was a little scared now.

"Keyarra, did you hear me?"

I nodded my head.

"I like verbal answers."

"Yes, I heard you…. you'll go slow."

Derek leaned forward and put one knee on the bed.

"Wait, don't you want me to turn around?" I asked, quickly.

He smiled, his tongue swiped across his bottom lip. "Naw. I wanna see that pretty ass face, when you cum on my dick."

I took a deep breath and watched as he slid the tip up and down my slit. He attempted to ease it in, but the pressure made my hand fly up his abdomen, to stop him.

"You want me to stop?" He asked.

I didn't answer him, my mind was racing, and I could hear my heartbeat in my ears.

"Keyarra, you have to talk to me baby. I'll stop, if it's too much."

"No." I finally spoke. "I want you to keep going."

"Ok. Do me a favor and move your hand." He said, calmly.

I dropped my hand and grabbed the edge of the bed. He slowly pushed himself in, and I had a flashback of a familiar pain. But I wasn't going to stop him; I wanted to feel every inch of him.

"Shiiiit, you tight as fuck, Key." Derek groaned, as he moved in and out of me slowly.

The pain was still there, but it was starting to subside, and pleasure was taking over.

"You sure I'm not hurting you?"

"No, please keep going!" I moaned.

Derek grinded into me more, taking my breath away. Pain and pleasure charged through my body, and I was tingly everywhere. He pushed more inside of me, causing me to grip the bed.

"Mmmm, you feel so good." He groaned, again.

He leaned forward and kissed me. I used that as a distraction, for the pain that was creeping up again. He lifted my left leg and placed it in the crook of his arm, which allowed him to go deeper.

"It's so big." I moaned as he stretched me out more.

"I know, and you're taking it so well." He voiced in my ear.

"Fuckkk, Derek!"

"Mmm hm, take all of me Key."

I had the sudden urge to pee, and I was about to panic.

"Oooo wait, I think I have to pee."

"Naw, that's not pee."

"No, no it is!"

I tried to push him back, but he didn't move; he put more weight on me and started sucking on my ear.

"You wet as fuck, you about to cum! Cum on my dick, Keyarra!"

I started moaning and shaking, uncontrollably.

"That's right, just like that." Derek egged on.

The sensation of him sliding in and out of me, mixed with his voice directly in my ear, had me damn near fighting him. Derek lifted up slightly and looked between us; I was literally gushing everywhere. I was trying to push him back but once again, he didn't budge. I felt tears sting to my eyes.

"Oh, fuck!" I called out.

I looked down, and a stream of fluid shot straight out of me and onto Derek. He looked back up to me in amazement.

"You a squirter, Key?" He asked bewildered.

I was so embarrassed I could cry.

"Not that I knew of." I whimpered, out of breath.

I just came hard as hell, and I was still shaking.

"I knew you was wet as fuck man; I could feel that shit at the beach."

Derek now had every inch of him inside of me. He continued his vigorous strokes; I clawed at his back, as I tried to match his stroke.

"Mm hm, fuck me back Key, I love that."

"Derek please, I'm about to cum again." I moaned.

I was still coming down from the 1st one.

"And imma make you keep cumming all over this dick!"

I started to moan loudly, and I arched my back; Derek took my nipple in his mouth, and bit down gently, which caused me to involuntarily, clench my muscles in my vagina; Derek looked at me, surprisingly.

"Shit!" He growled, slowing down his pace. "You tryna make me bust this nut girl!"

I continued to squeeze, as I came violently again.

"Fuck, Keyarra!" He roared.

Derek pulled out and came in his hand. I watched as he bit down on his bottom lip and jerked the rest of his cum out.

"Woooo shit." He mumbled.

Derek got up and walked into his bathroom. I was lying in the bed winded. I tried to catch my breath and gather my thoughts. I couldn't believe that just happened, but I didn't regret it, not one bit. The sexual tension between us finally exploded and it was amazing.

"You ok?" He asked.

I didn't even hear him come back into the room.

"Yes, are you ok?"

"Better than ok." Derek smiled.

"Good, me too. The condom broke I guess?"

"Yeah I felt it when you came the 2nd time, you were tight as fuck, Key! I wasn't expecting that."

"Hmm. Why did you cum in your hand?"

"I didn't want to cum on you."

"Why?" I asked, curiously.

"I respect you too much for that."

"You can respect me a little less, next time."

"Next time?"

"If you want it to be one."

"I mean, next time, can be right now."

I was tired as hell, but I wanted another taste.

"I'm ready!"

Derek licked his bottom lip and walked over to his dresser. He had 3 more condoms in his hand. He twirled his finger, motioning for me to turn around and I obliged. I stretched out, arched my back and put my ass in the air.

"Damn, that's a beautiful arch you have." He complimented.

I felt his finger glide across my opening quickly and it took me off guard. I wasn't the biggest fan of fingers down there, but I didn't protest.

"Mmm and you still wet."

I heard the foil rip, and the anticipation was killing me. Suddenly, I received a hard smack on my ass.

"Oh!" I yelped, but I liked the stinging sensation. "Do that again." I requested, lustfully.

"You liked that?"

"Yes." I said, slightly moving my ass cheeks back and forth.

"Yeah I see you're gonna be a problem." He chuckled, then delivered another hard smack.

"Oh shit!"

He did it two more times, and now I was hornier than before. I was expecting another one, but instead, I felt Derek's soft lips kissing where he had just laid his hands.

"Mmmm." I hummed.

"You have a tattoo?" He asked, surprisingly.

I always forget that's back there.

"Yes, I got it last year."

It was a small tat of a butterfly, in the upper corner, of my left ass cheek.

"You're just full of surprises."
I felt him kiss it then he smacked that very spot.
"Derek please." I begged.
"Please what?"
"Please fuck me!"
"Can I taste it first?"
I was about to yell no, but I needed to keep my cool.
"Nooo, I want to feel your dick." I whimpered.
"You gonna get that, but I want you to feel my tongue too."
"Next time! Please make me cum on your dick again."
Instead of replying, he rammed himself right inside of me; I felt like the wind had just got knocked out of me.
"SHIT!" I yelled.
Derek gave me a few seconds to adjust before he started to thrust in and out of me. I went to grab the top of the mattress in an attempt to not have him so deep.
"Stop running! This what you wanted, right?"
"Mmm hmm."
He smacked my ass.
"That's not an answer!"
"Yes...yes this what... I w-wanted."
I started to throw my ass back on him.
"Mm hm, throw it on me, Key."
I did that steadily, until I felt myself ready to cum again.
"Oh Derek, I'm about cum!" I damn near yelled.
"I know, I can feel it. You so damn wet. Wet me up! Wet this dick up!"
I could feel my wetness once again gushing out of me.
"Ahhhhhhhhh, shit!" I screamed.
My orgasm ripped through me, viciously.
"Got damn! I can't wait until you let me taste this water park, Key."
Derek had a tight grip on my waist, and he was still fucking me silly.
I felt so weak, but I wasn't about to tap out yet. I wanted to make Derek cum.

"This pussy feel good?" I asked, seductively.

"You know it do…. talk your shit! You know you got some good ass pussy…. I'm mad I ain't been in this…. but I'll tell you one thing." I felt Derek ball up my hair in his hand and he jerked me back a little until his mouth was at my ear.

"This pussy ain't going nowhere." He continued. "You not running from me no more." He gritted.

"No…no, I'm not going anywhere." I moaned breathlessly.

"I want you…to feel me…every…time …you…move…tomorrow." Derek delivered a stroke with each word he spoke. I cried out in pleasure. Derek and I were bucking intensely. The noises I started to make sounded like gibberish, my eyes were rolled into the back of my head, and I was on the verge of another orgasm. I clenched my muscles and Derek inhaled sharply. He released my hair, gripped the top of my ass cheeks, and continued to fuck me.

"There you go again! Tryna make me nut!"

"Derek…I'm cumming…I'm cumming…. cum with me!" I hollered.

"I'm cumming baby!" He grunted.

We came in unison and I'm almost certain, we woke the neighbors up, with the way we yelled out. I collapsed on the bed and Derek collapsed right on top of me. I heard him say something, but I was exhausted; before I knew it, I drifted off to sleep. I'm not sure how much time had passed, but I suddenly felt myself being lifted. My eyes slowly opened, and Derek had me in his arms.

"What are you doing?" I asked, tiredly.

"I gotta change the sheets, it's like a puddle over there." He joked.

"I'm sorry."

"Don't be, imma get a mattress protector just for you." He smiled, as he laid me on the little couch in the corner of his room.

"Shut up."

He disappeared out of the room, and he returned a few minutes later. I watched as he put a towel down, then new sheets over top of it. I was trying to stay awake, but my eyes were so heavy. I turned my attention to the big window and admired the scenery as a distraction; the moon was out, and I had the perfect view of it. Derek walked back over to me and went to pick me up again.

"I can walk." I stated.

"You sure? You passed out on me."

"Yes, I'm fine."

I wrapped myself in the blanket he put over me and I went to stand up; just for me to collapse, right onto the damn carpet; I was mortified!

"Oh shit, you good?" Derek asked, while trying to muffle his laughter.

I just laid there and groaned; my body was sore all over. A few seconds later, he gathered me off the floor.

"Stop being so hardheaded." He laughed.

He laid me down and got under the covers with me. Pulling me to his chest, I fell asleep to the sound of his heartbeat.

"Shit!" I gasped as I opened my eyes abruptly.

Another nightmare

"Hey, you're ok." Derek comforted me, as he placed soft kisses on the side of my face.

He looked concerned, so I assume he witnessed me trying to fight out of my sleep; I just hope I didn't say anything.

"Did you have a bad dream?"

"Um…yeah…but it's fine… I hope I didn't scare you." I said, still trying to catch my breath.

"Naw, you didn't. I was just trying to wake you up."

I looked over at him and the moonlight shined over his beautiful face.

"What time is it?"

Derek looked over at his phone.

"It's only a little after 3, you can go back to sleep."

"I don't want to."

One I was scared to, but I also wanted him again.

"Why?"

I sat up slightly and pulled his face to mine. I stuck my tongue in his mouth, and we made out, intensely.

"I want you." I whispered against his lips.

My hand was massaging his hard on through his boxers.

"Say less."

Derek quickly grabbed the condom off his nightstand and before I knew it, he filled me up. I don't know how many rounds we went before I passed out, yet again.

My eyes opened and I closed them again quickly, because the moon was now replaced by the sun, and it was beaming in on me. I tried opening them again slowly, so they could adjust. I looked around the room and Derek was nowhere in sight, but I did hear the shower on. For a quick second I thought to go join him.

"Let me calm my horny ass down." I said out loud.

I noticed a bottle of water on the nightstand next to me, along with some Tylenol and my phone. I laughed at the Tylenol, but I was going to take two because my body felt like I was in a brawl. I grabbed my phone and saw that it was almost 9. I had at least a dozen missed calls from Tre, some from an hour ago. He also texted me a bunch of times saying how sorry he was, and to please call him.

"Damn, I cheated on him, for real." I said holding my face in my hands.

I instantly felt bad, but no regret. What happened with Derek last night, was something I will never forget, he touched me in ways that I never thought I could be. He was gentle, but dominant at the same time, and I loved it. I heard the water cut off and I immediately looked at my reflection in my camera; hot ass mess. I put a little water on my fingers and tried my best to clean my face. My hair was spiraled all over the place, as usual; I quickly finger combed through it, the best I could, and put it up in a bun again. I grabbed the water again and swished it all around in my mouth, in hopes that it would get rid of any morning breath I had. I wrapped covers around because I was still naked, and I was feeling shy again. The bathroom door opened, and Derek walked out, with a towel wrapped around his waist, and he was drying his hair with another one. He looked like something out of a movie, the way the steam from the hot shower followed him; he was like a dream.

We locked eyes and he smiled.

"Good morning love, I didn't expect you to be up this early." He greeted.

"Me either, the sun was a little bright."

"Oh, my bad."

He walked over to the window and closed the curtains.

"Better?"

"Yes, thank you."

He walked over to me and leaned down to kiss me, but I quickly covered my mouth.

"I have morning breath." I mumbled out.

"Keyarra, stop playing with me."

He removed my hand and kissed me. It was sensual and I was ready to take his towel off. He pulled back and said,

"Yeahhh, you do have morning breath."

"Derek!" I screeched, re-covering my mouth and he burst out laughing.

"I'm joking baby."

He pecked my lips twice and walked away still chuckling.

"That's not funny."

"It was. What do you have planned today?"

"Nothing really. I guess, help G with dinner, but that's it."

"Ok. I wanna see you after dinner." he stated, nonchalantly.

"Why?"

He looked over at me funny.

"What you mean, why?"

"I don't know…. I thought maybe you got what you wanted and…"

"And what? I was gonna hit it and quit it. Keyarra, I literally kissed your ass last night! I wouldn't do that, just to not fuck with you again…. you and your brother think really low of me."

What does that mean?

He dropped his towel and put on the boxers he just took out of the drawer; my mouth started to water. I see why the girls who have had sex with him, would lose their shit because that thing would dick-matize you.

"Hey, focus horn ball." Derek said, snapping me out of my dirty thoughts.

I laughed.

"It's not funny Key, why would I fuck you, then leave you high and dry?" he asked, seriously.

"U-um, I d-don't know; all those other g-girls...."

"What did I tell you about stuttering? Don't be nervous around me, especially after last night.... that nervous shit went out the window, when you threw your ass back on me."

"I'm sorry."

Derek was turning me on, in the worst way, I could tell he was a little upset, but I liked it. I wanted him to fuck me, while he was mad at me.

"And fuck those other girls Keyarra, they don't have shit to do with us......Wait, is that why you asked me, if I wanted you to turn around?"

I nodded my head. He blew out a frustrated breath through his nose. He walked over to the bed and sat down.

"Come here."

I secured the sheet around me and climbed into his lap.

"Don't compare yourself to those other girls. I told you I was going through some shit, and they were just jump-offs. That's not what this is, if that's what you're thinking. And don't say I got what I wanted, like you didn't ask to cum on my dick...you got what you wanted too."

He had a point, I initiated it. And I 100% did think that we were going to have sex, then everything would just be a little awkward between us; but, Derek was talking to me like we weren't both, in full blown relationships.

"So, what is it then?" I questioned.

"I don't know, but I know your ass not going anywhere, and I mean that shit."

Derek leaned in and kissed me. We started to moan a little and I was ready to have him make me yell out his name until we heard a knock on his door; my stomach dropped. I was about to panic because I knew it was Tia.

"Oh my God." I whispered.

"Chill, just go in the bathroom." he said, calmly.

I hopped off him to scurry into the bathroom and closed the door, leaving it open just a crack. I watched Derek go answer his door, I couldn't fully see Tia, because he was blocking her.

"And, where the fuck you been at?" he asked, angrily.

"1st, don't come at me like that, I told you where I was." She fussed.

"Tia, I had to text you numerous times to get a response from you, then you turned your location off, and I told you not to ever do that shit."

"It was an accident, Derek." She whined.

"Miss me with that shit, where were you?"

"I told you; I was with Keyarra, Chris, and Tre."

Oh shit!

Derek swiped his hand down his face.

"You were with Keyarra and Tre?"

"Yes, I chilled with them until Chris got off of work."

"Interesting."

"Derek, I don't know what the issue is, but I don't like how you're questioning me, all of a sudden."

Tia was sounding convincing as hell, I would've believed her!

"Ard, man whatever."

"Are we still having brother/sister day?" she asked, sweetly.

"I don't know. I'm a little disgusted with you right now. Go get ready and I'll let you know."

"Why would I get ready, if we aren't going anywhere?"

"Tia, you're really testing my patience."

"Ok, grumpy!"

Derek went to close the door, but Tia stopped him.

"Why do you have scratches all over you?"
I covered my mouth!
"Because I was fucking." He admitted, bluntly.
"Um, ok ew, and is she still here? Does she know it's brother/sister day? She can't come with us, Derek!"
I heard him take a deep breath.
"Bye Tia!"
And with that, he slammed the door right in her face. I walked out of the bathroom and just stared at him. He looked frustrated when he saw me, his expression softened.
"Your homegirl gonna make me put my foot in her ass."
I laughed softly. "Don't do that."
"I promise you I am. I think I liked it better when she was anti-social."
"Cut it out, she was miserable though."
"Yeah, true"
He went to his closet and laid some clothes out. I went to get my phone, and Tre was calling me again.
"That light skin nigga kept calling you too."
"Um, yeah I saw."
I watched as the call ended and a message popped up.

Tre: I called GG, she said you were fine, but I just need to hear your voice please call me!

I felt Derek wrap his hands around my waist, and kiss alongside my shoulder blade.
"I can run you home real quick." he offered.
"No, I can take an Uber."
"You and these damn Ubers."
Derek smelled so good. I traced a small scratch on his arm, I turned around to face him and that's when I saw the others.
"I'm really sorry about the scratches."
"Don't be, I like rough shit and apparently, so do you."
"Stop." I said, shyly.

"Mm hm. You surprised me, multiple times last night. You kept up and barely tapped out."

"I didn't want you to think I was lame."

"I wouldn't have thought that."

My phone lit up in my hand, I looked down and read the message that appeared across my screen.

My bestie: Hey girl, sorry I didn't get back to you. Is everything ok? I need your help though, he probably won't ask but if he does just please tell Derek I was with you Chris and Tre last night…. I'll explain later."

I didn't even notice that Derek was looking down at my phone as well. His eyes got dark and he gently pushed away from me. He started to walk towards the door, until I hurried and got in front of him.

"W-w-wait, where are you going?" I asked.

"To do exactly what I said and put my foot up her ass." he fumed.

"No, you can't do that!"

"Why?"

"Because it'll look weird, and I just broke girl code by letting you see that message."

"Girl code is broken because you're fucking her brother."

"Um, true. But still, you can't say anything!" I pleaded.

I stood on my tip toes and pulled him down to me, kissing his lips softly.

"Just calm down, Tia isn't doing anything reckless."

"And how do you know that?"

"Because I do. I'm not sure why she's lying, but I'm sure it's harmless."

"Yeah whatever." he said, calming down.

"What's brother/sister day?" I asked.

"It's when I buy her a bunch of shit, but she got a lot for Christmas, so probably just go to the movies or something."

I wish Matt and I did that.

"Oh that's nice....um, do you think I need a Plan B?" I asked, nervously.

He furrowed his brows.

"I really don't remember how many times we had sex and if you used a condom every time." I continued.

"If that would make you comfortable, but I was pretty careful."

"OK, and I never put my clothes in the dryer."

"I did, they are right there on the couch along with your jacket." he pointed.

"Oh, thank you."

I walked over to the couch and my clothes were folded neatly, in the corner. I looked behind me, and Derek was peering at me, in anticipation of me dropping my sheet. I dropped it and gave him the perfect view of my ass. I quickly got dressed and went to put on my boots, that were still a little wet.

"I can get you some new ones today."

"Derek, you don't have to do that, you brought me 3 pair of sneakers for Christmas."

"You like sneakers." he shrugged.

"I do but you weren't even fucking with me like that."

"That doesn't mean I wasn't thinking about your hardheaded ass, you got me a gift too though."

My butterflies fluttered.

"I wouldn't not get you anything but I will get new Uggs, thank you though."

"Fine. Do you just want to wait here, until we leave out?"

"No, I don't want Tia busting in here or something."

"She won't"

"I just rather leave now."

"Ok. Sounds like she is still in the shower. She takes a while." Derek went to the door and looked down the hallway. He motioned for me to come on. I hurried past him, and he followed behind me, as I made my way to the door. Derek stood in between the frame and the door as I called for my Uber.

"It's 6 minutes away." I said.

"Ok, call me when you get home safe."

"Ok, I'll text you."

"I said call me." he said, sternly.

"But you'll be with, Tia."

"What did I just say?"

"Ok, bossy."

"Thank you for staying the night with me."

"Thank you for…. everything." I smiled.

"Anytime."

He reached for my shirt and gently pulled me towards him. He leaned down and kissed me. He was so good at that; I could kiss him for hours.

"I'll see you tonight, ok." he whispered.

"Ok, goodbye Derek."

I started to walk away, when I felt myself being whipped back around by my arm, towards him right into his arms. He could've fucked around and gave me whiplash because he did it so fast. I'm just glad it wasn't on my arm, that was still a little sore. His eyes were piercing into me, and I couldn't read his expression.

"I don't like goodbyes." he expressed, lowly.

"What do you mean?"

"You said, goodbye Derek! That's the last thing my mother said to me…. "goodbye Derek, I love you" ….and I never saw her alive again. So, goodbyes seem very….permanent to me now, therefore, I don't like the word, goodbye." He explained.

My eyes teared up a little.

"Derek, I'm sorry. I didn't know."

"I know, that's why I'm telling you."

"Ok, well um, I'll see you later?"

"Perfect, thank you, and yes you will."

He kissed me again quickly, then released me. I slowly backed up and turned to walk away. I didn't know that was the last thing she said to him. I don't even remember what mine said to me, but I was also a little younger. I waited for the elevator and got in, every damn muscle in my body hurt, Derek wasn't joking when he said he wanted me to feel him every time I moved because I sure

353

as hell was. That Tylenol wasn't doing shit! I opted to wait outside instead of the lobby. I wanted to get some fresh air. It was cold, but I enjoyed it. My Uber pulled up and I got in.

"Good morning, miss." he greeted.
"Good morning." I smiled, brightly.
"Looks like someone had a good night sleep."
"It was the best!"

I leaned my head back and closed my eyes. The memories from last night flooded my mind and I couldn't help but smile. Derek was right, I wasn't going anywhere. I do feel bad about cheating, but Derek didn't seem too concerned about him cheating, so maybe I shouldn't be either. All I know is, that boy had me hooked, and he didn't even know it yet.

FEBRUARY
DEREK

"Good morning, Carmen." I smiled.

"Good morning, Derek."

She eyed me suspiciously, like she had been doing every week at our sessions. I had been in these good ass moods, and that's thanks to Keyarra's ass. Since December, we had sex multiple times a week; I couldn't get enough of her. Just seeing her face makes my day better, honestly. It was her smile that really did it for me; it would light up a room. I've had sex with a lot of girls, but it's something different about her, she made feel different.

"I see you're still in your chipper mood." Carmen took note.

"Yeah, just happy to be here."

She looked at me like, nigga please.

"Are you ready to tell me what has had you in such a good mood, these past few weeks?"

"I feel like you will be disappointed in me."

"Derek, if our personal relationship has started to affect your ability to tell me things that pertain to your therapy, then maybe we need to find you new consultation, so you can be properly treated."

"Ard, calm down, don't go all ethical on me."

Carmen has become like a maternal figure to Tia and myself the past few years, so telling her that I started having sex with someone else besides Katrina, made me nervous. Because we have put a lot of work in to ensure that I keep to one person.

"Um, I had sex with this girl…. or I should say, I've been having sex with this girl."

"Hm, I assume you and Katrina, are still together."

"Yeah."

"Have you been actively having sex with Katrina, as well?"

"Yeah." I said, putting my head down.

"Derek, look at me."

I picked my head back up.

"Did you think I would be upset with you?"

"Yes."

"Listen, I have been trying my best to separate the personal and professional relationship that I have developed with you and your sister. I expect you 2 to do the same as well. But just to let you know, as your friend and your therapist on the contrary, I am very proud of you."

"Why?" I asked, surprised.

"You had such doubts when you came back to Baltimore. You thought you were going to get with any girl that looked at you for longer than 10 seconds. And if you're telling me that after 8 months, you had your first slip up, then that is something to be very proud of. I remember when you would miss sessions with me because you were off acting on your impulses. Don't dwell on your mistake."

I didn't think of it like that at all, but I had to tell her everything.

"I appreciate you saying that, it makes me feel better for sure, but it wasn't a mistake"

"How so?"

"I wanted it. Like that's all I thought about for a long time, then it finally happened, and I can't stay away from her. She got this pull on me, that I can't explain."

"Is this the girl you kissed a while back?"

"Yes."

"Ok, when did you sleep with her?"

"Dec 26th."

"And it has happened since then?"

"Multiple times."

"Ok, so why not break up with, Katrina?"

"Because she has a boyfriend."

"Who has a boyfriend?"

"Keyarra."

Got damn it!

Carmen gave me a surprised look. I was not ready to tell her that yet.

"Keyarra? Like, Tia's best friend, Keyarra?"

I remained silent.

"Derek, you have been withholding a lot, and I'm not sure how I feel about it."

"I know, I um, didn't know how to tell you."

"Why would you and Keyarra, being interested each other be something that you wouldn't want to tell me?"

"I don't know."

"Hm, so you both are cheating?"

"Something like that"

"It's exactly like that."

"Ok."

"So you like her?"

"A lot."

"Then what is so hard about breaking up with, Katrina and pursuing, Keyarra?"

"I told you, she has a boyfriend."

"That she doesn't want to leave?"

"I get that impression."

I told Keyarra a few times that I don't like sneaking around with her. I want to be more open about our situation. It may have seemed like I was moving fast, but we aren't strangers, so I don't see what the issue could be.

"Ok, so why can't you make the first step and end things with Katrina, and maybe that would entice, Keyarra to end hers.... that's if you guys are on the same page."

"That's the thing, I'm not sure if we're on the same page."

Keyarra knows that I want her, more than just sex too. I want to try being in a relationship with her, but she seems very hesitant whenever I bring it up.

"Well, I think that's a serious conversation, that you two should have. Even though being sexually active with her isn't the worst thing in the world, it's still imperative that you still stick with one sexual relationship, at a time. If you don't, there is a possibility it could re-open a door that you don't want to go back in to, if you understand what I'm saying."

"I do."

"Great." she smiled.

Carmen and I finished up our session and I felt so relieved that I could share with someone about Keyarra and me. I was going to take her advice and sit Keyarra down tonight to tell her how I was feeling. I heard a knock at the door and got up to answer it.

"What's up bro?" Matt greeted me.

I dapped him up and let him in. Matt had texted me while I was in session and asked if he could stop by if I wasn't busy. I didn't have class on Fridays, so I told him to slide through.

"What's good with you?" I asked, sitting down on the couch.

He sat on the recliner, that was on the opposite side of the couch.

"Nothing much, I figured you be in the house. I just got done working on something with my dad, and it didn't take long. So, I'm killing time til Rin get out."

"Look at you, in a relationship and shit." I teased.

"Shut up."

"How's it going?"

"It's cool. I feel like we doing the same shit we did before we made it official."

"It be like that."

"She's all excited for Valentine's Day, I don't know what the fuck for."

"What you mean?" I laughed.

"I'm not no romantic ass nigga; she gonna get some flowers, candy, and dick…. that's that."

I couldn't stop laughing because Matt, was dead ass serious.

"You gotta do a little extra man."

"See, that's why I didn't want to do this relationship shit. It's too many expectations."

"Yeah, it can be a little heavy, but just think of something fun to do, and just be extra nice to her…. Shar seem like she not hard to please."

"She's not. I'll think of something. What you gonna do for, Katrina?"

"Now, be lucky you don't have to deal with that one, she is very hard to please. Imma just buy her some shiny shit and take her to, Oceanaire."

"Oooo, Oceanaire, sounds good" Matt said.

"For the love of God, please don't take Shar the same day, Katrina would lose her shit."

"I got you bro." he laughed.

My waterpark: I can still see you tonight right?

Of course…. I miss you

My waterpark: You just saw me this morning lol

So….

My waterpark: I miss you too see you later

Ok stop texting in class

My waterpark: Yes Dad

You can call me daddy if you want

My waterpark: In your dreams…. also I have a surprise for you

I don't like surprises

My waterpark: I don't care, talk to you later

"Who got you over there smiling like that?" Matthew asked.

"Mm, this shorty."

I've been trying my hardest not to lie to anyone, so I answer as honestly as I can.

"You just met her?"

"Naw, I've been known her…. just be flirting and shit through texts."

"You hit?"

I looked over at him and smiled.

"Say no more bro."

Matthew wasn't a fan of Katrina, so he damn sure didn't care that I was cheating on her, but just like everyone else, he just didn't want me falling back into my old ways.

"I got it under control though." I re-assured.

"I believe you, you seem a lot calmer since you've been back."

In Cali, I was always on 10, all I thought about was pussy, and if I couldn't get it, I was not the nicest person to be around. I do think I've come a long way, when Katrina and I 1st got into a relationship, it was hard because she was across the country. So, I have gone longer periods of time without it, but I never want to go through that shit again. I was having full blown withdrawal symptoms, and I didn't like it, not one bit; I felt like a feen. I was calling, Carmen, all hours of the night, but she and Tia helped me through. I'm not sure how long I can go now because even if Katrina was on her period, I was running red lights on her light days; so I've never had to go a full week, since I've moved back. I understand what Carmen was saying about re-opening a door because between Katrina and Keyarra, I was having sex damn near every day. And I can see where that might cause a problem.

"Yeah, I've been cool. Katrina been making me hit these blunts more; her moods have been so up and down lately, but besides that I'm straight."

"You still smoking with Chris?"

"Here and there, but he been falling back because he tryna get into the academy, so he gotta clean his system out."
"Can you picture that nigga as a cop?"
"Honestly no, he is ridiculously smart. He could be useful somewhere else. He could work for NASA or some shit, not no damn Baltimore City Police Department."
"I guess."
"What's the real reason you don't fuck with him?" I asked.
"I just don't."
This nigga!
"I'm telling you he cool, he's good for Tia, too. She been so damn nice lately."
"I've noticed."
"It's only 12, what you tryna do til these girls get out?" I asked.
"Wanna go hoop?"
"Yeah."
It was still cold outside, but it was the best time to hoop, in my opinion.
We hooped around Loch Raven rec, until it was almost time for school to let out. Katrina was supposedly going to see her father for the weekend, so I was free to spend it with Keyarra, if she could get away.

Keyarra told me to come pick her up from the park at 4, which I thought was late because she gets out at 2:45. I was waiting for her for a few minutes, when I saw her skipping down the street with a bag.
"Hi Derek." she smiled.
"Hi love." I said, as I caught her in my arms.
She wrapped her arms around my neck and exhaled; she seemed to be in a very good mood.
"I always feel better when I'm with you." she said, just above a whisper.
"The feeling is mutual, but is everything ok?" I asked, as I kissed softly along her neck.
"Mmmm, yes. How was your day?"

"It was cool, even better now, though."

"Therapy was good?"

"Yes, you thinking about going yet?"

"Um, no."

I have mentioned to Keyarra that Carmen is very easy to work with; she didn't like her last therapist, so she stopped going.

"Well, you just let me know when you're ready."

"Surely will. Are you ready for your surprise?" she asked, getting out of our embrace.

"Yeah, but are you spending the night with me?" I questioned motioning towards her bag.

"Yes...but not at your place." she smiled, wide.

She couldn't keep still; she was very excited.

"Surprise!" she yelled, taking what looked like a key card out her pocket.

"What's that?"

"Derek! It's a hotel key. You said you wanted to stop sneaking around. I figured, for one night we won't have to!"

I wasn't sure what to say.

"Did you have plans after you saw me tonight?" she asked, meekly.

We usually spent a few hours together, maybe had sex in my car, or she would sneak me into her room when G was out, or downstairs for the night. Matthew was spending most of the time at Rin's, so that made it easier.

"Naw, it's not that."

Keyarra stared at me, then it was like a lightbulb went off in her head.

"Shit! You don't like hotels."

"Yeah, they're not my favorite."

"I'm sorry, I totally forgot. It's fine, we can do something else."

"No, uh we can go. We just gotta change the sheets."

"Derek, you look physically uncomfortable, it's cool." she laughed.

"You paid for this right, we're not going to waste it."

"I promise it's fine."

"And, I told you, I don't like repeating myself."
I picked up her bag and put it in the back. I opened the passenger door for her to get in. She slowly walked over; it looked like I killed her mood. As she got in, I slapped her ass hard.
"Ow!" she yelped.
"Stop acting like you don't like that shit." I said, closing her door. We drove back to my place, so I could grab clothes; then we went to Target, so I could get sheets.
"How did you get a hotel?" I questioned.
"The same way I got my tattoo, and piercing."
"And, how is that?"
"I have a fake ID."
"That's still a thing?"
"You have no idea."
She handed me this ID and her learners permit, when I stopped at a light. The ID said she was born in '94. The exact same picture that was on the permit was on the fake ID as well; I had to admit, it looked identical to a real one.
"Keyarra, if it wasn't for your body, there is no way that would work. You have a baby face."
"No I don't." she pouted.
"Yeah, you definitely look like a 22-year-old, when you do that." I laughed.
"Shut up."
"So, is that how you and your alcoholic friends get liquor?"
"No, no one besides you knows. Tre, would run me dry, if he knew."
"Sounds like he has a problem."
"Speaking of a problem..."
I glanced over at her quickly. "What?"
"I know you and I have been together a lot lately, and I just didn't want it to interfere with your..." she paused.
"With my what?"
"I don't think recovery, is the right word."
"It is."
"I'm not interfering with that, am I?"

"I actually wanted to talk you about that, but we can do that at the hotel."

"Derek, we don't have to keep having sex. I just like being around you, we can chill tonight."

"You brought me to a hotel, for me not to fuck you? Yeah ok."

"I'm serious."

"I know you are love, and I appreciate your concern."

We pulled up to the Sheraton hotel in Towson.

"So, you came here, right after school to check in?" I asked.

"Yes, then I had to come back to the house and get a bag real quick."

"You put some thought into this. I guess you got tired of me covering your mouth, so you won't scream when I make you cum."

"Derek, quit it."

We walked through the lobby and onto the elevator. She hit the button for the 7th floor, and we walked to room 712.

"Did you request this room?" I asked.

"No, why?"

"It's your birthday."

"Aww, I didn't even notice."

We entered the room and it looked clean, but I didn't trust that shit. I proceeded to strip the bed and change the sheets, and I wiped down everything in the bathroom.

"You should apply for a job here." Keyarra laughed.

"I'm just being careful. You've never seen hotel nightmares?"

"No, I haven't." she continued to laugh.

"Well, the shit is gross, and I don't trust those maids. They fake clean, so they can get through as many rooms as possible."

Keyarra could not stop laughing.

"I told your paranoid ass, we didn't have to come."

"I hear you. What you want to eat?"

"I wanted to take you to, Stoney River."

I stopped what I was doing and looked over at her.

"Keyarra, are you trying to take me on a date?"

"Um, maybe. But it was more so to make up for your birthday, since I didn't see you."
Katrina took me to Philly for my birthday, last month. We stayed the whole weekend. I can be done with hotels for the rest of the year for real. I sat down on edge of the bed and motioned for Keyarra to come here. She walked over and straddled me.
"I don't want you spending your money on me." I said, peering up at her.
She started playing with my hair in the back and I leaned into it more. I loved when she did that.
"I remember saying something similar to you, for my birthday, and you did the opposite."
"That's because I'm grown and can do what I want."
"Well, my ID says I'm grown, so I can do what I want too."
I laughed; I leaned back and fell on the bed taking her with me. Our lips found each other and after a few minutes, I was ready for her to be gripped around my dick. Our kiss intensified, as my hands made their way up her shirt and in one swift move, I slid it off.
"Derek wait, we were supposed to talk about this first."
"We'll talk after." I said, removing my long-sleeved tee.
She gave me a disapproving look, but she didn't fight it, thankfully. Keyarra, sat up and started to undue my belt.
"Can I lick the tip?" she asked, seductively.
"I told you already, you can taste mine, if I can taste yours."

I had been begging Keyarra to let me give her head, but she was being stingy. She tried to suck my dick a few times, despite me telling her how I feel about that. I told her, if she let me lick it just once, then she could as well, but even that didn't sway her. That was for the best because it was no way, I was just doing one lick; I'm going to devour her, when she gives me the chance, I wanted that waterpark all over my face. She removed her bra, and I bit my bottom lip; she had the prettiest breasts I had ever seen, and the piercing just did something to me every time. She leaned forward, so I can catch one in my mouth.

"Mmm, bite it." She requested.
I did as she asked, and she shuddered. I continued to lick and nibble on both her nipples. She was squirming around, so I sat up and wrapped my arms around her waist to keep her still.
"What I tell you about moving around so much?"
"I can't help it."
She took my face in her hands and kissed me deeply, as she started to grind against my erection.
"Can I ride it?" she whispered, against my lips.
"You can do what you want."
I wanted to tell her it was hers because that's how I genuinely felt.
We took our bottoms off and before I could suggest a condom, she was sliding down on to me, and it took everything out of me not to nut. Keyarra's wetness and tightness felt new to me every single time. This wasn't the 1st time we went unprotected, but I tried to limit it. I was strapping up more with Katrina, but we also sometimes went without.
"Damn." I hissed.
She started to slowly ride me, and I had my hands at her waist. We held eye contact, as she bit down on her bottom lip and picked up her speed. I could already feel her dripping.
"You so wet man." I said, arching my head back slightly.
My nut was building, but there was no way I was cumming this fast.
"It only gets wet like this for you." She purred, in the sexiest voice.
SHIT!
"Chill Key, you tryna make me nut."
Her voice could do that to me. Keyarra placed both her hands on either side of my head, she pressed her chest against mine, and I could feel the tiny balls from her nipple rings. At this point, she was riding me like her life depended on it, and all you could hear was the gushy noises from her wetness.
"Damn Derek, this dick so good." She moaned in my ear.
"Mm hm, I can feel you about to cum."

Keyarra always got extra wet when she was close to cumming. I wrapped my arm around her waist and started fucking her from the bottom. I thrusted in and out, in and out, in and out, as fast as I could.

Keyarra was yelling.

"Yeah, let me hear you girl!"

"Fuck Derek, I'm cumming!"

"Cum all over my dick!" I demanded.

She started to shake and moan wildly. I was about to flip her over and go into missionary, when she hopped up and turned around. Without so much, as a second thought she slid right back down onto my dick, but in reverse. I loved that about her; Keyarra, could keep up and go round after round with me.

"Damn, you ready huh?" I laughed.

"Mm hm, I think you've created a monster."

Keyarra, planted both her feet on the bed and started leap frogging on my shit. I watched that little butterfly move right along with her luscious ass cheeks. The sight alone was threating to pull a nut out of me prematurely.

"You showing the fuck out in this room." I groaned.

I watched as she continuously bounced up and down. She lasted longer than I expected, she would stop just before she got to the tip, then move down again, until my entire dick disappeared inside her. Keyarra, had me gripping the side of the bed; I've never done that in my got damn life. She started flexing her muscles around me every time she slid back down, and I was about to nut.

"Keyarra, I'm about to bust."

"Me too, tell me when." She moaned loudly.

Keyarra, leaned forward and grabbed my ankles; she continued to move her ass up and down. I've had my experiences with a fair share of women, some have been damn near twice my age, and they haven't done things like this.

"Just like that Key, don't move." I gritted, then smacked her ass. I was about to cum hard as hell, and she was too.

"Derek, Derek…." she cried out.

She was splashing everywhere.

"Oh shittttt, I'm cumming, Key."

I held her by her waist, tightly, and without any thought, I released my seeds, right inside of her.

"FUCK!" I yelled out, as I jerked until I was done cumming.

We sat still for a second to catch our breath. Keyarra jumped up and ran to the bathroom; I hope she didn't think peeing was going to get rid of all the kids I just shot inside her. I heard the toilet flush then water running. She walked back to the bed slowly and cuddled up next to me. I wrapped my arm around her and sighed.

"I fucked up, I'm sorry." I finally said, after some silence.

"It's ok, I take my pill every day and I can take a Plan B."

"It's not good to keep taking those, Key…that one time was enough."

"Ok. We just have to be more careful and not get caught up in the moment."

"Key, you know this isn't what I meant about me being tired of us sneaking around, right?"

"Kind of. I thought you got tired of the muffled moans and car sessions."

"I am, but we are still sneaking, but just in a hotel now."

She sat up and looked at me. "So, what do you want? You want to stop, altogether?"

"Is that what you want?"

"No, I can live without sex with you I guess, but I do really like being in your presence."

"So, how can we explain us spending time together. Either way, they are going to think something is going on, whether we are still having sex or not."

I was trying to get Keyarra, to say what I was thinking, to see if we were on the same page.

"Um, I'm not sure."

I sighed. "What if I break up with Katrina, and you break up with, Tre?"

She looked a little surprised.

"You want to be my boyfriend?"

"I mean I told you before that we don't have to jump into anything if you don't want, but you mentioned earlier about my recovery. I'm doing really well with that, but it's not the best for me to be involved with more than one person at a time."

"And you want to be involved with me only?"

"Yes."

"Why?"

"We can chill without having sex. I've never had that before, honestly. All Katrina and I do is argue and have sex. I love sex, don't get me wrong but I think it should be more to a relationship then that. You're really like a breath of fresh air to me, Key."

"That's how I feel, too."

"I'm happy to hear that."

"But I don't know if I can break up with Tre, right now." She said, sadly.

"Why not?"

"He's going through a lot right now. His parents are divorcing, and it's senior year; and I'm his prom date and it's just a lot to put on him."

"Keyarra, he's the quarterback, he can find another prom date. All that other shit, sounds like excuses to me."

"How are you just ok with leaving Katrina assed out like that?"

"Because, me and you would look better at prom, with our matching dimples." I joked.

I had deep dimples on both my cheeks, but Keyarra only had one on her left side, which I thought was the cutest shit.

"It's not funny, Derek." She said, seriously.

"It's not, but I'm being honest. Listen, either I care about someone enough to not lie to them, or I don't care enough about them to lie; either way, I don't like to lie and lately I've been lying to a lot of people that I care about."

She stared at me, and I can tell she was processing everything I said to her; I pulled her back down to me.

"I want to go to prom with you…. have loud sex with you…. even argue with you." I said lowly, in between pecking her lips.

I made my way to her neck, and she giggled.
"I will think about it, Derek." She laughed.
"I'll take that answer for now."
I pulled her in for a kiss and before I knew it, I was inside her again, strapped up this time. We never made it to dinner!

It was the middle of the night, and I watched as Keyarra struggled in her sleep again. We had only spent the night together a few times, but this was the second time I saw her have a nightmare. She had distress written all over her face; I heard her murmur, please stop, more than once. I wanted to hear more to see if she would give away what she was dreaming about, but I didn't like seeing her like that. Tia mentioned to me that she heard Keyarra talking in her sleep a few times, telling someone to stop. We were both concerned but didn't know how to go about the situation. I almost slipped up and told her that I also witnessed Keyarra having a nightmare.

I started to gently shake her, as I placed soft kisses all over her face; I didn't want her to wake up scared, like she had before. Her eyes fluttered opened, as she looked around, relief washed over her face when she realized where she was.
"It's ok baby." I comforted.
"I'm sorry." Her voice cracked.
"Don't be sorry, tell me what your nightmares are about."
She shook her head no.
"You can tell me Key, maybe if you talk about them, they won't occur so often."
"I can't." She whispered.
"Yes, you can!"
Keyarra pulled me towards her and kissed me. She pulled the covers from over us and placed her hand on my semi-hard penis.
"Don't do that, Keyarra." I protested pulling away from her, "don't try to shut me up with sex, Katrina does that shit to me, and I don't like it."
"I-I'm..."

"Don't say you're sorry, either. It's fine, but I'm just letting you know. I understand that you don't want to talk about your nightmares, so I'm not gonna press you, right now but just know that I'm worried about you and I want you to talk to me or someone about them soon....ok?"

She nodded her head.

"I didn't hear you."

"Yes Derek."

I put the covers back over us and kissed her forehead. She pulled my face and kissed my lips.

"Thank you." she said staring into my eyes.

I know people say shit about my eyes but hers put me in trance often.

"I got you Key....always."

She smiled then wrapped her arm back around my waist, placing her head on my chest.

"Derek, I'm going to break up with him this weekend." she voiced, quietly.

That was music to my ears.

"And I'll break with Katrina, this weekend too...deal?"

"Deal."

"And Derek?"

"Yeah."

"I really love listening to your heartbeat."

I chuckled. "Ard, Dahmer." I joked.

"Shut up." She laughed.

Sunday morning, I was going straight to Katrina's house and breaking up with her. She probably wasn't going to take it well, but it had to be done.

I watched as my phone rang for the 4th time by Keyarra. I had missed her previous calls because I didn't know what the hell to say. We ended up spending most of the day together Saturday, and decided we were going to break up with Tre and Katrina, the next day. She had plans to meet Tre, in a public place around 12 to end things with him, I offered to come and watch from nearby, but she declined and insisted that she would be fine. I told her to call me when everything was done, but I had got wrapped up in my own shit with Katrina. I texted Tri to let me know when she got home, so I could stop by, she responded almost immediately, and told me she was, already. I wondered why she hadn't been told me that, but I wasn't sweating it. The conversation didn't go the way I thought it would earlier.

"What's up Tri, how was your trip?" I asked as I sat on her bed. I wanted to stay downstairs, but granny was there today.
"It was good, my dad says hi."
"Cool, what did y'all do?"
"A little of everything." She stated, simply.
Katrina looked really tired, and she didn't seem like herself. She wasn't as energetic as I thought she would be to see me, but that's cool because maybe she is feeling the same way I'm feeling, and this will be an easy conversation.
"Cool, cool, so um, I wanted to talk to you about something."
"Ok, I need to talk to you about something too, but you can go first."
"Ard, um I had been thinking...that we should just...uh..."
I was nervous for some reason, but I couldn't beat around the bush.
"That we should just go our separate ways." I continued.
She grinned. "You've said that before, Derek."
"I know, but I mean it this time, like I don't think we are good for each other anymore."
"Who told you that? The bitches you've been fucking?"
Katrina was extremely calm, and it wasn't sitting right with me.
"Um, no."
"So you are fucking someone else?" she asked, with a raised brow.

"Yeah." I answered, honestly.

She just stared at me then stood up, she walked over to her dresser and started rummaging through it. I stood up because I wasn't sure what the hell her crazy ass was about to do.

"This is what I wanted to talk to you about."

She handed me this large plastic baggie, that had 5 pregnancy tests in it. I examined them and they all had 2 lines on them, one even clear as day, said pregnant. I looked at her and she had tears in her eyes. She walked over to me and lifted her shirt, just above her stomach, she grabbed my hand and placed it there; I felt a small bump.

"I'm pregnant Derek, you can't leave me. I need you. We're going to be parents."

I was in shock; I just felt her stomach some more in disbelief.

"Tri, I-I um…. I don't know what to say."

"Say that you're happy! I was so scared to tell you." She said, as tears fell from her eyes.

"Is it mine?"

She looked up, and her face broke up more while fresh tears fell.

"Derek, yes, it is!"

"How far along are you?"

"Just over 4 months."

My mind was racing, how did I not notice? I mean, she had a very small bump, but I still should've known. Flashes of us having sex with her shirt on, or her getting angry at the smallest things, went through my mind.

"Homecoming?"

She nodded her head slowly.

"The Plan B didn't work, I guess."

I walked back over to her bed and just stared at the tests some more.

She came to sit next to me and laid her head on my shoulder.

"Derek, I know I've been a bitch, but I promise I will be better. I'll be better for you and for our child. Just please give me a chance to prove it."

I still didn't have any words. Katrina sat up and turned my head to face her.

"Do you remember before we were in relationship; we talked about how we didn't want our future children to be raised in broken homes because of the things we had to go through growing up.... screaming parents and thinking that we had to choose sides." She asked.

"Yeah."

"I still don't want that, and I know you don't either. Let's give this a real shot. I don't care about you cheating, we can move past that. We can be a family. I can't go through this alone!"

She leaned forward and kissed my lips softly, she pulled back and she stared into my eyes, before she leaned in again. I accepted and kissed her back.

"I got you Tri, we're gonna figure this out."

"Thank you baby."

She wrapped her arms around my neck, and I embraced her.

How in the fuck am I going to tell Keyarra this?

TIA

It was 7 in the morning, and I was getting ready for school. Derek said he was going to drop me off, but he went for yet another run. He had been doing that damn nearly every day, for the past few weeks. I tried to ask him a few times if everything was ok, but he said he was cool. It's like one minute he couldn't stop smiling, then the next, he was in a bad mood. He was either over Katrina's or locked himself in his room; he even missed a few Sunday dinners, which was a bad sign. I was going to try my hardest to talk to him on our ride today. We just got back on decent terms, after my little stunt I pulled a few months back. I lied and told him I was with my friends, when I was really with, Matt. Nothing happened between us, but we were just enjoying each other's company, and time got away from us, my phone was on silent, so I didn't even see Derek or Keyarra's missed calls and messages until later that night. I texted Keyarra back, but she never replied, and when I called she didn't answer. I was going to go home but I ended up crashing at GG's, but I stayed in Keyarra's room, and Matt dropped me off home early, G didn't even know I had been there. I didn't cheat, but I still felt bad about lying to Chris. Shit, I lied to everyone, Keyarra and Derek; how Derek knew I was full of shit, is still beyond me; I guess he just has that intuition. Keyarra asked me where I was, and I told her that I spent the night with

Chris alone and that I knew Derek would be pissed if he knew that so that's why I threw her and Tre in the mix. I don't think she fully believed me but shit that was the best I could come up with and I was thankful that she didn't question it any further. I asked her if she was ok because her messages seemed like she was upset but she said she was fine and that she stayed with Tre for the night. I heard Derek's room door close, I walked down the hall and gently knocked.

"It's open." he said, from the other side.
"Hey, I'm ready when you are."
"Ok, we can leave in like 10."
"Cool, how was your run?"
"It was good."
I walked further into the room and looked at him. My brother was stressed, it was all over his face.
"Derek, what's going on?"
He was sitting on his couch on his phone. He looked over at me and sat the phone down.
"I fucked up, Ti."
"Ok, well you know I will help you with whatever".
"You can't help me with this."
"Are you um, feeling like you are slipping or something? I've helped you through those before."
"Naw....Katrina's pregnant." he said, faintly.
"Excuse me?"
Derek inhaled and exhaled deeply "Katrina, is pregnant."
"Derek what the fuck?" I shouted.
"Yeah, that's what I said."
"Is she keeping it?"
He squinted at me and turned his head slightly.
"What kind of question is that, Tia?" His calm tone was filled with anger, but I didn't care.
"Derek, you can't have a baby!"
"Well I am. Let's go, so I can drop you off."

I was feeling hot all over and my voice was caught in my throat. There was no way in hell, this was happening. For a while, I thought he was getting over her, but now he was spending all his free time with her, and this explains it. She trapped my brother, and I am livid! Derek got up and walked past me.

"Derek wait!" I said following him.

"I don't wanna talk, Tia."

"Are you even sure it's yours?"

"I can't determine that right now but considering the fact we don't use condoms that much, then it is a strong possibility."

"How can you be so stupid, Derek?" I yelled jumping in front of him.

"I think you should watch who you're talking to, Tia." he said, menacingly.

His eyes got dark and his nostrils flared. That shit didn't phase me; I've seen it many times.

"Derek, I don't give a fuck about you being mad! You can do a DNA test, now!"

"Why would I put her through that? I'll do that when the baby is born; until then, I'm going to proceed, like this baby is mine!" he shouted back.

"But Derek!" I pleaded.

"But nothing! I'm not putting her through the shit mommy went through, when she was pregnant with you. Our father loves telling me I'm too young to remember, but I remember everything. How mommy would cry because he refused to show up to the appointments, how devastated she was when he missed your birth, Tia! She never let him live that shit down, all the way until the day she died. If I carry Katrina like that and this baby is mine, then I'm the one that missed out! And that shit is not happening! That girl could make my life a living hell, if I dog her while she is pregnant, so I don't need any shit from you or anybody else, about the way I'm handling my fucking business." He screamed.

Derek was seething! I don't think I've ever seen him THIS angry before. Tears poured from my eyes; everything he said was true. Our mother brought up every single time she could, about how DW treated her when she was pregnant. I felt terrible for her, that always added more fuel to my fire, when it came to how I interacted with him. My mother made one mistake and he took it out on her, time and time again, but Katrina was different! That bitch is a snake, and my brother was too blinded by a fat ass and a pretty face to see it; that baby isn't his and I can feel it in my soul; I'm willing to put that on my mother's grave.

"Whoa whoa, what's going on?" DW asked, as he stepped through the front door.
What the fuck was he even doing here?
It was a Friday, and he usually came on Saturdays.
"Does he know?" I asked Derek.
"Naw."
"Do I know what?" DW questioned.
I stepped back and motioned for Derek to spill it.
"Go ahead!" I urged.
Derek just shook his head and sat on the couch.
"Katrina, is pregnant." Derek revealed.
DW sat his bag down.
"Ok, I thought it was some real heavy shit."
My mouth dropped. "What?"
"To be honest, I thought this would've happened as soon as y'all touched down here." He admitted.
"You can't be serious right now." I said, in disbelief.
"Tia, I had a baby by the time I was Derek's age, so it's not the most uncommon thing."
I could not believe what I was hearing.
"I don't know why I thought you would say something useful." I sneered.
"Tia, chill." Derek said.
"No, I'm not going to fucking chill! Your son is supposed to better than you! He's supposed to finish college and be the boss of some

financial firm or some shit. Not changing diapers and shacking up with some HOE!" I yelled.

"Tia, watch your mouth! And stop yelling at our dad!" Derek said standing up.

"He's your damn dad, NOT MINE!" I pointed. "He's a sorry ass excuse for a father and a man." I yelled.

"That's enough, Tia!" Derek yelled.

"Whatever. Fuck both of y'all for real!"

I grabbed my bag and ran out the door. Tears continued to stream down my face, as I raced down the hallway. I was starting to breathe heavily, so I needed to calm down. I stopped in the lobby and called Chris; it rang but he didn't answer.

"Ughhh" I groaned.

I called Matthew next.

"What's up, Ti?"

"Are you busy? Can you come take me to school?"

"Uhhh yeah, you may be late, though.... everything ok?"

"Not really, but it's fine. I just need a ride. If you're busy, I can call an Uber."

"Naw, you good. I'm on my way. Give me like 15 minutes."

Not even 15 minutes later, Matt pulled up. I hopped in and he pulled off.

"What's going on?" He asked.

I wasn't sure if Derek had told Matt or not about the baby, and it wasn't my business to share.

"I got into a fight Derek and DW."

"About what?"

"Same shit; he's not my father and how much I hate him."

"You said that?"

"In so many words."

"C'mon Ti, that's not ok."

"Pease don't start. I just want to get to school and forget about this morning."

"I understand, but you can't be disrespectful."

"I know you're not talking about being disrespectful. The man who was blacked out drunk, how many times in G's house?" I snapped.

I wasn't for anyone's shit today!

"Tia don't take your anger out on me. I'm just saying! But imma leave it alone because you're tripping today."

We rode the rest of the way in silence; he pulled up to the front of the school and I got out, as quickly as I could.

"Thanks." I said quickly and closed the door.

I walked into the school, and I had never been so happy to be here.

I looked down at my phone and saw that Chris called and texted me. I texted him back to meet me after school; I wasn't even going to attempt to make it to homeroom. I just headed in the direction of my 1st period. I waited in the hall until the bell rang. There was a girl walking in my direction. I saw her around school a few times, and she always had a mug on her face, but I didn't know her name.

"Cute boots." she complimented me as she walked by. I noticed how she looked me up and down with a slight smirk.

It was the beginning of March, and it was still a little nippy outside, so I had on my Michael Kors, heeled, Chelsea boots.

"Oh, thanks."

She smiled at me but it didn't reach her eyes; there was something about the way that she looked at me that I didn't like. She seemed a little ratchet to me, with her stale weave, that was fire engine red; it reached all the way down, past her butt. The bell rang and I shook off my thoughts. I hoped school went by slow for once because I wasn't ready to see DW or his dumbass son.

I was waiting outside near Chris's car until he was done getting changed from basketball practice. Thankfully, he didn't have to work today, so I was trying to stay at his house, for as long as I could tonight.

"Hello, Ti-baby."

That voice always gives me a bad case of the chills. I turned around slowly, and saw the pain in my ass, Darren, standing there.

"Do not...call me that. And that is my last time telling you."

"Your attitude makes my dick hard."

I went to smack his ass, but he caught me by my wrist and squeezed tightly.

"Get the fuck off of me!" I yelled.

Since it was late, there wasn't a lot of people around.

"I really can't wait to stuff that pretty little mouth of yours!"

Fear washed over me because his eyes were sinister. As I struggled to get out of his grasp, a car came screeching into the parking lot. I thought someone saw what was happening and was coming to help.

"I bet they shut your prissy ass up." he sneered.

Three girls dressed in oversized hoodies and sunglasses hopped out the car, just as he let me go and shoved me to the ground. Before I could get up, the girls approached me and started to bank me. They hailed hits left and right; I tried my hardest to defend myself, but one kicked me right in the stomach and I swear, she cracked a rib.

"Go the fuck back to the west coast, bitch!"

KICK!

"Where's all that mouth now, hoe?"

PUNCH!

"I guess you didn't believe me, when I said he was mine!"

I started swinging and kicking wildly. I kicked one bitch right in the stomach with my heel.

"You dumb bitch!" she yelled.

"Hey, hey! Stop that!" I heard the voice of a man, who I assumed, was coming out of the school.

I received one last blow to the head, before the girls took off back to the car. My vision was blurry, but I saw a flash of something red!

"Tia!!!" I heard Chris yell.

I was weak and my body was on fire.

"Tia Tia, what happened! Somebody get some help!" He screamed.

I felt him by my side, but his voice was becoming faint.

"Hold on Tia. Just hold on...."

Everything went black.

"My daughter is laying in a hospital bed, and the best you can tell me, is that y'all are doing the best you can do? Go pull some fucking cameras and get the little deviants that did this to my child!" DW shouted.

"Derek, you have to calm down and let them do their job." GG said, softly.

I assume he was on the phone because I didn't hear any response to his loud ass. I tried to open my eyes, but they hurt so bad. I groaned, and I instantly felt a presence around me.

"Baby girl, baby girl, can you hear me?" He questioned.

I just nodded my head slowly, even that hurt to do.

Those bitches really fucked me up!

"THANK THE LORD" GG praised.

"Ti, we're here. We're all here" Derek said next.

I heard beeping noises, and I could feel that I was in a gown, so I was in a hospital. But I don't even remember how I got here.

Tears stung to my eyes, as my mind started to flood with what happened to me.

"Don't cry Ti, you're ok now." Derek comforted.

"I'll go tell everyone she's awake and go get the doctor." GG said.

I attempted to open my eyes again and although it hurt, I was able to open them, and my eyesight slowly adjusted. I scanned the room. Derek and DW were at my bedside.

"How bad is it?" I asked, hoarsely.

"It's not too bad, Ti. Let the doctor tell you." Derek answered.

A few seconds passed and I saw GG come in, with a pretty brown skin woman, who I assume was the doctor.

"Hello, Ms.Williams, I'm glad to see you're awake. I'm, Dr.Wallace."

She quickly washed her hands then approached my bed, she took a little flashlight out her pocket and quickly flashed it, in both my eyes.

"Perfect. If it doesn't make you too uncomfortable, can you tell me how you're feeling." She asked, politely

"Just pain…. everywhere…. hurts to breathe." I mumbled out.

"OK, I'll get you something for that. So, you have a bruised rib, which is why it is painful to breathe. We did a CT scan and you have no brain injuries or any other internal injuries, which is the best news possible. You do have a mild concussion, so I want to keep you overnight, just so you can be monitored. Besides that Tia, you just have some bumps and bruises that will heal with time."

Those weak hoes couldn't even do any real damage!

"You are a tough cookie." she continued.

"Damn right she is." Derek threw in.

They all lightly laughed, but I didn't find anything funny.

"I will get meds for you and besides that, you just need to rest. Any questions from anyone?" she asked, as she looked at everyone.

"No. Thank you, Dr." DW said, as he shook her hand.

He smiled at her and I swear, she blushed. If I could throw something at him, I would.

"Can I have water?" I asked before she left the room.

"Absolutely. A nurse will be in with your meds and water in a few minutes."

She disappeared out of the room and we all just kind of sat in silence.

"How long was I out?" I finally asked.

"About 4 hours." Derek answered.

"How did I get here?"

"An ambulance. Chris, rode with you and he called me."

The mention of his name made me furious. Another lady walked in. She was white, with long brown hair, pulled into a ponytail; she introduced herself as nurse, Stephanie. She told me that she would be administering my meds through my IV. We watched as she did it, then she poured me some water.

"Just give me a buzz, if you guys need anything else." she said cheerfully and exited the room.

I finished the 1st cup quickly; and went to pour another.

"I got it, baby girl." DW said.

He helped with the water and handed it to me.

"Thanks. Um, can I see my face?"

He hesitated for a second, then looked over at GG.

"Baby, maybe you should wait for a day or 2…. Just until the swelling goes down." GG said.

"Let me see my face, please." I urged, seriously.

My father dug his phone out his pocket and went to the camera. He faced it towards me, and my eyes instantly welled with tears. Both of my eyes looked swollen and purple, and my bottom lip was busted.

I'm going to kill those bitches!

"Remember Ti, the doctor just said it's bruises, it will heal up." Derek reassured.

I heard a faint knock, and I looked at the door. Keyarra was standing there with tears in her eyes.

"Tia." she cried.

"Hey." I said, faintly.

"I'm so sorry! I should have stayed after school with you."

"It's not your fault."

My eyes went from her to Matthew, at the door and he looked just as pitiful as Keyarra did.

"What's up Ti. I'm glad to see you're awake."

"Thank you."

"Imma step out, so everyone else can come in." DW said.

"Me too." GG said, as she followed him out.

"Who's everyone else?" I questioned.

I got my answer a few seconds later.

Sharin and Christian stepped in the room.

"Ti-baby." he said, as he rushed to my bedside. "I'm so happy you're ok; you scared the shit out of me!"

"Yeah Ti-Ti, you had us on the edge of our seats." Sharin chimed in.

Anger started to run through my veins.

"Please leave." I said, lowly.

"Huh?" Chris asked.

"You heard me…. get out!"

"Tia!" Derek said.

"Tia, what did I do?"

"This is your fault!"

"How, I don't understand!"

"You said I had nothing to worry about, you said you handled it, but look at my fucking face, and look at where the hell I am at!" I said, in a more elevated tone, as tears threatened to fall again.

"Tia, I don't know what you're talking about." Chris said, with confusion all over his face.

"Lisa! Lisa, the bitch with the red hair and some other hoe banked me."

"You saw them, Tia?" Keyarra questioned.

"I told you he was mine! That's what she said, and I saw the girl with red hair earlier, in the hallway. I saw her shoes when she kicked me in the fucking stomach; they were the same tired ass Js that she had on this morning!" I explained furiously.

Pain radiated through my body, but I didn't care, I was pissed!

"Lisa? Lisa wouldn't do this. She's not that kind of girl." Chris said.

"Did you think she was the kind of girl to cheat on you?" I asked, vilely.

I saw the pain on Chris's face when I said that.

"Exactly! And that nigga Darren was there too. He set me up; he knew those bitches were coming, you dragged me into whatever dick swinging contest y'all have been having, and look!!! You let this shit happen and I want you to leave. NOW!" I shouted.

He stared at me for a few seconds before he got up and stormed out the room. I narrowed my eyes onto Sharin, next.

"AND SHE'S YOUR COUSIN!! SO, AS FAR AS I'M CONCERNED YOU WERE IN ON IT, SO YOU CAN GET THE FUCK OUT TOO!"

"Tia, chill." Matthew said, as he stepped in front of her.

"You can step as well. As a matter of fact all y'all can get the hell out!"

My head was pounding, and my ribs were on fire. I overdid it and now I was paying for it!

Matthew just shook his head; he turned around, grabbed a crying Sharin's hand and they left. I looked over at Keyarra and pointed to the door. I wanted everyone out. When she didn't move, Derek walked over to her and whispered something in her ear. She stared up at him, then looked back over at me.

"I love you Tia, and I'll be back tomorrow." She stated, then she went to leave the room; she slightly bumped into Derek, and it didn't look like an accident to me. I watched as Derek followed her with his eyes, until she disappeared. He looked a little more upset now.

"Tia, you've been on one today, hospital bed or not. I get that you're upset, but that's not right, those are your friends. But they not gonna hold it against you. You're clearly not thinking straight."

I gave Derek the death stare. "I meant you too. I want you to leave"

"Oh naw, I'm not going anywhere. You might scare them, but not me. Your big brother will be right here with your mean ass."

"Shouldn't you go check on your child's mother or something?" I hissed.

"I already did. Now just because I'm in here, doesn't mean we have to talk. Take your ass to sleep."

He plopped on the chair in the corner and got on his phone. I didn't have the energy to fight him, I was too tired. Today has been the day from hell!

It had been a little over 3 weeks since I was attacked, but I'm almost fully healed. My face was back to normal, I still had a few bruises, and my ribs still ached, but besides that, I was good. I still hadn't gone back to school because I used the excuse of not feeling safe. I was an honor roll student, so my grades didn't suffer too much. Keyarra brought most of my work home and the teachers were very accommodating. I got the news that Lisa, Darren and the red head girl who I learned her name was, Shanae, were all expelled; my sperm donor was also pressing charges. But that wasn't enough for me, I wanted my lick back, but that will come in due time. I ended up apologizing to everyone except for, Chris, because fuck him! I was in Keyarra's room waiting for her to come home from school. I spent most of my time there during my recovery because one, GG was able to watch me, and two, it was still some tension between Derek and I, even though I apologized. He looked so unhappy lately, and I hated that for him. I can admit, I'm proud of him for stepping up, but just the thought of Katrina being around for the rest of our lives, made my ass itch.

"Hey Ti." Keyarra said, walking into the room.
"Hey, how was your day?"
"It was good. Since spring break starts, your teachers didn't hand out any homework or anything."
"OK cool. Thanks for doing that for me, these past few weeks."
"It's no problem. Tre asked me to prom today.... again."
"Damn again, what did you say?"
A few days after I was released from the hospital, Keyarra told me that she broke up with Tre. I was happy for her because she didn't seem happy in that relationship; she said that she wasn't too upset about the break-up, but I could tell something was bothering her. I would press down on her, but she insisted she was fine. One thing that bitch gonna do, is keep a secret!
"I finally said yes because he looked so damn sad. But I told him I didn't want to get back together. He's going to school in PA; it just makes sense for us to end things now." she explained.
"Yeah I get it. I'm glad you decided to go because our dresses are almost done." I said, excitedly.

Keyarra, Sharin, and I were getting our dresses made for prom; I had been working very closely with the designer. The girls gave me full control. They just told me what color they wanted; well, Keyarra didn't, she said she trusted me. I had been having the time of my life; I know I was getting on the designer's nerves but, oh well.

"Have you talked to Chris?"

"No, he calls every day though. It's annoying."

"Why haven't you blocked him then?" she asked, with her hand on her hip.

I remained silent.

"That's what I thought, you ain't fooling nobody. Tia, who you gonna go to prom with if you're ignoring Chris?"

"Girl, I will find another date or I will go by myself."

"You're not going by yourself."

"Whatever."

"Um, you cool with Sharin coming up?"

I sucked my teeth.

"She been downstairs the whole time? "SHARIN, GET YOUR ASS UP HERE." I yelled.

Even though I apologized, she has been very skittish around me. I heard light footsteps coming up the staircase. Sharin slid into the room.

"Hey Tia." she said softly.

I rolled my eyes.

"So, I can't be Ti-Ti anymore because I cussed you out, one time? Girl I had a concussion." I said, playfully.

A smile crept on her face.

"Hey, Ti-Ti."

"Thank you, that's better. How was school?"

"Good, I'm ready for break"

"I bet. I'm going to go back after break."

"Yay, class is so boring without you." she cheered.

"Yeah, yeah. She's coming back. Sharin, tell her!" Keyarra said.

"Tell me what? I questioned.

Sharin looked a little hesitant.

"Rin don't make me cuss you out again. Tell me what?" I urged.

"We know where Lisa is going to be tonight."

My eyes lit up, like a Christmas tree.

"For real?"

"Yeah. Keyarra and I were going to go pay her visit, but we thought we should see if you want to come."

"Hell yeah, I wanna come!" I said, jumping up.

The sudden movement made me wince.

"See, you're doing too much; you can't go out there wild'n, Tia. You're still healing up." Keyarra fussed.

"If you think I'm not about to drag her ass, then you're the one that's wild'n."

Sharin laughed.

"I knew we shouldn't have told you." Keyarra said, rolling her eyes.

"You keep enough shit from me. What time we going?"

"Um, Chris said he would take us when we were ready." Sharin mumbled.

My eyes reached the sky.

"Why can't we get, Matt?"

"Because boo said if he finds out what we're up to, he's gonna kick all our asses." Sharin explained.

"Fine, whatever. I'm just ready to go. What about, Shanae?"

"No one knows where she lives and honestly, her and Lisa aren't even friends, I think she just recruited her. The bitch is ghetto and just likes to fight." Keyarra said.

"What about the 3rd girl?"

"As far as we heard, she is just a friend of Shanae's, but she wouldn't give up her name when she was at the station." Sharin answered.

"At least the hoe not a rat." Keyarra stated.

"So, them bitches don't know me from a can of paint and banked me?" I asked out loud.

"Looks like it, but Lisa about to get hers." Sharin said.

"So, you cool with setting up your own peoples?" I asked.

Sharin scoffed. "This has been a long time coming. Blood ain't always thicker than water. Lisa tried to tell the school that we didn't live together, so that I would get kicked out. If it wasn't for my auntie setting me up with the magnet program, my ass would not be at Parkville. So, fuck her." Sharin said, seriously.

"Heavy on, fuck her!" Keyarra agreed.

We got ready and our childish asses were so excited. We went down the steps and were out the front door, when we ran straight into, Matthew. He eyed us, suspiciously; we were all dressed in sweats and sneakers.

"What are y'all up to?"

"Nothing, about to go chill with, Chris." Keyarra said, quickly.

He looked over at Rin, who was avoiding his eye contact.

"Ard. Let me talk to you for a second, Rin."

"Matt, Chris is waiting! We gotta go" Keyarra whined.

"Ok, tell him she'll be one second."

Before Keyarra could protest any further, he backed Sharin into the house.

"Shit." Keyarra hissed.

"What?" I asked.

"Sharin is wrapped around Matt's finger, and she can't lie for shit."

"Damn, she about to get us caught up"

"Let's hope not."

Chris started to approach us and I turned away, slightly. I hadn't laid eyes on him, since the hospital; he looked good a hell.

"Hey y'all, what's the hold up?" he asked.

"Hey Chris, we're waiting for, Rin"

"Cool. Hey Ti." he greeted, apprehensively.

"Hi." I said, without bothering to turn in his direction.

"Uh, I'm glad to see you're doing better."

"Thank you."

"Do you think I can talk to you for a minute?"

Sharin suddenly came out the door.

"Let's go...now!" she said, rushing down the steps.

"Hey Chrissy." she said, passing him and hopping in the car.

"What happened?" Keyarra asked, once we all got in and Chris pulled off.

"He just asked where we were going, and I told him to chill with Chris, but he kept asking why were dressed like that especially, Tia. Girl, what you don't wear sweats or something?" she asked me.

I hate that Matthew knew me so well.

"Not really."

"I was nervous as hell; y'all better not get a scratch on y'all." Sharin said.

"She won't get the opportunity." I spoke.

Chris looked at me through his rearview.

"Be careful Tia. Your brother will kill me if he knew I drove y'all."

"Ain't nobody thinking about Derek, he got bigger things to worry about."

"Got that right." Keyarra mumbled.

I wonder what she means by that.

"So, what's the plan? Where are we catching her at?"

"My home girl's mom does her hair, around the corner from her house; she walks home from there. I know what way she takes; not many people go that way because it's a little creepy, but it's the fastest way." Sharin divulged.

The sun was setting, and we all were kind of silent as we waited. Chris kept glancing at me through the rearview; I knew I would have to talk to him eventually, but I really didn't know what to say. Blaming him for the fight was a little silly, but who else could I blame? I told him several times that I didn't want any problems, but I just feel like he brought them to me.

"She just texted me and said that Lisa is leaving now. Let's go, so we can cut her off." Sharin said.

We got out and headed behind these houses, towards the woods. Creepy is right; why the fuck would anyone walk back here? It wasn't too dark outside, but the pathway wasn't well lit, so it appeared to be dimmer. We hid behind these bushes for a few more minutes. Sharin kept peeking, until she finally whispered. "Here she comes. Tia, you go first."

I walked from behind the bushes and stood on the pathway. She froze when she saw me.

I smirked. "Hey girl."

She looked like she was about to piss herself.

"Where's all that mouth now, hoe?" I questioned, repeating what one of the girls said to me.

"T-t-tia, I'm really sorry about what happened to you."

"You mean, you're sorry about what you did to me?" I questioned, approaching her slowly.

"Ye-yeah, Christian wasn't even worth all that. I was jealous and I'm sorry."

"Girl, sorry don't mean shit to me now."

Her eyes got big, I looked behind me and saw that, Keyarra and Rin had come from behind the bushes.

"Don't look scared now.... you wasn't scared when you jumped my sis." Keyarra spat.

"Sharin, please, we're family. Don't do this." She cried.

"Toughen the fuck up, nobody even touched you yet, and you crying." I snarled.

Before she could respond, I swung and punched her right in the mouth, blood instantly spewed from her lip. She stumbled back then charged at me; I moved out the way and the goofy hoe fell right to the ground. Keyarra kicked her, then Sharin followed up.

"Wait a minute y'all, I don't wanna bank her." I interrupted.

"What?" Sharin screeched.

"But Tia, she needs this ass whopping." Keyarra said.

"She does, but I don't believe in that whole banking shit. That's for weak bitches. I appreciate y'all, but I want to bust her ass myself."

Sharin kicked her one more time.

"Ard, I'm done." she said, stepping back.

"Get up!" I demanded.

She laid on the ground groaning.

"Please don't make me say it again." I growled.

She stumbled to her feet and soon as she stood, I punched her back to the ground. I rained punch after punch on her, until I was satisfied, plus my ribs were starting to ache.

"You did all that and Christian still want this ghetto ass barbie, dumb bitch." I spat and walked back to the direction of the car.

I overheard Sharin say something to her in a different language. I didn't even know she was bi-lingual. We made it back to the car and Chris sped off.

"Y'all didn't kill her, right?" he asked.

"Naw, Ti-Ti did all the work. She got off easy; we didn't bank her." Sharin said.

Chris glanced at me once again, in the rearview, I kept eye contact this time, until he focused back on the road. We got back to GG's house and got out the car.

"Thanks." I said to Chris, walking past him.

"Tia wait..." he said, grabbing my hand to stop me. "Can I please talk to you?"

I looked over at Keyarra, and she nodded her head lightly, then walked away with Sharin.

"What's up?" I asked.

"Um, how you been?"

"I've been fine"

"Ok. My brother misses you. He thinks you don't want to be his friend anymore."

"You are so full of shit. Devin is not thinking about me." I laughed, lightly.

"He is but, so is his brother." he said, looking down at me, with sad eyes.

"Christian, I don't know what to say."

"Say that you forgive me. I didn't mean for none of this to happen. I never thought Lisa was capable of some grimy shit like that."

"I know and I'm trying not to be mad at you, but I am. I wanted so bad to have a good school year; I've fought every single year, since the 9th grade. I didn't want to look back at high school, and that's all my memories consisted of. I thought this year would be different. I was close too, but now...." my voice trailed off, I felt like I was about to cry.

"I'm so sorry, Tia. If I ever thought I would be dragging you into something, I would've never pursued you.... please forgive me. You being mad at me, has had my head all fucked up."

He grabbed my hands in his and kissed all over them.

"Please Tia." he pleaded.

"I forgive you, Christian."

He smiled widely, scooped me up and swung me around. He pressed me hard, causing me to wince.

"Ouch, not so hard, Chris."

"Oh shit, I'm sorry." he said, putting me down.

"It's cool. My ribs are still a little sore."

He just shook his head.

"Again, I'm really sorry, Tia. I'm sorry you got hurt. Seeing you on the ground like that, damn near broke me."

"Yeah, Derek told me how upset you were."

"I was very beside myself; did you get the flowers my brother sent?"

"I thought they were really from you.... so, I um...threw them away." I said, looking down.

"Damn Tia." he laughed.

"I'm sorry. I'm a straight up asshole, when I'm mad."

"I see. I'll try my hardest to stay on your good side. He wanted to give them to you in person, anyway."

"Ok. Besides everything, how have you been?"

"Um, ok I guess, I'm over the school year though. I think I have senioritis or some shit."

"I'm actually ready to go back, having a month off was a bit much."

"I would love a month off." He expressed.

"Have you accepted Utah's offer?" I asked, taking him off guard. The happiness I saw on his face disappeared.

"Uh, I actually did, but I'm going to rescind."

"Why Christian?"

"Because I can't leave them Ti, I would worry my ass off there. I wouldn't be focused."

"What did your mother say when you told her?"

"She was so happy."

"Did you tell her how you were feeling?"

"Yeah, she just brushed it off and said everything will be fine."

"Then believe her."

"Tia, I really don't feel like talking about this right now."

He pulled me towards him and leaned back on his car; he held my face in his hands.

"I missed you so much, Ti-baby."

"I missed you too, but what happened to your hands?"

I removed my face and took his hands. I examined his knuckles and they looked a little bruised.

"Darren."

My eyes got big.

"You fought him?"

"We dog walked his ass, Ti."

"Who is we?"

"Derek and Matt."

I was shocked.

"Wh-when? Why the hell no one told me?"

"Derek didn't want us to say anything, so don't mention it."

"Was he bad?"

"Yeah, it'll take him a lot longer to recover, than you did. After Matt and Derek did them, me and him went toe to toe. Can't lie, he took that ass whooping though. He held on long as he could."

"Did you feel better after?"

"You still weren't fucking with me, so no; do you feel better after getting at, Lisa?"

"Um, hell yeah."

"I figured." He laughed. "Listen, even though she deserved it, I think it's tough that you didn't want to bank her."

"I like a fair fight." I shrugged.

"I feel you. So, are we like back together orrr..."

"Change your Facebook status to, it's complicated." I joked.

"Ahhh, c'mon Tia, now you just busting my balls."

I cracked up. I leaned in and kissed his lips, lightly.

"Thank you for taking care of Darren."

"Anytime. So, back to my question."

"Wouldn't say we're back together yet, but we good."

"Ok, so are we back on for prom or do I have to beg you to do that too?"

"Mm, I don't remember you asking me to prom."

He hung his head in defeat. "You really playing."

"I'm serious. But, if this is you asking me, then I'll give it heavy consideration."

"You are something else."

He leaned in slowly and pressed his lips against mine. We engaged for a few seconds, before I pulled away. I don't know why, but I was hesitant. I let my guard down with Chris and even though it wasn't his fault, I just still wasn't fully comfortable yet. He looked at me with concerned eyes.

"Ok, we're not there yet, and that's fine. I'm just glad you're not mad at me anymore." He spoke.

"Thank you for understanding."

"No problem. It's getting late. Can I call you when I get in the house?"

"Yes."

"Cool."

He kissed my lips again and walked me to the door.

"I'll talk to you later."

"Ok."

"And Ti-baby, go put your hands in some ice."

I looked at my knuckles, and they were getting swollen; I hadn't even noticed.

"I will." I laughed.

I walked in the house and....

"Chris and Tia sitting in a tree, k-i-s-s-i-n-g" Keyarra and Sharin sang.

"I hate y'all so bad." I said, rolling my eyes.

"Y'all are the cutest." Sharin gushed.

"Yeah yeah, where is Matt? Did he say anything?"
"No, he downstairs helping GG fix something." Keyarra answered.
"Ok cool, imma go get in the shower."
Before I reached the steps, I turned towards them again.
"Hey Rin. What did you say to her?"
"I told her that if she opened her mouth about this, then word will get back to our, Amah; she would be shunned!"
"Ok bad ass." I praised.
"Yeah girl, I got your back"
"When me and Rin get our nails done, she be shocking the shit out of them when she bust out in their language." Keyarra said.
"I bet. Ard y'all, I'm out. I'm tired."
"I bet you are, Kill Bill." I heard Keyarra mumble.
"Girl, fuck you." I said going up the steps.
I started my shower and felt myself rushing because I didn't want to miss Christian's call. I don't know who I was fooling because I knew I was going to take that boy back.

Spring break flew by, and I was waiting for Keyarra to come down the steps. I was actually walking to school with her today; it was early April, and it felt pretty good outside.
"Ready?" She beamed, coming down the steps.
"Why the hell you so happy?"
"It's just...a beautiful day outside."
She was being weird.
"Yeah whatever. Let's go"
"Tiaaaa." GG sang, coming from the kitchen.
"Why are y'all in such a good mood?" I asked, kind of annoyed.
"Oh hush, grumpy. Just excited for your 1st day back, are you nervous at all?"
"To be honest, a little; I don't want to slap anyone for talking slick about the fight."

"You certainly will not." GG said.

"Yeah Ti, you saw how many people wrote on your wall and all the nice things they said. Some didn't even know you." Keyarra reassured.

"Yeah, I guess. It's just nerves. Can we go now?"

"Tia why don't you change your shoes, your feet will hurt." GG said.

"These wedges are really comfortable, I'll be fine."

"If you insist. Love you two. May the Lord cover you." GG said, as she hugged us.

We left out and headed towards the school. Keyarra was texting on her phone a lot.

"Who the hell you texting this early?" I asked.

"Tre." she answered, quickly.

For some reason, I was irritated. Like she begged me to walk and now, was barely paying me any mind. I think my nervousness, mixed with this bullshit, was putting me in a bad mood. I noticed Keyarra couldn't hide the smile on her face.

"Girl, if you don't tell me what the hell is going on; you've been on 10, all morning. What Tre proposed or some shit?"

"Shut the hell up, you know that's not happening. I'm just so excited for school."

"You are such a fucking liar, stop talking to me." I snapped and walked ahead of her.

I heard her snicker. We walked the rest of the way in silence. I could see the school in the distance and my stomach started doing somersaults.

"Keyarra, I think I'm gonna go home."

"You absolutely will the hell not."

"I feel like imma throw up."

"You're not, how about this? I'll walk you to homeroom, just like the 1st day, and if you're still nervous after that, then GG can come get you."

"Ok." I agreed, softly.

She linked arms with me, and we crossed the street. I noticed a lot more kids outside than usual; they were like in a crowd. Some turned around and stared, some gave light smiles, while some waved. I wasn't sure how to feel. Most of the school knew about me being attacked, so maybe they assumed I wasn't coming back, since I had been gone so long. I suddenly heard this loud music.

I'm digging you (baby) I'm feeling you (yeah)
And you know what's up (you gotta know what's up)
Said I'm big on you (ohh) and I'm wanting you
So tell me what's up (so just tell me what's up)

It was the lyrics from, "U Know What's Up", my favorite song, from the, "Save the Last Dance", soundtrack. Keyarra's face had to hurt because she was smiling so hard; she grabbed my hand and led me through the crowd. Everyone had their phones out and was recording whatever was ahead of us. Keyarra pulled me in front of her and took my bag off my shoulder, then she pushed me forward, until I saw Devin standing in front of me. He was on the end of a long red carpet, except this one was pink, with rose pedals decorated down it.

"Hi, Ti-baby." He greeted, approaching me.
"Hi Devin, it's been so long." I said, crouching down to his level.
"Here are your new flowers."
He handed me an assortment of flowers then hugged me around my neck. My eyes stung with tears.
"Thank you so much, these are beautiful."
"You're welcome, my brother has to ask you something."
He took my hand and walked me down the pink carpet. My mouth dropped when I saw what I was looking at.

Rae, Nelly, Tre, and Sharin who could hardly keep still because she was so excited, along with about 4 other students held these large white signs; and they each had a word on it, spelled out in pink paint.

TI-BABY WILL YOU GO TO PROM WITH ME?

Devin let go of my hand and ran over to his mother, who was also recording. Christian was standing next to her, with a bouquet of pink and white roses. He looked so handsome. His springy curls were perfect, as usual, he had on a long-sleeved white shirt, with a pink bow tie. I was floored. I couldn't stop the tears from running, as I walked towards him; my legs felt like jelly.

"Hey, Ti-baby." He greeted me, lowly.
"Hi." I choked out.
"Is this a better way to ask you to prom?"
I just nodded my head because I didn't feel like I could form words at the moment.
"So, should I take that as a yes, you will go with me?"
"Yes, I will." I sobbed.
He picked me up and I wrapped my arms around his neck, I cried into his shoulder. I heard loud cheers from all around. I finally peeked up and saw everyone. GG, Derek, Matt, Keyarra, and even DW were standing there with their phones out, chanting and cheering. Keyarra and GG were in tears, right along with me. What I thought would be a bad day, turned out to be the best day of my life, so far!

PROM

KEYARRA

I was sitting in my room, and it was a madhouse; there were people everywhere. My room had been transformed into a full-blown salon. Tia, Rin and I were all getting ready for prom. We had hair stylists, a make-up artist and even our dress designer, all crammed into my room. GG couldn't stop crying and she was taking so many pictures; everything was just becoming a little overwhelming. The thought of walking down the steps and not meeting Derek really was dampening my mood; the last conversation we had kept replaying in my head.

"So, what are you saying Derek?" I asked furiously.
"I'm saying that imma try to thug it out with, Katrina."
Derek had just told me that she was pregnant, and I felt like the wind had been knocked out of me. I was excited at the thought of something developing between us. I felt so safe with him, but now all I feel is rage.

"You do know I just broke up with my boyfriend for you, right?"

"Yeah, but Key, you weren't even happy in that situation. So, what was the point of you even staying with him?"

"What's the point of you staying with her?" I shouted.

"Keyarra, stop yelling! The point is, she's having my baby, and I just don't think it's right leaving her."

I couldn't help but laugh and shake my head.

"You know what, that's cool. You and your family have fucking fun."

I tried to leave his room, but he blocked my path.

"Don't leave like this Key, I'm sorry. I want us to still be cordial. We both agreed that we enjoyed each other's company, so that doesn't have to change."

"Fuck you Derek, you really played the shit outta me. All that stuff you said was just pillow talk, huh?"

"You know damn well it wasn't; I told you, I don't lie to you. I meant every word I said. I was going to break up with her, but she hit me with the pregnancy shit and I just...."

I put my hand up to stop him.

"Derek, what if I'm pregnant right now? What would you do huh? Did you forget that you bust inside of me as well...you couldn't be with both of us!"

He looked like he was at a loss for words.

"Exactly, so save the bullshit. Remind me to go get tested, since you out here slinging raw dick to everyone; can't believe I fell for that cute shit you were talking." I fumed, pushing him to the side and walking out of the room.

I heard his footsteps behind me, as I made my way to the front door.

"Keyarra, for what it's worth, I really am sorry."

I swung around meeting him and his sympathetic eyes; he almost got me but the rage I felt wouldn't allow me to fall for the bullshit.

"It's not worth shit, GOOD-BYE Derek!" I spat, leaving out the door and slamming it behind me.

"FUCK MAN!" I heard him yell, followed by the loud sound of something breaking.
I stood on the other side of the door and the tears that I had been holding back fell freely. I'm not sure why, but I felt like my heart was broken. The only thing I knew for sure, is I would never trust another man again; the hurt they cause, is just too much for me.

"Ok, tell me what you think beauty."
My hair stylist handed me a handheld, trifold 360 mirror, so I was able to get a full view of my hair; it was so beautiful, and just how I imagined. I wanted to go for a princess look. My hair was curled all over, but some hair was braided and pulled back, into a loose French braid, that sat on top of the curls. She added some tracks, for a fuller and elongated look. There were also pearl bobby pics, that were placed throughout my hair.

"It's perfect, thank you so much."
"It fits you so well, sweetie." She complimented me.
I got up and let Rin get in the chair next; she was getting a half up half down style. She had so much hair that there was no need for any extra to be added. I watched as Tia was getting the finishing touches on her make-up; she went old Hollywood. A dark red lip and a light smoky eye; it complimented her shoulder length, glamour bob. It was dressed in deep waves and she accessorized it with a crystalized, claw hair pin on the left side.

"You look so pretty, Ti." I complimented her.
"Thanks, so do you. Your hair is pretty."
"Thank you." I smiled.
"Ok baby girl, you're up next." the make-up artist said to me.
I sat in the chair and let her go to work. She finished in no time. I told her I wanted a very natural look; nothing too bold. Even though my dress wasn't my favorite color, I still wanted my make-up to be grey and glittery. She gave me exactly what I wanted. My eyes were adorned with a grey eye shadow, and she put this

shimmery liquid over top. I had on a light pink lipstick, with a
glittery gloss on top, as well.

"Oh girls, you 3 are so perfect." GG gushed.
Sharin's make-up just got done. She went with a defined cat eye;
she also had a shimmery, orange eye shadow and nude matte
lipstick.

"Thank you." we said in unison.
It was time for our dresses. When Tia asked if she could design
them, Sharin and I let her have at it. She footed the entire bill,
which Sharin cried about countless times. We had several fittings
and each time, she cried. Sharin had been so emotional, if she
hadn't taken several pregnancy tests that came out negative you
couldn't have told she wasn't carrying my niece or nephew. Our
dresses were taken out of their garment bags, and our mouths
dropped. They were breath taking, and to think this came mostly
from the mind of Tia, showed just how successful her future in
fashion would be.

Sharin's dress was satin and light orange, in color. It was strapless
and beaded, along the bust line; it was mermaid style, with a high
dramatic slit, that got wider as it went up; it stopped at her upper
thigh.

Tia's was this shiny, black velvet, with a little bit of a train. Hers
was also strapless, but with a deep v cut; it must've had a built-in
bra because she was well lifted and supported, from what I saw in
her fittings. Her split wasn't as wide as Rin's, but you could see
that she had a red fabric on the inside that would complement
her red lip and red bottom heels.

Mine screamed me, in every single way; pretty and simple. I told
Tia to surprise me with a color, and when I first saw the dark sage
she had picked, I fell in love. It was spaghetti strapped, with as
sweetheart neckline. The entire dress was sequined, which is the

next best thing to glitter, to me. My split was in the back and stopped just after the back of my knees.

"Ughhhh." Sharin groaned, in a cracked voice fanning her eyes to stop her tears.

"Aht, you better not." I warned.

"Yes, let's not." the make-up artist chimed in.

We were all helped into our dresses, carefully. The photographer was told to come upstairs and take pictures. We all wanted to come down, at the same time. The entire living room gasped, as we walked down the steps; it was filled with our dates and their families. We posed on the landing before we joined the guys. They all looked so good; they each had a matching bowtie or tie, that matched us perfectly. I noticed that Chris's tux was also black velvet; he and Tia could have been on the cover of a magazine. They truly deserved that cutest couple win.

"You look absolutely gorgeous." Tre complimented.

"Thanks, you look great."

"Thank you for still coming with me, I couldn't imagine prom without you."

I blushed. "I'm sorry for giving you a hard time about it, I've just been all over the place."

"I understand, me too. I've had my plate full with you two."

"Who's two?" I asked, confused.

He paused.

"College…. between all the applications and everything. I feel like I neglected you, so I get why you wanted to end things."

"Oh. Well, let's just have a good time tonight."

"Cool."

He put on my corsage, and I pinned on his boutonniere. GG had outdone herself with the house; she had a backdrop and everything. There wouldn't be a need to take pictures at the venue.

"Can I take a picture with you real quick, before I go?" Derek asked.

He looked so fucking beautiful. His fade was perfect, his hair had grown out a little, so he had a small, curly fro. His suit jacket was a deep, dark purple and it had some type of pattern imprinted. His black, slim fit dress pants and patent, leather loafers topped off his look.

"Sure."

He knew it would look weird if I refused. We stood on the backdrop and posed; I felt his hand on the small of my back.

"You are breath taking." He murmured.

There was so much chatter, that I knew only I could hear him.

"Thanks."

"Key, I know you are still upset with me but..."

"Please stop, I don't want to talk about this here."

"Ard. I guess I'll see you at the prom."

"Ok."

We stared at each other for a few seconds, and he looked like he wanted to kiss me right here, in front of everyone. He stepped back and walked away. I followed him with my eyes, until I locked with Matt, who was looking at me strangely. I looked down and walked in the opposite direction.

"Ard y'all, I'm out, I'll see everyone later." Derek announced.

He had to go meet Katrina at her house and they would leave from there. I felt myself rolling my eyes. I'm just ready for this night to be over already.

TIA

We walked into the aquarium and the set-up was stunning. The theme was Under the Sea, and it was very fitting. There were turquoise, blue, and white decorations everywhere.

"Parkville, did better than I thought they would." Christian stated, admiring the decorations as well.
"Very true, I'm glad it wasn't at the Ravens stadium, like it had always been in the past."
Apparently, we were the 1st class to vote against having it at the stadium. When it came to a vote, most of the class voted for the aquarium. After exploring and taking pictures in the dolphin room, we finally made it to a table.
"Ready to get lit?" Tre asked.
He pulled out a flask from his jacket pocket.
"Can't you wait to do that after prom?" Keyarra asked, annoyed.

"C'mon, it's prom. We didn't drive, we can all indulge." He responded.

He tried to pass the flask around discreetly and we all declined, even Matthew.

"So be it, more for me." he said, taking a long chug from the flask. I just shook my head. That boy had a problem, for real.

"Why did they have to put our middle initial on our ornaments?" Sharin asked out loud.

Each student had a dolphin shaped ornament; mine read,
Tia N. Williams.

"I should start calling you, Nicki." Christian joked.

"Um, I think not."

We heard, "Panda", by Desiigner, come on.

"Let's go y'all, we not sitting here all night." Christian exclaimed.

We all hopped up and hit the dance floor with our classmates. About a half hour later, I heard a few gasps and whispers. I turned to see what everyone was looking at, and there was Derek and Katrina, fashionably late. I can't lie, they both looked damn good; they looked like they should have been on a runway. Her dark purple, long sleeve dress clung to her, hugging her stomach, showcasing her 7-month belly, which I'm sure that's what the whispers were about. Derek told me she had been concealing her belly as much as she could, with oversized clothing. She was carrying kind of small, so you wouldn't have thought she was due in 2 months. Derek also found out that she was having a boy; even though he still wasn't fully himself, he was excited at the thought of having a son.

"What's up y'all." Derek greeted.

"Hi." Katrina said, as nice as she could.

We greeted them back.

"We have 2 more seats, if you guys want to sit with us." Tre offered, quickly.

"You guys are kind of in the center and I would like to off to the side...thanks though." Katrina politely declined.

Keyarra and I gave each other the side eye; I'm sure we are thinking the same thing.
Phony bitch!
"Yeah, I'll go get us a table, and I'll back in a little bit." Derek said.

They walked away and I saw the back of her dress; it was completely exposed. The cut out showed her bare back, all the way down to her lower back. She had a long, sleek ponytail that was flowing down the middle. The print of the dress matched Derek's suit jacket. It was very pretty. Even though they were putting on a good show, I could see the unhappiness in my brother's eyes. I recently found myself praying more since I've been back in church, and I must admit it felt good too. I've never prayed so hard on anything in my life, but every night, I pray to God that he pulls a miracle, and not have my brother be the father of that baby.

DEREK

"Are you having a good time?" Katrina asked me.
We had been sitting at this table for the past half hour, she didn't want to do anything. Not dance, not eat, not shit.
"If you are, I am."
"I am." she smiled, then leaned in to kiss me.
Katrina had been really trying to be better. The last few months, she was a different person; she reminded me of the girl I first met. She had a pretty easy pregnancy, no morning sickness or anything, she also had this glow that she embraced. She knew having her swollen belly, on full display at the prom, would cause some commotion; all night, people approached us to say congratulations; a lot of them complimented her on how radiant she was.

"Well, I see why you didn't do spring cheer." Courtney said.

"I'm sorry coach, I really wanted to tell you."

"It's fine, you look almost angelic."

"Thank you so much, we are very excited." Katrina gushed.

"I'm sure you two will be amazing. I have to send you a gift."

"We'll let you know when the baby shower is."

Tri and I had talked about a baby shower several times. But the truth was, neither one of us had a lot of family or friends, so paying for an expensive hall seemed ridiculous. I offered to have it at my place, but she didn't want that. We hadn't come to an agreement yet, but we needed to soon.

"Baby, they are going to announce the queen soon. I'm going to use the bathroom." She said, when Courtney walked away.

"Ok, I can walk you."

"No it's fine, I can manage."

I helped her from her seat and watched as she walked off.

"Finally nigga, you got a minute alone. I hate these damn dances; our old asses shouldn't even be here." Matthew said loosening his tie a little, as he sat in an empty seat.

"Money talks." I laughed. "But my bad, all she wants to do is sit here. I'm like, we could've sat in these clothes at home."

"For real though. Rin was cool at first, but now she has a little attitude about something. I don't have time for guessing games though."

"These girls man...they a headache." I said, shaking my head.

"Tell me about it."

Matthew and I chopped it up for a few more minutes, before Tri came back, she looked a little annoyed now.

"You ok?" I asked.

"I'm fine. After they announce queen, I would like to leave."

"Uh, ok"

"Ard man, I'll talk to you later. Katrina, I haven't got the chance to tell you, but congrats on your pregnancy." Matt said.

"Thank you." She responded, dryly.

He walked away and she sat down.
"You sure you ok?" I asked.
"I said I'm fine." She snapped.
"Ard."
I wasn't about to play guessing games with her ass, either.

All night, I tried my hardest to keep my eyes off Keyarra; she was so gorgeous. She had this good girl aura, but I knew how she was behind closed doors; it was like the best of both worlds. I'm still pissed on how things ended between us. Her blowing up the way she did was confirmation for me, that she was feeling me like I was feeling her, but I blew it. She kind of stayed to herself for most of the night. Tre was off, probably getting wasted, and Rin and Tia were with their dates. I wanted so bad to be here with her.

"Alright ladies and gentlemen, it's about that time, we are ready to announce your prom king and queen." a teacher announced from the stage.

"Parkville's 2016 Prom King is, Christian Richards."
I clapped along with everyone else, as he went on stage to get his crown.
"Ugh, I don't wanna take a picture with him." I heard Katrina scoff.
"And drum roll please...your 2016 Prom Queen is..."
Katrina stood up.
"Keyarra Devore!" He announced.
Everyone looked over at her and she sat there frozen; I knew she wasn't a fan of attention. I heard she was nominated, and she wasn't thrilled, but everyone assumed Tri was going to win. I heard Katrina scoff again.
"What the actual fuck?" She said out loud.
"C'mon queen!" Christian encouraged, from the stage.
Rin and Tia were cheering, as they pushed her forward. She finally made it to the stage and took her crown.

"I can't believe this." Katrina said, in disbelief.

"It's cool babe, you have 4 years of crowns and sashes."

"I don't give a fuck. Prom queen is really the only one that matters." She lashed out.

I took a deep breath; I knew this nice girl shit was an act.

"Ok, well it's nothing you can do about it, so let's not let ruin the night."

"Whatever! I'm ready to go. But I have to use the bathroom 1st, this got damn baby has me going every 30 seconds."

"Aye, watch your mouth man."

She rolled her eyes and stalked away. I decided to walk around for a few minutes; I felt myself becoming annoyed. Students were still enjoying the last few moments of prom and that's when I laid eyes on Keyarra, again. She was sitting at the table by herself, and she looked sad; I couldn't help myself.

"Why is the prom queen, the prettiest girl in the room, sitting here all by herself?" I asked, sitting next to her.

She smiled lightly. "You better not let your child's mother hear you say that."

"I'm not too worried about that. What's up with you. Why you sitting here looking all sad? You not having a good time?"

"I am."

"Lies."

She sighed.

"I feel like I should be here with you." She admitted, quietly.

"That feeling is again mutual.... next time?"

"Next time." She laughed. "Derek, I'm sorry about some of the things I said. I was upset, but that's not an excuse."

"You know who my sister is; I've heard worse, I'm not sweating it. I'm sorry that I hurt you. I promise that's the last thing I ever want to do to you."

"It's fine...I get it now."

We stared at each other for a few seconds, our connection was strong as hell, I was so drawn to her. I was about to say fuck everything and tell her let's get out of here. I just wanted to lay up with her.

"Derek, I want to go now!" Katrina urged, when she walked up to where we were sitting.

Her eyes were glossy, like she was about to cry, and she looked like she was in pain or something. I stood up and put my hand on her stomach.

"Are you ok? Is it the baby?"

"No... I-I just want to leave...please."

"Ok, let me get your stuff."

"I have everything, let's go!"

She walked away but as she passed Keyarra, she glowered at her; I assume it was because of the queen thing.

"Ard Key, enjoy the rest of your night."

"Ok, I hope everything is ok." she stated, genuinely.

"Thanks."

I hurried after Katrina. I hope she was in a better mood when we got back to my place. I don't feel like the headache tonight.

TIA

I sat down and my mind was boggled from what I had just witnessed. I saw Katrina, smack the dogshit out of Tre; they looked like they were arguing, but I couldn't hear much. All I heard was, you will keep your mouth shut, and she stormed away. Me and him made eye contact; he just gave me a somber look, then walked away.

"You good, Ti-baby?" Chris asked, sitting next to me.
"Yeah...yeah I'm good." I responded, shaking off my thoughts.
"Your feet hurt yet?"
I was the only girl who hadn't taken their heels off yet.
"A little."
"I can massage them back at the room." Christian said, but in a very suggestive tone.

I think tonight was going to be the night. He hasn't told me he loved me or anything, but I could feel it. After we made up; we had been inseparable. It was weird because technically, we weren't back together, but everyone assumed we were. I mean, we had won cutest couple. An editor from the yearbook told me that I had won most fashionable, but also Chris and I won cutest couple. Since you could only be featured in one superlative, so others could get a chance, they gave you the option to choose. Without thinking, I said cutest couple. Christian was fine with it because that's what he voted for too; he had also won for Future President of the United States. We all had won one actually. Rin, got Best Personality, Tre was Most Athletic, Keyarra, settled for Best to Take Home to Mom and Dad; but she had also won Future American Idol.

"You seem eager to get back to that room."

"I am."

Christian's mom got us a room downtown for the night. She knew that he was practicing abstinence , so she trusted that nothing would happen, but how he was looking at me suggested otherwise.

"Before we get back to the room, I want to give you something." I spoke.

"What is it?"

I dug in my small purse and handed him the tiny, folded up piece of paper. He unfolded it and examined it quickly. I watched as his eyes got big and his mouth went ajar.

"Tia, what the hell is this?" he asked.

"It's a check, what does it look like?"

"I-I-I know b-but it has my name on it and it's for $10,000."

"Actually $9,999. Derek said something about depositing anything over 10 gets investigated or something like that."

Chris was still staring down at the check in shock.

"Christian, look at me."

He looked at me but his eyes were all over the place, he could barely focus. I took his hands in mine and stared into his eyes.

"I care about you a lot and I care about your future; this money is to help you. The thought is for you to maybe take some and get a PI started on your sister's case, and maybe that will give you a little peace of mind. Then give some to your mother, so she can stay ahead on her bills. Hell, I really don't care what you use it for but, just make sure it helps you in a way that will make you more comfortable in Utah. I don't want you to ever look back and regret not going."

"Tia, I um…I can't take this money."

"You can and you will."

"It's your father's money."

"Boy please, I have money that I don't touch. The first time I really touched it, was for all this extra shit I wanted to do for those dresses. Otherwise, it just sits there; I can't think of anything better I want to use it on."

"I don't know what to say."

"Just say, thank you."

He pulled me forward and our lips crashed into each other. It was deep and passionate.

"Tia, I love you."

"You can't say that after I just gave you a check, it's like I paid you to say it." I laughed.

"I promise I was going to say it anyway, I really do. And not just in a romantic way; you have really been one of the best things that has happened to me, in a long time. The thought of leaving you troubles me, almost as much as the thought of leaving my siblings and mother."

"I'm not worth giving up your future for."

"I feel otherwise but thank you for this. I'll go."

I flew into his lap and embraced him.

"You're going to be amazing." I whispered.

"Thank you. I'm ready to go if you are."

"I am."

"Ok, let me go grab something, then I'll be back."

He got up and walked away. I sat there patiently and waited for him to return.

"So, I have to ask you something." Rin said, replacing Chris's now empty chair.

Her expression was a little difficult to read and her tone was throwing me off.

"Um, ok."

"Tia N?"

She pointed to the N on my ornament. "That stands for Nicole. Like Matthew's Nicole, right?"

My heart dropped and I knew I looked like a deer caught in headlights.

"Mmmm that's what I thought, I'm so stupid. I should've known because as soon as you got here, he started acting odd as hell."

She wasn't looking at me, she was looking in Matthew's direction where he was talking to Keyarra.

"Rin, listen."

"Did you cheat on Christian?" She questioned, her head snapping back towards me.

"No, absolutely not! Soon as we got together everything was over between Matt and I."

Rin looked hurt, but also angry.

"So, he finally got with me because you and Chris got together, basically?"

"Sharin, you and I both know that Matthew is not going to do anything he doesn't want to do. I begged him for years. I'm not gonna lie, I begged him when I first got here, but he still didn't budge. He told me about you. That he liked you a lot, but he didn't want a relationship with either one of us, at the time. I wanted to dislike you so much, Sharin, but I couldn't. As our friendship developed, I felt bad, I felt really bad, and I have to tell you, I don't feel bad about shit. I'm sorry if I hurt you, that was never my intention."

Her eyes watered and she just shook her head.

"Does Christian know?"

"No."

"I think you should tell him."

With that she got up and walked away. I felt terrible, I was willing to go to my grave with that secret, but now I had to tell Christian. I hope he doesn't hate me.

KEYARRA

I was sprinting down the hallway, looking for the familiar apartment number. I haven't been here since the day Derek dropped the pregnancy bomb on me, but now I was going to drop a bomb on him. I knocked at the door several times, when I didn't hear anything, I knocked again, louder. I finally heard the locks being undone. Derek opened the door, and he looked surprised. It was the morning after prom, and I rushed here from downtown in an Uber. I know I looked crazy as hell; I washed as much make-up off, as I could, but it was still some glitter and shit. I had un-done my braid and combed through my tracks and threw it up into a bun, as usual.

"Keyarra?"
I pushed past him.

"Is she here? Did she tell you?" I asked frantically.

"Is who here?"

"Katrina!"

"Yes, she's in my room. What's going on?"

"COME OUT HERE KATRINA!" I yelled.

"Keyarra, it's 7 in the morning, stop yelling and tell me what's going on."

"She didn't tell you, did she? I knew she wouldn't!"

I was out of breath and my adrenaline was rushing; I was antsy and couldn't stop pacing.

"Tell me what, Keyarra!?" he boomed.

I suddenly ran down the hallway and opened his room door. Katrina was standing in the middle of the room; she had on an oversized tee and nothing else.

"Get dressed and bring your ass out here!" I yelled.

I felt Derek jerk me back by my arm.

"Yo, what the fuck is wrong with you?"

I tried to break free from his grasp, but no luck.

"Derek, tell her to come out here now!"

"I don't know how many times I have to tell you that I don't like repeating myself. Tell me what the fuck is happening!"

"I'm trying to give that trifling bitch the chance to tell you first!"

Derek pulled me into the living room, and forcibly sat me on the couch.

"1st, calm the hell down and don't get the fuck up and 2, watch your mouth…Katrina, come out here!"

I was fuming. My leg was bouncing, and I was trying to keep in mind that this bitch was pregnant. Katrina slowly came out of the room with the same tee, but with some shorts on now. She looked petrified, which was a first for me.

"Tell him!" I urged.

She still was quiet.

"You claim to be this solid ass bitch but can't tell him what the fuck you need to. You're a pussy!" I yelled.

"Yo, one of y'all better start talking, before I really lose my temper in here." Derek said, calmly.

"Derek, this shouldn't be coming from me, but this morning, Tre told me, that he is almost 100% positive, that Katrina's baby is his!"

Derek looked at me like I was crazy.

"What?" He questioned.

I looked over at Katrina.

"Tell him Katrina. Tell him how you 2 have been sleeping together, for over a year! Tell him how he thinks that's his baby because he slept with you unprotected the week of homecoming!"

Derek turned to look at a now crying, Katrina.

"Damn Tri, that's what we doing?"

"Derek…" She cried.

"Is it true?" he asked, cutting her off.

"I made a mistake, but this isn't his baby."

"You made a mistake and fucked a nigga for over a year?"

She stood silent.

"I mean, I know I'm not perfect and I cheated too, but having another nigga thinking that's his baby is crazy."

"Derek, he's always drunk. He doesn't know what the fuck he's talking about."

"He was pretty sober this morning." I spoke.

"SHUT UP! SHUT THE FUCK UP!" She yelled.

"No, you shut the fuck up! I'm not even mad you was sleeping with Tre; I'm mad you got Derek, out here looking crazy. I knew you were a petty bitch, but not a grimy one."

"I guess we can't be too upset Key, we were sleeping together."

Derek revealed nonchalantly, as he sat on the couch next to me. I wasn't planning on disclosing that.

"What?!" Katrina screeched, in disbelief.

"Yeah, she's who I cheated on you with, but it was only for a few months. I mean, if you count kissing, then that was almost a year ago." He shrugged.

Katrina approached the couch, and I stood up. I didn't trust that bitch.

"I told you don't get up; she's not going to touch you." Derek said to me.

I sat down with my eyes trained on Katrina still. She looked taken back by the way I listened to him.

"But Derek, you told me I didn't have to worry about her! It could have been anyone else, but not her! She is always in my fucking way! I didn't even want to do this shit; it went too far, and I got stuck." She cried.

"What the fuck are you even talking about?" I asked.

"You know what I'm talking about!"

"No, the hell I don't. He told me you came on to him, after he made it clear that he wanted to date me. And after we got together, y'all just never stopped fucking, at your request."

"It's what you deserved." She said icily.

"Deserved? Bitch, I haven't done shit to you!"

"You try to act innocent, but you know you're just a sneaky hoe."

I stared at her in confusion because for the life of me, I had no idea what the hell she was referring to, she got closer and I was ready to hop up again, but Derek got up first and stood in front of me.

"Ard, I think it's time for you to leave."

"But Derek, what about us? What about our baby?"

"I'll be there for the baby IF it's mine, but as far as us. I'm good."

"It's your baby!"

"There's a possibility of that, but until I know for sure, I would like for you to leave."

"I'm not going anywhere." She protested.

"Oh, but I think you are." Tia said, startling all of us.

We didn't even hear her come in.

"I knew you were a hoe; I knew you were a sneaky and conniving bitch!" She spoke, as she slowly walked closer.

Tia's eyes danced with excitement; she had been waiting for this, for a long time.

"Derek, don't let her talk to me like that!" Katrina whined.

"That's not really my problem anymore." He responded, coolly.

"You can't do this to me, we've been through so much. You're putting stress on the baby."

"No, you're putting stress on the baby. I'm asking you to leave and you're refusing."

Suddenly, Tia grabbed her by her hair and pulled her by it.

"Get the fuck off of me." Katrina struggled.

"Tia....she's pregnant." Derek stated, in an elevated tone, but still calm as usual.

Tia let go of her hair.

"I suggest you leave; she can only hold back but for so long."

Derek walked away and disappeared down the hall.

"You have 2 seconds to get your shit and get the hell out." Tia warned.

"Matter of fact, I'll do it for her." I said getting up, sprinting towards Derek's room.

I went into Derek's room and balled up all the shit of hers I could find. I saw a little blue duffle bag and stuffed everything in there, including her prom dress. When I came back, Katrina was on the floor, in a ball crying and holding her stomach. Tia stood over her with her arms folded.

"This is some pathetic shit." Tia said, shaking her head.

I opened the front door and threw the bag out.

"Time to go, phone is in your bag." I said.

"Katrina, I would love to put my hands on you, but you are pregnant, and I don't wanna go down for killing a baby, so please get up and take the little dignity you have left, and leave." Tia encouraged.

After a few seconds, she finally got on her feet and headed out the door. I slammed it so hard behind her.

"So, what happened?" Tia asked, immediately.

"You didn't hear it?"

"No girl, all I heard was Derek asking her to leave. I didn't need to hear shit else."

I burst out laughing.

"Well, why you call her conniving and a hoe?"
"Because she is, and I feel like it just fit."
I could not stop my laughter.
"Spill it." She urged, quietly.
"Tre told me that Katrina's baby is his!"
Tia gasped loudly.
"BITCH SHUT UP!" She squealed.
"Yes, and they have been sleeping together for over a year. He had been begging her to tell Derek the truth, but she had been refusing. And last night, he told her that he was going to tell me."
"Oh shit, that's why she slapped his ass!"
"When?!"
"Last night, I saw them together and she smacked the shit outta him. His face was red and everything."
"Wow." I said shaking my head.
"Are y'all done?" Derek asked, returning from, I assume Tia's room.
"Brother, I'm so sorry." Tia said, going to hug him.
"It's cool." he stated, embracing her.
He walked into the kitchen and got some water. I couldn't tell what his mood was.
"Did you tell her about us?" he asked, turning around and leaning on the counter, taking a sip from the bottle.
I froze.
"Us?" Tia questioned.
"Yeah, us." he said, pointing between me and him.
"Uh no, she left that part out."
"Tell her Key, then come holler at me in my room." He stated, walking away.
Asshole!
Tia cocked her head to the side.
"Well?" She asked.
"Um, Derek, and I kind of been...messing around."
"Giiiirl, you couldn't resist, could you? I knew it, all he gotta do his flash a smile and panties drop." She joked.
"Shut up, it's more than that.... I think."

"Well, go find out what it is. I'm going to bed, I'm exhausted." she said, attempting to walk away.

"Wait, why you here so early?"

"Chris had to take his brother somewhere this morning and I just wanted to sleep."

"Mmm, why didn't you get any sleep last night?"

"Girl, go worry about my brother and not me."

She disappeared down the hall and into her room.

I can't stand these damn, Williams' siblings.

I walked back to Derek's room, and he was laying on his bed on his phone.

"Come here." He said, while still typing.

I came and sat on his bed.

"Take your shoes off and lay down with me."

I did what I was told and cuddled up under his arm; head on his chest and listening to my favorite sound; his heartbeat.

He put his phone down and leaned over to kiss the top of my head.

"Are you ok?" He asked.

"Yes, are you?"

"Ummm, I'm not sure how I'm feeling."

"I understand. I'm sorry this happened."

"It is what it is, thank you for looking out."

"Of course."

"You gonna miss, Tre?"

"No."

"Cool, so what's up with us?"

"Derek, you could still be having a baby, let's find that out first."

"Doesn't matter if I am or not, we gonna be together either way."

"We'll see." I laughed.

He pulled me closer and before I knew it, I was knocked out.

JULY
DEREK

"Yes, I will be there." I spoke dryly, into the phone.
"Derek, I'm due any day now and if you miss the birth, I will never forgive you."
"I could care less about you forgiving me or not. I will be at the hospital tomorrow." I said, hanging up.

It had been damn near 2 months, since I found out about Katrina treacherous ass. Now I know what Granny B meant about that whole apple from the tree bullshit. I really don't fuck with none of them because they had me walking around looking dumb as hell; but I blame myself, I knew better and ignored the signs. A part of me was hoping this baby wasn't mine because I don't want to have any dealings with Katrina, for the rest of my life, but in the same breath, I did want to be a dad.

I was at GG's house to pick Key up; I used my key to let myself in. I went up the steps and knocked at Keyarra's door; I had been on her ass heavy, since that day she revealed everything. I wanted her bad and I wasn't going to let up.

"Hi." She smiled.

"What's up?"

I pulled her towards me and stuck my tongue down her throat.

"Quit it, Derek." She said, pulling back but she had a smirk on her face.

"I have to stick something somewhere." I quipped.

Keyarra had been holding out on me. I hadn't had any since prom night and I felt like I was losing my mind, but I didn't have the urge to have sex with anyone else, besides her.

"You're doing so well, why ruin it?"

"Man whatever." I said walking past her.

I sat on her bed and instantly had flashbacks of me blowing her back out on it.

"You ready to go?" She asked.

"Yeah, but if you had something else in mind, we can cancel the movie." I said lowly, as I eyed her up and down.

"You wish. Let's hurry before anyone gets home."

"I told you I'm tired of this sneaking around shit."

"I know. Just until my birthday; we can tell everyone then. I mean, that's if the baby isn't yours."

"You really not gonna fuck with me, if the baby mine?"

"I don't do baby mama drama, I'm too young for that. My next boyfriend, I'll just have to find at, Morgan."

Keyarra had got accepted into Morgan State University and was slated to start in the fall.

"Yeah ok, keep playing." I warned.

"Calm down. Here, distract yourself with this until I get back, I have to go to the bathroom, I don't want to use it at the theater."

Keyarra tossed me this yo-yo. I recognized it as the old one that I used to play with all the time.

"Yoooo, where'd you find this?"

"In the attic."

"What were you doing up there?"

"I just like to make sure nothing gets too dusty or anything."

Upstairs felt like a shrine to our mothers, I never went up there.

"I was a beast at this." I said, practicing with the toy.

"I thought you would like that, better then solving math problems, right?" she said, walking out the room.

Keyarra had me so backed up, that I had started writing out multiplication problems instead of doing them in my head. Carmen was thrilled that I had gone without sex, but I was pissed off. Keyarra was lucky that I'm changed, the old me would be busting a few girls down, until she came around; I also enjoyed a challenge though.

I was trying to remember some of the old tricks I used to do, suddenly the yo-yo snapped off the string and rolled under the dresser.

"Old piece of shit." I mumbled.

I got on the floor and reached my hand under the dresser feeling for it; I struggled for a few, until my hand landed on what felt like a book. I slid it towards me, to see what it was. It was grey and it read journal.

"I know it's something about me in here."

I know I shouldn't read it, but I really wanted to know how Key was feeling; she was so bashful around me now, it was like we went backwards. I quickly skimmed the pages and looked at dates, until I found the date I was looking for.

"Derek did things to me that I didn't know were possible."

"I almost screamed out I loved him."

I smiled because my ass almost said the same thing. I skimmed some more.

"We have been spending so much time together but I don't know if it's just about the sex."

"The way he looks at me gives me butterflies all over."

"I ruined everything; I tried my hardest not let my jealousy show but I can't help it. Derek is really mature and I wanted to prove I was too but clearly I'm not and now he not fucking with me."

"I can't believe he's having a baby, I feel like my heart has been stepped on."

"I don't even want to go to prom, fuck prom"

"I'm so happy I told him about the baby, I thought he wouldn't believe me. Hopefully we can start over, I'm a little apprehensive about moving forward but I'm pretty certain what I want to do no matter if the baby is his or not"

That was her last entry a few days ago.
"Shit, I'm not going anywhere, so she better get used to the idea of possibly playing step-mommy." I said out loud.
I was about to put the journal back, when it slipped out my hands and fell to my feet. The pages spread open, I picked it up and a word caught my eye.

"Kill"

I skimmed over the page and it actually said, kill myself. The year was, 2012.

"I feel like shit, I tried to kill myself but I threw all the pills up. The thought of GG finding me like that made me physically ill. I'll just have to live with what I've done."

"What the fuck?" I mumbled.

"The abortion has me fucked up in the head but I couldn't carry my brother's sibling, there was no way I could go through with that."

"Brother's sibling?" I questioned.
I kept repeating brother's sibling because my mind wasn't fully comprehending what that meant. I skimmed back some more.

"It hurt so bad, I can't believe he did it. I lost my virginity to Mark and I can't stop crying. I feel so dirty, he kept saying how I felt like my mother. I screamed for him to stop but he just hit me so many times. I begged him to not do this just for him to laugh. I can't believe he raped me."

I felt rage race through my entire body, and I started to shake as I re-read that last part, over and over again. My vision blurred, and I almost felt like I was going to throw up. I could hear myself breathing heavy, I couldn't read anymore.

"What are you doing?"
I looked up at Keyarra and she had fear written all over her face. "What the fuck is this?" I asked.

KEYARRA

I closed my eyes, as my ears started to ring with pain. I was counting in my head, hoping to wake up from another nightmare. This couldn't be real; it can't be real. I worked so hard to conceal it. I want to wake up!

"KEYARRA!"

The yelling of my name made me open my eyes and reality set in. This wasn't another nightmare; it was real! I looked at Derek, and he looked like a different person. His eyes were as dark as the night sky, and he looked red. I saw a vein protrude from his neck and he was breathing so hard, like a rabid dog. Hot tears started to cascade down my face, as I tried to think of what to say next.

"Keyarra, you better answer me. Is this shit real? Did Mark rape you?" he asked, in a tone that sent chills up my spine.
I couldn't speak. Derek approached me and looked me in my eyes.
"Did he rape you?" he asked again, slowly.
I finally nodded my head up and down. Derek's face was now mixed with hurt and anger. I put my head down and I felt like I could pass out. I wasn't sure what was about to happen.
"How many times?" he finally asked.
"Too many." I whispered.

Mark had repeatedly raped me, for at least a year; every chance he got. At one point, I stopped fighting him because it hurt less that way. He told me that I clearly wanted it because I got wet for him. I was disgusted with myself because I didn't understand why that would happen; I didn't want it. I didn't want to lose my virginity to him, I didn't want to have sex with my brother's dad, I threw up just about every time after it would occur, because it wasn't right. Then when I got pregnant, I couldn't deal with life. I knew terminating the pregnancy would mess me up because I never wanted to get an abortion in my life, and I was right. It led to suicidal thoughts, and I tried but failed. I felt like trash, and I didn't want to look anyone in the face; that's why I cut Tia off and isolated myself. One look at me, and she would've known that something was wrong.

"Why didn't you tell anyone?"
"I couldn't"
"Why?"
Silence. Derek gently lifted my face up.
"Keyarra, why didn't you tell anyone?" He repeated.
I stared at him, and anger took over his face again. He let me go, then attempted to walk past me.
"W-w-wait, where are you going?" I asked frantically, pulling him back by his arm.
"You're not saying shit, so imma go find out myself."

"No, no, no please, you can't. No one can know. You can't say anything." I pleaded.

"You're out your rabbit ass mind, if you think I'm not telling my dad, then paying that sick fuck a visit." He yelled.

"Please Derek you can't...he's dangerous."

"What you mean dangerous?"

Again, I was silent.

"Keyarra, you better start fucking talking." He spat.

"He's the reason Matt, got into the accident." I sobbed.

"What?"

"Mark did it! He was upset because I fought him one day, and he told me I would regret it. Next thing I know, Matthew is in the hospital, his intention was to kill him. Mark told me he did that to his own son, i-imagine what he would do to GG, or one of y'all. Derek, that's why I couldn't tell you g-guys, I had to protect y'all. He threatened y'all every chance he could; that's why I let it go on so long. I can't bear to lose another person I love. I would do it over again too, if it means that y'all are safe. P-Please Derek, please don't tell anyone. Matthew can't know!" I cried, uncontrollably.

I don't even know if he understood everything I said because I was so distraught. He pulled me into his arms and wrapped them around me, as I sobbed into his chest.

"Ssshh, calm down. Keyarra, you know I can't keep this shit to myself. He violated, in the worst way."

He sounded like he was trying to hold back tears.

"Derek, if you care about me the way you say you do, you won't tell anyone."

"That's why I have to say something baby. I can't hold this secret for you. Is this what your nightmares are about?"

I nodded yes. He let me go then lifted my face by chin to look into his eyes, they were still dark, but I could see the pain in them as well.

"Look what it has done to you Keyarra, you cut off your family and that hurt all of us. This shit been destroying you from the inside

out. I've seen the way you flinch sometimes, when I touch you in a certain way. You may think you're over it, but you're not. This nigga still around, and you not gonna be able to heal from this bullshit, until something is done about him."
He was right, but I was scared; it was his word against mine. He told me so many times that no one will believe me.
"Derek please, no one can know." I begged one more time.
"Too late." a voice from the doorway said.

My stomach dropped.

MATTHEW

I watched as Derek let Keyarra go and she stared at me. She looked like a kid, that had just got caught, with their hand in the candy jar. I had been listening at the door and heard damn near everything. The type of fury I was feeling was foreign to me. I had a temper, but this was different. I had murder on my mind.

"Matt, listen." Derek said.
"I'm not listening to shit!" I snarled, turning around.
Fuck Derek! Hearing him call my sister baby, and how he touched her, made me want to go toe to toe with that nigga, but I had bigger fish to fry. I walked into my room, slammed the door and locked it. I heard the sobs from Keyarra, and a knock at my door.
"Matt, open the doorman, we gotta talk about this shit." Derek called out.

I ignored him and went to my shoe boxes in the back of my closet, until I found the one I was looking for. I pulled the small handgun out and checked to see if it was still loaded; it was. I had only used it once, but just to practice. The piece of shit, who I used to know as my father, gave it to me because I was the man of the house, and I needed to protect it. What I didn't know was that it needed to be protected from him. When I heard Keyarra say he had raped her, it made me want to curl up in a ball and cry. How the fuck didn't I know? How the fuck didn't I see it? Visions of Keyarra, locking herself in her room when he came over, or how she would look visibly shaken up, after disappearing to God knows where, started replaying in my head. The thought of that pussy touching my sister, added fuel to my fire; he was good as dead. I tucked the gun in the back of my waistband and swung the door open. Derek was still standing there, I pushed past him and headed down the steps.

"Matthew, where you going?" He asked, hot on my trail.
"Stay out my business." I fumed.
"I don't want you doing something fucking stupid!"
"Nigga fuck you." I snapped, turning around.
We were inches away from each other's faces. We stared each other down; the anger in his eyes matched mine.
"I know you're pissed about what you just heard, but we gotta handle this shit the right way."
"Imma handle it."
"By doing what?"
Keyarra was slowly descending the steps; tears were streaming down her face. My heart broke, all over again. I turned back around to leave but Derek grabbed me by the arm; I turned around and swung on him, connecting with his face.
"MATTHEW!" Keyarra screamed.
She rushed to Derek's side and gently held his face in her hands. The look they exchanged didn't sit right with me, they clearly had some deeper connection.

"I'm good Key." He assured her softly
He slowly tore his gaze from her to me. I braced myself for him to follow up, but he didn't. He stood up straight to face me again, he was furious, but Derek had better control then I did.

"Ok, you got that. Imma let it slide because I know you're upset."
"Upset? Nigga I just found out my little sister was RAPED by my fucking father, and on top of that, my best friend been fucking her as well. So fuck being upset! I'm way past that!" I seethed.
"Nigga don't look me in my fucking face and act like you innocent. How you think I felt when I found out about you and, Tia?"
What the hell?
"Yeah nigga I knew. I'm not dumb, by any means. I let the shit rock because Tia seemed like she was content with whatever y'all had going on. But once she got here it clicked for me and I didn't like how you were carrying her, but again, I let it rock; especially since she immediately took to, Chris. The difference in our situations is that I genuinely care about your sister, and I wanna be with her. You played mine like a fiddle, and I've been wanting to fuck you up for it, but she made out better in the end."

I didn't have anything to say. I hate that he thinks I don't care about Tia because I did; I still do. I slowly turned back around to leave.
"Matthew, please!" Keyarra cried.
I stopped.
"Please stay. I promise we can figure this out together. I need you!"
I turned back around to look at her. She reminded me of our mother, she favored her so much. My sister was a good kid, always had been, that's until her innocence was taken from her. She turned into someone else, and now I know who is responsible for it. I have to make him pay for that. I pulled the gun from behind me and revealed it. Keyarra's eyes got big and fresh tears formed again.

"Matthew d-don't." She begged.

"Why you ain't tell me, Key? I would've believed you." I said in a cracked voice.

Tears now were falling from my eyes; my stomach was in knots. I can't believe I failed as a big brother.

"I wanted to tell you, but I couldn't. He tried to k-kill you once and you are the most important person to me. I wouldn't be able to live with myself, if something else happened to you."

"Keyarra, how am I supposed to live with myself, knowing this shit happened to you, and I didn't do anything about it?"

She just stared at me.

"Give me the gun, bro." Derek said.

I looked over at him. He knew that shit wasn't happening. He lunged at me and I was able to shake him off. I pointed the gun directly in his face. If Derek was scared, he certainly didn't show it. He slowly moved in front of Keyarra, blocking her path and view.

"Nigga, you supposed to be my brother and you pointing a gun in my face."

I didn't budge.

"Listen, as much as I want to dare you to do it, I'm not because we got other shit to worry about."

He reached behind him and gently pulled Keyarra by her hand next to him.

"Look at her!" He urged.

My eyes moved to her, and she was trying not to hyperventilate; I know the gun scared her.

"We made promises to our mothers, that we would protect our sisters. If you go do this dumb shit, and end up in prison or worse, then what? Who is she gonna have? She needs you bro, you thinking out of anger and trust me, I get it. I'm pissed too, but we gotta be smart about this. Don't do this, Matt."

I wanted to break down and cry. I feel like this was my only choice. I couldn't take back what happened, but I was about to make it right, the only way I knew how.
"Looks like you've been doing a good job at taking care of my sister, so continue to!"

With that said, I shot two shots into the ceiling; I knew the sound would be deafening for them and give me the time I needed to leave. I rushed out the door and hopped in my truck. I raced like a bat out of hell. Mark lived in the city, but still on the east side. I'm thankful I didn't run into any cops because the way I was speeding, surely would've gotten me pulled over. I barely put my truck in park before I hopped out. I went to open the screen door, but it was locked, which was rare. I banged on it hard; it rattled loudly. I heard the main door opening.

"Son, what you doing here?" Mark questioned.
"I need to holler at you, let me in!"
"Now is not the best time." He said, looking behind him.
I shook the handle to his screen door again.
"Let me in." I demanded.
"Stop shaking my shit like that."
He looked behind him again, then unlocked the door. I swung it open and rushed past him. I started pacing back and forth because, now I was nervous. I had a plan in my head, but all that went out the window.

"What's going on son, what girl got you all worked up now?"
"I'm not your son." I mumbled.
"What?"
"I SAID, I'M NOT YOUR FUCKING SON!" I yelled.
"Boy, you better calm the hell down. What the fuck is wrong with you?"
"Imma ask you a question and you better answer the shit truthfully."
"Ok, and that is?"

He looked a little nervous at this point. Mark was only 5'11, so I had some height on him, and a little more muscle too. I know he wasn't scared of me, but I think he knew I could beat his ass, if it came down to it.

"What you do to my sister?"
"Huh?"
"Nigga, you fucking heard me! WHAT DID YOU DO TO MY SISTER?"
"Matthew, calm down."
I pulled the gun from my back and held it at my side.
"Tell me to calm down again." I warned.
He eyed the gun.
"Matt, I told you to only use that, if it was necessary."
"Trust me, it's necessary. Now answer my question!"
"Nothing happened, that she didn't want." he said, wickedly.
His response took me back. I cocked the gun back because this nigga was playing with his life now.
"Say that again?"
"Your sister is a lot like her mother.... a whore."
POP!
I shot him in his shoulder. Blood spewed everywhere.
"Fuck!" He yelled out in pain.
I heard something drop upstairs.
"Who the fuck is upstairs?" I asked him.
He was too busy attempting to add pressure to his wound.
"Whoever is upstairs, you better come down now! Or imma start shooting into the ceiling."
I didn't hear any movement.
"5,4,3..."
"MATTHEW, DON'T!" Mark yelled.
"2...1"
"Wait." a female's voice called out.
"Come down here bitch!" I called out.

I heard soft footsteps coming down the steps and I got the shock of my life when I saw a full-blown pregnant, Katrina. I was so confused.

"What the fuck are you doing here?"

She was shaky and her bottom lip was trembling.

"Katrina, what the fuck are you doing here?" I yelled.

"Stop yelling at her!" Mark grimaced.

"Nigga, shut the fuck up! Before I shoot you in the fucking face"

"Please don't." Katrina said, in a shaky voice.

"Then start talking!" I demanded.

"He's the father of my child." she finally said.

I was floored. I looked back at Mark, who was bleeding profusely.

"So, you just a pervert? You like fucking teenage girls, huh?"

"I told you, your sister wanted it; she came on to me, so many times, until I finally gave her what she wanted."

"She would never do that!"

"She did! That's why I went after Tre, she wanted what me and Mark had, and she seduced him." Katrina interjected.

This dumb bitch!

"Shut your dumb ass up! You sound stupid. How old was she when you first touched her Mark? What, 12? 13? She wasn't thinking about sex, she wasn't thinking about you nigga. She looked at you like a dad, and you took advantage of her. I should blow your fucking head off!" I shouted.

I was radiating with rage! This nigga was a predator, and the thought that we shared the same blood, made me sick to my stomach.

"Her body said otherwise." He spat.

I walked over and hit him on the nose with the gun, instantly breaking it.

"Aaaahhhh!" He called out and fell to the ground.

Katrina attempted to run over to him, until I pointed the gun at her.

"Back the fuck up." I gritted. "He wanna call someone a whore but look at you. You have three different niggas thinking that they are the father of your bastard baby."

"Don't call my baby a bastard!" She snapped.

"Fuck you and that baby!" I yelled.

Mark groaned and found his way back to his feet.

"You know Matt, I always thought you were a real pussy. I never thought you would use that gun and look at you."

He had this devil-ish smile on his face, which confirmed to me, this nigga was sick in the head. He had a gunshot wound plus a broken nose but was smiling.

"When you survived that car crash, I thought damn, this little nigga a fighter, you just might be mine." He continued.

I honestly forgot about that.

"Why did you do that foul shit?" I asked.

"Because I don't take no for an answer." He stated, darkly.

"So my sister seduced you, but she told you no, then you punish her, by trying to kill me?"

He didn't say anything because he knew it was bullshit.

"That's what I thought, you raped my sister because you're sick. You sat with us at dinner tables and taunted her. You made her life a living hell, and she internalized it to protect her family from your evil ass. But she won't have to go through that any longer."

I raised the gun again and my finger hovered over the trigger.

"I'll say hi to your mother for you." He sneered.

"You won't see her where you're going." I shot back.

I closed my eyes and went to pull the trigger. I heard Katrina scream and some sort of splashing sound.

"Oh God, my water just broke!" She cried out.

I looked over at her, and that's when he charged at me. He was trying to get the gun; we tussled around the kitchen, knocking everything over in our path.

"I won't.... hesitate ...pulling the trigger...on you son." He grumbled.

I focused on trying to get it out of his grasp. All I could hear were the screams from Katrina, then I heard two more shots.

POP! POP!

To be continued....

Made in the USA
Columbia, SC
16 December 2024

49614573R00248